CONTINENTAL NEXUS

A NORTH AMERICAN NOVEL
FOR ENGLISH-SPANISH BILINGUALS

J.D. FARRELL

1627 North 24th Place
Milwaukee, Wisconsin 53205

Copyright © 2002 J.D. Farrell
All rights reserved

Cover Design by Shelby Keefe
Text Design by Georgene Schreiner
Edited by Linda Andrews

No part of this book may be reproduced or utilized in any form or by any means, electronic or mechanical, including photocopying and recording, or by any information storage and retrieval system, without permission in writing from the author.

06 05 04 03 02   5 4 3 2 1

ISBN: 0-9715161-0-3
Library of Congress Control Number: 2001097431

First Printing 2002
Printed in the United States of America

Published by Whirling Words
Project Coordination by Printstar Books
Milwaukee, Wisconsin   www.printstarbooks.com

1627 North 24th Place
Milwaukee, Wisconsin 53205

Dedication

*To Joannah,
who did most of the work.*

*And to Ofelia, Dulce, and Bridget,
who shared the experience.*

*And especially to Efigenia, who somehow
managed to transplant the matriarchy.*

NARRATOR'S NOTE

During the seventh and eighth decades of the twentieth century, a group of people whom I began to think of as "the Alvarez clan" became my neighbors on the near west side of Milwaukee's inner city. The character known as "Noise" does the service work on my pickup. The character known as Miguel is a loyal drinking companion. The characters known as Isabel and Concha share my predilection for gardening. The character known as "Loco" is a colleague at the local tech college. He researched the Alvarez family history and encouraged me to use it as background for this, their story.

None of these, of course, are their real names. The village of Jachalco in the Mexican state of Puebla is also a fiction.

SIGNIFICANT LOCATIONS IN THE STORY OF THE "ALVAREZ CLAN"

EARLY ALVAREZ FAMILY

Natalia Alvarez   =   liaison with
1847-1918   Jean Batiste Leduc
                        1841-?

Pascual Alvarez
1865-?
(disappeared)
=
Catalina Jiménez
1867-1906

Rodolfo Alvarez
1885-1936
=
Sacramento Robles
1887-1958
(raised two nephews, Federico and Rogelio Robles, as
well as her own sons; see Robles family tree)

Juan Alvarez	Antonio Alvarez	Ramón Alvarez	Guillermo Alvarez
1904-1983	1905-1973	1907-1937	1910-1920
(see separate family tree)	(see separate family tree)	(see Gómez family tree)	(drowned in laguna accident)

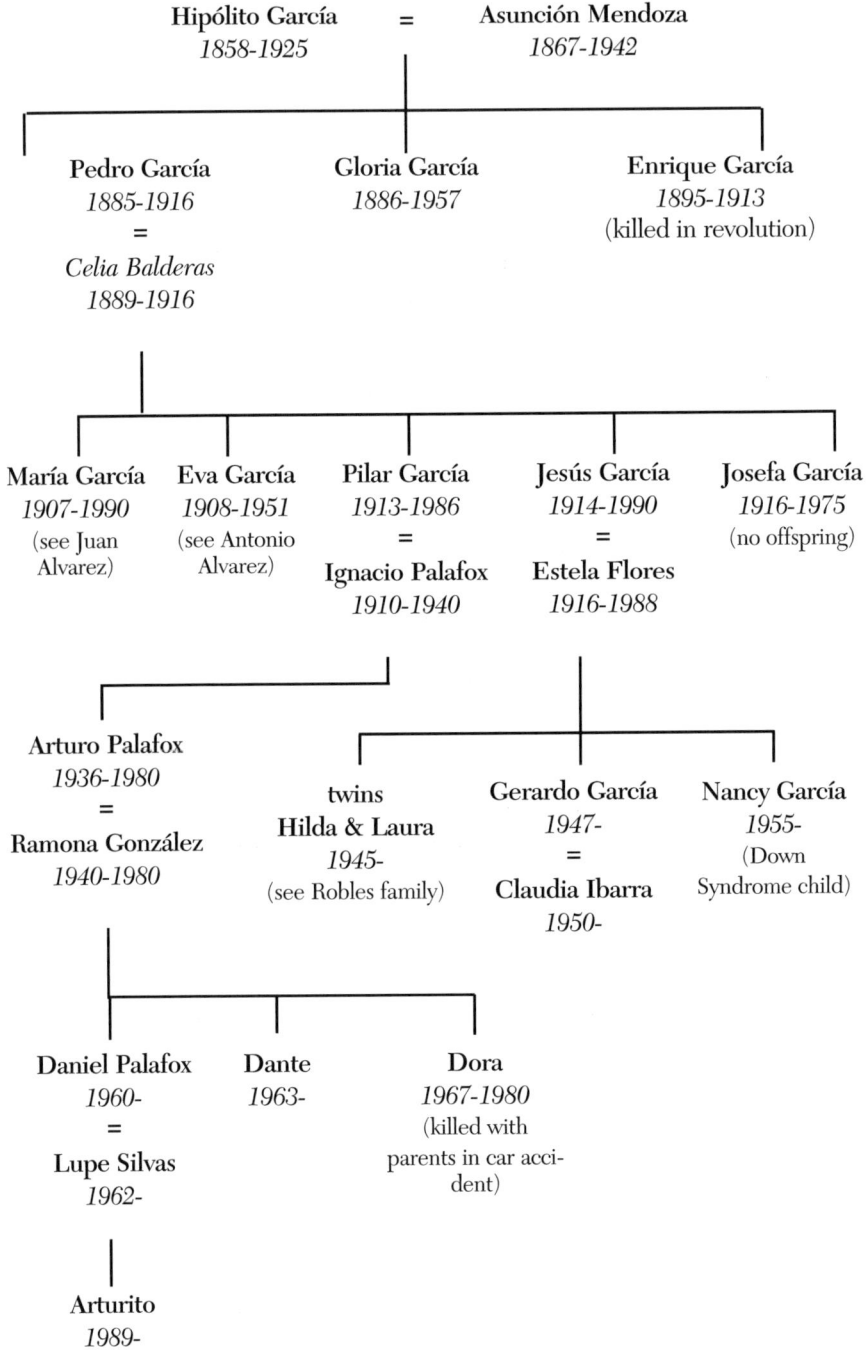

ROBLES FAMILY

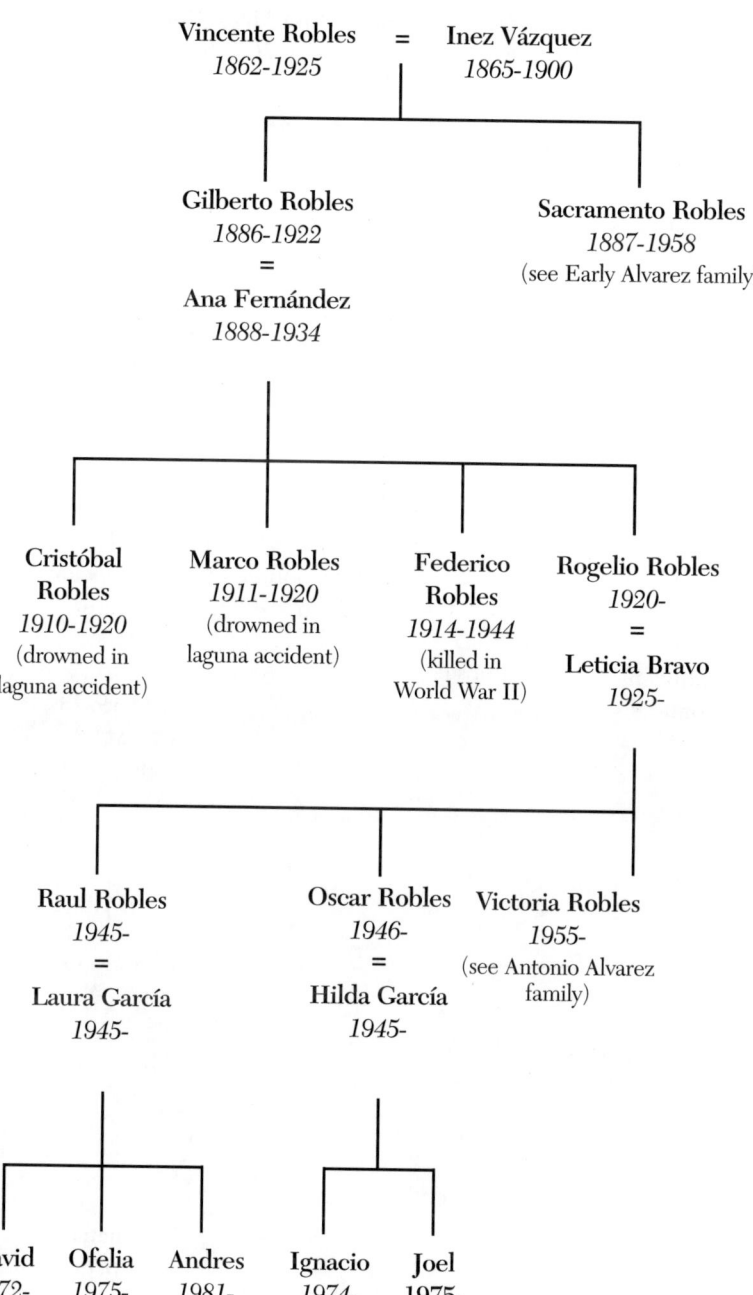

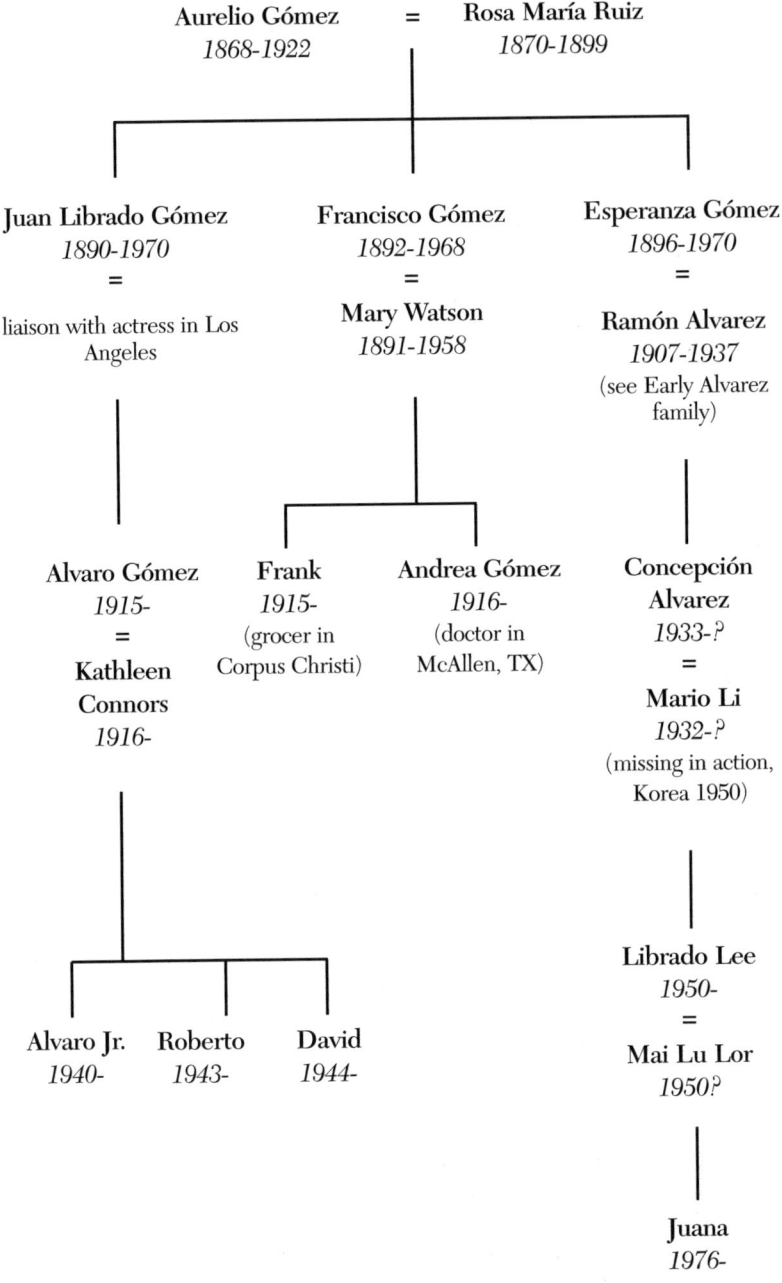

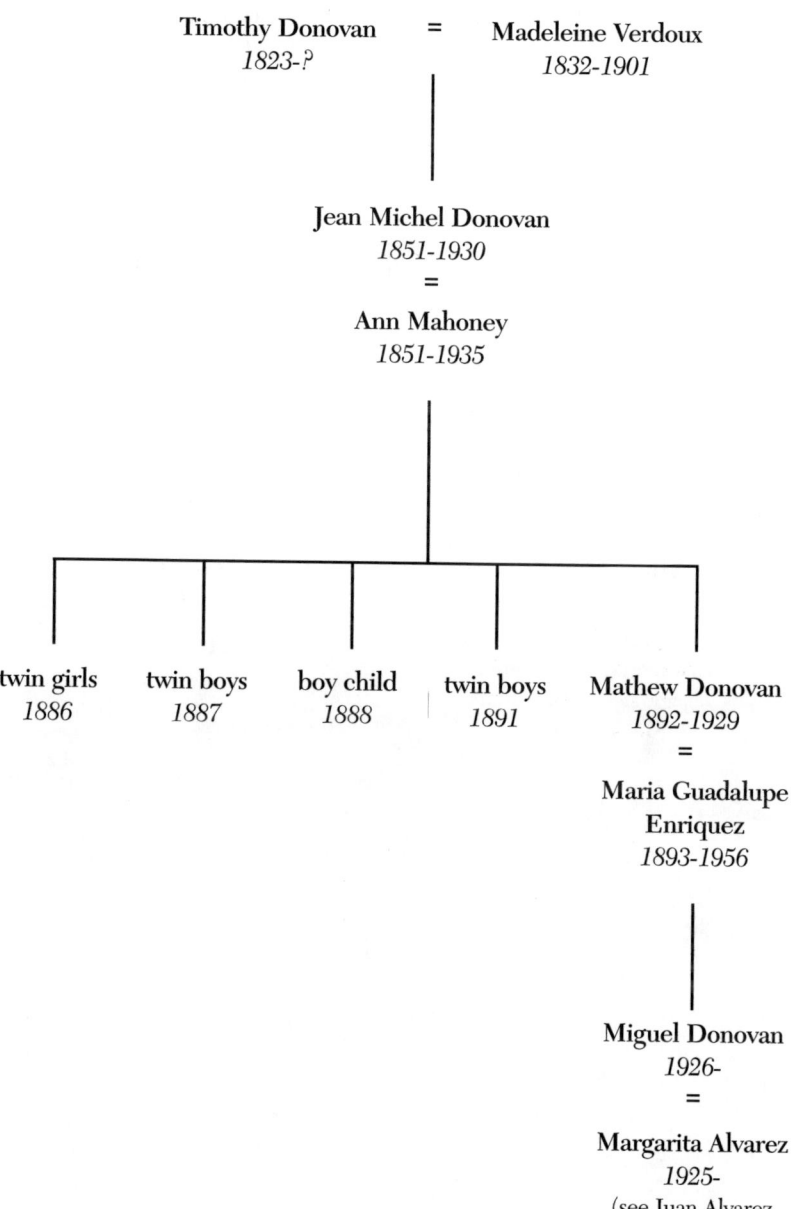

JUAN ALVAREZ FAMILY

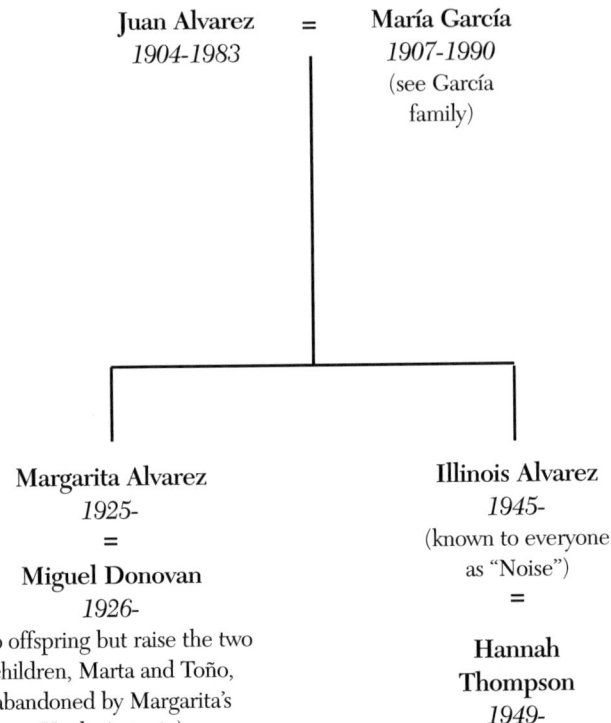

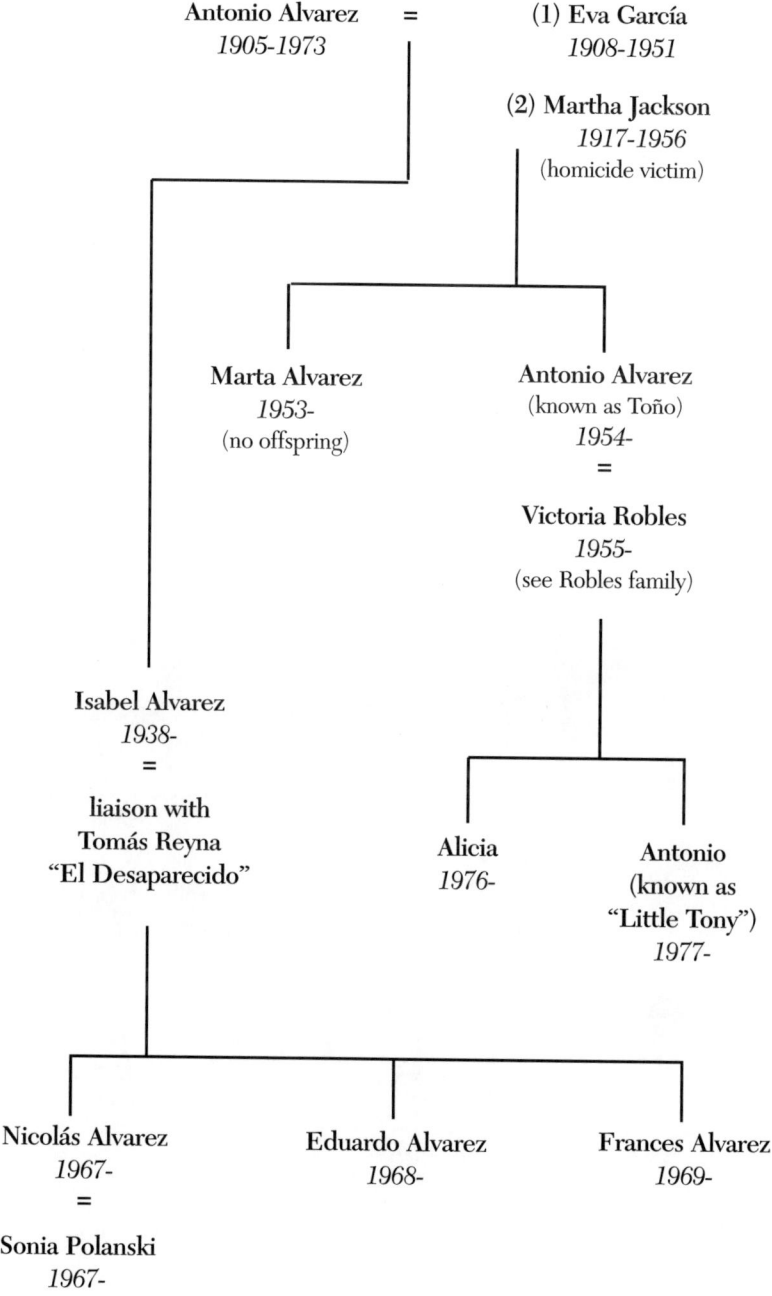

BOOK ONE:
THE PRIMORDIAL OOZE

CHAPTER ONE

THE ODDS WERE VERY LONG.

Consider. One tiny sperm cell. One in a trillion that it would even get properly ejaculated. And even that done, one in a billion that a receptive vagina would be there for it. And even that done, one in a million that it could navigate and flagellate its way through the uterus. And even that done, there was a 50 percent chance of error when the fallopians were reached and breached. And barring a mishap there, the likelihood was very small that there would be an ovum in the tube willing to meet the tiny sperm halfway, so to speak. Even then, the probability was very low that the ovum would be penetrable. And even that done, and the zygote achieved, the prospects for implantation were not very good.

And yet it happened.

For the second time in the course of their intercourse, and following an interval of twenty years, our happy couple beat the long odds.

Such was not, of course, their intention. They had no concern for the fate of one tiny sperm cell. They were entirely ignorant of its struggle. They gave no thought to the formation of zygotes or the probabilities of successful implantation. Quite the contrary. These two were single-mindedly concentrated on a quite distinct outcome.

CONTINENTAL NEXUS

All their effort, all their striving, was toward the blessed event itself.

Ejaculation.

But I anticipate. Some background is required.

Know, then, that he of the tiny sperm cell was Señor Juan Alvarez and she of the receptive vagina was Señora María García de Alvarez. The union of these two was thoroughly sanctioned por las dos leyes. That is to say, they were in fact husband and wife. So in what follows, there is no suggestion of anything improper. No indeed. Our happy couple did nothing wrong. Rather, as often happens with humans, they did much more than they had intended.

To the facts of the case then.

It was a Friday night. Juan and María had passed a quiet evening in the living room of their Chicago home, listening to the radio. First some music. Then some boxing. At ten o'clock, a news program began. That cued the abrupt departure of María, saying as she left, "No quiero saber nada de esa guerra. Luego me dan pesadillas."

Upstairs she stopped by the east bedroom to exchange a goodnight kiss with her daughter Margarita. Then she walked down the hall, past the never-used guest room, soon to be a nursery, to the master bedroom. She removed her makeup, then turned out the light, and took off her outer clothing. She slipped into a nightgown and only then removed her underclothes, justifying her nakedness as she did every night, "Por si acaso me quiere usar Juan." Which occasionally he did. A couple times a month. Some months more frequently, if the widow Cándida, who lived a block from where he changed buses on his way home from work, was inaccessible. And truth told, María was feeling menos molesta about her sexuality as she aged. Although she still recited her act of contrition after each encounter—just in case she had felt something that "Dios no permite."

Meanwhile downstairs, Juan was making what sense he could of the English language news. The war in Europe appeared to be going well. The Allies were celebrating their entry into Paris. France was going to pin some kind of medal on Eisenhower. As he turned off the radio, Juan did his own summary of the report. "Parece que ahora sí, los están chingando a esos alemanes; al rato les toca su turno a los japoneses." The last clause was somewhat personalized, since his cousin Federico was with the marines in the Pacific.

At the top of the stairs, Juan paused at the east bedroom. He knew by the patch of light below the door that his daughter was still reading. But rather than entering to say good night, he merely issued a parental warning in passing. "No te quedes muy noche, Hija. Se te va a acabar la vista." Margarita responded, "No Papá. Hasta mañana, Papá." Juan mumbled his own, "Hasta mañana," and continued down the hall.

A few minutes later, he was lying beside his wife, staring at the ceiling. He tried to focus his thoughts on the war news, but the image of the widow Cándida kept insinuating itself. It was hard to explain her appeal. Physically she was less attractive than María—older, shorter, stouter. But in the bedroom she did things. Juan could picture some of those things, and he began to do so. She also let a man do things. Juan could remember some of those things, and he began to do so. More than anything, she did not try to hide her body. And now . . . now . . . a su mecha . . . now she was giving him a hard-on.

At the same time, María was busy telling her beads. Although "beads" is a mild inaccuracy. Early in their marriage, Juan had once found María in bed with a rosary entwined around her fingers and "por poco se explota." Which did not, of course, deter her from her devotions. She simply began counting on her fingers.

Anyway, on the night in question, since it was a Friday, María was reciting the sorrowful mysteries. She had just started the "Aves" for the crowning with thorns and was about to launch into another silent "Santa María" when Juan turned onto his side and nudged, no . . .

"Madre de Dios" . . . poked her . . . con su miembro. A signal admittedly lacking in subtlety. But quite effective. María responded immediately. Not in panic however. She had done this before. Hundreds of times. What was called for was lubrication. As quickly as possible. Before Juan became impatient and attempted a dry entry.

So while he engaged in what for him constituted foreplay, nibbling her ear with his lips and rubbing her thighs with a rough hand, María shut down her rosary and pulled up her nightgown. Then, asking forgiveness for what she was about to do, she started the fantasy that she used to achieve lubricity.

In the fantasy, she is a young woman dressed in only a black, satin-and-lace negligee. She enters a bedroom lighted by a single candle on the dresser. On the bed there is a young Juan, lying on his back covered by a sheet. Music is playing—something by Agustín Lara. She goes to the bed and kneels. Juan turns to her. They kiss passionately. She rises. With a regal gesture of her arm, she flips aside the sheet. Crossing her left leg over his, she straddles him, sitting on his thighs. She slips her arms inside the negligee and lifts the top of the garment above her head so as to form a tent. She raises the front edge of the tent and lets it drop onto Juan's chest. Now she is alone with her lover. She caresses him—with her hand, with her mouth, with her hand, with her mouth. She plays with him—little pumping motions. She rubs her breasts against him. Soon he begins to drool. She raises herself onto her knees and then, ever so slowly, lowers herself over him. She will take him in. She will enclose him. She will enfold him. She will encompass him. He will be her captive.

Finally she could feel herself begin to open, to loosen . . . yes . . . Gracias a Dios . . . to moisten. And none too soon. For Juan (in the flesh now) had just hoisted himself atop her and was already pressing for entry. María adjusted her position so as to accommodate him. Then she went limp. Now it was up to him. She made a quick calculation as to where she had interrupted her rosary and took up the count.

Juan, meanwhile, had abandoned the widow Cándida for a more cinematic fantasy. He is naked, sitting on a bed, observing a woman who bears a remarkable resemblance to a young Dolores Del Rio. She is admiring herself in a full-length mirror. Casually she undoes the bow on her black negligee and lets it drop to the floor. She is now clothed in only a black satin panty. She signals for Juan to rise. He positions himself behind her. Still observing herself in the mirror she pushes her butt against his penis and begins to rub. Juan reciprocates. He reaches around and plays with her breasts. As the two become more intense, she stretches her head back and to the side, asking for his mouth. He complies. She begins an assault on his tongue that continues until he pulls himself away, gasping for air. As he does, she calls his attention to the mirror. She reaches down, pushes her panty below her buttocks. Then she bends forward. This is more than Juan can handle. He is so taken with her beauteous, bounteous behind that he manages a paltry four thrusts and must rush to get inside as the semen starts to ooze.

Fortunately, in the real world of María's vagina, no such crisis occurred. The tiny sperm cell got off to a very smooth start. Made even smoother, perhaps, because of something that happened to María. For in fact, as Juan waxed more and more enthusiastic, María concentrated less and less on her "Aves." She started to sweat. Her respiration increased. Then her hips began to reach for Juan's thrusts. Now her prayers were but recordings that she was playing back to herself. At the end there was a wave. It rolled up from her extremities and through her body until . . . until . . . "Ave María, llena de gracia." As always, María was restrained in her excesses. Nevertheless, the last words escaped her. And though it was a mere whisper, Juan, who was already returning to his everyday self, immediately became accusatory. "¡Estás rezando!"

Certain of the imminence of another lecture on the evils of commingling sex and religion, María quickly responded, "Por un hijo, Juan. Por un hijo."

A statement not entirely untrue. Years before, when her one child, Margarita, was already seven or eight, and it appeared that she would never again conceive, María began to have scruples about persisting in sexual activity. She had consulted a priest. A real priest. Who spoke Spanish. And knew about sin. He had reassured her that as long as she undertook the act with the intent to conceive, no evil was involved. Whereupon María had made a solemn pledge to the Virgen that she would always welcome another pregnancy.

Which was all well and good. In the land of guess and maybe. But a month later, that pledge became a source of solemn indigestion. And while the physiological side effects were indeed weighty, they were as nothing compared to the welter of emotions.

While breaking the news to her husband, María was able to maintain a semblance of control. But then she gave way to hysteria as she thought of the social consequences. "Voy a morir de vergüenza" became the major theme of the pregnancy. She could not look at Juan without repeating that phrase. Or one of its variations. "Todo el mundo va a saber que yo, una mujer de . . . bueno . . . de bastantes años, y todavía haciendo esas cosas ¡Dios me libre! ¿Qué va a pensar la gente?" And before the second trimester was over, "Ya ni modo. No puedo salir de esta casa. Tienes que inventar algo para decirles a los vecinos, Juan."

Juan's comportment also underwent some adjustment. People said he looked taller. He took up whistling. He began talking to strangers at bus stops, explaining, without anyone asking, that he was hurrying home because "Mi señora está en estado." He even stopped visiting Cándida. At least at the beginning of the pregnancy. Later, of course, when María was really big, it was understood that he

BOOK ONE, CHAPTER ONE

would take his needs elsewhere.

And so with one thing and another, in the fullness of time, a man child was born to María García and Juan Alvarez. The latter determined to have his way in the naming of the boy. No, he would not be a second Juan Alvarez. Nor would he be named for his grandfather. Nor for any other male relative. Nor for any idol of the silver screen. He would have an uncompromisingly northern name. A name guaranteeing his right to take root in Gringolandia. He would in fact be named for a state. "Con un nombre así, los desgraciados van a pensar dos veces antes de deportar a mi hijo," reasoned Juan. And what state would be more appropriate than that in which the boy had been born?

Such was the origin of Illinois Alvarez.

Alas, as with a great many human plans, this one went askew. As Illinois Alvarez grew and went out into the world to take his place, people began to do things to his name. Starting in fact in early childhood. All the kids in his neighborhood pronounced the name of the state so that the last syllable rhymed with "poise." And the fact that the name comprised three syllables made it just too much of a mouthful. In short, before he had reached his sixth birthday, Illinois Alvarez had become just plain "Noise."

Alas also, by the time he had reached sixteen, he and his father had grown so far apart that Juan would have welcomed the deportation of his son.

But that's another story.

CHAPTER TWO

LONGEVITY WAS OFTEN NOT AN OPTION.

Consider. In their environment, at any moment, humans may confront any or all of the following. Billions of bacteria, seeking an opening into the flesh or an entry into the food supply. Virillions of viruses, intent on committing mayhem whenever the immune system happens to nod or even yawn. Gadzillions of gnats, ticks, bees, fleas, and pismires, capable of piercing and poisoning a body. And all that without even mentioning scorpions, tarantulas, and black widows.

None of the above, however, had brought Celia Balderas and Pedro García to their separate, but related and nearly simultaneous, encounters with mortality. Something much less predictable had caused Pedro's blood to be seeping into the dust of a trail near Cuautla, Morelos. Something much more capricious had caused Celia's blood to be oozing into the sheets of a birthing bed within that same town.

For it is sad but true that very few of us are cut out for the life of a hermit. So. Any calculation of longevity must also factor in the mischief of history. At birth, we are dropped not only into an environment, but also into a context. We become members of such predetermining groups as family, village, nation. There are power centers in place. Certainly political. No luck there. Probably political and religious. Worse luck there. Possibly political and religious in concert. Reconsider the hermit option. These centers define our range of movement and choice. The range can vary from the modestly permissive to the massively restrictive. The defining is done by regulations, rules, statutes, directives, encyclicals, commandments, injunctions, proclamations, and the occasional papal bull.

Folks shape themselves to the context as best they can. But accommodation has its limits. So one day in Delano, California, a woman reaches the point beyond which she will not be bullied and begins to chant, "Huelga. Huelga." Or one day in Anenecuilco, Morelos, a man can no longer tolerate la vida hincada and begins to yell, "Ya basta, hijos de la chingada."

Which brings us to Emiliano Zapata and his Plan of Ayala. At once a program for land reform and an impassioned call to arms to implement that program. Down with the traitor Madero. Break up the haciendas. The land for the campesinos who work it.

Pedro García taught some of the sons of those campesinos. He understood their need to share in the wealth that their labor created. And never would they have a real share until they had ownership. Until they had land. So. A political revolution was insufficient. An economic revolution was also required. It was not difficult to construct a rational justification for Zapata's cause.

But all that was mere logic. Far more motivating was the emotional rush that accompanied the conviction that the revolution was the great historical event of his lifetime. To be there and not to take part was unthinkable. There was, of course, the considerable presence of Celia Balderas. It was she who made bearable his otherwise thoroughly ordinary life. He would somehow have to make her understand. What was happening was greater and grander than any personal relationship. He simply had to participate.

CONTINENTAL NEXUS

Longevity al carajo.

I know. I know. I am ahead of my story. Some background is required.

Know, then, that in the year in which Porfirio Díaz decided that the Pax Porfiriana would be more beneficial to his country than effective suffrage, Asunción Mendoza seduced Hipólito García. He was from Morelos, twenty-six, a prematurely balding schoolteacher with a passion for books and ideas. She was from Puebla, seventeen, with a passion for economic security and upward social mobility.

When Hipólito learned that Asunción was with child, he agreed to do the honorable thing, and the two were joined in matrimony por las dos leyes. They first set up house in Cuautla, Morelos, where he was teaching. Some years later they moved to Puebla. There were three offspring of the union. Pedro was born a mere five months after the wedding. Gloria was born the following year. Enrique came along some nine years later, a sort of romantic hiccup.

Returning then to the historical context.

From the beginning, the revolution rained disaster on the García family. The youngest son, Enrique, had inherited all of his mother's willfulness and none of her good sense. Not long after the publication of the Plan of Ayala, he asked his parents' blessing on his own plan to join Zapata. Since they were not supporters of Zapata's cause, and since Enrique was only seventeen, they refused. A quarrel ensued. The parents remained adamant. It got nasty. References were made to the size of certain parts of Don Hipólito's anatomy. There was even speculation that the parts might be missing. Blows followed. Enrique made a sudden, unannounced visit to Pedro in Cuautla. There he borrowed a horse from his brother and set off to join Zapata.

The next day a friend of the family brought him back to Pedro's home. Apparently something along the road had spooked the horse.

BOOK ONE, CHAPTER TWO

The young man had been thrown. But not cleanly. His foot had caught in a stirrup and he had been dragged for some distance. His spine had been fractured, and there were numerous other injuries. He was quite dead.

The day that Enrique García had ridden off to join Zapata, Pedro had come within a heartbeat of yelling after his brother, "Espérate. Voy contigo." Then the moment passed. He waved and yelled, "Adiós." What stayed him in this moment of temptation was a beautiful woman named Celia Balderas. She and Pedro had met shortly after he had begun teaching in Cuautla. At that time she and her younger sister, Reina, lived with their widowed mother, Eulalia, in a state of poverty bordering on la miseria. Eulalia had always assumed that her attractive daughters would one day fall victim to another kind of proposal. Consequently, when Celia announced that a young man had chastely proposed marriage, and that the young man was a teacher, and the son of a teacher, the mother was nearly speechless. This condition, fortunately, was only temporary. She recovered and gave her consent. The union was sanctioned por las dos leyes early in the last decade of the Pax Porfiriana.

In the next few years it became evident that Pedro and Celia had a prodigious talent for procreation. María García, whom we met in the previous episode, was born ten months after the wedding. Her sister Eva followed her by a mere eleven months. Then there were a series of miscarriages. Five years after Eva, another daughter, Pilar, was born, followed the next year by Jesús, and then two years later by Josefa.

All that propagating did not, however, occupy all his time nor satisfy all his needs. So. In the year that Victoriano Huerta seized control of the capital and assassinated Madero, Pedro García also rode off to join Zapata.

He had pictured himself as a warrior. He had visualized himself plotting tactics. He had fantasized about leading men to the attack. What he had never imagined was that others would scrutinize his background and conclude that he was better suited to lesser tasks. To his considerable shame, he became a supply officer.

With Huerta as the common enemy, Zapata, Villa, Carranza, and Obregón cooperated. Together they eventually drove the federales out of the capital. Then the wraps came off each one's special agenda and collaboration ceased. Carranza and Obregón retired to the Gulf Coast. Zapata returned to Morelos. Villa had neither the aptitude nor the appetite for politics. Soon his position in the capital became untenable. Obregón returned. Villa left for the north. Carranza was installed as president. He dispatched General Pablo Gonzalez to Morelos to eliminate the Zapatistas. Cuautla was taken. Not for long. But in the time that the town was occupied by the Carrancistas, Josefa García was born. Pedro, knowing the due date, requested and received permission to go to his wife.

Zapatista patrols were operating in the area around Cuautla. Pedro was temporarily assigned to one of those patrols. The plan was for him to slip into Cuautla while the rest of the group was reconnoitering the villages in the region. He would learn what he could about the strength of the federal garrison. If it did not seem too risky, he would also visit his family. Then he would rejoin the scouting party.

For Pedro, the patrol was like a long-awaited holiday. For three glorious days, he would ride with real soldiers. For three glorious days, he could cuss and fuss about every irritation, just as they did. And there was always the chance of encountering the enemy. Not likely, his companions told him. Pero, ¿quién sabe? If they did meet the enemy, Pedro promised himself that he would get off at least one shot. Then no one could say later that he had not taken part.

All went uneventfully, until the day that Pedro was to set out on his personal mission. That afternoon the patrol rode into a village where they were to make night camp. A detail was sent to secure the perimeter. Pedro went along. In the course of this duty, the detail surprised three federal soldiers who had probably strayed from a foraging party. Shots were fired. One of Pedro's companions was hit.

Outnumbered, the federales opted for prudence and fled the scene. While his companions dismounted to assist the injured man, Pedro inexplicably set out in hot and solitary pursuit. This was reported later to the patrol's ranking officer. He concluded that Pedro had been using the incident to cover his departure.

The officer was dead wrong. Pedro's intent was to destroy the enemy. With a pistol! Against three men with rifles! Who, as they turned in their saddles, were astonished to find that they were being chased by a lone warrior. At first this was merely annoying. But as the minutes passed, and their horses became lathered with sweat, it got to be downright irritating. Finally at a rise in the trail, they turned, fired a volley at their pursuer, and then continued their escape.

The probability that two of the three projectiles would strike their target was certainly minuscule. But that is what occurred. At virtually the same instant, one bullet slammed into the trapezius muscle of Pedro's right shoulder, while a second sliced through his left thigh, severing the femoral artery. He fell from his horse.

Now we enter the land of guess and maybe. Maybe, had he stayed on the trail, he would have been found by his companions. Instead, half-crazed with pain, he staggered to his feet and made a feeble attempt to recover his mount. In doing so, he stumbled off the trail. He tripped and rolled into a shallow ravine. Maybe, if the pain in his leg had been greater, he would have attempted to stanch the bleeding in that wound. Instead, because his shoulder hurt more, he spent his last conscious minutes tending the less serious wound. So the blood continued to ooze from his leg and mix with and muddy the dust of his patria chica. Little by little it slowed. And then stopped.

Meanwhile, his wife was involved in her own life-and-death struggle.

On the same day that Pedro and the patrol left the main Zapatista camp, Celia's labor pains began. Pedro's sister, Gloria, took the children to the Balderas home. Celia's sister, Reina, went to fetch the doctor. He was not available. He had been summoned to the local barracks to attend to an injured federal officer. The doctor's wife was hurrying off to visit relatives, but she paused long enough to scribble a note, which she left on the desk in the doctor's study.

Throughout the day, Celia's labor waxed and waned. Her mother, Eulalia, sent for the neighborhood midwife. The woman arrived. She scrubbed. She examined the patient. She delivered the bad news. It was not a standard presentation. What was pressing against the cervix appeared to be a shoulder rather than the baby's head. A physician's services would be required. Reina made another trip to the doctor's home. He had not returned. She stopped by the home of a second physician whom the Garcías sometimes consulted. This man was out of town and not expected back for several days.

In the evening the midwife was summoned again. She noted that the contractions were neither more proximate nor more intense. Nor had dilation of the cervix increased significantly. "Mañana será," she pronounced, "Pero más les vale traer a ese doctor. Y temprano."

At daybreak Reina hurried again to the doctor's home. He was not there. She went to the barracks, intending to send in a message, but she was driven off by threats and insults.

By then Celia was one large mound of pain. Again Eulalia sent for the midwife. "¡Por Diosito Santo! Haz algo por mi hija, Señora." It was the plea of one mother to another, and it did not fail. Some brief but intense negotiation followed. Eulalia agreed to pay one hundred pesos more than the midwife's usual fee. Then an image of the Virgen of Guadalupe was lowered from the wall. Eulalia pressed her hand to the image and swore that she would not hold the midwife responsible for what might happen to her daughter.

The patient's extremities were tied down. An herbal analgesic and a small dose of laudanum were administered. Then a pep talk: "Lo que voy a hacer te va a doler, Señora Celia. Probablemente te va a lastimar. Pero tenemos que sacar a la criatura. Yo voy a hacer lo que tengo que hacer. Te va a doler bastante. Tú, grítame como te dé la gana." Then the midwife prepared her instruments. She scrubbed. Finally, with Eulalia and Reina restraining the patient, she attempted to readjust the baby's position.

Maybe the moment was exactly right. Maybe the midwife's skill was actually up to the task. Maybe it was the liters of sweat that poured from her brow and arms. Maybe it was simply outrageous luck. In any event it worked. There were gasps, grunts, screams, howls, prayers, and curses. But in less than three hours, Josefa García was born. Head first.

Then the wailing began. Josefa, of course, because she had just been properly whacked on the bottom. Eulalia, because finally her daughter's agony had ended. Reina, perhaps because another strong argument had been made in the case for virginity. The midwife, obviously, out of unmitigated relief.

The wailing was intense. But necessarily brief. Much remained to be done. First the midwife administered a substantial dose of laudanum to Celia. Then she and Eulalia began the cleansing of the new mother, a process involving about equal parts of hygiene and ritual. Meanwhile Reina cleaned and comforted the infant.

Later, with order once more in the ascendancy, Eulalia found a bottle of brandy and poured a generous congratulatory cup for the midwife. This was firmly refused, until Eulalia agreed to join her. Then there was some small talk and the midwife took her leave. But not before delivering a stern admonition that Celia be examined by a doctor.

Everyone saw the wisdom in that. But Celia appeared to be resting easily, and everyone was exhausted from the all-night vigil. Consequently, no one went for the doctor. Consequently, he returned from the barracks and took a leisurely siesta before reviewing his messages and learning that he was needed at the García home. He arrived about five in the afternoon to find Eulalia nodding in her chair beside the patient's bed and Celia hemorrhaging. He did what he could, but at that point, only a transfusion would have saved her, and he knew of such things only by hearsay. Celia died later that night.

María, Eva, Pilar, Jesús, and Josefa García were orphans. Their grandma, Asunción Mendoza, was beside herself. For years and years she had scrimped and squirreled away every possible peso from her husband's salary in order to make the downpayment on an apartment building in Puebla. In the same year that Porfirio Díaz had moved to Paris for his health, she had finally achieved her goal. Since then she had continued her frugality, using the rental income to pay off more than half the principal. She had calculated that in three more years, the Garcías would own the building outright. Now, without warning, there were five children needing food, clothing, and shelter.

Asunción raged at and wrestled with her fate. She contorted and distorted the data. But there remained two indisputable facts. The children's other grandma had barely enough for herself. And there was no one else.

The addition of five people to the family would require considerable reorganization. Fortunately, Asunción was blessed with considerable organizational ability. Once resigned to her destiny, she immediately began defining functions and assigning roles. There would be a need for economic support. That role clearly belonged to her husband, Hipólito. He would have to take on some additional private students for tutoring. There would be a need for the standard parenting services. Someone would have to see to the feeding, clothing, bathing, comforting, and everything else involved in nurturing and nutrition. At age thirty, Asunción's daughter, Gloria, was still single and with no prospects. She would be the careprovider. Finally there would be a need for planning and administration. That role belonged to Asunción herself.

And over the years she played her part quite well. The children never suffered hunger. They all received an adequate education. Except for Josefa, each of them found a suitable marriage partner. And in the end, Asunción was able to leave to the three youngest the apartment building clear of debt. In fact it was in that very building that one day Illinois Alvarez would find a home with his Aunt Pilar.

But that's another story.

CHAPTER THREE

SPEED IS IN THE EYE OF THE BEHOLDER.

Consider, for example, geologic time. Millennia count but little. Centuries even less. Years hardly at all. Counting is done in epochs and periods and eras. Pleistocene and Pliocene. Devonian and Silurian. Paleozoic and Precambrian. In this sort of reckoning, a meter of tectonic movement is a very big deal. It might be the equivalent of a jog in human time. Or possibly a scamper. Maybe even an outright sprint. Anyway, what we have in geologic time is a tectonic plate called the Cocos, hell-bent for the Caribbean at the prodigious pace of three or four centimeters a year.

Or to picture it from the perspective of the Caribbean. To your immediate north, the continent of North America and half the North Atlantic Ocean, sitting on one plate, just daring anybody to even nudge, much less budge it. To your immediate south, the continent of South America and half the South Atlantic Ocean, sitting on another plate, trying to bump and bully its way north. And then along comes the Cocos, this rowdy randy runt from the Southwest, attempting a move onto your turf by sticking its hot little magma-filled whatever under your lip and undergoing subduction. If you get my drift.

This kind of environment promotes geologic events. Such as

volcano formation. So it is that across the North American continent, at roughly the nineteenth parallel, where the Caribbean and North American plates meet, there appears an irregular line of potentially explosive peaks with names like Parícutin and Popocatépetl. At the far eastern end of the line, the highest of these peaks, Citlaltépetl, overlooks a village named Jachalco. About which more presently.

Geologic events are not renowned for their predictability. A volcano can begin to ooze from a mere crack in the ground. From there it can spurt and spew to a height of two hundred meters in a fortnight. Then it can slip into a siesta mode for a few hundred years. Only to detonate at the advent of an earthquake. Once again active, it can bluster and belch until it blows itself to naught and gone, with only a crater to mark its geologic passing.

Folks inclined to put an anthropic spin on geologic events can, however, take comfort. For one effect of all this activity is to turn the inside of the Earth into the outside. And in so doing, a volcano helps to produce soil. From time to time, ash and pumice and scoria rain down on the lands beneath the peaks. There they mix with the obsidian chips and sand and whatever else has blown in on the wind. The resulting composite is just close enough to real soil so as to tempt a campesino to try to grow something on it. It is also close enough to non-soil so as to break the heart of one who tries.

Not that Illinois Alvarez was in any danger of having his heart broken. For no one could possibly have mistaken him for a campesino. Although yes, he was breaking a sweat in a field near Jachalco, Puebla. Yes, he had a basket of seed corn strapped to his shoulder. Yes, he had a planting spade in his left hand. Yes, he was plodding along a row marked for seeding. Yes, he was thrusting the spade into the ground at more or less regular intervals and casting two or three seeds into the opening behind the spade. Yes, he was closing the gash in the earth by a swipe of his right foot. And thrusting again. And casting seed again. And again with the foot. One two three. Pala clavada. Semilla echada. Hoyita tapada. Just as his cousins had shown him.

With one enormous unequivocal difference. The labor of the cousins was a thing of beauty. Every step had cadence. Every motion of the arm exuded fluidity. Every movement exhibited elegant, envy-arousing rhythm. In contrast, the exertions of Illinois displayed only dull, deadly drudgery.

So what was Illinois Alvarez doing in a cornfield at the far southern end of North America? Sembrando maiz is the obvious answer. But how did he come to be there? For Jachalco is a long way from Chicago, where we observed, so to speak, his conception. And no, he had not been deported.

Here again, some background is required.

Know, then, that in the year of the massacre of Tlatelolco, Illinois Alvarez took to the road for a muddle of reasons that we will not attempt to sort out here. Suffice it to say that his intent was to visit his mother's family in Puebla and his father's family in the ancestral village of Jachalco. For in Jachalco, his father, Juan Alvarez, had been born and raised. His grandfather, Rodolfo Alvarez, also. And the grandfather's brother-in-law, Gilberto Robles, as well. And this Gilberto had fathered a boy named Rogelio, who in his turn had fathered two boys, Raul and Oscar Robles. And these last two were the pair referred to earlier as the cousins of the "envy-arousing rhythm."

Returning to the cornfield then.

It was a Sunday afternoon in the early spring of the year following the Tlatelolco massacre. Noise had arrived in Jachalco on the afternoon bus from Puebla. He had stopped by to say hello to his Uncle Antonio and then proceeded to the Robles home. In the course of two earlier visits, he had struck up a friendship with Raul and Oscar Robles. In this early phase, the relationship was based more on a mildly incredulous fascination than a commonality of ancestors. Noise could not believe that his two cousins, one of them his age and the other a year younger, could already carry themselves with the same calm dignity as their father. The Robles brothers could not believe that their gringo cousin, nearly twenty-four, could still behave like a volatile adolescent.

Noise accepted an invitation to Sunday dinner. Present also was Raul and Oscar's sister, Victoria. She attended secondary school in a nearby town, and she and Noise had not previously met. The introductions were hardly finished when she began battering him with questions.

"¿De dónde vienes? ¿Siempre hace frío allá? ¿Cómo pueden caminar los coches sobre la nieve? ¿Es cierto que no hay tortillas allá? ¿Te gusta la música? ¿Conoces a los Beatles? ¿Quién mató al presidente Kennedy?"

A native Spanish speaker would have needed considerable verbal dexterity to keep pace with the effervescent adolescent. Noise had no chance at all. He was just about to stagger and stutter into a response, when Victoria bailed him out by suddenly shifting to his first language, "I am learning English. You will help me, yes? You will teach me, yes? In five years I want to speak a perfect English." Noise was so relieved that he immediately agreed.

Following dinner, the women cleared the table and the men gave Noise his first lesson in pulque drinking. Pulque is the name for the fermented juice of the maguey cactus. As the Robles cousins had expected, Noise proved to be an avid learner. He tried pulque plain, and then with strawberry flavoring, and then with pineapple flavoring, and then with orange soda, and then with cherry soda. All of which loosened his tongue. His Spanish improved remarkably. Unfortunately, he also made a promise to help in the field the following day. A promise he remembered with forlorn regret on Monday morning when, at six o'clock, his cousins dumped him from his bed with an unceremonious, "Órale, Primo. El sol nos está ganando."

La Señora Robles showed a little compassion. She offered a cup of coffee and a conchita along with an "Ay M'hijo" and a "Pobrecito" or two. Noise managed a couple sips of coffee. Then he was escorted out the door to the remolque. He struggled to a sitting position on a sack of seed corn just as the horses started to move.

The field to be seeded that day was about a kilometer from the village. It stretched from north to south for some four hundred meters. Noise was assigned the first row and given a short course in technique. It was a three-step process. Pala clavada. Semilla echada. Hoyita tapada. Not too difficult. Even for a city boy. Make a hole. Put in the seed. Cover the hole. Noise tried it. Then again. And again.

He was klutzy. Borderline inept. The cousins concealed their amusement behind enthusiastic praise.

"Así se hace, Primo."

"De estilo, Primo."

"En dos días vas a ser maistro."

Then with Noise occupied and out of their way, the cousins began the day's work in earnest. In a matter of seconds, they had moved past him and down the field at a magnificently measured and effortlessly efficient pace. He was astonished. The spade always opened the soil to the precise depth. The seed always fell precisely into the opening. The hole was always precisely covered. All with a maximum of accuracy. All with a minimum of effort.

Ruefully Noise returned his attention to his own row. He tried to achieve some rhythm. To no avail. The spade went in too deep. The seed fell next to, rather than into, the opening. He kicked dirt onto his other shoe, rather than over the hole. Pala errada. Semilla regada. Hoyita fallada. With some grit but little grace, he plodded ahead.

Frustration grew. Suspicion set in. There was something the cousins hadn't told him. A trick they had not shared. He stopped to observe them. What could it possibly be? They were following precisely the three steps that they had shown him. The spade goes into the ground. The seed goes into the hole. The hole gets covered with soil. The spade goes into the ground. The seed goes into the hole. The hole gets covered with soil. ¡Chingao! There had to be a trick.

From the start, his body had been oozing and losing moisture. Now he began sweating profusely. Soon he was panting. He forced himself to further exertion. The voices of derision resounded in his brain. Pala clavada, Primo. Semilla hechada, Primo. Hoyita tapada, Primo. A crazy cracked recording that went on and on. He was getting dizzy. He noticed a small tree a few meters ahead next to the field. He dropped the spade and the seed basket. He stumbled to the tree and lay down in its shade. The sky above him was spinning. He closed his eyes.

Little by little his breathing returned to normal. It's the oxygen depletion because of the altitude, he reminded himself. It was small solace. Even less consoling were the jeers of his cousins as they passed him on their second lap of the day. "¿Ya mero?" Raul called out cheerfully. Noise sat up and answered, "Ya merito." But the attempt to sound jaunty died in his throat. Oscar yelled, "¿Así trabajan en Gringolandia?" Noise pretended not to hear. He tried to get to his feet. He staggered a few steps toward his row and sat down again. It was another half hour before he could resume his task.

For awhile, it went a little better. He forgot about rhythm and concentrated on accuracy. He guided the spade into the soil to the proper depth. He virtually counted the seeds into the opening. He covered the hole slowly and carefully. The cousins lapped him. He ignored them. They lapped him again. He held to his pace. At ten o'clock, Raul called him to brunch. "Ven a almorzar, Primo. Para trabajar bien hay que comer bien." The cousins had each finished seven rows. Noise had not finished one.

He expected the raillery to continue during brunch. It didn't happen. The cousins ate their enchiladas and drank their beer in total silence. Noise began to feel nervous. "¿Qué tanto vamos a terminar hoy?" he asked. "Todo," was the answer from Raul. Noise was sure he had misunderstood. "¿Todo el campo?" Raul patiently explained. "Sí. Son treinta y cinco surcos. Es lo que llamamos una tarea. O sea, para dos sembradores, es un día de trabajo." Noise let out a soft whistle. So that was it. The cousins' apparent nonchalance was a mask. In fact they were locked into a real endurance test. Clearly they could not expend energy on small talk.

Without appetite, Noise washed down two enchiladas with a soda. Then a brief rest. Then back to work. Then more trouble. His digestive system shifted into reverse. Maybe from the intensity of the sun. Or the jolt of the enchiladas. Or a residual effect of the pulque from the previous evening. Or all of these in concert. Whatever the case, he experienced a total loss of control. He started shaking. Then sweating. Great beads of liquid oozing from his head and torso. Really scary stuff. Actually sweating bullets. Then icy chills. And more sweat. And more chills. He retched. Again. From deep within. He barfed. Again. From deep within. Copiously. Gushes of the stuff. The enchiladas had grown and multiplied within his stomach. Then more wrenching retching, producing nothing. Finally it slowed to a stop. Again he stumbled to the shade tree and collapsed. For the next hour, death seemed like a probable and not totally unwelcome outcome.

Then a curious calm took hold. Body weakened and resigned. Brain active and unpredictable. Ground tilled and primed for seeding.

BOOK ONE, CHAPTER THREE

He replayed all his wanderings from Chicago to Jachalco. All that centrifugal energy now collapsing back into the self. And the self totally detached. Cut loose from its groundings. Sinking into the soil. Entering the shell of the Earth. Down through the mantle. On to the core. To the very innards of the planet. Sensing the convulsing energy. Taking the pulse of the elemental churning forces. And then returning with the currents impelled toward the surface. Murmurs and tremors bouncing about the crust. Oceans and continents and all they contained drifting with the whim of the energy. Without a goal. Without a plan. Nobody's fault. No one asleep at the switch. There was no switch. That was okay. That didn't mean that it was all without purpose. It just meant that purpose was not a given. People had to imagine and create their own purpose. Out of the stuff that bubbled up from the Earth. Out of the stuff that bubbled up from the self.

While Noise was achieving his modified version of nirvana, the less blessed cousins continued their stoic tread up and down the field. North to south to north to south. Pala clavada. Semilla echada. Hoyita tapada. The sun climbed to its zenith. There were still more than a dozen rows to complete. They persisted. Step by step by step. Row by row by row. About one o'clock they took a water break and stretch. Then again to the task. By two o'clock they were pausing at the end of each row to flex their hands and arms. Sweaty, grimy, cramped, fatigued, determined, they held their course. Pala clavada. Semilla echada. Hoyita tapada. Then it was almost done. Shortly after three o'clock they began their last lap.

And marvel to behold. Noise too, at last, arose from his reverie to finish his row.

He stayed until Thursday. But not to further an agricultural career. Instead he was cajoled by the charming Victoria into making good on his promise to assist her in learning a perfect English.

Noise had no idea where to begin. But after a brief conversation, he identified one area that required some remediation. Victoria could not correctly produce a "th" sound. Every "think" sounded like "sink." "It's all in the tongue placement. Look." He then demonstrated the need to extend the tongue beyond the front teeth. Click. "Sank you" instantly became, "Thank you." That's great. Thank you. That's terrific. Thank you. Success led to excess. Innocently he taught her to say, "This is the thing." Locura. Frenesí. Every conversation now started with, "This is the thing." He had unwittingly created a compulsive linguistic monster. The response to "¿Cómo estás?" began with "This is the thing." "Pass the tortillas," was preceded by, "This is the thing." Finally the Thursday bus for Puebla arrived and he made his escape.

But he kept going back. To tutor Victoria. To help Raul and Oscar. To get better acquainted with Rogelio and Leticia. But more than anything, to absorb the warm feel of the Robles home, so unlike the atmosphere of the house where he had grown up in Chicago.

And soon the García twins, Laura and Hilda, began to accompany him to Jachalco. And not long after that, Raul and Oscar Robles began to ignore Noise and focus on his pretty cousins.

But that's another story.

CHAPTER FOUR

RANDOM WAS ALWAYS THE RULE.

Though the rule was ignored early on. Consider Copernicus, Galileo, Kepler, and others of that ilk and era. Luminaries of heliocentricity. Discerners of celestial symmetries. Heralds of heavenly harmonies. Splendid lads all. Not for them the evident inconvenience of misguided meteorites. Nor the inconvenient evidence of aberrant asteroids. No indeed. None of that. Everywhere they looked they encountered congruity. Sweet lovers of ethereal euphony. If one of them had been fatally mauled by a rock from space, he would have died trying to prove that it had been launched by an irate neighbor.

Then came Sir Isaac and the Royal Society and the rest of that mafia. Newton. Apoplectic apologist of universal ordurous order. The cosmos could now be made to behave not only musically but mathematically as well. A place for everything and everything in its place. Anything awry would be righted by God, and if God wasn't up to it, Newton was there to advise. Quite properly so. God, after all, had merely purveyed the creation. Sir Isaac had provided the stuff to hold it together. The fable of the fruit falling from malus sylvestris which led to his attack of gravitas contains a major error. Ironically the error is numerical. For in fact, so massive was Sir Isaac's cranium, that it attracted and was battered by an entire bushel of windfalls.

But the universe would not be still. Not only were there subsequent discoveries of entities both larger and smaller than anything Sir Isaac had allowed for. Those novel entities also began to behave badly. Even worse, their indiscretions proved to be intelligible. Setting Newton aside, Einstein unriddled the orbit of Mercury. Planck and Heinsenberg guaranteed uncertainty. The floodgates opened. Antimatter appeared, in a manner of speaking. Black holes entered the picture. Or rather, someone finally noticed them. Eventually the concepts included such lovelies as superstrings, virtual particles, and speculation about something called a naked singularity.

Here at last we find ourselves in a universe where it is easier to accept that somewhere on the planet at every moment the sky falls on someone. A lot of it is pretty ordinary stuff. Ruptures, fractures, hernias, hemorrhoids. Some of it is a bit more exotic. At least in name. Embolisms, aneurysms, sarcomas, melanomas.

Fortunately for the species, most of that mess targets the senior set. But the juniors don't escape entirely. Understandably, most of the items on their list cluster around the themes of sporting competition, chemical experimentation, and vehicular velocity. But here, too, we occasionally encounter the exotic. In the case of the Alvarez and Robles families, it was a crater lake cum maelstrom.

Which brings us back to Jachalco. Within walking distance of the village, there are a number of huge holes in the earth. These are apparently the craters of anciently extinct volcanoes. Their sides are generally precipitous, but in a few instances, the rim has collapsed, and a zigzag path provides access to the bottom. In one of the more shallow of these craters, a spring has effused, creating a small lake. The local people call it la laguna. And if we can believe these citizens, at the very center of the lake, there is a people-eating maelstrom.

But I anticipate. There are family matters that require elucidation.

BOOK ONE, CHAPTER FOUR

Know, then, that Noise's paternal grandfather, Rodolfo Alvarez, and his wife, Sacramento Robles, had produced four sons. Juan, whom we have already met as Noise's immediate progenitor, was the oldest. The other three in order were Antonio, Ramón, and Guillermo.

Next door to the Alvarez family in Jachalco lived Sacramento's brother, Gilberto Robles, with his wife, Ana Fernández. These two also had four sons. But somewhat younger. Cristóbal, the firstborn, was the same age as Guillermo Alvarez. Marcos was next. Then came Federico, mentioned in an earlier episode as a marine in the Pacific War. The baby was Rogelio, whom we met in the preceding episode as the father of Raul and Oscar and Victoria Robles.

Returning then to the incident of la laguna.

It was a Sunday afternoon in June. The children had gone off to their sports. The adolescents to soccer. The younger group for a swim. Baby Rogelio to his siesta. Ana and Sacramento were making plans for the evening meal. Rodolfo and Gilberto were resting on the patio of the Robles home, between them a bottle of rum that Gilberto's father, Don Vicente Robles, had liberated from the hacienda. Nothing unethical in that, mind you. Don Vicente was the mayordomo, and consequently the keeper of the keys, at the hacienda. He and the hacendados had an unspoken understanding that he would have an occasional need for a bottle. The rum, however, was doing little for the conversation. Rodolfo had no inclination toward either strong drink or strong opinion. Gilberto bravely bore the burden for both.

It was the year in which Venustiano Carranza had attempted his unsuccessful walk to Veracruz. In fact, Carranza's recent demise stirred a comment from Rodolfo. "Primero matan a Madero. Luego a Zapata. Ahora a Carranza. ¿Hasta cuándo va a parar esto?"

Gilberto emptied his glass and poured himself another three

29

fingers. He appreciated the deference shown by his brother-in-law. It was merited. For he was an avid, albeit skeptical, reader of history. In fact he habitually referred to history as la mentira colectiva. Rodolfo's remark, nevertheless, had evoked a pronouncement in him. "La revolución siempre consume a sus creadores." This was punctuated by the very substantial pause that it deserved. Then, "Y te digo una cosa. Al rato le toca su turno a Villa. Y a Calles y a Obregón si no se cuidan."

"¿Piensas?" This from Rodolfo was very strong doubt.

"De ley, hombre. Aquellos y más. Acuérdate de nuestra revolución del siglo pasado. Hagamos una lista: Hidalgo, Allende, Morelos, Guerrero, Iturbe. Por mencionar solo a los más destacados." Gilberto paused and drank to the fallen legends. Then he moved to another continent. "Los franceses pasaron por lo mismo. Mandaron al rey Luis a la guillotina. Y en poco tiempo le seguían Danton con sus discipulos. Luego Robespierre con los suyos. Todos terminaron en la misma violencia que ellos mismos habían creado. Es como si fuera una ley de la historia."

The digression into French history produced a silence of several minutes. Then Rodolfo countered with what for him was a broadside. "A mí se me hace que la revolución de los gringos fue distinta. Washington por lo menos se murió en la cama."

This time the response was so delayed that Rodolfo began to think he had scored a knockout. It was not to be. "¿Pero cuál revolución, hombre? No hubo ninguna. Cuando los norteamericanos declararon la independencia, ya no eran ingleses. Por su manera de pensar, por su distinta cultura, ellos ya constituían un pueblo independiente de Inglaterra."

Rodolfo was preparing himself for a verbal battering. Instead the conversation ended abruptly. At the moment that Gilberto said "Inglaterra" the small door in the zaguan opened, and his son

BOOK ONE, CHAPTER FOUR

Federico, one of the swimmers, staggered through the opening. The boy was dirty and scratched and bruised. Much more disturbing was that he was simultaneously hyperventilating and trying to scream. Gilberto embraced the boy and yelled for Ana and Sacramento. Rodolfo raced to get the horses. It took him a full ten minutes to bridle, saddle, and return with the mounts. In that time the others were able to learn only that something had happened at la laguna.

Rodolfo and Gilberto covered the three kilometers to the lagoon at a controlled gallop. They left the horses at the top and stumbled down the slope. After a brief search, they found the clothing of Rodolfo's son, Guillermo, and Gilberto's two sons, Cristóbal and Marcos, piled on a tree branch near the water's edge. There was no sign of the boys. The two men climbed back to the top, rode to the nearest village, and made some inquiries. No one had seen their sons. They returned to the lagoon and rode around the perimeter, calling out the boys' names. Then they descended once more and did a complete circuit of the lake, again calling for their sons, to no avail. Finally with the coming of dark, the ride home was no longer avoidable.

Meanwhile, Ana and Sacramento slowly calmed Federico. They hugged his trembling body. They stroked his wounded limbs. They soothed his pounding chest. They blessed and kissed and caressed and cuddled and rocked him. They murmured and mumbled countless M'hijos and Pobrecitos. Little by little the shudders became less violent. When he was able to drink, they gave him some warm milk laced with rum. Still it was a full half hour before he achieved coherence. Then it soon became clear that he had very little to tell.

The boys had arrived at the lagoon in the early afternoon. The eleven-year-olds, Cristóbal and Guillermo, and the ten-year-old Marcos were accomplished swimmers. It was their job to teach the six-year-old tagalong runt Federico. They had promised their parents.

And they made an effort. Brief. Perfunctory. And Federico tried to learn. As long as they remained in the shallows. But soon the older boys were coaxing him into deeper water. He balked. Then the verbal abuse began. "¡Maricón! Vete a jugar con tus muñecas. ¡Pinche chillón! Te vamos a poner un vestido cuando lleguemos a la casa." Federico fled.

Once he was safely out of the water and into his clothes, he turned back to the older boys to fire off a salvo of his own. "Que los coma el remolino." He had heard people talk about the maelstrom. He did not have a clear concept of what it was. But when he yelled the word remolino, it sounded offensive, and he was pleased. He grabbed his slingshot and went off to hunt birds.

On previous swimming excursions, the older boys had sometimes tried to scare Federico by feigning a drowning. Consequently even when he heard the shout, "¡Auxilio!" he hardly looked up. Eventually, however, he tired of his solitary hunting and meandered back to where earlier the four had undressed. He could see no one. A fear began at the edge of consciousness. He could easily believe that they had abandoned him. But they would not have left their clothes. He stood at the water's edge for a minute and screamed, "¡Cristóbal! ¡Marcos! Ya sálganse. Me están asustando de de veras."

Only the big people would know what to do. He started running to the path that led to the rim. At the top he was already exhausted, but he forced himself to go on. As long as he was moving, the horrifying probability could be kept at bay. Staggering, stumbling, falling, crawling, he dragged himself to Jachalco.

The bodies were raised the next day. There were no marks or clues indicating the cause of the drownings. So, of course, there was much ado in the land of guess and maybe. One hypothesis was cramps. But was it likely that three swimmers would experience cramps simultaneously? Another conjecture was a game of chicken.

BOOK ONE, CHAPTER FOUR

This was more credible, since the boys were prone to such mutual dares. But would they take their game to such an extreme? Most people simply raised their level of belief in the people-eating maelstrom.

A bitter conclusion for six-year-old Federico. For weeks following the tragedy, he wandered around his home mumbling to himself, "Yo no tuve la culpa."

He received no help from his parents. At first his father was busy with the funeral. He brought the bodies home. He notified relatives. He arranged for the church services and burials. He saw to it that the mourners had food and drink. He led the funeral procession. But when all that busywork was finished, he did not reach out to his wife and surviving sons. Instead he withdrew into himself. He did not neglect his work, but he did it in the manner of an automaton. He only spoke to answer a question. He ate very little. He lost his taste for strong drink. Within two years, he was dead of cancer.

Federico's mother, Ana Fernández, was also mightily traumatized by the tragedy. The day after the drownings, her breast milk went sour, and baby Rogelio had to be abruptly weaned. Not long after the funeral, she began to converse with imaginary people whom she almost always encountered in doorways. She became a sleepwalker, on some occasions wandering around the village in her nightgown. Although she was still in her early thirties, her menstrual cycle never resumed.

Rodolfo Alvarez had his own peculiar symptoms. He seemed to lose all sense of purpose. Frequently, instead of going to work in his fields, he would loiter around the village for an entire day. He would stop people to ask them if they had borrowed his hoe or machete. If he met the same people ten minutes later, he would question them again about his missing tools.

Only Sacramento Robles allowed the sorrow to embrace her fully and thereby withstood the shock. During the week following the funeral, she was as disoriented as the other three parents. But then a reaction set in. She began to feel trapped in her house. There was never enough to do. She cooked. She prepared the masa and made the tortillas. She fed the Robles and Alvarez families. She washed dishes. She scrubbed and cleaned the house. She did the laundry. She ironed. She mended. She bathed the little ones. She tended to their hurts. She fed the chickens and turkeys. She gathered the eggs. Finally at ten o'clock, she went to bed. But by four o'clock the next morning, in her words, "La cama me lastima." There was simply not enough work.

Eventually she began helping in the fields. After the breakfast dishes had been washed, she would prepare a torta for Federico and a bottle for Rogelio. Then she would grab a diaper or two and a hoe, and off the three would go for a few hours in the milpa. There she would find a tree with a sturdy branch within her reach. Using her rebozo, she would fashion an hamaca for the baby. With a piece of rope, she would improvise a swing for Federico. Then she attacked the weeds.

She would hurry down a row of corn or beans until the little boys could no longer observe her face. Then she would allow herself to grieve. Tears only at first. Oozing from her eyes. Mixing with her sweat. Falling to the soil. But always hoeing. Hoeing. Devastating the weeds. Destroying the weeds. Hateful, ugly, life-sucking weeds. When she was sure that the boys would no longer hear her, she would let herself sob and moan until the hurt was once again at a manageable intensity.

On Sundays, Sacramento would find an opportunity to slip away from the village and visit the panteón. There, for an hour, she would sit beside the small crosses that marked the graves and talk to the boys about what was happening in Jachalco. Later she would kneel, and while her tears fell on their graves, she would ask the Virgen of

BOOK ONE, CHAPTER FOUR

Guadalupe to keep them safe in the afterlife. Then she would hurry back to her work.

And so, with weeding and weeping, the summer passed. By harvest time the pain in her chest had lessened. Again she began to have hopes and plans for her children. Which now included Federico and Rogelio.

Ana Fernández did not reject her two remaining sons. Nor did she ever discuss transferring them to the care of their aunt. She merely started acting as if all the boys were the children of Sacramento, and she, Ana, an extra member of the household, who assisted in their care. And because Ana lived for only another twelve years, Sacramento became in time the only abuelita that Rogelio's children would ever know.

But that's another story.

CHAPTER FIVE

BEGINNINGS ARE NEVER UNAMBIGUOUS.

In some cases for transparent reasons. Consider the selection of a starting point for cyclical phenomena. The tides. The phases of the moon. The seasons of the year. Any whim will do and all whims are equally valid.

Or the life cycle itself. Conception. Gestation. Birth. Accretion. Pubescence. Maturation. Reproduction. Decrepitude. Death. The last two items are not, of course, phases of the cycle in a strict sense, but rather a way of getting the individual actors off the stage, once they have finished their reproductive struts and frets. Some species do this with admirable efficiency. In salmon, for example, decrepitude and death follow immediately as consequences of reproduction. Other species, humans notably, allow the individuals to lollygag along in decrepitude for decades. Often to the considerable consternation of their offspring.

In any event, what remains clear is that the selection of a starting point for cyclical processes depends on the caprice of the selector. But suppose that the universe allows for linear as well as cyclical processes. And suppose that the formation of our solar system was such a linear process. We hypothesize a sort of elemental cloud that densified as it rotated. The center of the cloud began to accumulate

BOOK ONE, CHAPTER FIVE

matter by gravitational attraction, until it formed a massive glob, which eventually became luminescent. The glob continued to rotate and densify until it went nuclear. Voilà. But whence came the elemental cloud? We postulate that it formed from some even more inchoate matter. But where did that stuff originate? Stop. Let's assign the beginning point to some event of the process. But which? The moment of luminescence? The instant of nuclear fusion? We can, of course, define "beginning" in such a way that only luminescence or only fusion meet the terms of our definition. That, however, constitutes redundance, not incipience.

And if the question of beginnings is problematic in astrophysics, imagine the ambiguity it takes on in matters of the heart. Case in point, Natalia Alvarez and the Frenchman. Who would hazard a guess as to when that affair commenced. Was it the moment of the first bold eye contact in the market, she intent on staring down an ogler. Or the moment when he, after disarming her with a warm, blue-eyed smile, asked her name. Or when he lingered with the hand touch as he paid for the half kilo of petits pois. Or perhaps none of these. For he had already been observing her at a distance. The purchase of the petits pois was mere pretense.

In any event, le fait initial was certainly not the day we observe her aboard a burro on the road from her home village to Jalapa. For on that occasion, she was already carrying a two-month-old babe in her rebozo.

Here again I anticipate. A family update is de rigueur.

You will recall that Illinois Alvarez y García was the son of Juan Alvarez y Robles, who in turn was the son of Rodolfo Alvarez y Jiménez. Note the use of the two surnames. Standard Hispanic practice. By custom, an individual introduces himself by giving the family name of first his father and then his mother. Know, then, that it is something much more serious than an oversight when I tell you that the father of Rodolfo Alvarez was known as Pascual Alvarez only. Even more appalling. He received that surname not from a male progenitor but from his mother. Her name, as you have certainly already guessed, was Natalia Alvarez.

Returning then to the road to Jalapa.

It was a Sunday morning, a few weeks after the fourth anniversary of the battle of Puebla. Natalia was bouncing along on the burro's behind, trying to prepare herself for the reunion with Jean Batiste Leduc, her baby's father. The consequences of the encounter could be enormous. For her. Even more so for her son. And she was so unsure of herself. So overwhelmed. So alone. Her Aunt Teresa, with whom she stayed in Jalapa, would willingly have accompanied her. Belatedly upholding what remained of the family honor. But with predictably disastrous results. There would have been accusations. Hysterical tears. Denunciations. Possibly even threats. Then an attempt at a grand-style exit. No. Better to go alone. She would confront Jean in all her helplessness. He would respond to her vulnerability. Or, if not, then surely he would be moved at the sight of his son. Love would call to love. The child was fat and fair with lovely green eyes. If others could not resist the charm of those eyes, how could the father?

There were no grounds for doubting Jean Batiste. Unless you counted the lengthy hiatus in the relationship. That had begun with Natalia's return to her village in the eighth month of pregnancy. She had gotten very fat. It had become advisable to escape from Jean's disapproving gaze. Then there had been the long final weeks, and the labor and delivery, and the ritual rehabilitation following the birth. Finally the customary forty days had been completed, and the midwife had pronounced her fit. Now she was once again rushing to her lover's embrace. Well, at least rushing at the best pace that a burro could maintain over an eight-kilometer trail.

BOOK ONE, CHAPTER FIVE

The burro, Ney, for so he had been named by Jean Batiste, had carried Natalia to Jalapa at least a dozen times, and she felt a genuine compassion and admiration for him. Every few kilometers, she would dismount and walk beside him for some distance. Twice she stopped to nurse Pascualito, giving the burro time to graze the scrub grass around the magueyes that lined the trail. As the baby pulled on her engorged breasts, she watched the donkey search out and crop the barely visible vegetation. "¡Qué aguante!" she said aloud. "Se afama por su estupidez. Pero son ignorantes los que dicen eso. ¿Quién no quisiera tener el aguante de este pobrecito?" Ney of course did not respond. But neither did he let her down.

Jean Batiste had let her down. There had been only two letters during the nearly four months that they had been apart. Not even letters really. More like notes. Pensando en ti. That was about all. And the last one already six weeks old. She had expected so much more.

Justifiably so. For whatever event may have constituted the beginning of the romance, there was passion enough in the early days. Jean had followed up the encounter in the market with a series of visits and gifts. La Tía Teresa had reacted somewhat in the manner of Zaragoza at Puebla. Initially she had positioned herself to resist the Frenchman with all her limitless courage and all her limited might. Then, not much later, she had found the same position indefensible and had begun to counsel accommodation.

To the extent that time allowed, Natalia accommodated. She was still attending la escuela de comercio in the morning and helping her aunt with the sale of produce at the market stall in the afternoon. But she did have some time available in the late evenings.

Jean Batiste was a lieutenant in the French expeditionary force assigned to the garrison at Jalapa. Since the French were in firm control of the capital, and since most of the country had already been pacified, his duties were fairly routine. He too had some time available in the late evenings.

Aunt Teresa chaperoned. At least initially. She counseled restraint. Then things began to heat up. She counseled caution. Then the affair began to get out of hand. She disappeared. But not before confiding to her niece every anticonceptive trick known to the women of that era. This lively performance included a demonstration of several techniques for achieving coitus interruptus.

One thing led to another. One evening Jean arrived shortly after Natalia had finished her bath. She invited him into her room. Seated on the edge of her bed, with only a dressing gown covering her virtue, and with her hair hanging limp and slightly damp on her shoulders, she projected the aura of half-vamp, half-virgin, just as she had calculated. She was tantalizing. She was enticing. She was irresistible. Men of lesser passion would have fallen to their knees and gone directly to a declaration of love and a proposal of eternal bliss. Jean Batiste fell to his knees and went directly to the clitoris, easing her back onto the bed, so that he could better concentrate his efforts. This was not, of course, part of Natalia's plan, but she was not about to haggle over specifics. Soon she was moaning and groaning and calling him a diablo. Undeterred, he brought her to orgasm, dancing as it were on the tip of his tongue.

Then, while she continued enthralled in her passionate response, he hastily freed his member from his clothing and entered her with no undue ceremony. So intensely aroused was he that, even had she recalled the instructions for coitus interruptus, it would have been too late. Within seconds, he had had his way with her.

From that day forward, there was no inhibition and little restraint. The mere sight of each other could provoke a frenzy. In a matter of seconds, they would be panting and pulling at each others' clothes. On rare occasions, when circumstances had kept them apart for a few days, they would vanquish the separation with two or three couplings in the same evening.

The swoon that had overtaken them lasted for several months. The end of the beginning occurred when Natalia was forced to acknowledge that her problematic period was more than a mere tardanza. She was, in fact, pregnant. The word she used to describe her condition was embarazada. Jean Batiste, demonstrating Gallic nicety, insisted that she refer to her condition with the word encinta. To please him, she acquiesced. In most matters she began to acquiesce. She was terrified of losing him. "Yo sé que me vas a dejar" became the refrain of many a conversation. "Cuando esté gorda ya no me vas a querer." He attempted to reassure her with a phrase he had memorized, "Jamás te abandonaré."

The pronoun and verb were virtually identical in French. Equivocation entered with the adverb. Had he been obligated to utter the French word, jamais, he might have been more inclined to keep his promise. At least there would have existed the resonance of moments of interaction with his mother or aunt when the word had been spoken solemnly and unconditionally. The strength of the cerebral synapse formed on those occasions would have reverberated and evoked a sense of duty and a sensitivity to consequences. Jamais would have resounded with: Thou shalt never. Jamais would have echoed centuries of honoring the female.

But the Spanish adverb carried no such resonance. Jamás was empty. Jamás was neutral. Jamás was a word that could be used to have your way with une ingenue provincial.

At the outskirts of Jalapa, Ney called to another burro that was tied to a gatepost. Natalia kicked him impatiently. The end of her solitude was at hand. She was in a hurry to be done with confronting the world alone. A few more minutes and Jean Batiste would take her into his arms. Together the two would face and face down all of life's importunities.

It was not to be. Since the previous month, Jean Batiste Leduc and his regiment had been reposted to Veracruz. Furthermore, their stay in that port would be brief. Soon they would be recalled to France to face the saber-rattling Prussians. The sergeant who spoke with Natalia was, however, conscientious enough to remember une lettre that the lieutenant had left for Mademoiselle. She was so stunned that she accepted it.

There were no tears. Not while the French could see her. Not while anyone could see her. She stayed in town only the time necessary to nurse Pascualito, buy herself a torta, and water the burro. Then they were back on the trail.

About halfway home she made a stop. A most significant stop. She put her baby down in the shade of a capulín. Then she abandoned herself to the moans and sobs and tears which had been welling up inside. This went on for several minutes. Meanwhile Ney, who had drunk copiously in Jalapa, began to relieve himself. This too went on and on until Natalia could not help noticing. "A fuerza me tienes que ganar, ¿verdad?" Ney did not respond, but he had given her an inspiration. A spitefully delightful inspiration. She found a sharp flat stone and dug a hole near the capulín. Into the hole, she put the unopened letter from Jean Batiste. She lifted her skirts, pulled down her drawers, squatted over the hole, and pissed. Then she kicked the loose dirt over the hole, picked up her baby, mounted the burro, and went on.

Two years later, she was again living with her Aunt Teresa in Jalapa, and working at the market for her room and board. She would rise early and open the stall so as to catch the early trade. Later Teresa would join her for the busy hours. In the lazy afternoon, they would each catch a nap. Natalia would then stay to close while her aunt went home to cook.

Her life might have continued in a repetition of just such days,

BOOK ONE, CHAPTER FIVE

had it not been for Don Antonio Quiroz, who entered the market one day to buy some flowers. He was passing Aunt Teresa's produce stall when Natalia's voice caught his attention. "Perdón Señora, permítame hacerle la cuenta." She then proceeded to enumerate the purchases that the Señora had just made, specifying the price per kilo of each, calculating the cost per item, and adding that amount to the total bill. There were fifteen items, and she did the account at a pace that Don Antonio could barely sustain. No pencil and paper. No abacus. No calculating device of any kind. He positioned himself where he could observe her unobtrusively. What a gem. Not only was she efficient; there was no hint of servility about her. She exuded dignity. And she found ways to support the dignity of her customers. Suggesting items that might have been forgotten. Pardoning error with a genuine, "No hay cuidado."

He introduced himself. He was the administrator of the hacienda of Jachalco, and he was in need of an administrative assistant. They discussed the job duties, concluding that she was probably overqualified. They discussed salary. It was most generous. She mentioned her son, expecting the conversation to come to a polite end. It did not. The boy would be as welcome as she. But where was Jachalco? Don Antonio drew a map. Then he explained that he was leaving for home on the stage the following morning. Natalia and Pascual were packed and waiting for him at the station.

The first year, she returned to Jalapa and her home village for Noche Buena and Año Nuevo. She did so again the following year. But reluctantly. After that, she went back only for funerals. By the third year, Jachalco had become her home.

She worked long hours, but the job was not onerous. Little by little, she took on all the bookkeeping for the hacienda. She also handled a major portion of the business correspondence. On occasion, she even substituted for the governess.

CONTINENTAL NEXUS

She found ways to charm and disarm the women of the hacienda. But she preferred the society of men. She went to work in pants and smoked cigarettes. She loved talk of commerce. She was an excellent listener. She learned. In time, she became a speculator in grain. From that activity, she saved enough to purchase land from the hacienda. Eventually she owned twenty hectáreas, which she passed on to her grandson Rodolfo.

Was she Don Antonio's mistress? The question is best left in the land of guess and maybe. Perhaps she was, and he was prematurely infertile. Or perhaps they had an improved formula for coitus interruptus. Or maybe there was no basis for the rumors. What is certain is that she had no more children.

What is also certain is that Don Antonio took a keen interest in her son Pascual's education. And for a time, the young man also flourished. He became an accomplished guitarist. He was a regional champion at jaripeo. He succeeded wonderfully at his studies and could have become a superb accountant and administrator. But at school, he joined a political faction of supernationalists. He became obsessed with the idea of ridding his bloodline of any sign of French ancestry. To that end, he married a village woman with strong indigenous features and a braid that hung below her waist. With her he had three children. The second and third died as babes. The eldest was Rodolfo Alvarez, whom we already know as Noise's grandfather. One day when Rodolfo was about seven years old, his father walked out of Jachalco and never returned.

But genetic slippage is a fact of life. Pascual's great-grandson, Illinois Alvarez, was blessed with pale grey eyes, which women would find decidedly hypnotic.

But that's another story.

CHAPTER SIX

AT TIMES THERE WAS ENOUGH.

Do not make light of that. If you live in a time-place of plenty, praise your gods. Abundance permits a wealth of human foibles. Even competition. But dearth has been the more typical predicament of the species. And enough is all that stands between us and Darwin's damnation. For when the fittest are selected, there is scant cause for rejoicing. Even if you are one of the fit.

Selection is as capricious a reaper of species, as death is of individuals. Consider a case. Two species of antelope share an environment containing tall grass and short grass. One species eats only short grass. We will call them the specialists. The other species eats both tall grass and short grass. We will call them the generalists. One day a plague of locusts appears in the region. The locusts consume all the tall grass, thus creating a scarcity for the antelope herds. What follows? Because of their greater efficiency at cropping the short grass, the specialists will outcompete the generalists for the available food.

Notice what happens. The selective pressure is such that the antelope with the wider range of adaptability are eliminated. Why? Because, in this instance, the selective pressure favors the specialists. Are they, therefore, the fittest? Given the selective pressure, yes.

Does this result diminish the long-range survivability of the antelope? Probably. But such is selection. Indifferent as to outcome. Inexorable as to execution. Blind as to consequences.

But stop there. Alter the data just slightly. At the moment when the locusts do their worst and move on, posit an abundance of short grass in the environment. How distinct the outcome. Now everyone is selected because there is enough.

Sacramento Robles might have been baffled by talk of selective pressure. She had probably never heard of Darwin. But she knew quite a lot about survival. She was well informed on the topic of feeding habits. She was encyclopedic on the question of, "Is there enough?"

That was the very question Sacramento was wrestling with as she went about her morning chores. As usual, she had gotten up at four o'clock. After crossing herself and saying a short prayer, she had dressed, fussed with her hair briefly, and splashed some water onto her face. Then she had shouldered the pail of nixtamal and started for the hacienda. There the hacendados had a generator-powered mill that ground the corn for the villagers.

At the mill, she watched with her usual, well-concealed awe as the machine magically turned the soaked corn into tortilla dough. Her wonderment was directed mostly at the machine's efficiency and power, which daily saved her hours of time and effort. But there was something else. Near the top of the mill's grinding chamber, there was a tiny defect in the housing. When the mill was loaded to near-capacity, the yellow juices of the nixtamal oozed out through this tiny opening. Sacramento recalled the morning when, observing these juices, the notion had flashed through her brain that the corn was bleeding. She had censored the thought and quickly pushed it aside. But the sensation had lingered and left her uneasy. Bleeding corn! A novel fancy. Not sinful. But surely dangerous. People who

BOOK ONE, CHAPTER SIX

suffered from novelties soon lost their way.

When the masa was ready, Sacramento again hoisted the pail onto her shoulder and hurried off to her kitchen. With the distractions of the molino safely behind her, she was soon back to fussing about the future of her sons. It appeared that the two oldest were destined for a double wedding in the late summer. That certainly raised the question of, "Would there be enough?"

There would be enough affection. Of that Sacramento was quite sure. She had met the García girls, María and Eva. She had questioned them about their home life. She had listened to their patter and chatter about the future. She had watched them interact with her sons. They were very immature. They were credulous beyond belief. Often they were downright silly. But they were also caring, forthright, and generous. They were perfect for her sons. But what was she to make of the Mendoza woman who was their grandma?

Sacramento and Asunción Mendoza had only recently become acquainted, and they were still at the sniffing and sniping phase of their relationship. In time that would change. In time the two would develop a sincere and profound dislike for each other.

But yes, again I am ahead of my story. Allow me to tie up some loose ends.

You will recall that the mother of Illinois Alvarez was one María García. You will also recall that her parents had died during the revolution. She and her siblings had been raised by their Aunt Gloria under the tutelage of their grandma, Asunción Mendoza.

Know, then, that this very same Asunción Mendoza considered herself one of that special class of humans that she referred to as los civilizados. This status brought with it certain responsibilities. One of which was to inform and instruct the less fortunate. So it was that waiters, drivers, porters, clerks, and even street sweepers were occasional recipients of a dose of her wisdom. Another duty was to pro-

47

mote a sense of civilizado in her descendants. So it was that she seldom went anywhere without her oldest granddaughters, María and Eva, who were expected to observe and emulate the behavior of their Abuelita. A third obligation was to vacation somewhere outside the city around Easter time. Accordingly, in the years following the revolution, Asunción began a series of spring visits to relatives in Jachalco.

The first spring visit coincided with the funeral of Gilberto Robles, who had died of cancer. The funeral drew Asunción's attention to the Alvarez family. She immediately discerned the presence of a pair of very marriageable young men. She herself would soon have a pair of very marriageable granddaughters. And time was not on her side. Her rapidly aging husband no longer worked at the academy in Puebla. His earnings from tutoring private students had dwindled to nearly nothing. There was still the rental income from the apartment building they owned. But that could provide adequately for perhaps five people. She was stretching it to support eight.

Asunción began to gather data regarding the Alvarez family. Then she drew up a sort of socioeconomic balance sheet. Predictably, by her standards, Juan and Antonio Alvarez were not great prospective husbands. They had minimal formal education. They were stereotypically rustic. Certainly they were dull. But they were also moderately prosperous. They were, by all accounts, passably industrious. And most importantly they were, Dios los bendiga, available.

The following spring, Asunción set out for Jachalco, strategically committed to matchmaking. She was, however, still a little vague about tactics. Her granddaughters were not. They too, it turned out, had noticed the Alvarez brothers. At a quinceañera, they found a way to become acquainted. By the end of that second spring holiday, María and Eva were imploring their Abuelita for a return to Jachalco during their summer vacation. Asunción could imagine nothing more dreary. But since it suited her plan, she reluctantly consented. She would use the time to ingratiate herself with the Alvarez family and begin the negotiations.

Sacramento Robles was not oblivious to all the maneuvering. But she did nothing to abet or hinder the young people's schemes. She had her own troubles. The memory of the laguna disaster had not faded. Now her brother was dead. Her sister-in-law was an invalid. Her husband had withdrawn into a premature dotage. Including her widowed father, she had nine mouths to feed. And then there was this business of her two oldest sons going north.

Regrettably, their plan made sense. The yearly labor of the village had a traditional rhythm that the revolution had upset. Late winter was the season to prepare fields for the new crops. There was an abundance of work. This pattern continued into the spring and early summer, when the seeding, cultivating, and weeding were done. Late summer, by contrast, was a slow time. Then, and on into the late fall, was the season when previously the Alvarez men would have looked for day work. That had provided income for the family until harvest time. But the day work had been at the hacienda. And because of the social and economic upheaval caused by the revolution, grain production, which was the main enterprise of the hacienda, had almost ceased. In fact there was so little activity that Don Vicente's position as mayordomo was becoming tenuous.

Returning then to the masa on its way to becoming tortillas in Sacramento's kitchen.

It was early on Tuesday morning of Easter week, in the year in which Plutarco Calles had accepted a demotion from the maximato to the presidencia, while he completed his plan for institutionalizing the revolution. It was also the year of the García girls' third spring holiday in Jachalco. Sacramento had just eased the masa pail off her shoulder and onto a table. She paused to catch her breath. It was unusual for her to tire so easily. Again it was the fault of that Asunción Mendoza woman, who had come calling the previous evening.

Sacramento paused to replay the scene. She had been in the process of preparing her nixtamal for Tuesday's tortillas. She had already shelled the criollo corn into the cooking bucket. She had added the required lime water, whose caustic properties aided the cooking and softening of the kernels, so as to facilitate grinding. She had placed the bucket onto the anafe and stoked the charcoal. She had looked up. There was the Mendoza woman, her head covered by a black shawl, as if she had gotten lost on her way to church.

"Buenas tardes. Te asusté."

"De ninguna manera. Buenas tardes."

"Pensé que aquí iba a encontrar a mis nietas."

"Sus nietas aquí. ¿Pero por qué?"

Perhaps Asunción had overexerted herself in her search for the girls. Or possibly she had found something accusatory in Sacramento's reply. Whatever the motive, without any prodding or prologue, she had launched into a litany of praises for her granddaughters. By her accounting, they were not only favored with a surfeit of faith, hope, and charity. They were also generously endowed with prudence, justice, fortitude, and temperance. They were blessed with all the beatitudes listed by the evangelists, besides a few that had gone unmentioned. They possessed an excess of modesty, an exorbitance of purity, and an extravagance of chastity. Their virtues would have sufficed to create a whole new bevy of venerables, raise several of them to the rank of blessed, and achieve the canonization of at least one or two.

Then, by an association that eluded Sacramento, the older woman had thrown herself into a condemnation of the revolution and all its works and all its pomps. The revolution had killed the sons whom she had counted on for support in her declining years. True, her children had been stupid. But she could have protected them from their stupidity, had it not been for the demagogs and their prevaricating rhetoric. Predictably, a major share of this vituperation was directed at Zapata. That poor son of Morelos was charged with every form of human perversion. He was guilty of necrofilia, coprofilia, and every other form of filia short of sodomizing a porcupine.

At one point, Sacramento attempted an interruption, "Está usted muy agitada, Señora. Le voy a preparar un té para los nervios." But it had no effect. The diatribe got old. The tea got cold. Then suddenly, almost in midsentence, Asunción had arisen and taken her leave.

Sacramento returned her attention to her task. The comal was hot enough. But she was not satisfied with the masa. It had come from the mill much too crude. She scooped a glob of it from the pail and dropped it onto her metate. Then with her neclapile, she began grinding it to a finer consistency. When it met her standards, she began shaping bolitas. She counted out twelve. One by one she flattened them in her tortilla press, removed them carefully, and placed them on the comal in three rows of four. When they had cooked on one side, she turned them. When they were done, she stacked them in a basket and covered them with a large cloth napkin to keep them warm and clean. Metate. Manos. Prensa. Comal. Canasta. Milling. Shaping. Pressing. Cooking. Stacking. This process was encompassed in the verb "tortillar."

Ordinarily Sacramento enjoyed this early morning task. It produced the tortillas which were the most important item in the family's diet. It also had a slow, steady rhythm which was calming. But on this day, the formidable figure of Asunción Mendoza loomed in her memory. And then, just as Sacramento was turning the last batch of tortillas on the griddle, there she was again. In the doorway. Like a nightmare that will not be pushed aside.

For a moment there was awkward silence. Then the two women greeted each other with constrained courtesy. Asunción appeared nervous. She began to babble about the weather. This went on for several minutes. Sacramento crossed her fingers. Perhaps the older woman wanted nothing more than some small talk. Perhaps she was leaving for Puebla and had merely stopped to say good-bye. It took only a few more minutes to dash those hopes. Very shortly Asunción had bullied the conversation into line with her personal agenda.

"Tus hijos, ¿no te han dicho nada de sus planes?"

"Planes. ¿Como de qué?"

"¡Planes! ¡Planes! ¿Que nunca hablan de su futuro?"

"Pues sí. Han hablado mucho de que van al norte. Durante los últimos meses no han hablado de otra cosa."

There was the opening. Asunción drove in a wedge. "Se me hace que sería muy conveniente tenerlos casados primero."

"Casados. ¿Pero por qué? ¿Qué prisa tienen ellos para casarse?"

Asunción ignored the feigned lack of comprehension. "Ponte a pensar, Sacramento. Están solos. Se van al norte. Se sienten mas solos allá. Empiezan a buscarse compañeras. Unas gringüitas listas los agarran. Con el tiempo se casan allá. ¿Y luego qué? Las nueras hablando otro idioma. ¡Dios nos libre! ¿Cuándo vuelves a ver a tus hijos? ¿Cuándo te vienen a visitar?" She paused to achieve the full dramatic effect of the transition. "En cambio, casándose con mis nietas, aquí los vas a tener por lo menos en las fiestas de diciembre."

Ahí estaba el detalle. Asunción had touched the very core of Sacramento's fear. Her sons would go north and never return. Or they would return with strange wives and children who could not even communicate with her. She poked at the wood under the comal. She was not ready to share her fear with the other woman. So she changed the topic. "¿Sus nietas saben guisar?"

Asunción was unflappable. "La más grande, María, hace maravillas en la cocina. Su hermana . . . " she shrugged and gestured to indicate más o menos. "Pero esas muchachas no pasaron su niñez en la cocina. Las dos terminaron la secundaria en Puebla." There was the slightest pause. Just enough to allow for a transition, without permitting an interruption. "Tus hijos trabajan en el campo, ¿verdad?"

Sacramento noted and admired the parry and thrust. But she had a ready answer. "Sí, Señora. Trabajan las veinte hectáreas que mi esposo recibió de su abuela, Doña Natalia, en paz descanse." She paused to allow for appreciation of that half of the family fortune. "Y también trabajan las veinte hectáreas de mi Papá." She was about to mention horses and mules. Then she caught herself. Asunción had probably counted them already. Suddenly she felt lessened. She had given away enough. This woman had no right to be questioning her. It was time for some assertion. Her next words took on the tone and volume of a pronouncement. "Hay algo que usted tiene que entender, Señora. Yo no voy a obligar en nada a mis hijos. Ellos van a decidir. Y no importa lo que decidan, ellos saben que pueden contar con mi apoyo." As far as Sacramento was concerned, the conversation had ended.

Meanwhile, in blissful ignorance of these machinations, the young people dallied toward the nuptial precipice. First María's wiles pushed Juan over the brink. Antonio proved to be a more difficult case, but once Juan had fallen, he too toppled over the edge.

The wedding was held in Jachalco on a weekend in August. The civil marriage was celebrated quietly by the immediate families on Friday evening. On Saturday morning there was a church ceremony attended by the extended family. That was followed by brunch.

The main item on the brunch menu was chicharrón. This was, of course, the cut-up and fried-down carcass of a hog. The animal selected for the occasion was a one-hundred-seventy-kilo sow, one of several being raised by Hipólito García in Puebla. The sow's best days were behind her, and her fate was sealed by a substandard reproductive performance. She had produced only two piglets in her last litter.

At the evening meal, a few dozen additional relatives and friends were present. The dinner menu featured mole poblano. The turkeys that graced the mole had also come to their end because of a selective pressure involving procreative inefficiencies. First, the flock was screened, and two toms, whose wattles and combs indicated that they were still bursting with reproductive zeal, were pardoned. Then the remainder of the toms, eight to be precise, joined two rather senior hens at the butchering block.

Virtually the whole village came for the dance that followed dinner. Sacramento's father, Don Vicente, had ordered "suficiente pulque para que se hundiera el estado de Puebla." But by Sunday morning, it was all gone. Fortunately, he had anticipated just such a demand. An additional shipment arrived on Sunday morning, and the party continued well into that night.

Following a quincena of connubial bliss in the Alvarez home, and then another quincena in the García home, the newlyweds packed and migrated north. And a little west. To Los Angeles.

But that's another story.

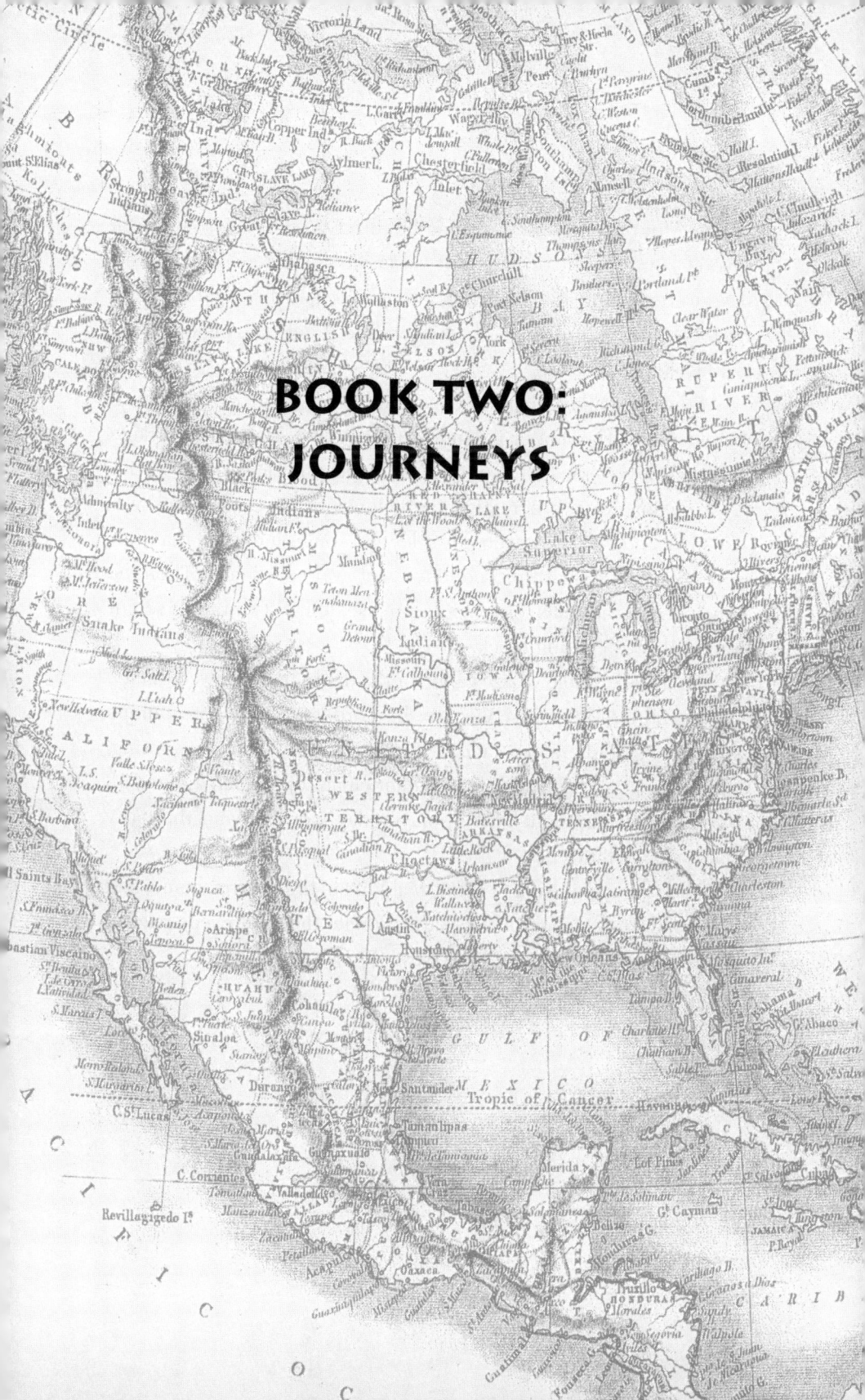

BOOK TWO: JOURNEYS

CHAPTER SEVEN

When she finally reached the river, Concha was gasping for breath. The caminata from the camp, five kilometers to the south, had been terrible. Only the labor pains had made it possible to ignore her mistreated feet. She fought off the pain with the panting technique that her cousin Andrea had shown her. It was all happening much too fast. She could feel herself opening more with each step.

She forced herself into the stream. It would not be a difficult crossing. Here at this season, the river spread itself wide and shallow. It was neither grande, as the people to the north called it, nor bravo, as the people to the south gave it name.

Step by step, she struggled to midstream. There the pain brought her to a full stop. She could no longer resist the urge to push. She started to scream, then fought to regain control. She spread her legs, one foot firmly planted in Gringolandia and the other just as firmly in Mythico. She grabbed the next scream halfway up her throat and used the energy for a giant push down. Then she panted, as she had been taught. She wanted to pause, but one wave had barely subsided when the next one rolled over her. Again she pushed. And panted. And tried to pause. And pushed. And panted. And tried to pause. And pushed. And then . . . there was the baby.

She caught the child in her two hands, grateful for once for the long arms which her mother had so often ridiculed. She regained her balance, waded to the north bank of the stream, and lay down in the sand. Immediately she began talking to the infant as she cleaned his face. She pinched his tiny nose and patted his behind until he unleashed his first wail. Then she made a check of his parts, admiring his little widget and counting his digits, until she had assured herself that nothing was missing. "Es un milagro," she said aloud. "Sin exagerar, es un milagro." Finally she wrapped the boy in her chal and put him to her breast, but he had barely begun to nibble when he drifted off to sleep.

Soon the placenta was birthed. She pushed it into the river with her feet. Then she found a bush that provided some shade and lay down to rest. There was still a half-hour walk to the road and nearly another hour to town. But that would keep until the sun was lower in the western sky.

Two days later, Concha and her cousin Andrea took the child to the municipal building to be registered as a native of Texas. The birth was stated to have occurred at Andrea's home. A quite credible assertion, since cousin Andrea was a practicing physician. The mother was stated to be Concepción Alvarez, residing at the time at Andrea's address. The father's name was recorded as Mario Lee. The address given was that of his aunt in Corpus Christi. Concha attempted to have the name corrected to read Mario Li, but the registrar assumed that she was in error, since the Civil War general had certainly spelled it Lee. The child was given the name Librado Mario Lee, Librado being the name of Concha's favorite uncle.

A week later the baby was again registered, in the town south of the river, but this time as a native of Tamaulipas. With the exception of the mother's place of residence at the time of birth, the recorded information was consistent with that in the Texas registry.

It behooves us now to link this Concepción Alvarez to the

Jachalco family of the same surname. In a nutshell, her father was Ramón Alvarez, the younger brother of Juan and Antonio, who had married the García girls and carried them off to Los Angeles. But though the family connection is straightforward enough, the retracing of the lines of causality, which converge at the moment of the child's birth in the river, is a celebration of sinuosity. Humor me.

The formation of a self by an individual human is a halting, faltering process of trial and error. Guided by genetic endowment, the newborn begins to interact with the others in the environment. The infant notes that certain actions generate approval, others disapproval, and still others indifference. The child's response is a sort of, "Aha, I am such-and-so." Time passes and the process continues. The toddler pushes the envelope of such-and-so. Usually there is feedback, approving or disapproving or indifferent. Gradually, the response of the child becomes, "Aha, I am a little more *such* and a little less *so*," or "I am a little less *such* and a little more *so*." Eventually, if all goes well, we have a young person capable of evaluating the feedback and confident enough to assert, "Whatever you may say, I am still *such* and *so* because I choose to be."

On the surface, it may appear that the child and the adults are pursuing a common purpose with compatible perspectives. But there is an undertone of discord. For while the child is avid for the acquisition of a self, the adults are keen on assigning to the child a role within the group. And when the group is a family, the roles are few.

As Ramón Alvarez was to discover, for children in a family, birth order is nearly everything. The firstborn will be the lady or lord of the manor, however mean or magnificent the manor may be. The nextborn will be the challenger, pushing the firstborn to achievement, and in the process, also becoming an achiever. The lastborn will be everyone's darling, pampered and petted from birth until long after infancy. Any sibling unfortunate enough to be born between the second and the last will be assigned the ill-defined and unrewarding role of extra child.

Enter Ramón Alvarez. He was no less gifted than his older brothers. He was probably a harder worker. But he was also the thirdborn of four. He was, and always would be, the extra child.

Now as any two-score-or-better veteran of our common wanderings can attest, humans maintain most tenaciously their most fallacious beliefs. So it was with Ramón. When his older brothers and their brides removed to Los Angeles, he was sure that, at long last, it was his turn to shine. Now that he was out of their shadow, his own sweat and toil would be noted and praised. Finally his invisibility would end.

It was not to be. That first fall, after Juan and Antonio went north, Ramón husked corn seven days a week from sunrise to sunset, trying to do the work of three. At the end of each long day, with the last of his energy, he would feed and water the animals. Only then would he slump into a kitchen chair for his supper. His mother would be there. At the comal, warming tortillas. But instead of asking how his work progressed, she would chatter on and on about his brothers. A daily, seemingly endless, conjecture about their lives in California. It did not take long for the tortillas to acquire a bitter taste.

But eventually the harvest was completed. The workload became lighter. Ramón began to have time for romance. The first beguiling glances came from a local enchantress named Beatriz.

Euphemizing egregiously, one might declare Beatriz a tease. She could be kissed copiously. She could be embraced excessively. She could be fondled profusely. But she had standards. All kissing must be mouth to mouth. All stroking must be above the waist. All clothing must be left in place. At least a dozen young Jachalcanos claimed to have had their way with her. One or two may have been ignorant of precisely what that meant. The rest were lying. Ramón was one of

BOOK TWO, CHAPTER SEVEN

the liars. Beatriz reciprocated by spreading the story, not apocryphal, that he had once been spanked for pissing in the horse trough. It was time to broaden the range of his search.

About a two-hour ride from Jachalco was the town of San Isidro. There Ramón began attending the Saturday night dances. But for only a few weeks. Ash Wednesday brought the dancing season to an abrupt halt. That would have been penance enough. But then on Palm Sunday, his grandfather, Vicente Robles, died of a sudden massive stroke. The family began the observance of the customary year of mourning. No dancing. No fiestas. By the end of that protracted period, Ramón was ready to serenade the first female who smiled at him. Unfortunately, the first was Virgen Palacios.

She was from San Isidro. Her father was a successful grain merchant, and the family lived quite comfortably. On occasion, Virgen had stayed with relatives in the capital. Where she had attended the theater "tres veces en menos de un año."

She was a confusion of quirks and foibles. She did not dance. But she loved dances. The ambiente. The noise and movement and laughter. She and Ramón would sit and commune under the watchful eye of her mother.

She was much given to raptures. She could become giddy about the words of a popular song. She could babble at length about romantic love. Ramón pronounced her fresh and innocent.

By their third encounter, she was confiding everything to him. "Tengo que confesarte algo, Ramón. Yo ya he tenido tres novios. Y los tres eran malos. Todos querían aprovecharse de mí. Bueno. No aprovechar. ¿Cómo quiero decirte? Me querían apurar. Apenas empezábamos a hablar y me querían abrazar. Y no nada más abrazar. Me querían besar. ¿Tú crees? Y me apretaban para besarme. A veces yo tenía que gritarles. Y entonces, sí, me dejaban. Pero me asustaron mucho." She paused, but Ramón made no reply. He was too busy congratulating himself on not having made any premature advances. She continued, "Y ahora tú. Tú eres tan lindo, tan bueno, tan respetuoso. Tú eres todo lo que estoy buscando."

After that, of course, it was time to meet the rest of the family. So. One Sunday morning a few weeks later, Ramón attended the Palacios brunch.

Her father was forthright to a fault. "Nosotros queremos mucho a nuestra hija, joven. Pero no somos ciegos. Reconocemos que la muchacha que Dios nos dio no es normal. Ella es sencilla. Aparenta ser mayor. Y por cierto tiene veinte años. Pero sigue siendo una niña. Y siempre lo será." He paused, took Ramón's silence for concordance, and continued his lecture. "Mire, joven. Esta muchacha tiene la cabeza llena de fantasías y caprichos. Ella se puede casar solamente con un hombre capaz de cumplirle aquellos caprichos." Then he lowered his voice by several decibels for the main thrust. "Además será un hombre capaz de buscarse a otras mujeres para sus necesidades. En fin, el hombre que contempla matrimonio con mi hija, tendrá que contar con bastantes recursos." The voice resumed its pontifical mode. "Ahora bien. Usted se da cuenta que es preferible terminar con estas tonterías lo más pronto posible. Así ella tendrá menos tiempo para hacerse ilusiones, y le va a doler menos el desenlace."

Ramón lost his appetite, found his hat, and took his leave. Virgen came to say goodbye. She squeezed a wad of paper into his palm. "Me van a mandar con mis parientes otra vez. Aquí está la dirección." She was, in fact, sent to the capital that same week. Ramón begged and borrowed and saved and followed her a month later. But the address Virgen had given him proved to be either erroneous or fictitious. "La vida es una pura chingada," concluded Ramón.

His stay in the metropolis was not, however, a total loss. On the third day there, he gave up his futile search for Virgen and discovered a cabaret. And inside the cabaret, he made a further discovery. If you were callous enough about how you flashed your money, but then deliberate enough about how you surrendered it, you could dance with a woman, most of whose parts were still in place, and who, for an additional fee, might invite you to a hotel to inspect those parts a little more closely. Ramón managed one of those inspections. Then a cash flow crisis ensued. He hopped a freight for Veracruz, got off in San Isidro, and walked home. His mother, Sacramento, would not allow him into the house until he had bathed.

The long days in the field resumed. But now, as he went about his work, there was a little more bounce in his step. This did not go unnoticed by his mother. She began a campaign to get the local availables to work their wiles and guiles on her son. But either they were wanting in wile or lacking in guile, for Ramón ignored most of them and ridiculed the rest. Following the next harvest, he spent a whole week in the capital, learning about and from la mujer nocturna.

Meanwhile, his cousin Federico slowly acquired the skills of farming. The boy was intelligent, eager, and conscientious. When he was fifteen, he could be entrusted with the care of the animals. Ramón began to visit the cabarets several times a year.

One of those visits altered the course of his life. It happened when he was almost twenty-four. He was in the train depot of the capital. He noticed a woman struggling with two suitcases. The handgrip of one had broken. She was trying unsuccessfully to carry the bag under her arm. Ramón offered to help. "Gracias, joven. Usted es un caballero como los de antes."

That was effusive enough to get his attention. He took a closer look. She had one of those cherubic faces that give the lie to a woman's age. But she was probably a very well preserved thirty-something. She seemed familiar. Someone from his dream life. His body began to feel warm.

She also had been taking his measure. Her next words, all candid and plain on the surface, were calculated to produce precisely the bewitching effect which they in fact achieved. "Voy a tomar el tren para Monterrey. Regreso a mi casa en Reynosa." A significant pause. "Y usted, joven, ¿a dónde va?" As he thought about it later, it seemed to Ramón that his mouth had begun to work before his brain. That perception, of course, was erroneous. But he did appear entranced, as he heard himself answer in a calm clear voice, "Yo también voy a Monterrey."

The train trip north gave them a chance to exchange biographies. Her name was Esperanza Gómez. She had come to the capital for the birth of her first grandchild. After helping her daughter through the first forty days, she was now returning to her home in Tamaulipas.

She had been married very young to a soldier, who, reportedly, had covered himself in glory while dying at the battle of Zacatecas, leaving Esperanza with a baby daughter and no visible means of support. At the time that Ramón met her, however, she was hardly the classical defenseless widow. Her daughter's husband was a colonel in the military. Of considerably greater weight was her older brother, Librado, who was some sort of paramilitary operative for the Maximato in the northern states. In a mob north of the border, he would have been called an enforcer. The title he gave himself was enviado armado. An appropriate designation, judged by its effect. Governors removed their sombreros when they spoke with him. It was he who owned the house in Reynosa where his sister Esperanza lived.

In Monterrey, Esperanza bought a loaf of bread, a half kilo of cheese, a kilo of grapes, and two liters of wine. Then she and Ramón checked into a hotel. From which they emerged a day and a half later, following a meager amount of sleeping, a moderate amount of eating and drinking, and an inordinate amount of fornicating. From there they went on to Reynosa and more of the same.

BOOK TWO, CHAPTER SEVEN

The infatuation lasted for more than a year. Then, to their considerable consternation, they discovered that they were in a family way. Adjustments were not made gracefully. Esperanza had always inclined toward the fleshy. As the pregnancy advanced, the last suppleness of youth vanished. Even after the birth, she continued to stouten appreciably. By the time the child could walk, strangers who saw the two together invariably assumed that Esperanza was the little girl's grandmother.

Ramón turned away. The reverberation in his brain proclaimed, "Otro chingadazo más." He tried to mask his reaction. And he was never unfaithful. But the relationship grew strained. He began to frequent a neighborhood cantina. His evening interests shifted to drinking and playing cards.

He fancied himself a superior poker player. The evidence for that was scant. The local competition was mediocre. And still he lost as often as he won. But he had a real gift for selective memory. On successful evenings, he would buy two dozen sweet rolls and proudly bear them home. A silly excess really. Unless there was company. Otherwise a few pieces would be eaten during the next day or two. The rest would go stale and end as rather expensive food for the chickens.

Meanwhile, the child named Concepción Alvarez was thriving. Her mother called her "Mi sorpresa" for her ill-timed arrival and "Mi chimpancita" for her long arms. But for the most part she found the little girl a nuisance. That however did not translate into neglect. Quite the contrary. The more Esperanza saw her daughter as an inconvenience, the more guilty she felt. And guilt translated into attention.

To Ramón, the baby girl was a daily joy. But in very measured doses. When he returned from his day's work, he would play with her intensely for fifteen or twenty minutes. Then he would eat and go off to his cheap whiskey and cards at the cantina.

One night, when Concha was almost four, he did not return from his card game. Esperanza expected the worst. The following morning she roused the neighborhood to a search. One of the searchers located his body in an alley. He had died from a number of knife wounds. The police were called. They poked and puttered about. They posed a few questions to the man who had left the card game with Ramón and who had been seen with him at the bakery. They plodded about the area. They paused for some posturing. Finally they pronounced the murder unsolvable.

Not long after the funeral, Esperanza's brother, Librado, arrived from Los Angeles. He had come to help his sister through what he assumed would be a difficult time. He was shocked at how little Ramón's death had affected her. But he stayed. For his own motives. And for the niece, Concha, who would stir his paternal instincts as not even his own son had done.

The Gómez family was originally from Ciudad Juarez. There, Esperanza and her two brothers were born. Librado was the oldest. Librado Juan to be precise. Before he had celebrated six years on the planet, he had been dubbed Juan Diablo. His version of several years later as to how and why the nickname went something like this. "Es que me tenían en un circo muy reducido. Me sentía muy apretado. Yo necesitaba un circo más amplio. Con elefantes más enormes y tigres más feroces."

Perhaps. But some of the misadventures were cruelly outlandish. On one occasion Librado purported to have misunderstood an explanation as to how chickens were cooked on a rotisserie. He caught two of his grandma's hens, poured kerosene on them, and set them afire. In their last terrible moments of life, the birds did turn round and round. But when they stopped, they did not look like anything Librado wanted to eat.

BOOK TWO, CHAPTER SEVEN

His mother died when he was nine. Grandmother Gómez agreed to take in Esperanza and her brother Francisco. But when it came to Librado, she put her foot down. He was sent packing to his Uncle Pablo Gómez in Los Angeles. Who, with nary a child of his own, hadn't a clue as to what to do with the nephew. He bought Librado a horse, showed him how to bridle the beast, and left him to figure out the rest.

Had Solomon and Socrates consorted and conspired in a plan to harness Librado's energy and turn it toward some good, they would not have come within a continent of what Uncle Pablo achieved by dumb blind luck. True, the gelding he purchased had already seen his best days. True, the horse had been mistreated terribly during his working years. True, on the date of sale he was not worth even the five dollars that Uncle Pablo had exchanged for him. Yet he was a prince among nags. He was a king among equines. For he was the inspiration for virtually all of Librado's education.

Far from hyperbole, this is, if anything, an understatement. Librado became a reader so that he could exhaust the world's literature on horses. He learned math so that he could haggle more effectively regarding the cost of his horse's food. He studied nutrition so as to better care for the beast. And along the way, of course, he learned responsibility.

He taught the first horse to cross its legs and bow on command. One of Uncle Pablo's neighbors was so fascinated by this trick that he traded an old, but still healthy, mare for the broken-down gelding. The mare was still in her reproductive years, and, when Librado got a job at a livery stable, he found a way to mate her with a stallion that was boarding there. The colt that resulted from that pairing became his constant companion for the next twenty years. Librado named him Bucéfalo.

Time passed. Librado grew to manhood. Except for some daredevil riding, he might have led a rather uneventful life. But in his early twenties, he began making friends with people who knew people who were fomenting revolution in the South. It was not long before he and Bucéfalo had joined the Obregón forces in Sonora.

He quickly became famous for his horsemanship. Soon he was making himself useful as a messenger. He would ride day or night through any terrain and any weather. To that audacity he gradually added circumspection. As time passed he became known and trusted by the general's staff. By revolution's end, he was not only a bearer but an enforcer of the word. Whenever a matter of delicate diplomacy needed executing, it was not long before one of the officers would ask, "¿Qué está haciendo Gómez?"

The fighting flamed and sputtered, ebbed and flowed. But eventually the forces of Carranza and Obregón swept all before them. Guaymas, Mazatlán, Guadalajara, the capital. When Villa took control of the metropolis, Librado did not join his companions in Veracruz. Instead he got permission to take some leave. He returned to Los Angeles, where he fell in love with a would-be actress. He left her pregnant with the instruction, "If it's a boy, name him Alvaro."

He was in Querétaro for the constitutional convention. There he met Calles, who had already checked his background, and who almost at once put him on the payroll. That was the beginning of the assignment to the northern states as enviado armado.

Most of the work was routine. Twice a month he stopped by an office in Monterrey to pick up instructions. Then he would visit a mayor or a governor, deliver messages, and sometimes carry back responses. Usually the meetings were amicable, but occasionally he would have to remind someone of the perils of intransigence.

The year that Calles began his presidency, Librado made the rounds of the northern strongholds to ensure that everyone was in step. He visited Tijuana, Hermosillo, Juarez, Chihuahua, Saltillo,

BOOK TWO, CHAPTER SEVEN

Monterrey, Laredo, and Matamoros. In the words telegrammed from the capital, his tour was "un éxito total." The message accompanied a sizable bonus, which was used to purchase the house in Reynosa.

During his travels, he made notes regarding certain incorrigibles in local political circles. "Gente terca," as he phrased it. In the course of a second coast-to-coast trip during Calles' third year, he saw to it that a few of these individuals came to a bad end. That brought an even bigger bonus, which he used to purchase a ranch near Reynosa. A larger consequence of that second Tijuana-to-Matamoros trek was that no one ever again underestimated him. For the next eight years, he never opened a door for himself, except at home.

If he had an opinion regarding his sister's liaison with Ramón Alvarez, he kept it to himself. He tried to teach the younger man a better approach to poker. But the lessons were sporadic and ineffective.

In fact, the two men interacted very infrequently. In the year following Concha's birth, Cárdenas assumed the presidency, and Librado could foresee the day when he would be unemployed. He went north and helped prepare a safe house for the ex-presidente. Then he began his retirement in Los Angeles.

In spite of his repeated and extended absences during Alvaro's growing years, Librado had a good relationship with his son. On that account, he remained in California for almost three years. But he was still too energetic to be a city dweller. When he heard of Ramón's demise, he returned to Reynosa. There he dedicated himself to the nurturing of his land and his niece.

From six to fourteen were the years of Concha's formal education. She acquired numeracy and Spanish literacy at the local school. Outside of school hours, there were enrichment activities featuring Uncle Librado's curricula: anecdotes, English, and equestrianism.

Two of the three actually proved to be useful in Concha's later years. There was never much call for daredevil bareback riding. But her skill as a raconteur was occasionally helpful. And, of course, English literacy became a major asset after she went north.

Not that utility was ever her uncle's concern. He taught what he was good at doing. Consequently, he taught enthusiastically. Consequently, he taught successfully.

His greatest enthusiasm was, of course, the horses. "Para captar la pura sensación de la vida, no hay nada como montar un caballo. Y el gusto es doble, si uno lo hace con confianza. Y triple, si uno lo hace con estilo."

The equestrian lessons occurred on the weekends, when Concha accompanied her uncle to the ranch. The skill at relating an anecdote was acquired over the years by observing and absorbing the technique of the master as he gave vent to his proclivity. The English lessons, on the other hand, were a planned, purposeful, daily task.

Which sounds a lot grimmer than it actually was. Librado's method was simplicity itself: hear the word, say the word. Or if the task involved literacy: read the word, write the word. Context and content were equally straightforward. The context was the environment. The content was whatever pertained to the particular milieu. So. Concha learned to say, "Good morning" in the morning. She practiced, "Excuse me" when she bumped into someone. She learned to say, "I'm sorry" when she spilled the beans.

It didn't hurt, of course, to have some patient relatives to practice on. One such was cousin Andrea Gómez. She was the daughter of Francisco Gómez, the brother of Esperanza and Librado. As a young man, Francisco had followed a railroad job to Corpus Christi. There he had married, reproduced, and prospered sufficiently to start a grocery business.

He had not been a grocer for long, however, when the Great

BOOK TWO, CHAPTER SEVEN

Depression swept across the continent. Soon the business could provide little more than subsistence for the family. Higher education for his children was out of the question.

Until Uncle Librado intervened. He announced that if either Andrea or her brother Frank would be willing to move to Los Angeles for a time, he, Librado, would pay for the schooling. Frank Junior wanted only to follow his father into the grocery business. So. Andrea was selected by default. She proved to be something of a phenomenon. In less than four years, she earned an undergraduate degree and entered medical school. In the year following Pearl Harbor, she started a medical practice in McAllen, Texas.

Concha and Uncle Librado paid their first visit before Andrea was thoroughly settled in. At the time Concha was an impressionable girl of eight. Her uncle was a patriarch of more than two score and ten. But even without the commanding style and tone, she would never have forgotten his words of introduction. "Esta señorita se llama Andrea. Ella es tu prima. Hija de tu tío Francisco, que vive en Corpos. Ella ya te ha visto. Pero de más chiquita. Por eso no te acuerdas de ella. Ahora sí, la conoces. No te olvides de ella. Ella es tu prima. Hija de mi hermano. Somos una familia. Siempre acuérdate de eso. Chanza que tengas suerte en la vida. Chanza que tengas muchas cosas. Pero sin tu familia, no tienes nada. Más bien no eres nada."

Andrea embraced her small cousin.

"I am very pleased to meet you," said Concha.

"Oh my god! She speaks English." Andrea was all delight and affection.

"She is learning," said Librado, "but she needs to practice more. And with more people. A propósito. During her summer vacation, could she visit you? No todo el verano. Digamos unas dos o tres semanas."

"Será un placer tenerla conmigo. Hasta un mes si ella quisiera,"

71

CONTINENTAL NEXUS

Andrea agreed.

So it was ordained. Each summer of the next six years, Concha spent a month or more with her cousin. In addition to English conversation, the visits afforded an opportunity to observe Andrea on her medical rounds. Very little was lost on the perceptive child.

Not long after the war, Andrea bought a home in McAllen. On New Year's, the Gómez family gathered there for the holiday. At one of these annual feasts, they began to plan for Concha's quinceañera, which would occur the following summer. Uncle Francisco's family would provide the food. Uncle Librado would supply the music and drinks. Andrea would see to the church arrangements. Esperanza would furnish the location. The Los Angeles contingent would be asked to contribute for the dresses of the damitas and the tuxedos of the chambelanes.

All their planning went for naught. In the spring Uncle Librado suffered a heart attack. As the year wore on, he mended somewhat. But very slowly. By the time he was able to leave the house on his own, it was already fall. Shortly after that, his son, Alvaro, came to visit and convinced his father that he would receive better care in Los Angeles. Concha was left a virtual orphan.

Most human feelings lend themselves to metaphor. Anger is a fire approaching flashpoint. Envy is an itching wound. Hate is a relentless hawk. But the death or definitive departure of a loved one produces a feeling of all-absorbing absence. And only that. There is no adequate metaphor. People speak of a physiological hollowness. Or they liken the experience to a psychic hunger. But these are just other ways of naming absence.

Concha got to know that feeling. For months she moped about like a sleepwalker. She ate little and talked less. She stopped caring for her clothes. She still went to the ranch to ride her favorite horse. But that served only to pass the time.

"Ella necesita un cambio de ambiente," declared Andrea. Esperanza was already convinced that her daughter would do herself harm. She made no objection to the doctor's proposed treatment. So. Shortly after the new year, Concha was packed off to Corpus Christi to work in the Gómez grocery.

Nothing changed. She still felt as if part of herself were missing. But there were shelves to stock, and errands to run, and customers to assist. So she was busy. And sometimes busy is the best we can be.

One morning just after she had opened the store, a girl, perhaps five or six years her junior, walked in and asked for a loaf of bread and postage for a letter which she placed on the counter. Concha found a stamp, licked it, and stuck it on the envelope. She noticed the return address. The first line said: Sr. Antonio Alvarez.

"Qué curioso," she said to the girl. "¿Cómo te llamas?"

"Isabel Alvarez, para servirle."

"Qué chistoso. Mi apellido también es Alvarez. Y mi Papá tenía un hermano con el nombre de Antonio. Y ellos eran de Puebla, este mismo estado a donde va la carta." She shook her head trying to recall more. "Pero no. Ahora que me acuerdo, me dijeron que los hermanos andaban por California. De todos modos, está curioso." She gave Isabel her change and thought no more of the incident.

The following day, however, Isabel was back. Concha was stocking shelves when a man tapped her gently on the shoulder.

"Perdone, Señorita. ¿Podemos hablar un momento?"

Concha was about to answer that she was busy. Then she noticed the little girl next to the man. "Ah. Tú eres . . . no me digas. Tú eres Isabel Alvarez. Hola. ¿Como estás?"

The little girl smiled. "Bien. Este es mi Papá."

"Yo soy Antonio Alvarez, Señorita. Mi hija me dijo que usted también se apellida Alvarez."

"Es cierto. Pero es un poco común el apellido Alvarez. ¿Verdad?"

"¿Cómo se llama su Papá, Señorita?"
"Mi Papá era Ramón Alvarez."
"¿Era?"
"Sí. El se murió hace muchos años."
"¿De grande? Digo. . . ¿Su Papá tenía muchos años cuando se murió?"
"No. No. Se murió muy joven. Yo tenía como cuatro años. Me dijeron que fue un accidente. Pero no creo. Por otras cosas que he oido, yo creo que lo mataron. En una cantina."
"¿Y como era él?"
"No le puedo decir exactamente. Tenía bigote y olía a licor."
"Bueno, perdone las preguntas, Señorita. Pero es que yo sospecho que su Papá era mi hermano."
"Me hablaron de que tenía hermanos. Dos por lo menos. Juan y Antonio. Y esos dos vivían en California. Es todo lo que yo sé de ellos. Ah. Y que vinieron del estado de Puebla. Nada más."
"Pues yo soy Antonio. Y anduve muchos años en California con mi hermano Juan."
Concha shrugged. "A lo mejor es una coincidencia, nada más."
"Puede ser. Pero lo dudo." He paused. "¿Su Mamá de usted está todavía?"
"Sí. Ella vive en Reynosa. Pero nunca mencionó de que había familiares de mi Papá en Tejas."
"Por no saber. Mire. Mi hermano Ramón desapareció de la casa en Jachalco, Puebla, hace como dieciocho años. Desde entonces, jamás hemos sabido de él." He paused. "El hombre que era su Papá, ¿no le dejó nada de recuerdo?"
"Mi Mamá me dice que solo me dejó su apellido. Y hasta eso de mala gana."
"¿Nunca le dijo nada de sus abuelos?"
"Chanza que sí. Pero de nombres no sé nada."

BOOK TWO, CHAPTER SEVEN

The inquisition was making Concha nervous. She was genuinely drawn to the girl Isabel. But the man who was threatening to become her uncle reeked of cigarettes and alcohol. And he was persistent.

"La próxima vez que usted escriba a su Mamá, pregúntele si ella no sabe como se llaman los padres de su Papá Ramón."

"Sí, lo voy a hacer," answered Concha. Then she pushed the conversation toward some small talk and goodbyes.

The following week, on the pretext of needing a dozen eggs, Isabel returned to the store. Concha greeted her with, "¿Cómo estás, mi tal vez prima?" But then she took a closer look. The child was a consternation of frets and jitters. A smile would start and then retreat. The eyes were threatening tears. The hands could find no place to rest. Concha stooped and wrapped the girl in her long arms. "Sí, vas a ser mi prima. Y si resulta que no, entonces vamos a ser las mejores amigas."

"¿De verdad?"

"Te lo juro."

That loosened the small tongue. "¿Usted no ha oído nada?"

"Nada. Estoy esperando una carta de mi Mamá. Y a propósito. Si tú y yo vamos a ser primas o amigas, no puedes seguir hablándome de usted."

Immediate concurrence. "Yo le dije a mi Papá."

"¿Dijisteis qué?"

"Que tú no eres una pretenciosa."

Concha laughed. "Tú me conoces mejor que tu Papá."

A month passed. The letter from Esperanza finally arrived. Antonio's suspicions were confirmed. Concha's paternal grandfather was Rodolfo Alvarez. The grandmother's name was Sacramento. Some uncertainty about her surname, but perhaps it was Robles.

There was a small welcoming celebration in the Alvarez home. Then a series of Sunday visits. Little by little a bonding occurred between Concha and her Aunt Eva. But the relationship with her uncle was always a bit strained.

Shortly after the welcoming, Concha's life took another twist. A young man moved into the house across the street from the Gómez grocery. His name was Mario Li.

The two first met when he entered the store to buy cigarettes. Concha was behind the register. While he waited for the customers ahead of him, he noted her handling of the transactions, first in English, then in Spanish.

"That's pretty good, the way you do that Mexican stuff. My grandma was Mexican, but I never learned none of it."

"I am from Mexico," she answered. "Why are you surprised?"

"Well I mean you don't look it. I mean you do. But you don't. I mean I wouldn't guess you were from there. I mean your English is pretty good," he finished lamely.

It was not an auspicious beginning. But Mario had at least three things going for him. One was Concha's need for the companionship of someone her own age. Another was her inexperience in matters of the heart. Then there was her unconscious yearning for a relationship that would fill at least a little of the void left by her Uncle Librado's departure.

As for Mario. He was a clutter of cultures and a jumble of genes. On his mother's side, he had a German grandmother and a Cherokee grandfather. On his father's side, he had a Mexican grandmother and a Chinese American grandfather. Which addresses only the question of genotype. As to phenotype, he was standard mixed-up American adolescent.

He was from Oklahoma. His divorced mother had put up with him until he had finished high school. Then, although he was not yet eighteen, she had shipped him off to his aunt in Corpus Christi. Within a month the aunt was giving him every encouragement in his plan to join the marines.

He was socially inept. But he possessed that awesome ability of many a lonely adolescent. He could find the words to state the personal in a way that suggested the intimate. Conversations consequently featured a great deal of, "Your hair looks really nice today." Or maybe, "You have the greatest smile when you're pretending not to be mad." Or even better, "Do that again with your eyes."

Enough of this can lead to an explosion. So. Of course it did. Late one summer evening, they found themselves alone in a remote corner of a park. And dark came. And neither made a move toward home. One thing led to another, until they just started removing each others' clothes.

Before that moment of warm embraces, Mario had sometimes boasted of supposed previous triumphs. After the encounter in the park, he was mostly relieved that he had not performed too badly. Concha too was relieved at her performance. But she was also stirred by her ability to arouse him. In fact in the weeks ahead, when body-bonding was reprised, it was usually she who initiated the action.

All might have come to a predictable fruition or frustration. Except that Mario had a passion that he had not revealed to Concha. He loved cars. Especially big cars. Especially big fast cars. And, since he had not the resources to acquire a love object of his own, he borrowed from others. Unbeknownst to them. Not to keep. The intent was never to steal. He just borrowed them. Drove them. And left them. To him the distinction was clear and real. Not so to the enforcers of the law. He had twice been arrested in Oklahoma. In the early fall, it happened again in Corpus Christi. A Buick Roadmaster, with the keys in the ignition and the engine still warm. How could he possibly say no?

The judge who heard the case had won a measure of local fame for handling adolescent misconduct in unorthodox ways. He gave Mario sixty days to join the Marine Corps or face a jail sentence. Since the young man's paperwork for enlistment was already being processed, the decision was hardly a strain.

Basic training followed. Then Camp Pendleton. Incorporation into the First Marine Division. More Training. In June of the following year, the North Korean army crossed the 38th parallel in force. In August, as a member of the Provisional Brigade, Mario Li disappeared into the Pusan Perimeter and was never heard from again.

Meanwhile, for Concha, destiny was not so well defined. She spent most of the fall in denial. At Christmas she returned to Reynosa bearing a letter from Uncle Frank to her mother. The gist of which was that Concha's presence in the Gómez home in Corpus Christi was no longer gratifying. A few days later, cousin Andrea confirmed what was already manifest. Concha was with child.

Reactions were as predictably outrageous as they were outrageously predictable. Her mother stormed, "Tenías que dejarnos en vergüenza. ¿Pero por qué no lo hiciste acá, y no en la casa de mi sobrino?" That was a constant theme. As was, "Tu tío Librado tiene la culpa. El quería criarte como princesa. Y mira el resultado. En lugar de princesa, ahora lo que tengo es pendeja."

That was straightforward. And easier to endure than the quiet disappointment of cousin Andrea. "Mejor que no está tu tío Librado, Prima. Todo esto lo hubiera matado."

Concha fortunately had a third alternative. The ranch. As the weeks passed, she began to make it her home, bunking with the cook who in days of yore had been a paramour of Uncle Librado. Or so the rumor went.

Concha would arise with the chickens and help prepare breakfast for the men. That didn't earn her any points with the cook. But washing the dishes did. "Tú fregando y yo fumando," the old woman would cackle. Then she would add, "¿Quién dijo que no hay justicia en esta vida?" punctuating the rhetorical question with a series of perfectly executed smoke rings.

Concha would also carry lunch to the men who were working too far from the ranch house to return for their noon meal. This was her favorite time. She could ride for several hours, not reappearing in the kitchen until mid-afternoon. Then she would help with dinner, again wash the dishes, and play a few hands of rummy with the cook. Being careful not to win. The old woman was a monstrously obnoxious winner. But she was a far worse loser.

So the weeks passed. Concha wrote many long letters to Mario. She sent them to his aunt in Corpus Christi. But the aunt never bothered to forward them. So there was no return mail. After a few months, Concha stopped expecting any. Occasionally she would visit her mother. Once a month she checked in with cousin Andrea, who was monitoring the pregnancy. The two would review the steps of the birthing process. Andrea would try to be upbeat. But Concha needed little reassurance. Physiologically she had never felt better.

Then one morning Concha awoke very early. Something had changed in the night. She was both enormously aware of her body and at the same time strangely detached from it. There were pains. But of such irregular intervals, and of such variant intensities and durations, that it was difficult at first to perceive them as pieces of a larger design.

Until noon she went about her duties routinely. By then she had begun to suspect that what she was experiencing were contractions. She delivered the lunch to the men who were working at what was called the north camp. She exchanged the usual pleasantries and rode away.

About a kilometer from the camp, she dismounted and tied the horse where she was certain he would be found. Then she gathered her energy, crossed herself, paused for a short prayer, and started walking north toward the river.

CHAPTER EIGHT

When Vicente Robles became the mayordomo of the Jachalco hacienda, early in the last decade of the Porfiriato, grain production was just barely showing a profit. The hacendados understandably wanted that to change. Vicente had already worked at most of the jobs in grain production. He understood the process from field to market. The bottleneck in the system was usually the shipping. And the key to shipping was a chief mechanic. One who could assure a steady movement of loaded rail cars from the local bodegas to the main rail line in San Isidro.

Hilario Fuentes was his man. A master of forge and anvil. A diagnostician who, folks said, could place his hand on a faulty engine and sense what was amiss within. Tenacious. Practical. Capable of command. But not disinclined to play with fire and metal. A foreman in a blacksmith's apron.

He became not only Vicente's lead mechanic but also a member of the family. He stood as godparent for Vicente's grandchildren, Juan and Antonio Alvarez. Lamentably, in the year of Antonio's baptism, a devastating crop failure occurred in the region. Jachalco was especially hard hit. With the trains at a standstill for want of product, Hilario grew restless. He was not inclined to sit and wait for better times. So. In the same year that Henry Ford began to manufacture the Model T, the Fuentes family relocated to Santa Monica, California.

Initially Hilario worked for a railroad line. He saved his discretionary income and purchased a building which he converted little by little to a car service and repair shop. For twenty dollars, he bought a Model T that a neighbor had ruined in a failed assault on a palm tree. He dismantled the car, forged his own replacement parts, and reassembled the vehicle. Following that experience, he could have repaired the Ford in his sleep. He opened his shop. The fame of his skill spread. Model Ts gathered from miles around. Business boomed. When the Alvarez brothers arrived in California, they found him in desperate need of mechanics. Both Juan and Antonio agreed to become trainees.

The brothers were eager to learn. They were encouraged to jump in and get their hands dirty. This suited their learning style, and they quickly acquired the skills of the trade. As mechanics.

But there was a customer service aspect of the job that Antonio could not abide. Occasionally there were know-it-all types who had to look over his shoulder as he worked. These were irritating. But bearable. Mostly they just got in the way. The truly obnoxious customers were those who insisted that their vehicles had a mysterious defect which no one could identify. Such a one was Mrs. Schwartz.

There came a day. A minor earthquake occurred in the early morning. Nothing more than a conversation starter actually. Antonio got to the shop about nine. Mrs. Schwartz pulled in about ten minutes later.

"It's the carburetor. I'm sure of it this time."

Antonio's interior monologue had nothing to do with his answer. "Sí, Señora. Ahorita lo vamos a componer."

"Can you fix it?"

"I will see." It was one of his six stock English phrases that got him through most crises.

Antonio adjusted the carburetor. He drove the car around the

BOOK TWO, CHAPTER EIGHT

block twice. He parked it. He pretended to tinker with the carburetor some more. Again he did two turns around the block and parked the vehicle. "It's good. It's good," he told her. She signed the bill and drove off.

Twenty minutes passed. There was a second earthquake. Somewhat stronger this time. About twenty minutes later, Mrs. Schwartz was back. Antonio again made a show of adjusting the carburetor. Again he took the vehicle for a drive. "It's good. It's good," he reassured once more.

About noon, another tremor struck the area. Strong enough to make the newscasts. And bring Mrs. Schwartz back to Fuentes Service and Repair. "It's the earthquakes that are doing it. I'm sure of it now," she announced. Antonio just stared at her. "Temblor," she said. It was a word she had learned from her maid. "Temblor," she repeated.

"Sí, temblor," replied Antonio as he began fooling with the carburetor again. He playacted the mechanic for ten minutes, then took the vehicle for another test-drive. He parked about five blocks from the garage and smoked a couple of cigarettes. Then he drove back.

"Finished," he announced. "All good. All good."

She left. But a half hour later she returned. "You didn't fix anything," she screamed. "You're not a mechanic. You don't know what you're doing. Where's the boss?"

Antonio understood the last word. "El patrón no está."

Her response was to scream another word that she had learned from her maid. "Pendejo! You can't fix a car. You can't speak English. What are you good for?"

"Tú pendeja," was his response. "El problema no está con el coche. El problema está con la pendeja que no sabe operarlo."

They were still screaming when Hilario returned from lunch and convinced Mrs. Schwartz to get a second opinion regarding her car.

He apologized copiously. He even tore up the bills. She left, somewhat mollified.

Next Hilario began a lecture on a few fine points of customer service. Antonio listened for two minutes and walked out. The next day he went to the railroad yard and found a job there. In time, that took him to Texas, where eventually he found employment as a stevedore in Corpus Christi.

Meanwhile Juan was doing much better. In part for reasons of character. But also because he had discovered a universally successful ploy in situations calling for English. "No comprendo." It was simplicity itself. You just say, "No comprendo." You repeat the phrase again and again until the other person tires of the attempt and concurs that communication is impossible.

This is not as easy as you might imagine. Sooner or later you will find yourself in circumstances where you know how to respond. You know what to say. The words are ready to leap from your tongue. In such a situation, it is enormously difficult to keep repeating, "No comprendo." But you remind yourself that one response will bring on the need for another. And even if you can finagle a second response, that will only bring on the need for a third. So. You stay with the plan. You maintain. "No comprendo. No comprendo."

Sooner or later you will also encounter an Anglo who speaks Spanish. But Juan learned early on that the "No comprendo" ruse could still succeed. Stay stubborn. "No comprendo." Most people who speak a second language do so with some unease. There are always small doubts lurking about the edges of consciousness. The speakers suspect the extent or the accuracy of their lexicon. Or they distrust the quality of their accent. It is really rather easy to tap this font of insecurity. Stay with the method. When they address you in moderately adequate Spanish, regard them with your blankest gaze and answer, "No comprendo." Usually their confidence will disintegrate in a matter of moments. In any case, stay stubborn. Nothing reinforces the message better than another, "No comprendo."

But what of the case of one who speaks your language fluently, who has no reason for self-doubt? Obstinacy can still overcome. But you must maintain. For such a one will try your patience. Perhaps to the extent of becoming offensive. He might even comment on your mother's propensity for mating with other-than-human primates. Resist your urge to respond. "No comprendo" carries the day.

Blessedly, most communication with the customers was handled by Hilario. Juan delved. María span. Life was a struggle. But rewarding. Before they had completed a year in California, their daughter Margarita was born. Juan was jubilant. For the christening, he invited everyone he knew. Plus a few. Mole poblano bubbled. Tequila flowed. Juan imbibed. His cup raneth over. He waxed munificent. He borrowed money and sent for an auxiliary supply of liquor. Without consulting María.

Deception was possible only until the next payday. Then the loan had to be repaid, and the grocery fund was short. Justice was stern and swift. The immediate consequence was that, for the next week, Juan was served a steady diet of beans, tortillas, and chile. The enduring consequence was that María assumed control of the family finances. This was a boon. Juan earned about thirty dollars a week. María stretched this meager income into a moderate prosperity. Not only that. She somehow squirreled away five dollars a week, with an eye toward eventual home ownership.

Time passed. Margarita was about four when the Great Depression started. By then Juan was the lead mechanic at Taller Fuentes. His job was not in danger. But his wages stagnated. Then the deportations began.

"Vamos a regresar," María pleaded. She was terrified of being trapped in a redada. "Vamos de una vez, Juan. ¿Qué estamos haciendo aquí donde no nos quieren?"

Juan had no more courage than she. But he was an inertia of habit and routine. He felt settled in California. He would not easily be moved. His daughter was learning to speak the language of the gringos. His friends and compadres were supportive. He had a satisfying job and a dependable paycheck. And there were a few more subtle considerations. The memory of his first walk with María in the waves of the immense Pacific. The feel of the afternoon ocean breeze on his sweaty brow. Tonterías. Sí. Pero bellezas también. "¿Además, qué cosa vamos a hacer en Jachalco? Si las cosas aquí andan mal, imagínate en Puebla."

María had nothing to combat that logic. In the end, the pressure to return came from an entirely unexpected source.

Hilario Fuentes had prospered mightily during his California years. Long before the arrival of the Alvarez brothers, he had begun buying up properties. By the time of the Depression, his rental income was such that he began to lose interest in auto repair. His plan was to sell the business to Juan.

"¿Cómo voy a comprar un negocio cuando apenas tenemos para comer?" was Juan's consistent response.

"No seas bruto, hombre. No tienes que darme todo de un jalón. Me vas dando un tanto cada mes. En diez años el taller es tuyo."

"¿Y si se chinga el negocio mientras?"

"No me debes nada. Yo me quedo con el edificio."

"¿Y los pagos que ya se hicieron?"

"Bueno. Eso sí es otro cantar."

"Lo voy a pensar," was Juan's way of cutting short the discussion.

That exchange or a semblance thereof was repeated a half-dozen times. The first occurred on the day that Hilario stood as godparent for Margarita's First Communion. The last took place about two years later. By then, Hilario had wearied of Juan's indecisiveness.

BOOK TWO, CHAPTER EIGHT

"No te puedo esperar mucho tiempo más, hombre. Como dicen los gringos, el momento ha llegado de cagar o quitarte del cagadero."

That was straightforward enough. And still Juan vacillated.

Hilario, of course, went ahead with his plans. And he made no attempt to dissemble. But Juan continued obtuse. Consequently he made little of it when his godfather declined an invitation to dinner. Then a few days later, Hilario and a stranger strolled through the garage as if inspecting the place. Finally Juan went to work one day and found his tools packed and waiting for him at the front door. Even an Alvarez could figure out what that meant.

The timing was not all bad. A month earlier a letter had arrived from Jachalco, bearing the news that Rodolfo Alvarez had fallen from a horse and suffered serious head and back injuries. Still Juan resisted. But now María decided to force the issue. She used a part of her savings to purchase the tickets. She showed them to Juan and held her breath. Predictably he stomped and fumed and kicked the furniture. She ignored him for a day, while he released his steam. Then she began consulting him regarding every detail of the move. Acceding to his judgment in all things. Swallowing her own contrary opinions. And when they stuck in her throat, swallowing harder. Little by little Juan came around and started taking charge.

Margarita's exuberance also helped. "¿De veras voy a conocer a mis abuelos?"

"Sí, M'hija. Y a los tíos y primos y a la abuelita de tu Mamá."

And so it came to pass. When the school year ended for Margarita, María sold their furniture, gave away their dishes, and packed their clothes. Then one morning they caught the train for El Paso.

For María the journey south was a true homecoming. Had it been possible to stop the train after leaving Juarez, she would have descended and kissed the ground. Some of the emotion derived from an understandably keen anticipation of once more being with her family. Less easy to account for was the beauty she discovered in the barren landscapes of Chihuahua. "Si es la misma ruta por donde vinimos hace diez años, ¿por qué no puedo recordar nada de esto?" she asked herself a dozen times. Eventually, of course, it came to her. "Pues sí. Es cierto. En aquel entonces eramos recién casados. No teníamos ojos para vistas y paisajes." A tender wave of recall flowed over her. She cried briefly. But even those moments were delicious.

For Margarita, it was like something out of her storybooks. Her fancy had always been full of far fantastic places. But her world of fact had never extended beyond Los Angeles and its adjoining counties. Now she was off on a trip of four thousand kilometers. Just saying the number made her head spin. Everything fascinated. But especially the names of the towns. Juarez, Chihuahua, Torreón, Zacatecas, Aguascalientes, Irapuato, Celaya, Querétaro. Those eight she memorized. And retained so well that, sixty years later, she could still wrap a story around them for the amusement of cousin Isabel's grandchildren.

In Puebla, Asunción Mendoza greeted María and Juan and their daughter with the formal courtesy of an aging matron. Not so María's brother Chucho and her sisters Pilar and Josefa. They were unrestrained in their welcome. Especially for their first and only niece, Margarita. In fact, the aunts went a little batty. They hugged. They caressed. They cuddled. They coddled. They pampered. Ignoring the fact that she was nine, they even tried to feed her. And there was no end to their astonishment at her ability to speak English. "Cuéntanos algo en inglés," they would plead. Margarita would comply while they sat mesmerized by the stream of unintelligible syllables flowing from her mouth. When she stopped, they would shake their heads and repeat, "Fíjate no más. Una sobrina nuestra. Hablando como una gringüita. No lo puedo creer. Estoy

BOOK TWO, CHAPTER EIGHT

oyendo, y no lo puedo creer."

A week of that in Puebla. Then it was on to Jachalco. And a slightly different scene. Grandma Sacramento wrapped the small girl in her arms and had a good, five-minute cry. Finally Margarita tired of the tears and turned to her mother. "¿Está triste mi abuelita porque vinimos?"

"No, M'hija. Estoy llorando de gusto," Sacramento quickly reassured. She dried her tears on her apron and started preparing something to eat.

The arrival of Juan set off a whole chain of family events. His father, Rodolfo, evidently convinced that his eldest son could now be assigned the responsibility for his mother, took to his bed, and remained there until his death eight months later.

Cousin Federico soon began talking about going north. He had been observing the year of mourning for his biological mother. Now that the observance was finished, and Juan was there to take over the fieldwork, the road was open. Or, as he succinctly put it, "Ahora me toca mi turno." The following year after the spring seeding, he left. For awhile he stayed with Antonio in Corpus Christi. Then he started migrating with the harvests in the Rio Grande valley. In Edinburg, Texas, he had a whirlwind romance with a Tejana, who taught him a basic English lexicon generously laced with profanity. When that ended, he enlisted in the marines.

There were happier events. In the fall of their first year back, María's sister Pilar married Ignacio Palafox. He was a pharmacist and the son of a dentist. Grandma Asunción pronounced him the catch of a lifetime. Late the next summer, a son was born to the Palafox couple. They named him Arturo. This infant made a contribution, albeit unwittingly, to Margarita's education. For it was in the course of helping change the baby's diaper that she discovered what every other ten-year-old on the planet already knew. So that's why little boys can stand up when they pee.

Margarita's formal education was much more troublesome. Jachalco had only a rural school, which terminated at grade three. So. The Alvarez confronted a true Hobson's choice. Margarita could live with her parents and not attend school. Or she could live with the García family in Puebla and attend school there. Which she did.

In a very short time the separation from her parents became unbearable. She loved her aunts dearly. And she had little trouble making friends. But the school building in Puebla was a cold, forbidding place. The teachers were too formal. And there was a dearth of books. Not textbooks. There were plenty of those. But Margarita needed more. She had already become a reading addict. History. Science. Even sports. And especially stories about long ago and far away. Where almost everyone was good, right from the beginning. And the bad people learned their lesson and became good before the story ended. Or they got their just desserts. And died in some really horrible way. But quickly.

Once each month, her mother came to visit and stayed for several days. Those visits were enormously stressful. Margarita felt obligated to act cheerful. Her mother was sensitive to the mood but blind to the cause. She would begin to question. That would provoke a dissemblance of feign and pretend. Which in turn would lead to some motherly anxiety. Then María would return to Jachalco all spiteful and quarrelsome. There would be a squabble with Juan about some cosmic trifle. That would be followed by an attack of guilt. Then she would blame her husband for the guilt. Something was very wrong.

Truth told, no one was happy with the way they were living. Juan too was having a change of heart. After ten years as a mechanic, he could not adjust to working again with horses and mules. But mostly, he missed his little girl. Finally, about two years after their return, he

BOOK TWO, CHAPTER EIGHT

looked at María across the Sunday morning breakfast table and asked, "¿Cómo vamos a ser una familia cuando estamos viviendo en dos pueblos?"

María caught her breath. She was fairly certain about what was to follow. But it was important that Juan say it first. So. All innocence, she inquired, "¿Qué quieres decir, Juan?"

"Vamos al norte otra vez, mujer. Yo sé que no te parece la idea. Pero tenemos que pensar en la niña. Ella no está bien, viviendo aparte." He paused and awaited the explosion.

It never came. Instead María responded mildly, "¿Quieres decir a California?"

"No." He paused to give the moment its due. "No. Esta vez, cuando digo al norte, quiero decir norte. Vamos a Chicago." He let it stand as if the idea had occurred to him out of the blue. In fact, while they were still in California, a compadre, who had moved on to the Windy City, had written to say, "En esta ciudad, hay bastantes oportunidades para mecánicos que saben trabajar." Juan had decided to put that declaration to the test.

And so it came to pass. After New Year's they went north as far as Corpus Christi. María assisted Eva during the last weeks of her pregnancy. Isabel was born in the late winter. Later that same month, as Cárdenas was busy expropriating the foreign oil companies, Juan and María and Margarita continued north to the city that smelled of cattle and steel.

They first stayed at a cheap hotel that rented by the week. They rested for a day, then began their search. María and Margarita for a flat. Juan for a job.

Predictably, the house search succeeded first. It was a clean but drab two-bedroom in a nondescript neighborhood on the south side. But there was a park nearby. And a grocery store owned by the Martinez family. And a church with a priest from Argentina who spoke Spanish. And next to the church a parish school. Public transportation was two blocks away.

Juan's success was a little less swift. And required a lot more diligence. The compadre who had recommended Chicago as a haven for mechanics had moved. No one knew where. That was a blind alley. Juan began walking into factory offices and announcing, "I mechanic. I looking for work." And getting nowhere. Sometimes there was churlishness. Sometimes there was courtesy. Mostly there was indifference. "No, nothing. Check back in a couple weeks," was a typical response.

Then toward the end of the first month, he caught a break. It was a sheet metal plant. The secretary took him to the foreman. Juan made his usual speech and prepared to leave. The foreman just stared and stared. Juan took a step toward the door. The foreman grabbed his arm. "Wait a second. You're from Mexico, right?" Juan nodded. "Why the hell didn't I think of this before? You start tomorrow. Seven o'clock. Tomorrow. Seven. Okay?" Juan agreed.

It would be months before he would understand why he had been hired. It turned out that the president of the sheet metal company was a man of remarkable foresight. He perceived Hitler's invasion of Austria as an indisputable signal that a general war would begin within a year. Then, he was certain, a conscription law would go into effect. His workforce would be decimated. He already had contracts to provide shell casings to the military. The numbers of those contracts would increase exponentially. But where would he find workers? He directed his foreman to offer employment to anyone looking for work who was unlikely to be drafted. They could sweep floors until the war started. That directive had been issued less than a month before Juan walked into the plant.

He did in fact sweep floors for awhile. And moved material. And packaged product. For that he was paid eighteen dollars a week.

BOOK TWO, CHAPTER EIGHT

Then one day an overhead crane malfunctioned. Juan asked if he could fix it. The foreman let him try. The problem turned out to be no more serious that a broken electrical wire. But it was enough to get Juan promoted to maintenance. After that he earned twenty-four dollars a week. Throughout the war, there was steady upward pressure on wages. By the time Illinois Alvarez was born, his father was earning slightly more than a dollar an hour.

María was also busy. The year that Germany invaded France, she went to the parish rectory to solicit the help of the Argentine priest.

"Padre, ¿cuánto tiempo va a durar esta guerra?"

"No sé, Señora. ¿Por qué me preguntas esto?"

"¿Más de un año?"

"Facilmente."

"¿Más de dos?"

"Casi seguro."

"¿Tanto como cinco años?"

"Es muy probable. ¿Pero por qué tienes que saber esto?"

"Porque voy a comprar una casa." She paused to pique his curiosity.

"¿Y qué tiene que ver la casa con la guerra?"

"Mucho, Padre. Por lo pronto mi esposo tiene un trabajo regular. Y mientras siga la guerra, lo va a tener. Después, ¿quién sabe? Ahora. Lo que yo he pensado es esto. Si la guerra sigue por cinco años, en estos cinco años nosotros podemos tener la casa pagada."

"Me parece que lo has pensado bien, Señora. Pero nadie puede tener la certeza de la duración de una guerra."

"Yo entiendo, Padre. Me conformo con su respuesta que cinco años es probable." She paused. "Ahora, usted me tiene que ayudar."

He was totally taken aback. She was going to ask him for money.

María noted his confusion, guessed correctly at the motive, and laughed. "No, Padre. Con el inglés. El propietario se apellida Novack. El no habla español. No vamos a entendernos nunca.

También hay muchos papeles. Contratos y impuestos y cosas por el estilo. De todo aquello yo no comprendo ni chispa."

The Argentine priest introduced her to a Mister Beltrán. This man had studied law for a time and earned small fees by acting as a paralegal counselor for members of the parish. He agreed to assist. It was time to sell the idea to Juan.

Of course, María had already begun that campaign. An innocent conversation about the weather could be maneuvered into a discussion of utility bills. And utility expenses were clearly interconnected with the physical condition of the housing. From there to the advantages of home ownership was not a long stretch. And that line of thought did not even touch the question of what could be done with the money saved on rent.

But Juan was a hard-nosed realist. One night he tired of the idle musings. "La verdad es que somos un par de coyotes aullando a la luna, mujer. ¿Cuándo vamos a juntar el dinero para una casa?"

It was the moment she had awaited. "Cierra los ojos," she commanded, "y abre las manos." She stood on a chair in her pantry and from the top shelf took down a cigar box. Back in the kitchen, she put the box into Juan's hands. "Ahora, abre los ojos." He did so. From the box he removed a stack of five dollar bills.

"Cuenta," she said softly.

He counted. There were exactly four hundred. He took a deep breath, "Pero, mujer, ¿dónde conseguisteis este dinero?"

"Son ahorros, Juan. Es dinero que tú ganaste en California."

"¿Cómo, en California?"

"Si, Juan. Cada semana me diste el dinero después de cambiar el cheque. Yo aparté un poco. Y aquí está."

It was too incredible. "Pero son dos mil dólares, mujer. ¿Cómo vamos a tener tanto dinero?"

"Aunque no lo creas." She paused to give him time to accept the miracle.

He shook his head again and again, "Dos mil dólares. Imagínate. ¿Ahora que voy a hacer?"

That was the moment. "Es tu dinero, Juan. Tú puedes hacer lo que quieras. Pero lo que yo quiero es que me compres una casa."

Had they been set up in the same manner, the oil barons in Mexico would have thanked Cárdenas for his expropriation.

The following week, with the help of Señor Beltrán, they made an offer to purchase. Mr. Novack was asking five thousand in cash for the property. Juan and María offered two thousand in cash and sixty payments of fifty dollars each. Novack twiddled his thumbs for awhile, but in the end, he accepted. The second week in December found the Alvarez family in their new home. By Christmas they had phone service. For Noche Buena they called Corpus Christi to wish Antonio and Eva the best of the season, and also in Juan's words, "para presumir un poco."

Meanwhile, Eva and Antonio Alvarez were making the transition to parenthood. They had been married fourteen years when Isabel was born. Understandably, Antonio was both relieved and proud. Not enough to become involved in diaper changing and midnight feedings. But at least for a few weeks, he abandoned his corner bar.

He was only mildly disappointed that the child had not been a boy. The key was that they had put behind them the doom of reproductive failure. Certainly there would be more pregnancies. Certainly one of the babies to follow would be a son.

Eva understood that she was the repository of these hopes. In an attempt to maximize the potential for another pregnancy, she stopped breast-feeding Isabel after only four months. Then she began to hold her breath as the day approached for her menses. And month after anxious aching month, she failed to conceive. A year passed. Then another. Gloom returned to the Alvarez home. The corner bar became once more a regular haven. When Isabel was six, there was one small glimmer. María called from Chicago to wail that she was undone, dishonored, destroyed. That, of course, was her way of announcing that she was unexpectedly expecting. And as we already know, Illinois Alvarez was born the following year. Antonio tried to give the event a favorable spin. "Mi hermano tiene cuarenta años y míralo." And Eva responded, "Y mi hermana, María, es mayor que yo." They renewed their attempt in a desultory way. But nothing came of it, and even wan hope could not be sustained forever. Eva turned forty. The illusion began to fade. Her health began to wane.

About that time, the family made contact with Antonio's niece, Concha. Eva rejoiced. At long last, Isabel had a cousin. And female. Not exactly the same age. But at least not an adult. Concha was outgoing. Perhaps she could help Isabel overcome her timidity.

The interlude was pleasant enough. But brief. Within a few weeks, Concha had taken up with the ill-starred Mario Li. Her relationship with Isabel was put on hold. And Eva's health continued to deteriorate.

She suffered, of course, from depression. Consequently, when she began to experience fits of fatigue, she assumed that it was part and parcel of the same syndrome. Then the digestive troubles commenced. Probably gastritis. It got worse. Possibly an ulcer. A change of diet would help. Easy on the hot sauce. Remission. She regained some strength. She even started planning a visit to the relatives in Chicago. Then a relapse. Intense abdominal pain. Back to the doctor.

The physician was of that ilk who believe that patients invariably exaggerate symptoms. So. Listen prudently and prescribe lightly. An antacid ought to suit the case. And, of course, a more potent antidepressant. Which tended to mask the symptoms. While the cancer continued to metastasize. Then the headaches began.

Concha knew nothing of all this. She was in McAllen, watching

BOOK TWO, CHAPTER EIGHT

her baby take his first steps and acting as secretary and occasional nurse's aide to cousin Andrea. By the time the letter arrived from Uncle Antonio, Eva was entering the last phase of her agony. The diagnosis was firm. Antonio spared none of the details. He was trying to care for his wife at home and becoming daily more desperate.

Concha showed the letter to Andrea. A collegial conspiracy ensued. "Lástima que no puedo ir contigo," sighed Andrea. "El caso está durisimo. El cáncer se ha extendido. Ya está en el cerebro y no se puede hacer nada. El chiste ahora está en manejar el dolor. Por lo que se entiende de la carta, el doctor no cree en la morfina. Es un estúpido. Pero yo conozco a mi gente. Tu tío va a respetar la palabra del doctor. Y tu tía va a sufrir las consecuencias. Sin necesidad. Mira. Yo te doy la droga. Y si se te acaba, háblame para más. Pero ponte abusada también. Tú sabes inyectar. Busca oportunidades seguras. Y ya sabes. En estos casos, el lugar indicado es detrás de la rodilla."

Concha packed some clothes and a good supply of diapers into which she wrapped the ampules of morphine. The next morning she and baby Librado caught the bus for Corpus Christi.

The arrival of Concha and Librado saved Isabel's sanity. The girl inclined toward the gloomy. Caring for her mother had magnified that sensitivity. Had she been forced to contemplate Eva's gradual demise, she might have become morbid beyond recovery. Instead she was given an opportunity to play at nanny. While Concha nursed Eva, Isabel attended to baby Librado.

It was a joyous task. The child already showed signs of independence. Changed and fed in a timely manner, he was very much his own little person. Exploring his environment, he always found something that piqued his interest. Yet he loved the adoration that Isabel showered on him. So much so that he soon entered his babbling phase. Antonio would notice and ask his daughter, "¿Qué tanto te platica?" She would invariably respond, "Me dice lo que está pensando."

Dealing with Eva was another matter altogether. The Alvarez home had become a house of horrors. Random ruled. Everything happened in a crisis mode. There was much screaming. Antonio was at the very end of his tether. A strong hand was required. Purposeful and caring. Concha provided that. By judicious use of the morphine, she began to help her patient deal with the pain. That allowed for the organization of a schedule. There was a time for medication. A time for visits. A time for rest. A time for hygiene. A time for bed changing. Regularity produced order. Order produced calm. Calm made it possible to discuss what was happening. Discussion produced understanding. Understanding produced planning. Planning produced more regularity. The sickroom became a place of repose.

People noticed. Especially the doctor who stopped by two or three times a week. "You are one hell of a nurse, young lady. When this is over, how about coming to work for me?"

For nearly two months, the agony continued. About the fifth week, Eva began to refuse food, and Concha did not insist. She was careful, however, to dirty some dishes each day, so that suspicion was not aroused.

And then mercifully it ended. In the wee hours of a late summer morning, with Concha holding her hand and mumbling prayers, Eva died.

The doctor was called to make it official. Then it was time to notify the Chicago folk.

Everyone there was expecting the news. So arrangements had already been made to attend the funeral. It was a first meeting for most of the cousins. Margarita exchanged warm embraces with Concha and Isabel. Noise responded to Isabel's shy smile by sticking out his tongue. His first reaction to baby Librado was, "Boy, there sure ain't much to him."

It was a whirlwind visit. Juan and Miguel could be absent from

BOOK TWO, CHAPTER EIGHT

work for only a week. All too soon, Concha and Isabel found themselves staring at each other across a very large and lonely kitchen table. Again and again, their common sorrow drew them together to share a salutary cry. Then Librado would come along and distract them with a lively but unintelligible story of a fumble or a tumble or some such feat of toddler ingenuity.

The cousins agreed that Isabel would visit Concha in McAllen at New Year's and again during summer vacation the following year. It was not much comfort, but it did remove a little of the sting from Concha's departure.

Meanwhile, Antonio wallowed in a slough of alcohol and guilt. Not just the usual guilt of the spouse who has outlived his partner. But guilt about the relief he felt at her passing. He had wanted her to die. Not only so that her suffering would end. But also so that he would no longer have to contemplate her pain. And endure the torment of knowing that he could do nothing. Nothing. Day after day after day. Nothing. Nothing. Nothing.

There was no one around to explain that such feelings were fairly normal. Consequently several months passed during which he continued to indict himself as a heartless aberrant, incapable of compassion and unworthy of absolution. And, of course, he continued to drink. Until he had drained the dregs from the cup of self-pity.

Then a woman entered his life. Not just any woman, but a spirit-breathing southern Baptist who said things like, "Ain't nobody got a right to feel as sorry for hisself like you be doing." And even more zealously, "You all the time telling about how you a man. If you a man, start acting like a man. Throw that bottle in the garbage where it belong."

Her name was Martha Jackson. Her ancestors had converged on North America from at least three other continents. But, culturally, she was all African American. She was younger than Antonio by twelve years. And conveniently a widow. And coincidence or whatever, her spouse had also died of cancer. She was a waitress at a diner near the docks where Antonio worked. Occasionally he went there for lunch.

At first, communication between the two was difficult. But for more than a quarter century, Antonio had been listening to English. He understood most of what he heard. Even his speaking was moderately competent. Especially when he was confident that his faulty accent and grammar would not be ridiculed.

Of course, there were times when the content of what he said provoked amusement. One such time was their first evening together when he told Martha, "You look more Mexican than me."

That put her in stitches. "Me, a Mexican? Not if I eat tortillas for the next ten years."

He tried to explain that he was referring to her skin color, which was a light shade of bronze. She laughed some more. "No honey, Martha Jackson was born a colored woman, and she don't need no changing."

Antonio was vaguely aware that he was being reproved. He had no idea why. But in any event, it was he who underwent conversion. In less than a month after he began dating Martha, he went from a shot and a beer to a Bible and a glass of Kool-Aid.

He fell in love. A blind adolescent infatuation, which he had never experienced with Eva, now overtook him at forty-seven. Against all rhyme and reason. She was everything he had never dreamed of. Confident. Competent. Independent. She insisted on keeping her job. She would not hear of Isabel calling her mother. When she had an appointment or a meeting, she told Antonio where she was going. But she never asked his permission. When she had a free day, and he was working, she never considered getting up to make his breakfast. And, between the sheets, she insisted that her

BOOK TWO, CHAPTER EIGHT

sexual satisfaction was as important as his.

The sex, in fact, was excellent. Once Antonio adjusted to the shock of dealing with a woman who was frankly proud of her body. And once he adapted to variety. With Eva, sex had always been a standard comida corrida. Now he was getting introduced to a whole menu. And even the menu varied from time to time.

Evidently she was satisfied with his performance. For in a few weeks, she began to talk of marriage. Antonio was head over heels in favor of that. And so it came to pass.

Within a year they had a daughter. They named her Martha and rejoiced in the Lord. A year later they had a son. They named him Antonio, and an adoring Antonio Senior became a regular righteous member of the Southern Baptist faith.

Never in his life had he even fantasized about such felicity. Each morning he went off to work whistling. The weight and labor of the day seemed not to touch him. Previously he had been happy to live from payday to payday. Now he began volunteering for overtime so that he could save for a down payment on a house. And, in fact, he salted away nearly a thousand dollars for that purpose.

It was not to be. One night about a week after Antonio Junior's second birthday, Martha was walking home alone from a church meeting. As she was passing by a bar, a man exited and greeted her, "Hey, Sister Harris, come here and talk to me." She ignored him. He started to follow. "Slow down, little Mama. I got to talk to you." She began to walk faster. He matched her pace. "Listen here, you black bitch, don't pretend you don't know me." She started to run. "Ain't no goddamn Harris woman too good for me," he yelled as he caught up with her. He grabbed her arm. She jerked away. He caught her again and slapped her. She fought back, scratching at his eyes. He screamed and gave her a mighty push. She fell. The side of her head banged into a sharp edge of the curb. She moaned once and then lay totally still.

An absurdity. Abysmal. Unmitigated. A man with alcohol-enhanced romantic inclinations. A woman pursued for resembling another. An unintentional homicide. An atrocity. More hurtful than anyone could possibly bear.

And yet Antonio did not despair. At least not immediately. He notified relatives. He made the funeral arrangements. He was solicitous toward the family and friends who attended the service. He patiently explained to his little ones that God had called their mother home, and that, when they wanted to speak with her, they should look to the heavens. But then ominously he began to ignore his children entirely.

For Isabel, that was the herald of despondency. She had already phoned McAllen to tell Concha of Martha's death. Now she called again to share her fears regarding her father. Concha calmed her by promising that she and Librado would go to Corpus Christi for the Christmas holiday, which was only two weeks off. "Pero no me falles, Concha," Isabel pleaded. "Mi Papá es capaz de cualquier cosa."

The Saturday before Christmas, Antonio stared at the kitchen wall for most of the day. In the late afternoon, he went to his neighborhood bar and began drinking. About midnight, he returned and tried to start an argument with Isabel. She locked herself and the little ones into her bedroom. For awhile, her father argued with the door. Then he gave up and started a bumbling fumbling but eventually successful search for his savings. He stuffed the bills into his pockets. With no looking back, he walked away from his family.

The following day, Concha arrived. Her uncle had not returned. On Christmas Day, the cousins called Chicago. Isabel related what had happened. Then Concha took the phone and explained that she had money to buy food for perhaps two weeks. After that, there might not be enough, even for milk. Aunt María was tearful. But hesitant to intervene. "Mira hija, aguántense lo más que puedan. Estoy segura que mañana o pasado mañana tu tío va a volver. El anda desesperado. Por eso se ha dedicado a la borrachera. Pero ya muy pronto va a reaccionar. ¿Cómo va a olvidarse de sus hijos? Tengan paciencia con él. Trátenlo bien cuando llegue. Pobrecito. Ha sufrido mucho." On and on in that vein.

But Concha would not be put off. She forced her aunt to confront the possibility of the ultimate outrage. "Si por desgracia no regresa antes del Año Nuevo, ¿qué hacemos?"

"En ese caso, háblanos otra vez."

New Year's came. Antonio was still missing. The next day María and Margarita and Illinois boarded a bus for the South. Forty hours later, they arrived to a less-than-festive reception in Corpus Christi.

Clearly something had to be done. Isabel was nearly eighteen. She could care for the little ones. But only with her father's financial support. How could she be left alone until he returned? And suppose he didn't. How long should they wait?

There were numerous vigorous discussions. From which María, Margarita, and Concha emerged in total agreement. Something had to be done.

Meanwhile cousins Illinois and Librado were getting acquainted. The process was not entirely smooth. Librado was small town. His strongest links were with books and adults. The world was vast and great with possibilities. Illinois was big city. His strongest connections were with companions of the street. His world was the few square blocks around his home. A world heavy with swagger and precepts of honor. Never rat. Stand by your friends no matter what. Don't back down to nobody. "I think my cousin will be a boxer someday," Librado told his mother.

The day of the Three Kings passed. Time was running out. Back in Chicago, Juan was becoming daily more restive. Soon he was calling his wife every evening, pressuring her for a decision. And complaining about the cold suppers he was eating.

María's response was always, "¿Y los niños, Juan? ¿Qué hago con ellos?"

"Que los traigas mujer. Mi hermano puede venir a recogerlos después."

But María always found a way to temporize. "Tengo el presentimiento, Juan. Estoy segura que mañana viene mi cuñado."

Eventually the foot-dragging made Concha suspicious. One day she arranged to accompany Margarita to the supermarket. On the way they paused at a park bench for some questions.

Concha's style was direct, "Prima, ¿cuál es el problema que tu Mamá tiene con los chiquillos?"

Margarita understood the precise intent of the question. But she was more given to diplomacy. "Tú sabes que la madre de Isabel fue hermana de mi Mamá."

Concha pushed forward impatiently. "Yo sé, Margarita. Y mi tío Antonio se atrevió poner a otra en su lugar."

Margarita's reaction was succinct. "Efectivamente."

"Además la otra no fue de nuestra raza."

"Eso también pesa."

"Y guatapeor, la otra tampoco fue de nuestra religión."

"Eso sí. Mucho peor. A mi me parece que aquella mujer, en paz descanse, tenía a mi tío embrujado."

For a moment Concha noticed the slightest sign of anger. But then just as quickly Margarita became her usual, unflappable self. "Mira, Prima. Comprende a mi Mamá un poco. Ella tiene sus prejuicios. Como todas los tenemos. Dejemos eso. Vamos a concentrarnos en el problema. Vamos a suponer lo peor. ¿Cuál es lo peor? Mi tío jamás volverá. No hay mas remedio. Los niños van a vivir con mis padres. Ahora. Ponte a pensar. Diariamente mi Mamá los va a ver. Diariamente va a estar recordando a su hermana y también a la otra que tomó su lugar. ¿Tú piensas que eso no va a afectar el trato que reciben los niños?"

So. There it was. As Concha had suspected. But with a wrinkle that had not occurred to her. The two sat in silence. A minute passed. Then another. Then, "Perdóname la pregunta, Margarita. ¿Tú nunca has intentado tener un hijo?"

"Desde el día en que me casé."

Concha looked directly and intently into her cousin's eyes and asked another. "¿Y cuánto tiempo tienes de casada?"

"Ya tengo como ocho . . . no . . . déjame ver . . . " She met Concha's gaze and stopped. Wordlessly the thought in her cousin's brain spilled over into hers. Lights flashed. Trumpets blared. Bells rang. An orchestra started to play. In a matter of seconds, Concha was rewarded by the largest smile she had ever witnessed on a human face.

And so it came to pass. Isabel spread the word among the neighbors that she and the little ones were going to Chicago with their aunt. By the fifteenth, even María conceded that Antonio's return was unlikely. The next day she gave up the vigil.

A teary farewell to Concha and her son. Then off to the North. Where Isabel would live with Juan and María and Noise. Margarita took the little ones on to Milwaukee. Where she and her husband Miguel lived. Then the new parents held their breath, hoping that Antonio would not return to reclaim his children. It never happened. The next time that Marta and Toño would see their father was when they went to Jachalco for his funeral.

CHAPTER NINE

When it came to trouble, the Donovans had never been noted for abstinence, and Timothy was a notable Donovan. Tim was an exile. That status had been earned in a donnybrook involving some of the local lads and some contentious uniformed Englishmen. The local lads were speculating about what might be found beneath Queen Victoria's petticoats. The English took umbrage. In the strife that followed, Tim vehemently lowered a bottle of Ireland's best onto the pate of one of the Queen's champions. Ordinarily it is a breech of good manners to advise others on questions of health. But this must be said. If you have never sampled Irish drink in quite this manner, forego the pleasure a little longer. The Englishman went to the infirmary and Tim to the colonies.

He arrived in Lower Canada in the year of the Act of Union. But he was restless, and creditors were bothersome. So. A decade later we find him in Toronto. The citizens there were celebrated for their enterprise and diligence. Timothy provided a counterweight to those excesses. When forced to labor, he was a fair-to-middling carpenter. But he much preferred betting on cards and dog fights.

Had he avoided his abbreviated amour with Madeleine Verdoux, Timothy might have escaped our scrutiny and joined the choir celestial in blessed anonymity. Alas! A brief indiscretion. A wee bit of wickedness. He barely recalled her face. For such a trifle, he was

BOOK TWO, CHAPTER NINE

condemned to paternité? His future beaupére thought so. Timothy applied his meager French. "Ce fut l'affaire d'un instant." The old man was not amused. Tim walked away. The old man reached for his rifle and fired a shot to get Tim's attention. Instead it got the side of his head, amputating most of his left ear. It was time to have a go at matrimony.

By then the blushing bride was six months pregnant. Following the wedding, she continued to live at home. Tim was permitted to stop by twice a week to inquire about her health. Eventually Madeleine delivered a baby boy. He was christened Jean Michel Donovan.

Having honored the child with his surname, Tim was informed that his presence in Toronto was no longer required. He objected mildly. The old man reached for his rifle. With the loss of his ear fresh in memory, and fearing the forfeit of some more valued portion of his anatomy, Timothy opted for prudence and departed for points west.

Time passed. From early on, Jean Michel displayed an instinct for business. As a young man he got a job in a bank. He saved his discretionary dollars and began speculating in railroads and western lands. He prospered. In the year that the Canadian Pacific completed the link of the maritime provinces with British Columbia, Jean Michel married Ann Mahoney. Almost immediately the two embarked on a mission to remedy the problem of continental underpopulation. Ten months after the wedding, they had their first set of twins. Identical girls. About a year later, identical twin boys were born. A single birth followed. Then there was a two-year hiatus. Evidently this was sufficient for a second procreative wind, because another pair of boys was soon in the offing. A year later the final Donovan was born. He was given the name Mathew, and it is his fate that we must now pursue.

Like all his siblings, Mathew was educated and encouraged to believe in his basic rights. The right to practice the religion of his forefathers. The right to speak his mind on political issues. The right to a regular and adequate return on his investments.

Mathew had no quarrel with the standard creed. Except that it packaged the world in a very small box. And he distrusted small boxes. When he was fifteen, he ran away from home.

For several years he worked at a paper mill in Sault Sainte Marie. Then he crossed over into Michigan and worked the boats out of Escanaba. He continued to follow the lake south, eventually to a railroad job with a home base in Milwaukee.

He was hired as a troubleshooter for the Upper Midwest. He had all the right virtues for the job. He was diligent, decisive, and determined. He paid attention to detail. He retained what he learned. He did well. He bought a house and began to look around for a woman to put it in order. In time he found one. But a very long way from home.

Because of his employment with the railroad, he was able to travel relatively inexpensively. On one of his annual vacations, he got as far as the Pacific Coast. There one Sunday morning, in a town named Santa Barbara, he went to church. Following the service, he was standing outside, admiring the local architecture in the manner of a tourist, when a voice next to him said softly, "You are not from here."

He looked and liked what he beheld. She was obviously a lady of considerable quality, if her bearing and style of dress were any indication. He blinked and realized that he had been staring. "Excuse me. I am conducting myself like a country bumpkin. I am from . . ." He paused. He had never really considered being from anywhere, and suddenly it was important. "I am from Milwaukee. Of course you have never heard of such a place."

"On the contrary. I know this is a place where the people drink

BOOK TWO, CHAPTER NINE

too much beer."

He laughed. "Aha. You have heard of it."

"It is the largest city in Wisconsin. It is located on Lake Michigan about one hundred miles north of Chicago."

"All correct. Except that we prefer to say that Chicago is about one hundred miles south of Milwaukee."

She understood. "Of course you would. How delightful!" She laughed. "I am Maria Guadalupe Enriquez."

"Mathew Donovan," he answered, restraining his urge to extend his hand.

"Mathew Donovan," she repeated. "It is a solid name. You are here on business."

"On vacation actually."

"But where is your family?"

"I have . . ." He paused again. Here was another deficiency that he had never considered. "I have no family."

"Really?" She seemed genuinely shocked. "But you are a very handsome man, Mister Donovan. Certainly you have not been exerting yourself sufficiently."

He could recall no moment in his life when he had been so thoroughly disconcerted. Nervously he looked around for a focal point. About twelve paces away stood a pair of sexagenarian females, staring at him in withering disapproval. They were dressed in a style similar to Maria Guadalupe. He realized that they were family members. One of them cleared her throat meaningfully.

"I must go," said Maria Guadalupe. "But you must come to see me," she added, handing him a card. "I think this afternoon is perfect. Tea at three."

"I will try." he managed to answer.

She joined her relatives and the three left in a private carriage.

He went to tea. Maria Guadalupe's church companions turned

out to be her mother and a maiden aunt. These two soon began an inquisition.

"What manner of business do you pursue, Mister Donovan?" asked the mother.

"I work for the railroad."

"You are a director, I suppose."

"Troubleshooter. Line foreman. They call it different things."

"I see. What precisely are the duties of a troubleshooter? Surely you are not required to use firearms."

"No, Ma'am. My job is to keep the trains running. If there's a problem, I go to the problem and fix it."

"It sounds very weighty. I suppose that it requires a great deal of work with your hands."

"At times. But the lads do most of the heavy lifting."

"Yes, of course." She looked at her sister, who then joined the interrogation. "You have a home in Milwaukee, Mister Donovan?"

"Yes. I bought a house about two years ago."

"Ah. Only recently. And the construction. Is it similar to the homes depicted in the books about Mister Lincoln?"

"If you are referring to log cabins, no, it's not. But it is constructed of wood."

"And are there still a great many savages about?"

"Well the Irish sometimes get a little out of line on Saturday night. But we get them up for church on Sunday morning."

He had nary a nick of intent to offend. It was a joke. Wasn't the best relief for social tension a touch of humor? Evidently not. For aught was surely amiss. And then he heard it. Over the thunder of the stony sexagenarian silence, Maria Guadalupe's lilting laugh. The mother and aunt were temporarily vanquished. But he would never recover.

The older ladies arose. The mother fired a parting shot. "I'm sure

BOOK TWO, CHAPTER NINE

you and Mister Donovan have a great deal to discuss, Maria Guadalupe. You seem to have a great deal in common." Acid dripped from the word "common."

What followed was a weeklong series of intense exchanges. Everything from family histories to personal creeds. With sidebars for confessions of gruesome pecadillos and anecdotes of dusty amours. All in an attempt to create the illusion of a "fresh start with a clean slate."

The Enriquez family had migrated to Santa Barbara from Guadalajara about a decade after the founding of the mission. At one time they had been large landholders in the region. But by the time of Mathew Donovan's arrival, unlucky family gamblers and grasping gringo neighbors had reduced their fortune to the value of the mansion in which they lived and a handful of family jewels.

Maria Guadalupe was the last of the Enriquez family. Never had she discussed with anyone how the family was to conclude its time on the planet. And yet she knew. As surely as if she had been handed a blueprint. To support themselves in their last days, her mother and aunt would mortgage the mansion. Still later, she herself would sell the remaining equity in the property. Then she would take the proceeds to a convent. The nuns would accept the donation and oversee the Christian demise and burial of the donor.

And then along came Donovan.

Surely Maria Guadalupe could resist this impulse as she had done with others in the past. But this time the temptation was distinct. It was not a courteous proposal that she relieve the tedium of her remaining years by linking her name to that of some equally sterile scion of another shriveled line of arid aristocrats. No. This was nothing of the kind. This was about couplings and mountings. This was about sweat, saliva, semen, secretions, and all the lewd juices of Eros. This was about lust.

Mathew Donovan was thirty-three. Maria Guadalupe Enriquez was thirty-two. There was no time and little inclination to posture or pretend. He confessed his relative poverty and professed his continued effort to overcome it. She confessed her predilection for ease and professed her willingness to strive against it.

"And there is one other thing you should know," he added apologetically. "I would like a child."

"Oh yes," she answered in a voice which had lost its customary control. "Oh yes, yes."

The mother pretended humiliation. "You propose that we take a common laborer into our family?"

"Not at all, Mother. He is not moving here. I am going to Milwaukee."

"You've taken leave of your senses. You will die there. You will find yourself surrounded by hordes of drunkards and herds of cattle. You will not endure six months."

"I will not be alone. And anyway my life here is not exactly a lark."

"Not a lark! Your father would turn over in his grave if he heard you utter such a philistine phrase." On and on. Huffing and puffing. Heaping hyperbole atop exaggeration in an effort to haul her daughter back from the brink.

But as the persistence of our species attests, prudence seldom prevails in a contest with passion. So. A year later we find Maria Guadalupe domiciled among the denizens of the heartland. And in a reproductive mode.

In less than three years, there were two pregnancies. The first resulted in a boy named Miguel. The second ended in a stillbirth. At that point the Donovans paused. And the question of additional offspring became moot, when, two years later, Mathew was killed in a train derailment.

Maria Guadalupe could have surrendered. She could have

BOOK TWO, CHAPTER NINE

packed and returned to California. Instead she dug in her heels, pulled back her shoulders, and said to herself, "I presume that the worst has now befallen me." The sentiment was correct, although a true heartlander would have said, "It can't get no worse than this."

In any event, she and Miguel eked out a living. There was a small settlement from the railroad. There were some meager savings. They owned their home. And as she never tired of telling her son, "You have been blessed with all your father's cleverness and all his courage."

The praise engendered pride, just as the mother intended. But in the years that followed, there were times when Miguel found himself wishing that his patrimony had incorporated a little less character and a little more capital.

It was the time of the Great Depression. For most people a time of loss. Jobs were lost. Savings were lost. Homes were lost. Innocence and arrogance were often casualties. At times even dignity and faith disappeared.

But even in that era, not all was grief and angst. Miguel remembered those years as a time of mutuality. There was no need to disguise poverty. Everyone was poor. Indigence was in style. Penury was high fashion. Once that was accepted, it was possible for neighbors to offer and receive assistance without shame. Barter and other forms of reciprocity became commonplace. Childcare was exchanged for cabbage and carpentry for coal. And almost anything could be shared, especially humor.

One of Miguel's favorite Depression stories concerned a woman who wanted to mail a letter. She tried to wet the stamp by dipping it into the soup. But her soup had gotten so thin that she had to leave the stamp in it overnight before it absorbed enough liquid to stick to the envelope.

Almost everyone in the southside neighborhood had a garden. Most people planted a variety of vegetables. But there were a handful of specialists. And occasionally these vegetative maestros would surprise even themselves with the volume of their harvest. Then the whole neighborhood would benefit. From a largess of legumes. Or a bounty of polebeans. Or a plethora of peas. Maria Guadalupe grew petunias and marigolds. Every summer people would remind her, "Mrs. Donovan, you can't eat flowers." And every year she would answer, "Yes, I know. But watching them bloom, I feel a little less hungry."

Easily the oddest recollection which Miguel had of those years was that of the Donovan's parlor guest, Mrs. Swenson. This good woman moved into the Donovan parlor about the same time that Mr. Roosevelt moved into the White House. She pushed the sofa into a corner which thereby became her dormitory. The rest of the room became her work area. Mrs. Swenson made quilts. The quilts were given to Maria Guadalupe in lieu of room and board. Miguel assumed that his mother had hit on this notion of a cottage industry to increase their income. But, of course, few people had money for fancy bedding. So the quilts were stacked higher and higher in the Donovan closets until the end of the decade, when a nephew turned up and took Mrs. Swenson away.

The Depression lasted for about ten years. Then the war began. And all the king's horses and all the king's men quickly had old Humpty not only up and humping. Egged on by arms production, he was soon humming along better than ever.

Miguel spent the war years attending the trade and technical high school. There he acquired the fundamentals of cabinetry and carpentry. He was equally adept at metalwork, but the feel and smell of sawdust were lifelong addictions. Two of his teachers recommended him to a small construction company. Within a year of graduation, he was gainfully employed as an apprentice carpenter.

When the war ended, a group of parishioners from Maria

BOOK TWO, CHAPTER NINE

Guadalupe's church journeyed to Holy Hill, outside Milwaukee, to give thanks for the successful conclusion of the conflict. Holy Hill is a locally famous place of pilgrimage. It features a lofty mound, rising above the surrounding farmlands. Atop the mound is a rather ordinary church, but with an accessible bell tower, allowing for propitious viewing of the countryside. Stretching down the hill from the church is a calvary with a stone walkway which some zealots prefer to traverse on their knees. There are also large grassy areas for picnics.

The initial pilgrimage proved pleasant enough, and the church group decided to return the following September. Eventually it became an annual event.

On the third trip to the site, Miguel accompanied his mother. The two were about to enter the church when a child caught Maria Guadalupe's attention. A robust toddler. Sartorially resplendent in a sailor's uniform. Pretending unease with, but actually eager for, the attention he was arousing. Clearly "el adorado de su Mamá." With him were two females also impeccably dressed and, by their ages, presumably the mother and grandmother. But both women had dark eyes, and those of the boy were a rush of grey. Maria Guadalupe squatted to better inspect them. "¡Qué preciosura de niño!" she exclaimed. The preciosura rewarded her evaluation by two darts of his tongue.

"Ili, te voy a matar si sigues haciendo eso," threatened the older woman.

"¿Cómo se llama?" Maria Guadalupe asked.

"Illinois."

"No me entendió usted. ¿Cómo se llama el niño?"

"Sí, entendí. El niño tiene el nombre del estado. El también se llama Illinois. Fue un capricho de su Papá."

"¡De verdad! ¡Qué simpático! ¿Lo puedo cargar?"

"A ver si se deja. Este niño es tremendo."

Maria Guadalupe lifted the child in order to better inspect the beguiling eyes. "Ojos que matarán los corazones," she proclaimed. The boy became fascinated by her earrings. It seemed a favorable moment for introductions.

The Illinois people were, of course, María García de Alvarez, and her children, Margarita and Illinois Alvarez, already well-known to us. They had come to Holy Hill on a tour bus from their Chicago parish. Maria Guadalupe's interest in Illinois came as no surprise. Women frequently stopped to admire the toddler. Many even stooped to pinch his chubby cheeks. What was mildly disconcerting was the reaction when María introduced both Margarita and the boy as her children.

"No puede ser, Señora."

"Sí. Es cierto."

"Pero Señora. Esta Señorita tendrá sus veinte años. Y el niño tal vez dos."

"Aún así. Son hermanos."

"Totalmente gracioso. Pero sí, tiene usted otros hijos."

"Ninguno."

"No me diga. ¡Pero qué fascinante!"

The exchange had barely begun. But Margarita recognized the signs. A major mutual debriefing was about to commence. Which would certainly include the deploring of a twenty-year-old daughter who had no prospects and no apparent interest in correcting that defect. She got Miguel's attention and asked if he wanted to take a walk. He agreed.

"Así mi Mamá me puede criticar con mas libertad," she explained when the two were safely out of earshot.

They walked in silence for some time. And began to discover a common predilection. Not only did each find the quiet quite congenial. Each could also sense that the other was untroubled by the silence.

BOOK TWO, CHAPTER NINE

A minor breakthrough. Someone else who could distinguish between serenity and stolidity.

But of course even serenity can be strained.

"Your little brother looks nothing like you," he said finally.

"You prefer to speak English," was her answer.

"Yes, I prefer it." He did not explain. The truth was that he felt uneasy about his Spanish. He had learned the language from his mother. Consequently he lacked a lot of the colloquial lexicon. In instances when other speakers said "muy seguido," he said "a menudo." When others would utilize "a veces," he said "de vez en cuando." English was safer.

After another pause, she said, "Your mother mentioned your family name. But I was distracted. Could you tell me again?"

"Donovan."

"Yes. Donovan. Miguel does not fit with Donovan. Tell me about that."

"It's not very complicated. My father was Irish."

"Was?"

"He died many years ago. In a railroad accident. I was a small boy at the time."

"And your mother is Spanish?"

"That's what everybody thinks when they hear her accent. But no. She's California Mexican."

"That's interesting. Have you gone to California to visit?"

"Never. My mother's family didn't like my father. Nobody ever explained this to me, but I suspect that my mother had to choose between my father and her family. And, of course, she chose my father."

"But why didn't they like him?"

"Who knows? He was Irish. He was poor. People back in those days had some pretty strange ideas." He paused. "How about you?

CONTINENTAL NEXUS

Do you know a lot about your family?"

"Tons of stuff. All my grandparents were from the state of Puebla. I still have one grandmother there. She lives with my father's cousin Rogelio and his family. In a village called Jachalco. It's a really interesting place. There is a huge hacienda there that was built before George Washington was born." She paused for a deep breath. "Then there's my mother's family in the city of Puebla. I have an Aunt Pilar, who is married and has, I think, just one boy. I have an Uncle Chucho, who has twin daughters. And I have an Aunt Josefa, and a great Aunt Gloria, who are what they call maiden ladies." She paused for a transition. "My mother's father was a very interesting man. He fought in the Mexican Revolution. He was an officer in Zapata's army."

"No kidding. Your grandfather was a revolutionary?"

"Yes. In fact he was killed in the revolution. Leading a cavalry attack. And on the same day, my Aunt Josefa was born. And my grandmother died giving birth to her. Isn't that amazing? My grandparents died on the same day. He was leading a cavalry charge, and she was having his baby, and then they were both gone. At the same time. Just like lovers in a story. I think that is really amazing."

"It is." He was thoughtful for a moment. "See, that's the kind of thing that I missed. I don't have a family history. My father cut himself off from his folks. Then my mother's family cut her off. And everything I know about history is out of a book."

"But books are wonderful too. I learned about Emiliano Zapata from books."

"I know. But you have a family history to go with it." He paused again. "Were you born in Mexico?"

"No. California. But we went back to Mexico once. When I was about ten. I think we stayed there about two years. Then we moved to Chicago."

"Do you go to school in Chicago?"

BOOK TWO, CHAPTER NINE

"I finished high school. Then I went to a secretarial school. Now I have a job. I work for a law office. Typing letters and filing papers. It's okay. Nothing great. But now I don't have to ask my father for money. How about you?"

"I finished high school. Now I'm an apprentice carpenter. My mother and I had some rough years, but now with my paycheck, we're starting to do a little better."

They talked about high school. She entertained him with stories about the nuns who had been her teachers. He regaled her with stories of accidents and near disasters in his high school shop classes. Eventually they drifted back to their separate groups. The day ended. They departed for their separate cities. On the bus ride home, he berated himself for not having worked up the courage to ask for her address.

During the next week, Miguel replayed this conversation with Margarita numerous times. Hoping for a sign. Seeking a clue. He really liked the attention she showed when he was talking. She was certainly courteous. Maybe a little more than that? Probably not. But definitely polite. Maybe even friendly? Maybe. But just politely friendly. Maybe there were a couple of moments when she was very close to really friendly. Well, maybe not close. But approaching close. Like when he was telling his high school stories. But no. That was probably just being polite. She did have a nice smile though. And she smiled a lot. Not that she was smiling at him. She just smiled when she felt like smiling. It wasn't meant for him. She probably smiled at everybody like that. It wasn't like a special smile.

After a week, the image began to blur. His recollection of the conversation turned vague. The feelings became fuzzy. But the impression remained. Carried forward because of an oddity of Miguel's brain. His profoundest most persistent memories were embedded in the olfactory aspects of his experience. He was one of those rare individuals who recall aromas. Margarita was a subtle scent of far-off lilacs.

"Let it go," he told himself. "We'll probably never see each other again."

Then at dinner one evening, his mother said casually, "I received a brief letter today from Señora Alvarez in Chicago. You remember the people we met at Holy Hill?"

Suddenly his heart was racing. He nodded.

"She has invited me to visit next month. You are invited also if you have time. I don't know quite how to respond. Of course I wouldn't go alone. But I don't want to obligate you." She gave him one of her most penetrating stares. "Tell me the truth, Miguel. Was the girl just too awful? If she was, we'll forget the whole thing."

By then he had regained some control. He gave the, "What can I tell you?" gesture with his right hand. "She was nice actually."

"You're not saying that just to please me?"

"No. She was really nice."

But his mother continued to fuss. "I really wish people would not toss around invitations like this. I never know what to do. If I say no, I feel like I'm being snobbish. If I say yes, I suspect that I'm doing so in order to avoid feeling snobbish."

At that point Miguel put in a most helpful word. "Why don't we just go and not think about it so much."

And so it came to pass. One Sunday in November, the Donovans took the train to Chicago and then a cab to the Alvarez home. The visit was less than a total success. Margarita's father, Juan, joined the party for dinner. He addressed Maria Guadalupe several times as Señora Donegal. Noting that she was from Milwaukee, he began quizzing her about the brewing industry. And of course he found her Spanish barely intelligible. And told her so. Much to his wife's dismay.

When the meal was finished, María suggested that a visit to one

BOOK TWO, CHAPTER NINE

of his compadres was long overdue. He agreed and left, but went instead to visit the widow Cándida.

Meanwhile back in the kitchen, the Señoras stacked the dishes and brewed a pot of coffee. Clearly they were anticipating a marathon tête-à-tête. Margarita and Miguel obliged by discovering a need to stretch their legs.

They walked in silence to the local pharmacy, slid into a booth opposite each other, and ordered strawberry sodas.

"I thought about you a lot," she began.

"No kidding. That's exactly what I wanted to say to you," he answered.

"Really? I'm so glad. I had this long list of things to ask you. And now I can't remember anything."

"I just feel good being here with you."

"That's the nicest thing anyone has ever said to me."

"I was afraid I wouldn't see you again. I forgot to get your address the last time."

There was another silence while they absorbed the significance of the words they had just exchanged. Amber lights began to flash in Miguel's brain. The pace was a little threatening. Even more unnerving was the emotional ambiguity. Neither he nor Margarita had even hinted at anything like a promise. But the air was supercharged with intimations and portents. It was time to insert a speed bump.

"What's your little brother doing today? I didn't see him at dinner."

"He's with his godmother. She lives about a block from our house. She came to get him this morning so my mother would have a chance to cook. And, of course, a nice long visit with your mother."

"It's really great for my mother. She doesn't have many friends. But what do you think they talk about for so long?"

"Families."

"You sound very sure."

"I am sure. That's all my mother ever talks about. And she knows everything. Every month she writes to her aunt and her sisters in Puebla and her sister in Corpus Christi and my grandma in Jachalco. She could publish a family newspaper."

"No kidding. How about you? Are you a letter writer?"

"Usually I just add my greetings at the end of my mother's letters. But I write to my grandma at Christmas. And to my aunts on their saints' days."

"Would you consider writing to a lonely Irish-Mexican in Milwaukee?"

"Are you serious?"

"Never more so."

"Then of course I will. But you have to answer my letters. Write a letter; get a letter. That's the only way I play. My mother thinks that's wrong. She says I'm an egoista. But no. If people don't have time to write me a letter, then they probably won't have time to read my letters either."

"You're a hard woman, Margarita," he teased. She giggled. Just as he had hoped she would. "You'll have to help me with the letter writing. I've never done anything like that before."

"It's easy. Just be yourself. Tell the person you're writing to how you feel and what you're thinking about. And if you have a really big gossipy secret, that's the best. I know that sounds awful. But it's true."

They lingered over the sodas for upward of an hour. Then they went for a long walk. It was almost dark when they returned to the Alvarez home. Las Señoras did a quick visual review of their children and exchanged a most revealing mirada.

The correspondence began later that month. Margarita led off. Her letter contained nary a hint of any big gossipy secret, but nevertheless covered four handwritten pages. Utilizing a rather oversized scrawl in his reply, Miguel managed to fill a page and a half.

BOOK TWO, CHAPTER NINE

There was a second exchange in early December, and Margarita wrote again that month. But Miguel skipped his response, since he and his mother were invited to dine with the Alvarez family on the Sunday following Christmas.

A holiday gift from Miguel to Margarita was, of course, a must. Maria Guadalupe selected a pair of classically elegant earrings. Which just happened to perfectly match the suit which the young woman had worn to Holy Hill back in September. The gift received all the praise that it merited. As did the gloves that Margarita had chosen for Miguel. The Señoras exchanged handkerchiefs. There was also a stuffed bear for "el niño de los ojos encantadores." Later that day, Illinois gave the bear a bath in the toilet bowl.

The letter writing continued into the new year. Margarita did her part enthusiastically. Miguel did his doggedly. The place in history of Heloise and Abelard as the premiere perpetrators of passionate correspondence was never in any danger. But the efforts of Margarita and Miguel were more efficacious. At least the consummation of their passion produced consequences much less bizarre. They became engaged on Valentine's Day. Then there was a small June wedding in Chicago. Margarita packed and moved north to Cream City.

She stayed home for the first year awaiting a first pregnancy. Each month brought great expectation and great disappointment. Then the word would go out to her mother and from her mother to the womenfolk in Corpus Christi and Puebla and Jachalco and sometimes even a comadre in California. Then a continental chorus of "Pobrecita" and "Qué lástima" would ensue, followed by, "Dios es grande. El próximo mes será." At the end of a year, Margarita started looking for a job.

It was a wise decision. She and Miguel would eventually have the large family they so much wanted. But it would be by a process of accretion rather than procreation. And even the first episode of that accretion was years in the offing.

The job she found was at a law office. Initially typing and filing. But the firm did have a handful of Spanish-speaking clients, and that number was growing. She began to translate documents. Soon she was doing language assistance for depositions. In time she became what would one day be called a bilingual paraprofessional. Her salary grew apace. She and Miguel began to save for the bigger home they would some day surely need.

Meanwhile, they continued unfertile. They began to borrow Illinois for an occasional weekend, just to have a child around. If they were in Chicago, they would take him to the movies. He loved the cowboy pictures, but even at the age of six, he showed his contrarian disposition by cheering for the Indians. If they were in Milwaukee, they would take him to a park and turn him loose. That suited him perfectly. All was spontaneous. Whatever structure there was to his play was self-imposed. For a few hours he would become moderately cooperative.

The only person who could consistently command his respect was Maria Guadalupe. She was sixty. She had a heart condition and circulatory problems, but she maintained her youthful appearance and still took great care with coiffure and clothes. Illinois was in love with her. The two were often coconspirators. He would refuse to eat his dinner. She would defend him. Then later she would give him money. He would run to the confectioner's for a quart of ice cream which her doctor had ordered her to avoid.

About the time that Noise celebrated his tenth birthday, Miguel stumbled into an opportunity to acquire the "bigger home" that he and Margarita had been saving for. One of his fellow workers on the construction crew was Pius Putterman. Pius descended from one of the old German families who inhabited Milwaukee's near westside. His father had thrived as a tool-and-die maker and had accumulated property in the neighborhood. But a diet favoring knackwurst, sauerkraut, and peppermint schnapps had facilitated his early entry into Valhalla. Being the only son, Pius became the unwilling inheritor.

The younger Putterman was an unambitiously able carpenter, who would gladly have spent the balance of his days driving tenpenny spikes into two-by-fours. Occasionally playing hooky, in order to wager on the ponies at Arlington Park. But now those halcyon days were gone. He was a man of property. And as beset as any Besitzer could possibly be.

His father still threatened him from the grave. His mother pretended to embody his father's ghost. And these two had married him to a woman whose principal grace was a set of unimpeachably Prussian genes.

Following the war, bedroom communities had begun to spring up all around Milwaukee. The pace of the exodus from the central city had been increasing for a decade. The Putterman womenfolk argued that soon they would be the only respectable burghers left in the city. For a time Pius was able to fend off their logic by pointing to the Kleisters and Brauns who lived down the block. Then the unthinkable occurred.

During the war years, families of predominantly African ancestry had been migrating from the rural South to the industrial North. This migration continued after the war. Eventually one of those families, the Trice family, bought a house just around the corner from the Puttermans. Arriving from work one day, Pius heard the news from his wife.

"You see what you've done. Now we will spend the rest of our lives surrounded by schwarz."

Pius bemused himself by imagining his seven properties surrounded by one family of newcomers. But he decided to have a look for himself. He met Mr. Trice and had some trouble with the

Alabama accent and rhythms. But nothing that a little effort couldn't overcome. And so he told his wife. "They seem like very nice people. And did you see that yard? It never looked that clean when old man Bauer was there."

"So," she steamed, "You are going to let the schwarz take over the neighborhood. And you expect me to live here with them."

Pius began carrying his woes to work. Miguel asked a few questions. "How many lots do you own?"

"Seven. Six with houses. There are two duplexes on forty-five-foot lots opposite each other on a corner. Next to one of those is the empty lot. And next to that is a single-family bungalow. That's what I want to sell."

"Four lots and three houses."

"Right. I need thirty thousand to put down on a place in Waukesha County."

"I only need one house," Miguel objected. "One of those duplexes would be perfect."

"You could rent the other two," Pius countered.

"Supposing I could. That still leaves the money question."

"Don't bullshit me, Mike. You're a journeyman carpenter. Your wife works for a lawyer. The two of you have no kids. I know you got some money."

The two higgled and harrumphed and haggled for most of the winter. Pius amazed even himself by standing firm. In the end they shook hands on the total package. Miguel paid cash for one duplex. Then he used that property and the house where he lived as collateral for a twenty-thousand-dollar loan. One of the law partners at the firm where Margarita worked agreed to co-sign and the deal was done.

In the early spring, Margarita and Miguel prepared to move. Maria Guadalupe had other plans. She declared her unwillingness to change her home. Then she backed up her statement by having a stroke. People who watched her recovery reassured her that it was a small stroke. But six weeks later, another occurred. After the second, she could no longer get out of bed. Margarita took a leave from work in order to nurse her mother-in-law.

Her patient declined precipitously. She stopped caring for her appearance. She either had no appetite or chose to ignore it. She began to commune more with the dead than the living. Once, during a visit from Illinois, she seemed to brighten a little. "Mi niño lindo," she slurred. But then in an instant the recognition was gone.

The funeral took place on a Wednesday. Only a handful of the parish faithful attended. Unless one counted Margarita's family, there were no relatives. Once more, Miguel received a jolting reminder of just how empty was his world.

Stuff kept happening. Maria Guadalupe had been in her grave only a few weeks when word came from Corpus Christi about the death of Martha Jackson. Followed, as we already know, by Antonio's seeming desertion of his children. After the new year, Margarita went south with her mother. Miguel began moving furniture to their new home.

The night that Margarita returned from Texas with Antonio Junior and Marta, she and Miguel stayed up most of the night. They drank coffee. They told stories about what had happened since they had parted. They even shared a romantic bath. But most of the night, they just sat beside the bed where the children were sleeping and watched.

Occasionally, there were two-line exchanges. Miguel, voicing his disbelief that they would be able to keep the children. Margarita, countering with more optimism than she actually felt.

"Of course your uncle will come for them."

"Maybe not. If he talked to the neighbors in Corpus Christi, then he knows the children are safe. Maybe he'll think it over and decide they're better off here."

And a little later.

"We can't let ourselves get too attached to them. It's just a question of time until their father shows up."

"Don't be so sure. He might be ashamed. He certainly should be. It's true that Isabel was there. And she is eighteen. But still. What he did was inexcusable."

And again a little later.

"Look at them. They're so beautiful. Nobody could just walk away from them forever. Of course your uncle will come for them."

"Even if he comes, it's not the end. We'll try to convince him to leave them here. If he still objects, we'll ask him to move in upstairs."

Understandably it took months for the gnawing fear to fade. But after a half year, Miguel began to let himself hope. By the following January, it was clear that all the agonizing had been needless. There was nary a peep out of Uncle Antonio.

The timing of the move to the duplex purchased from Pius Putterman could not have been more fortuitous. Marta and Toño arrived in the neighborhood with the Donovans. Their new neighbors assumed that they were the Donovan children. No one disabused them of that notion. Serendipity ruled.

The only downside to the new arrangements was that Margarita had to interrupt a promising career as a paralegal. Never was a sacrifice made with less regret. The new role possessed her entirely. She took to parenting so seriously, and doting on the youngsters so inordinately, that even her husband became a bit concerned.

"Te vas a enfermar, Mujer."

"No te preocupes, Miguel. Después de esperar tantos años, lo único que siento es un enorme alivio. Hasta en las desveladas."

The arrival of the children had provoked a resurgence of Spanish

BOOK TWO, CHAPTER NINE

in the Donovan home. After speaking English to each other for a decade, Margarita and Miguel had spontaneously reverted to the language they had first heard from their mothers. They used it to comfort the children. They used it to scold the children. They even used it to discuss the children. Asked to account for their behavior, the new parents would probably have responded that they were hoping to foster bilingualism in the little ones. But in fact the impulse went much deeper than that. This urge arose from their innermost innards. From the marrow where identity is molded. From the ground where the self has its center. From the core where the person is formed. From the very culture itself.

Meanwhile, from Margarita's mother in Chicago, the word went out to Jachalco and Puebla and even California as to the fate of the children of Martha Jackson. The response was a continental chorus of cheers for Margarita.

"Que Dios bendiga a tu hija, María."

"Yo siempre he dicho que tu hija es un angel, María. Ya está comprobado."

"Tu hija, María, es una santa."

But parenting does not promote sainthood. Like any new mom, Margarita was a fortress of safety and shelter. She tended. She clutched. She screened. She fussed. She planned. She cautioned. She shadowed. She clucked. The children were unaccustomed to such an overly protective environment. Predictably it reinforced their genetic proclivity toward stubbornness. Especially in the case of Marta.

Heralds and omens aplenty. Then the showdown occurred during her second year in Milwaukee when it came time for her enrollment in kindergarten. Marta announced that she would not attend. Instead she would wait another year. Then she and Toño would enroll together. Initially Margarita disagreed.

In a test of physical strength, an adult usually can coerce a five-year-old. But in a test of wills, a willful child will frequently prevail. So. On the first day of her formal education, Marta found a moment to escape from her classroom. She sat on the front steps of the school building and refused to budge until Margarita came to take her home.

Greater vigilance prevented another escape on the second day. So she pretended to sleep for three hours until Margarita came to take her home. By then she had been labeled a difficult child. On the third day she seemed to have a change of heart. She hearkened to instructions. She complied with requests. She was a model of conformity. At story time, the other kids formed into the customary semicircle. Not so Marta. She was rewarded for her cooperation by being seated on the teacher's lap. Whereupon she peed. At that point she was designated a very difficult child.

The contest continued for another week. Then Margarita wisely concluded that kindergarten was not uniquely suited to the fostering of intellectual development in a five year old. She started taking the children to the library. There they found the stuff needed for beginning English literacy. She herself improvised materials for Spanish literacy. The following year, sister and brother entered kindergarten hand in hand. Until their enrollment in high school nine years later, they would share labors and punishments and rewards. In moments of decision, it was easy to discern Marta's leadership. But mainly the two formed a friendly, albeit formidable, team.

CHAPTER TEN

Like most citizens of the planet Earth, Illinois Alvarez, by his early twenties, was firmly anchored in the everyday. Without much reflection, he acknowledged and practiced the standard faith. Life is a flow of commonplace events that ordinary folks confront in routine ways.

But what if the event were novel? Where was the model then? Again Noise followed the common wisdom. He went to the movies. He especially liked and occasionally imitated the tough-guy talk of the gangster flicks. But the situation in which he now found himself called for a touch of savoir faire. And for Noise, the suave gallant was a mighty stretch. Still, he tried. "Do you sometimes find yourself in need of intellectual companionship?" he asked the girl who had just occupied the bar stool next to him.

A reply in German would have disheartened him. A reply in muddled English would have discouraged him. Instead the answer came in melodiously accented and syntactically acceptable English. And disconcerted him completely. "You are a soldier. Why do you kill people in Vietnam?"

He held his ground for a moment. "Did I take a wrong turn on the autobahn? I thought this was Nuremberg."

She was relentless. "You think because you are here in Germany you are not so guilty?" He got up to leave.

"Sit down," she commanded. Sergeants rehearse for years to achieve such a tone.

He turned back to favor her with his most baleful glare. The movement took but a few seconds. In that interval she had gone from rage to repentance. "I'm sorry. Please sit down. Please."

The tears entangled. But the tone ruled. Echoings of his sister Margarita. Resonance of Margarita's mother-in-law, Maria Guadalupe. Reverberations of all the women who had tapped his chivalrous core and rendered him docile.

"I'm sorry," she repeated. "I know I cannot convince you with anger."

He sat down. "No problem. I trust anger. Anger is honest."

She wiped her eyes and forced a smile. "You like honesty."

He shrugged. "I'm old-fashioned." Then, "Your English is very good. Are you really German?"

"Bavarian yet. There is nothing more German than that. My aunt married a soldier after the war and went to live in Philadelphia. I went to visit her and stayed for two years of high school. Now I practice by talking to soldiers and tourists."

"And you start conversations by attacking people about Vietnam?"

"Generally I introduce myself first. My name is Greta Heilsam."

"My name, don't laugh, is Illinois Alvarez."

"Why would I laugh?"

"They named me after a state. Most people think that's funny."

"Illinois. It's a nice name. Were you born in Illinois?"

"Good guess."

"Then I congratulate you. At least you were not born in Virginia."

Noise roared his appreciation.

"There. You see? I made a joke. I am not so serious as you first thought." She paused to examine him more closely. Then, "You have wonderful eyes. They are much too beautiful for a soldier. You are a soldier, right?"

"Yes. I am a soldier. But I didn't start a war in Vietnam. Or anywhere else."

"Good. Tell me about being a soldier. I promise I will not fight with you."

"Okay. I'm a mechanic. I'm assigned to a snoop group along the Czech border. But I'm almost never with my unit. There's this colonel. He thinks I'm the only guy in Germany who can keep his jeep running. So I'm his personal driver. We go all over the southern part of the country inspecting bases. Then he makes reports on the combat readiness of the units. I keep the jeep purring. About every two months, he gives me a week off. That's when I come to Nuremberg. I have a small apartment a few blocks from here."

"And what do you do when you are in Nuremberg?"

"Most of the time I chase girls."

She laughed. "You do like honesty. Am I in the chase?"

"I thought you didn't like soldiers."

"I don't like war. Soldiers are okay. Most of them. Some of them are in love with their uniforms. This I don't like."

Noise refused to pursue that. Instead he asked, "Are you a student?"

"Yes. I study languages. And fine art."

"You mean painting."

"And sculpture and architecture."

"What will you do with all that when you finish school?"

"I will be a tourist guide. I will specialize in very rich tourists. I will meet a banker. I will marry him and live happily ever after."

They laughed together.

"Sounds like a perfect plan. You don't happen to know a female banker, do you?"

"There are none. You will have to marry a banker's widow."

Again they laughed. Noise said, "In that case I think I will wait for you."

"Good. It's all settled."

In fact some things were settled. They made a date for the next afternoon. A meander through the old city. Dinner. Much talk of food. Noise urging the improvement of German cuisine by the introduction of the chile pepper. Greta amused almost to hysteria. That started a long discussion of ethnicity. Especially his. By dessert time, she had a much-expanded, albeit very confused, concept of North America. Another stroll until twilight. Ending at the door of his apartment building. Would she come up? Yes, she would. A stairway to the third floor. Greta leading at a passion-inspiring pace. Pauses for the undoing of buttons and the groping of hands. Finally the front door. Inside one thing quickly led to another. And so began the first major entanglement of Noise's adult life.

Greta never declared her intent explicitly, but she began to make Noise her project. On his next leave, they did the museums and monasteries and the churches and castles of the Munich region. She had a tantalizing way of sharing her knowledge. Speaking of the number of churches and their embellishment, Greta explained, "The people who built and decorated these things were giving them the same attention that many people now give to their automobiles. You see what I mean? We haven't changed so much. We just pay attention to different things." For Noise, who thought of exhaust fumes as a sort of aphrodisiac, the explanation was resoundingly apt.

Once assured that Noise would be a willing participant, Greta became a manic organizer. In the same year as the Munich trip, they visited Cologne, Zurich, and Vienna. The last was part of a Danube tour that they took during his long leave. The following year, they invaded Italy. In one whirlwind week, they did Florence and Venice.

BOOK TWO, CHAPTER TEN

On his long leave, they spent a week in Rome. After a triumph there, Greta concluded that she indeed had a future in tourism.

Noise delighted in her enthusiasm. He encouraged her by questioning. He lauded the clarity and ebullience of her responses. He even made an effort to learn and retain the jargon of classical architecture. With moderate success. Twenty years later, he could still distinguish a Romanesque from a Gothic arch and a Doric from an Ionic column.

He did, however, find troublesome the concept of culture as a layer of refinement acquired by people through a propinquity to art objects. He was not incapable of admiring a statue of a dead Italian. But certainly he would prefer to enjoy a glass of wine with a live one. And of course there were matters of honesty. "What's the point of sculpting perfect human bodies?" Noise wanted to know. And his reaction to the David of Michelangelo was, "Sure he's beautiful. But he looks like he couldn't scratch, even if he knew what was itching."

Greta was irrepressible. She began taking books to his apartment. Fielding. Defoe. Dickens. Tolstoy. Twain. Faulkner. Noise tried them all. He could make nothing of *The Sound and the Fury*. He was already a fan of *Huckleberry Finn*. Dickens, in small doses, was fine but a bit predictable. *War and Peace* was grand. Defoe created the best overall collection of characters. But the crown jewel of the human imagination was *Tom Jones*.

Greta was unrelenting. One day she arrived with a volume of Shakespeare's plays. Which she conveniently overlooked when departing the following morning. Noise recognized the hook but took the bait anyway. Fortunately he started with *A Midsummer Night's Dream*. He became captivated. By virtually all the dramatis personae. But especially by the clowns. For the next several weeks, he solicited others' opinions on any topic by asking, "What say'st thou, Bully Bottom?"

The dream drama continued to be his favorite. But it was followed closely by *The Tempest*. This, too, produced a signature line. For some time, whenever self-reproach was called for, Greta would be treated to, "What a thrice double ass was I."

During his last year in Germany, Noise found a most suitable occasion for the Caliban quip. Greta had completed her studies and started a job at a travel agency in Munich. She sent him a postcard giving her address and promising a letter. Days passed. Then a month. Finally Noise got a week's leave. He decided on a surprise visit. At her Munich apartment, a tall European male answered the door.

"Was willst du?" the young man asked in an accent acquired somewhere south of Switzerland.

Noise was not a gifted analyst, but, in this case, not much of a gift was called for. "Are you the banker?" he responded, then turned and walked away. He heard Greta's voice ask who was at the door. He hurried around the corner and ducked into a tavern. There was a huge mirror behind the bar. He ordered a liter of lager and toasted his image, "What a thrice double ass was I."

It was a shock. But it was also serendipity at its best. Noise had been contemplating reenlistment. With Greta factored out, that temptation was easily overcome. He would go home. He would make a fresh start. He would begin to honor his father and mother. He would settle down. He would look for a steady job. He would start saving his money. He would become a responsible adult. Well . . . at least he would go home.

Once back on his neighborhood turf, however, all his resolve dissolved. During his time in Germany, his friend Kiko had opened a car service and repair shop. He was in need of Noise's talents for twenty or thirty hours a week. And as before, the pool hall beckoned. Soon Juan Alvarez was once again referring to his son as "ese inútil."

BOOK TWO, CHAPTER TEN

The deterioration of his relationship with his father was depressing enough. But the degradation befalling his cousin Isabel was heartrending.

Isabel had come to live with the Chicago branch of the Alvarez family when she was eighteen. For ten years she was a model member of the family. She was solicitous to please her aunt and uncle. She found and retained a boring repetitive assembly job and contributed half her weekly earnings to help meet household expenses. She attended church regularly. She kept herself sexually inactive. Then, without a herald or a harbinger, she gave up all that for a ne'er-do-well named Tomás Reyna.

It began with a few innocent hellos following the Sunday church service. It came to fruition amid the soiled bedding of a sleeping room in a boarding house for unattached males.

She was already deep into her second trimester when Noise returned from his military hitch. His father was attempting to push her away from the family. Noise allied himself with his mother and sister in opposition. That created a stalemate for the final trimester. Once the baby was born, however, the battle was rejoined. Soon the reproaches and recriminations were so constant and of such an intensity that Isabel begged her lover to take her away.

The two found a rundown apartment and moved in together. A second pregnancy commenced. But that was hardly the worst. As it turned out, Isabel had traded verbal reproof for verbal and physical abuse. She did her best to hide the lesions and bruises and welts and other evidence. But Noise stopped by from time to time. And he was not blind.

"¿Por qué te dejas, Isabel?"
"Es que me tiene amenazada."
"Y así vas a vivir toda la vida."
"A veces me trata bien."

"A veces es bullshit. He's supposed to respect you. ¿Entiendes? Te tiene que respetar. I'm going to talk to this sonofabitch. I'm going to find out if he's a tough guy all the time or just when he's punching out a woman."

Isabel implored him to do nothing. "Me va peor si él sabe que puse complaint contigo."

"No. No te va peor. De eso you can be sure."

Noise was as good as his word. He confronted Señor Reyna. He patiently and precisely described how Tomás and his huevos would each go their separate ways if anything untoward were to occur to Isabel or the fetus during her pregnancy. And Tomás heeded the warning. And his huevos remained attached and intact.

But that was still not the worst. One day when the second infant was about four months old, Noise stopped by the apartment. Tomás was not there. Briefly Noise admired the kids. Then he and Isabel exchanged some small talk while he started on the six-pack he had brought along.

At one point Isabel went to check on the little ones. Noise picked up a sports magazine and began to page through it. A letter fell out. He picked it up and examined it. The letter was addressed in a female hand to Tomás Reyna. The sender was Mónica Reyna in Fresno, California. When Isabel returned to the living room, Noise confronted her with the letter.

"¿Quién es esta Mónica?"

"Es su hermana. Como cada dos meses she sends a letter."

"Su hermana. ¿Cómo sabes?"

"El me dijo."

"Nunca has tenido la tentación to check it out."

"Me mata if he finds out que yo estoy revisando sus cartas."

"Pues a mi no me mata," Noise scoffed and started to open the envelope.

BOOK TWO, CHAPTER TEN

"Por favor, Noise. No lo hagas. Yo no quiero saber nada."

Noise stopped. He stared at her for several seconds. Isabel refused to meet his gaze.

"You know something, don't you? Lo sabes y no me estás diciendo." He tore open the envelope and scanned the letter. There were lots of newsy items about two small boys who were clearly the children of Tomás Reyna. The letter was signed "Tu esposa, Mónica."

"That goddamn sonofabitch! I'll break every bone in his ugly cheating body! I'll kill his ass!"

When the truth was out, it was almost exactly what Noise had suspected. Isabel had known for some time about the double life of her lover. But he had terrorized her into silence. And she was convinced that she had no options.

"I will take care of you, Isabel. You don't need this asshole. You have a family for christsake. Manda al infierno a este cabrón."

He went on at some length. Each time his anger rekindled, he invented a more delicious method of murdering Tomás. Fortunately some of the plots became so convoluted that Noise perceived the need for an assistant. He called the shop and talked to Kiko. His friend quickly recognized that Noise was on the verge of violence. He closed the shop and came to the rescue.

Kiko had but one argument to combat Noise's emotion. It was not overwhelming in its logic. Nor did he present it with any special flair. But he was tenacious.

"¿Por qué quieres dirty your hands con este guy?" Then he listened. Not to the volume of words. But for a change in the vehemence of the rage. As, little by little, the intensity lessened, he pressed his point more. "He ain't worth it, Noise. ¿Por qué te vas a meter con este tipo que no vale?"

After an hour or so, Noise was operating more on willfulness than wrath. "¿Entonces que? Just let him walk?"

Kiko continued patient, "Yo no dije eso. I just said he ain't worth it."

"But I already warned the sonofabitch. Ya lo hice. I can't just warn him again. I have to do something."

"So. Call the cops. La ley can take care of him. Pueden chingarle con bigamy or something like that. Comoquiera what he did tiene que ser illegal."

"No way. Estamos hablando de mi familia. It ain't nobody else's business."

They were thoughtful for some time. Then Kiko asked, "¿De dónde viene este pendejo?"

"De California. Fresno."

"¿Por qué no lo mandamos patrás?"

Noise reflected for a minute. "I like it. But we make damn sure he never comes back here."

And so it came to pass. When Tomás returned that evening, they were awaiting him with his bags packed. They forced him to confront the letter from his wife. When he tried to explain, they ordered him to shut up. They handed him his bags and drove him to the bus station. On the way, they recited the various phases of an excruciatingly painful execution which a certain tipo could expect to undergo if he ever again showed his face east of the Mississippi. They noted the volume of sweat that his body was generating and concluded that the message had been received. At the station, they insisted on purchasing his one-way ticket to Fresno. They walked him to the departure gate. They watched him board. They even waved goodbye as the bus pulled out.

Three days later Noise acquired a phone number for Mónica Reyna from Fresno information. He called. She answered, "Yes, Tomás is here. I'll call him."

"Not necessary," said Noise. "Just tell him that someone in Chicago called to make sure he got to Fresno."

BOOK TWO, CHAPTER TEN

So it ended. Tomás Reyna was never heard of again. In the years that followed, his name was never mentioned by any member of the Alvarez family. Instead he was always referred to as "El Desaparecido."

There remained, of course, the small matter of support for the widow and orphans. Like most of us, Noise was quick to promise and fickle to perform. Especially when the performance had to be sustained. Eventually he would have to find a real job with a regular paycheck. But that affliction would be faced only when every alternative had failed. In the meantime, he spent down the last of his mustering-out pay from the military.

That might have seen him through the summer. But fortune smiled on him sooner. In August the Democratic Party faithful arrived for their nomination convention. The anti-war believers also gathered to wreak havoc on the establishment. Each of these groups had its own motley assemblage of camp followers. There were flunkies and lackeys aplenty. There were harlots and strumpets galore. There were tribes and clans, brotherhoods and sisterhoods, levies and coveys in abundance. But the group that by far outnumbered all was the congregation of potheads. It seemed to Noise that every hashhound in Christendom had descended on Chicago.

A marketer's fantasy. Too many dollars chasing a dwindling supply of product. An orgy of inflation. Noise was only a delivery boy, pressed into service because of the unexpected boom. Yet, in roughly fifteen days, he squirreled away enough to buy milk and cereal and formula and diapers until Christmas. And pay the rent besides.

Fall came. Stuff kept happening. One day out of the blue, Noise got a letter from his cousin Concha in Los Angeles. The salient message of which was that her son Librado was now eighteen. He had registered with selective service and had been summoned for a physical examination. He would probably be drafted. Would Noise please write to him and convince him to go back to Reynosa rather than enter the military? She included Librado's address in San Francisco.

Noise put the letter into a drawer with some socks. In the following week, he took it out to reread several times. Each time he felt a little more helpless. Asking him to write any kind of letter was like asking an earthworm to whistle. And Concha was asking for something to rival Paul to the Corinthians.

And then it happened. With the plight of Librado still festering in his brain. With the long-term fate of Isabel and her children still far from resolved. On an ordinary day in November. The pivotal event of the pivotal year of his life.

He had been hanging out at the pool hall. Won twenty dollars. Lost twenty dollars. Just another day. Bored. He started for home. He's walking. He always walked. It's cold. There's almost no one in the streets. Five blocks from home. A rundown commercial area. Vacant and nearly vacant storefronts. He comes to the end of a block. About to cross the street. Stops. Looks right. On the cross street halfway down the block, a guy leaning against a phone booth. A regular at the pool hall. Jerry something. Small-time dope dealer. Looks left. A car. Cadillac. Closing much too fast. Passenger side window down. An arm. A hand. A gun. Noise takes a dive into a storefront entrance. Assumes the fetal position. Squeal of braking tires. Two shots. Bam. Bam. Definitely two. Squeal of accelerating tires. Roar of engine. Silence.

He begins a check of his parts. Heart pounding. Ears ringing. He moves his hands over his torso and legs. Nothing leaking. As far as he can tell. Deep, deep breath. Again. He gets to his knees. Listen. Silence. He gets to his feet. Peeks out. Nothing. Nobody. Just Jerry. Slumped against the phone booth. Noise starts toward him. Military style. Crouching against the buildings. Sprint. Pause. Sprint. Pause.

BOOK TWO, CHAPTER TEN

Sprint. Finally the phone booth. Jerry leaking from mouth and chest. Beyond repair. On the pavement between his legs a packet. Should he? Could he? Of course he would.

He starts to reach for the packet. Very, very slowly. The hair on his arm is standing straight out. His hand is two feet from the packet. Eighteen inches. A foot. Six inches. Two inches. One. The phone rings. He jumps a foot off the planet. He lands shaking. The phone keeps ringing. His heart is threatening to exit his chest. He orders his arm to move again toward the packet. Slowly. Slowly. His hand reaches the packet. He grasps it and begins to straighten up. His muscles are knotted. His body is cringing. He expects to hear a shot. Nothing. He jams the packet down the front of his shirt. He takes a step. Another. Another. Still no shot. The phone continues to ring. He starts to walk away. His heart keeps pounding. The hair on his neck is screaming, "Run! Run!" He forces himself to walk. A block. Two blocks. Little by little his brain begins to work again. Plan, it yells. You need a plan. Yes. Yes. First he would stop for a drink and check out the packet. Then he would work out the next steps. A bar three blocks from his house. He orders a triple brandy and goes to the men's room to give the packet a hurried review.

The bathroom door opened in. He stood with his back against it and removed the packet for a quick but closer scrutiny. There were three manila envelopes size five-by-eight held together by a heavy rubber band. He poked his finger into one of the envelopes. Unless he had totally lost his touch, the contents were a stack of bills. He shoved the packet back into his shirt and returned to the bar. He downed the brandy and ordered another. He desperately needed to talk to someone. Someone he could trust. If he had to hold this thing inside much longer, he was sure that he would implode.

He called up a list of people that he could confide in. It was a very short list. The only people who received more than a cursory blink were Margarita and Miguel. Margarita would probably find it necessary to moralize about whether he could keep the money. But Miguel would be cool. And cool would rule.

He phoned a cab to take him to the bus station. While he waited, he phoned his mother to let her know that he would be visiting his sister for a few days. An hour later he squeezed into the bathroom at the back of a bus to Milwaukee.

He opened an envelope and checked the denomination of the bills. They were all the same. All hundreds. He began to count. There were exactly a hundred bills. A rapid calculation. Ten C-notes for one large. "Holy shit!" That was ten large in just one envelope. He opened the second. It contained an identical sum. As did the third. "Holy turdballs of Jesus Christ!" Ten large times three. He grinned. He moved the number around in his brain. The grin grew and grew. He screamed internally but intensely. "That's more green than I've ever seen in one place!" He could barely contain his delight. He let out one further silent scream. Then he slipped the envelopes back into his jacket, returned to his seat in the coach, and gave himself up to fantasy.

Cars, of course, came first. A Porsche maybe. No. Better yet a Corvette. Anyway some sort of high-performance monster in which he could tool out to the coast and save cousin Librado from the generals and Uncle Ho. Stopping occasionally along the way for overly nubile hitchhikers whose erotic cravings could be gratified only by a graduate of the Greta Heilsam school of oral stimulation.

All right. All right. So that wasn't about to happen. But for sure he was going to leave town. Until the missing thirty thousand had cooled a bit. So a trip to San Francisco to rescue Librado did make some sense. From there, he could go on to visit the relatives in Puebla. Geography was not his long suit.

Isabel was a different tangle altogether. His luck was her luck.

BOOK TWO, CHAPTER TEN

Certainly she would share. But how? An outright gift was folly. When the cash had evanesced, the necessity would still remain. There had to be a better way.

Rephrase the question. What was her biggest ongoing expense? The rent. She had to stop paying rent. There. Solved by a jest. Cerebral flash. Maybe not all that facetious. Think about it. Who didn't pay rent? Home owners. Isabel a home owner? Another flash. The house across the street from the Donovans. Miguel owned it. And he, Noise, was on a mission for the acquisition. Sweet serendipity. It was as good as done.

He arrived at the Donovans in a total glow. He had his own key and let himself in. Miguel was alone in the kitchen. They shook hands and did an abbreviated abrazo. Miguel pushed a glass and a bottle of brandy across the table. Noise pushed the three envelopes back.

Miguel counted and calculated. "I'm trying to think of an explanation that doesn't make this illegal. You didn't rob a bank, because the money is divided too neatly. So it's a business deal. But it's cash. I guess the real question is how dirty it is."

"I knew you'd be cool. It was a drug deal. But not mine." Noise related the particulars.

Miguel nodded. "It's semi-legal. The law of finders-keepers. I like it."

"Good. It's yours. At least a good chunk of it."

"Mine! Why mine?"

"I want to buy the house across the street. For Isabel and her kids to live in."

Miguel scratched his head for a long minute but didn't respond.

"Is the money a problem?" Noise asked.

"Not really. A minor irritation at most. But what does she live on?"

Noise pondered and nodded. "I see what you mean. I didn't even think about that."

Miguel scratched his head some more. "We could help with the little ones. She could work part-time. But it wouldn't be enough." He gave the mix another cerebral toss. "Unless you'd buy the three places."

"What three places?"

"The house you mentioned. The vacant lot next to it. And the house next to the empty lot."

"I don't get it."

"You could let Isabel have the rent from the other house. She could rent the empty lot for parking during the winter and help herself by planting a garden there in the summer. That's what I've been doing."

"It sounds like a lot of real estate. How much?"

Miguel wriggled and squirmed and finally said, "Twenty-five."

Noise objected. "You're giving it away."

"Not at all. Just trying to smooth the road a bit."

"Well that's done then. Provided Maga agrees."

"That doesn't leave much for you."

Noise laughed. "What's the big deal? Money doesn't stick to me. If I take five or twenty-five, it'll all get away. Besides it's not like I had to work for it."

Miguel appraised his brother-in-law studiously. Clearly the young man hadn't a clue that he was about to perpetrate an act of enormous generosity. He was simply the same old Noise. Who on a good day could discern from whence blew the wind, but then would be just as likely to spit in that direction as any other. Miguel shook his head.

"What?" Noise asked gruffly. Silences made him suspicious.

"Nothing. I was just thinking about how most people would be . . . "

Fortunately Miguel was interrupted by the arrival of Margarita and the teenagers.

"Uncle Ili! Uncle Noise!" the two started shouting. There were hugs all around.

Noise said, "This is what I get for coming all the way from Chicago for a visit. Nobody home."

"Fuimos al cine," said Margarita. "What have you two been doing? You both look like the cat that swallowed the . . . " she noticed the stacks of money. "¡Ay Dios mio! ¿Qué pasa aquí?" She looked like she had just opened a closet door and discovered the corpse of the missing neighbor.

"Cálmate Mujer," Miguel ordered.

"Pero Miguel . . . "

"Take it easy, Maga. You're jumping to conclusions. Your brother found this money. Found. Do you hear me? Now give him a chance to explain. After you listen to what he has to say, you can make up your mind about the money." He motioned for her and Marta and Antonio to sit. Then a warning. "Nothing that is said here tonight can leave this house. Never. Ever. ¿Entendido?" Everyone nodded. He motioned to Noise. "Cuñado, it's your show."

Noise recounted the story up to his arrival at the Donovans. There he paused. A deluge of questions ensued. "Whose money was it? Could it be from the Mafia? Was he scared when he took it? Were there people following him? Was the Mafia in Milwaukee?" Noise joined them in the land of guess and maybe. "It could be that somebody saw me. And for sure somebody will start asking questions about the money. I'm going to get out of town next week. Just in case. But I don't want to draw anyone's attention by leaving in a hurry." He took a deep breath. "About today, I can say for sure that nobody followed me. I was in the bar for a half hour. I was in the bus station another half hour. That was more than enough time to do something, and nothing happened."

At that point Miguel came to the rescue. "That's enough questions for now. I want you to hear about a plan for using the money. This is what Noise and I talked about before you got here. I think it's a great idea, but we won't do it unless everybody agrees." He shared the scheme for the properties across the street.

Marta was the first to react. "You mean my sister Isabel would move to Milwaukee and live in the house across the street with her babies?"

"Exactly."

"Y sin aquel asqueroso que vivía con ella."

"That's right. Without El Desaparecido."

She looked at Margarita. "Mom, this is like a dream."

Antonio, as always, agreed with Marta. Noise looked at his sister. Margarita was also her predictable self. "It's perfect for us, Ili. It's probably perfect for Isabel. Even the timing is perfect. Our last renters moved out in September. So the house has been empty. It's clean. Isabel could move in tomorrow." She paused for a transition. "It's just that I don't like where the money came from."

Miguel interrupted. "That's not the point, Maga. Think of the good it can do. Listen. Thanksgiving is just a couple weeks off. You're already looking for donations for the food baskets. How about if we donate a couple hundred to the food pantry at church?"

Marta joined the attack. Inspired and relentless. "If God didn't want to help Isabel, then Uncle Noise wouldn't have been walking down that street when the bad man got shot. But he was there. So that means that God wanted him to have the money so he could do something good with it. It doesn't matter where it came from. That's done. Right now the money is sitting on our kitchen table. That means that God wants us to decide how to use it." On and on.

Finally Margarita said, "Voy a calentar algo para cenar." Which meant that she would not forego her scruples. But neither would she oppose their project.

At supper there was one more surprise. At least for Noise. Marta began rhapsodizing about the proposed proximity of her sister and nephews. "It's just like magic. One day there's four of us. And then the next day, eight."

"Seven," corrected Noise.

"Eight," insisted Marta.

Margarita glanced significantly at Miguel and then at Noise. "Isabel still hasn't told you?"

"Told me what?"

"Don't be hard on her. She was scared."

"What's going on?" Noise demanded.

"Isabel is pregnant."

"She can't be. She hasn't been with anybody since El Desaparecido."

"I know. It's his."

It was a shock. But there was so much positive energy in the room that Noise soon recovered his balance and the evening marched along smoothly. The next day they moved Isabel. Not exactly a Herculean labor, since her possessions consisted of a bed, a sofa, a couple of chairs, a dresser, and clothes for herself and the babies. By dark the movers were back in Milwaukee. Margarita was waiting for them with a meal of rice, beans, and mole rojo. Isabel was overcome to the point of tears. "Nunca imaginaba yo que algo tan bonito would happen to me."

"We think it's pretty terrific for us too," concurred Miguel.

"Y yo les traigo puros problemas," Isabel sobbed.

That drew the wrath of Margarita, "Cállate, Prima. Estás llorando por lo que ya pasó. Eso no vale aquí. Ahora tienes que olvidarte de todo eso. Tienes que ponerte a pensar en tus hijos. Y para ellos lo importante es el día de mañana. Ayer ya no vale."

"Right on, Hermana," Noise agreed.

Isabel shifted her attention to him, "Y tú, Noise. Tú eres tan bueno conmigo. Para mi tú eres like a saint."

"I need a drink," said Noise, reaching for the brandy bottle.

Everyone saw the humor in that. Marta took advantage of the moment to beg for permission to stay the night with Isabel. That achieved, she began pleading for permission to miss school the next day so that she could help acclimate her sister to the neighborhood. Eventually Margarita caved in on that plea also. About ten o'clock, each carrying an infant, the two sisters crossed the street with the air of a pair of maternal conspirators. The comadre talk lasted well past midnight.

Noise intended to spend a full week in Milwaukee. And he tried. He moved spare furnishings from Margarita's house to Isabel's. He took the women shopping for more furnishings. He fixed a leaky faucet at Isabel's and another that was only threatening to leak. Then he started on Miguel's truck. He changed the oil, replaced the coolant, inspected the belts and hoses, checked the brakes, rotated the tires, serviced the transmission, adjusted the carburetor, and tuned the engine. Thursday morning after breakfast he left for Chicago.

He hung out at Kiko's shop and the pool hall for a couple of days. Disseminating the word about his imminent departure for the coast. Garnering rumors about the defunct Jerry and the missing currency, which had already been inflated by the rumor mill to a hundred thousand. On Sunday night, he boarded a bus for California.

Three days with his cousin Librado in San Francisco. Then a slide down the coast to visit Librado's mother Concha. He told her about his attempts to influence her son's decision regarding military service. He also informed her about his real estate holdings in Milwaukee and offered to sell her a house if she ever decided to relocate. Concha asked about his plans. Learning that his schedule was mostly improvisation, she wondered aloud if he would like to visit her mother who was also, by marriage, his aunt. Sure, why not? Whereabouts? Reynosa? Where was that? Mexico. He was going there. It couldn't be too far out of his way.

Los Angeles to San Antonio. At ease. Riding the bus. Letting it happen. Watching the world go by. A state of California. A state of Arizona. A state of semi-awareness. Lethargic. Complaisant. Passive.

Then why did it require so much effort? Why the sensation of exertion? Why such a grind? Crossing the continent. Crossing the continent. Musings amuse. Cerebral giggle. He had planned but one continental crossing. Now he was doing a second. That constituted a double crossing. The continent was displeased. It was being cross. Quite understandable. When continents were double crossed, they became cross. Musings amuse. More giggles. Maybe even a single crossing caused displeasure. Crossing was going against the grain. For sure he was doing that. The lay of the land was all north to south to north. The Great Plains flowed north to south. The great chains of the Sierras and Rockies rolled south to north. And he was moving west to east. He was crossing the continent. At odds with the continental energy. Against the flow.

He grinned. He yawned. He slept.

In San Antonio, following Concha's instructions, he attempted to call her cousin Andrea in McAllen. But Andrea was in Corpus Christi for a funeral. He decided to visit Concha's mother another time.

He located a truck stop. A trucker loaded for Monterrey. Hell yes, for a hundred, he could ride there and back. Without being noticed at the border? That would be a bit steeper. Palms to grease, you know. Say another fifty. Deal.

From Monterrey, a bus to the capital. From the capital, a bus to Puebla. In Puebla the unforgettable welcome from his mother's sister, Aunt Pilar.

He knocked. The door opened. Amiably he extended his hand

and announced, "Hola. Yo soy Illinois Alvarez." Pilar looked at the outstretched palm as if it were her first experience with hands. Then very slowly a trickle of syllables formed into a flood of affection. "Pero, ¿qué es esto? Apenas ayer llegó la carta." She inspected him from toes to nose, finally fixing on the eyes. "De verdad eres mi sobrino. Mi hermana me ha contado cuantas veces de esos ojos." She embraced him. Fiercely. With an ardor which once would have aroused the jealousy of Greta Heilsam. Finally she pushed him away for another inspection. And further gushing. "Mira nada más esto. Ya ni tu Papá ni tu Mamá ni tu hermana tiene tiempo para visitarnos. Y aquí estás tú. ¡Ili! ¡Ili!" Then she noted that she had failed to introduce herself. She quickly corrected that and celebrated with another abrazo. From which he was eventually rescued by the approach of another woman who looked ten years the senior of Pilar but introduced herself as the younger sister Josefa. Her greeting was a muted, "¡Qué milagro! ¡Qué milagro!" and her abrazo was considerably more restrained.

Pilar hardly missed a beat. "Fíjate nomás. Cuando apenas ayer recibimos la carta de mi hermana. Pero entra, Ili, entra. Siéntate. ¿No tienes hambre? Claro que sí. Ahorita vamos a prepararte algo sabroso. ¿Qué te gustaría? Hay chorizo. Hay guisado de pollo."

He tried to think of the Spanish for "Don't make a fuss," but what came out of his mouth was, "Lo que sea."

"¿Cómo me vas a decir eso cuando tienes tantos dias viajando?"

"Ayer comí tacos. Y hoy en la mañana una torta."

"No te digo. ¿Qué te van a dar en el camino? No hombre. Yo estoy hablando de algo rico. Pásate a la cocina. Vamos a ver lo que hay. Mientras nos puedes dar razón de tu familia."

They eased him into a chair at the kitchen table. While Josefa prepared lunch, Pilar grilled him about his parents and sister and anyone else who had ever been honorably or dishonorably mentioned in a letter. Noise's answers were brief and consequently disappointing.

His predicament was alleviated sporadically by the arrival of family members. The first was a five-year-old who peeked at him from the next room for several minutes before entering the kitchen. The boy was introduced as Arturo's second son Dante. That led to a long listing of family members and their occupations and their relationship to each other. Soon Noise's head was spinning.

"Arturo es mi hijo. El único que tengo. El es doctor. El enseña en la universidad. Pero también consulta. Su esposa se llama Ramona. Ella es enfermera. Trabaja en una clínica. Por eso los niños están conmigo en el día. Y sus padres vienen a comer aquí en la tarde. Llegan aquí como a las tres." She was interrupted by the wail of a baby named Dora who required a change of diaper. Not long after that, the third child, Daniel, arrived from school. "Este es el mayor de los tres," explained Pilar.

The boy extended his hand like a grownup and announced, "Daniel Palafox y González a sus órdenes."

Noise was flabbergasted. "La gente me llama Noise."

"Yo sé. Tú andabas de soldado en Alemania. Noise es un apodo. En el ejército se usa mucho el apodo. Yo sé. Yo veo *Combate* en la televisión. En inglés se llama *Combat*, ¿verdad?"

Pilar scolded, "Daniel, estás hablando mucho."

"Pero quiero saber de la guerra. Las cosas que presentan en *Combate* son de de veras, ¿verdad?"

"No sé," Noise replied lamely.

"¿No ves el programa de *Combate*?"

"No. No lo conozco."

The boy made no attempt to hide his disappointment.

"Mejor haz tu tarea," recommended Pilar. She set a plate of huevo con chorizo in front of Noise and poured herself a cup of coffee. Then she resumed her family narrative. "Pues sí, ya conoces a mis nietos. Arturo y Ramona y estos tres ocupan el departamento al otro lado del pasillo donde entraste." She paused to organize her next surge. "En el departamento que sigue está mi hermano Chucho y su familia. Su esposa se llama Estela. Ellos tienen cuatro hijos. Las dos mayores son gemelas. Más o menos de tu misma edad. Se llaman Hilda y Laura. Luego un hijo, Gerardo. La bebita es la muchacha que no está bien. Es enfermiza, ¿me entiendes?"

Noise had no idea what he had just been told. But he nodded sagely, and that seemed to meet the exigencies of the case.

Pilar was indefatigable. "Las gemelas están terminando sus estudios universitarios. Gerardo es camionero. Anda por Veracruz. Chucho te puede explicar exactamente donde."

"Mi tío Chucho es mecánico, ¿verdad?"

"Sí, M'hijo. Tiene su taller en el terreno al lado de este edificio. Lo puedes ver en la tarde. A ti te interesa la mecánica también, ¿verdad?"

"Sí. Mucho."

She was obviously hoping for more, but he could think of nothing to add. He decided to try for a recap. "¿Y quién vive aquí, Tía?"

She gave him the sort of look that is usually reserved for slow children and incompetent adults. "¿En este departamento, Hijo?"

"Sí."

"Pues yo. Y Josefa. Y como hay una recámara desocupada, tú puedes quedarte aquí también. Si quieres."

"Y de la otra gente que mencionaste. Quiero saber quién es quién."

She gave him another of those looks and answered, "Hay solo dos familias, Hijo. Arturo y Ramona con sus tres. Y Chucho y Estela con sus cuatro. Aquí en Puebla no hay mas familia."

A key in the front door announced the arrival of Arturo and Ramona. Leaving Noise to exchange nervous smiles with her sister,

Pilar went to meet them. Noise could overhear.

"No vas a creer quien está aquí."

"Mi primo. Tan pronto. No me digas."

"Adivinastes. Ya llegó. Pero hay algo raro."

She lowered her voice. "Tu tía María siempre me contaba que este joven está muy descontrolado. Y lo que yo estoy mirando es que no sabe ni hablar casi."

Arturo chuckled softly. "¿Le ofreciste una cerveza?"

"¡Cerveza! ¿Piensas que tiene sed?"

Another mild chuckle. "Sí, Mamá. Tiene sed." He crossed the hall to his apartment and returned with four bottles each containing two liters of Orizaba's best. Thus armed, he entered the kitchen and greeted Noise.

More introductions. More abrazos. Then the brew. Arturo found two glasses and filled them. The customary toast, "Salud." Arturo sipped a thimbleful from his, while Noise drained off half a glass. Small talk. Another "Salud." Arturo sipped another thimbleful. Noise emptied his glass. Arturo poured him another.

Questions about his journey. Noise began to wax expansive. Recalling the happening later, he would attest that the first two-liter bottle had remedied thirst. The second had promoted inspiration. The third had produced fluency. That last assertion, of course, was outrageous hyperbole. What he achieved was not fluency but fervency. The effect, however, was about the same.

Arturo asked what had made the strongest impression on him during his travels. That was an easy one. "Los niños haciendo su lucha." Noise described the kids he had seen along the way shining shoes, hustling chicles, and in some instances forthrightly begging.

One thing led to another. Soon he was delving into memories of his own childhood. For some reason, the summer of the roaches rushed through his brain. When he and Kiko and the rest of the play group had experienced a sudden surge of interest in entomology.

It had started with the ants. The kids frequently observed them scurrying from crack to crack in the sidewalk. Occasionally there would be a wager on some outcome or other. One day a boy nicknamed Conejo showed up with a roach. He offered to bet a dime that his roach could go crack to crack in ten seconds or less. There were plenty of takers. But how could they accurately measure ten seconds? Not to sweat. Kiko Estrada had recently acquired a stopwatch via the five-finger discount.

Thus began the summer of their great content. Roach racing. To be sure, not the sport of kings. On the contrary. A most democratic pastime. Everyone had roaches, so anyone could play. But the group soon learned that roaches did not readily go crack to crack. When released, they might set off in any direction. Noise had the solution to that. A circle.

On any available pavement, mark a circle around a baby food jar. Have someone hold one end of a string in the center of that circle.

Attach a piece of chalk to the other end of the string. Then, using the string as a radius, scribe a large circle around the small one. That's it. Instant Blattidrome.

To initiate a competition, each of two or more kids captures a roach in a baby food jar. Overturn one of these jars in the small circle. Raise the jar to release the roach, simultaneously starting the stopwatch. Stop the time when the roach reaches any point on the large circle. Make a note of the roach's name and time. Then start the next roach. When all bugs have run, the winner obviously is the one with the least time on the course.

For the kids it became the all-consuming passion of the season. They devoted their playtime to racing or fantasizing about races. They cheated on their chores in order to give more time to the pursuit or ambush of swifter competitors. At night they dreamed of cornering and capturing Superbug. In the meantime, they spent most of their petty cash betting on the wrong roaches.

For the bugs, it was a matter of life and death. Losers were unceremoniously squashed. "Slow roaches die fast" was everyone's slogan. A couple kids had parents who played the ponies. Soon there were comments around the track about roaches who died in the gate or died in the stretch or died at the wire. But in these instances, the racetrack idiom was not mere jargon. These competitors actually did suffer the ultimate fate, crunched beneath a callous sneaker.

With a minimal lexicon but maximal energy and many a "¿cómo se dice?" Noise made the season live again. His listeners became concentrated, then fascinated, then hypnotized. About an hour after he had begun, Chucho's twin daughters arrived. But instead of being introduced, the girls were asked to hush so as not to interrupt the flow of the narrative.

Noise carried on.

The first notable champion was captured and raced by Lisa, the tomboy member of the playgroup. She named him Stinky, and for a week, he dominated the track. Then mysteriously, he began to run in circles and came to a bad end. A slow period followed his demise. For half a month no new champ emerged.

And then came Chuckie. Initially he was Conejo's pride and joy. His first day at the track he won five races. Kiko offered to buy him for a dollar. No deal. The next day he won three more races. Kiko upped his offer to two dollars. Sold.

It was a small fortune. The new owner needed a new strategy to recoup his investment. He announced that Chuckie would race for nothing less than a quarter. Outrage. He was threatening the entire enterprise. Nobody had been wagering more than a dime, and much more typically a nickel. Now the others would have to win three or four races just to earn a shot at Chuckie.

Kiko was adamant. The others struggled and scrambled to put together the requisite prize money, hoping that Kiko would deign to trot out the champ for an afternoon showdown. Once it was Lisa with a speedster named Alfie. Another day Noise challenged with a courser named Flash. It didn't really matter. Chuckie always won.

He was not the sleekest. He was not the fleetest. But he had a nose for the finish line. Regardless of how he was pointed, he ran straight for the chalk.

One day Conejo's older brother came by with a roach he called Dart. He would challenge Chuckie for a dollar. Kiko inspected the challenger and pronounced him the prize of the neighborhood. Was he for sale? At a dollar, no. Nor at two. All right. They would race. But for five dollars. Done.

The two met the following afternoon. By then there was action all around the block. People were giving three to one on Dart and finding the going tough. Kiko's grandmother bet her grocery money on Chuckie, but she stood nearly alone in her faith. And to be sure, Chuckie did little to justify her loyalty. He ran a rather average eight seconds. Dart, by contrast, was on a pace to cover the course in no more than five. Then, inexplicably, two inches from the finish, he turned and headed back for the starter's circle. Most of the neighborhood released a collective groan. Kiko's grandma squealed and peed in her drawers.

Everyone screamed for a rematch, and after the purse was doubled, Kiko agreed. So. On a Saturday morning, with at least two dozen fanatics crowded around the track, the rivalry was renewed. Dart was started first. In spite of a rather serpentine route, he covered the course in a respectable eight seconds. Chuckie, as usual, was slower but straighter. He crossed the chalk in seven seconds. Kiko was about to scoop him up when someone pushed Conejo who fell and landed on the champ. Kiko yelled foul. He might as well have yelled uncle. Chuckie had his victory. But Chuckie was also history.

They buried him in Noise's backyard under a small plaque that read: "Chuckie. You were the best." Kiko tried to revive the sport. Nobody showed any interest. Not then. Not the next summer. The circular lines faded from the pavement. The bugs went back to being pests. Roach racing, like Chuckie, was dead.

Noise concluded his story and looked around. Everyone looking back was looking pleased. "Maybe my Spanish isn't as bad as I thought," he congratulated himself. But that totally missed the mark. The relatives' reaction was about equal parts satisfaction and relief.

The García clan had pictured Illinois as a true gringo. He was the child of parents who had visited only once in the previous quarter century. And that for a funeral. He had been socialized and schooled with gringos. He had even served in the gringo military. When the letter had arrived announcing his visit, conjecture had abounded. Certainly he would be fastidious. Possibly pretentious. Maybe even arrogant.

Instead he appeared to be rather at home in their kitchen. He was sharing their food and drink. He was speaking a version of their language. And for the last two hours, he had captivated them with a tale of cucarachas. In his jeans and boots, he just might be a northern variation of their kind.

Time would prove the accuracy of that perception. And there would be plenty of time. Noise had intended a visit of possibly a year. He would stay for almost fifteen.

CHAPTER ELEVEN

The heart attack that felled Librado Gómez in Reynosa and compelled him to seek shelter with his son Alvaro in Los Angeles was a cruel blow. But with rest and measured exercise, he slowly began to recover his strength. Then another blow. Actually more of a slap in the face.

Librado frequently communicated with his grandsons in Spanish. His daughter-in-law, Kathleen, who spoke only English, resented his influence on her children. One day she informed him that she would no longer permit the use of Spanish in her home. Librado took exception on various grounds. Alvaro found himself in the unenviable position of arbitrator. His judgment was that domestic tranquility would be better promoted by siding with his wife.

The family was standard American nuclear. Librado's place at best would have been marginal. His weakened physical condition further undercut his standing. His lack of performance in the raising of his son rendered him morally compromised. He complied. What else could he do?

Internally, of course, he seethed. To be bullied by anyone was a disgrace. To be vanquished by a woman was outright dishonor. If a frontal attack was out of the question, there was still the option of scorched earth. He summoned his raiders. What else could he do?

The ensuing guerrilla was notable only for its excess of niggling and spite. One early attempt was directed at undermining the daughter-in-law's authority with the Mexican housekeeper. This worthy woman not only maintained her loyalty to the Patrona. She went out of her way to label Librado a viejo asqueroso. This, for his nocturnal use of a bedpan.

A few weeks later, there was a skirmish regarding a misplaced ring. Librado accused the housekeeper. She protested innocence but was dismissed. The ring then, mysteriously, reappeared. The housekeeper was recalled, but she had already acquired a more lucrative position.

In the next several years, a pattern emerged. An incident would occur. Verbal heat would follow. Kathleen avowing that she would no longer tolerate her father-in-law's presence. Alvaro pleading with his wife for continued leniency. "He's my father. I can't just throw him out."

As it turned out, he could. The time came for Alvaro Junior to celebrate his sixteenth birthday. A rite-of-passage event, announced Grandpa. The moment had arrived for professional instruction in the moves and modes of amor. He set Junior up with a call girl of his acquaintance.

Had the young man indulged himself and later bragged to his friends, whose loose lips then put his parents in the know, Librado would have been proud. Had the young man indulged himself but then raced in repentance to his mother's arms, Librado would have been chagrined but understanding. But when the youth beheld a goddess in a peekaboo gown over fishnet stockings and red satin underwear and fled to confess without so much as a tingling in his testicles, Librado was humiliated. He barely felt the pain of his own expulsion.

For about a week. Then the prospect of abysmal meals in dismal diners for the rest of his days unnerved him. He rushed off a note to his niece Concha, imploring her to come west and tend to his needs. He would see to the education of her son.

At the time, Concha was involved in the fallout from her paternal Uncle Antonio's desertion of his children. But with Isabel and her siblings safely ensconced with relatives in the upper Midwest, Concha bid a teary goodbye to cousin Andrea in McAllen and headed for the coast.

And thus it came to pass that her son Librado Mario Lee was raised amid the children of sun and beach. For the most part, he ignored them. For the most part, they reciprocated.

Uncle Librado immediately dubbed the seven-year-old "Tocayo" and declared him a total delight. He could not do enough for Concha's son. He began buying toys. A baseball glove. A football. Polite disappointment.

"¿Qué le pasa?" he asked the mother.

"Libros," she answered. "Le gustan los libros."

Off to the bookstore then. He returned with *The Tale of Peter Rabbit* and something called *Harold and the Purple Crayon*.

More polite disappointment.

"¿Qué le pasa ahora?" he asked the mother.

"Mira Tío. Este niño empezó a leer desde muy temprano. El está acostumbrado a libros mas avanzados. Pero no hay ningún problema. Si tú lo llevas a la librería, él sabrá escoger."

That brought relief. *Peter Rabbit* and *Purple Crayon* were exchanged for *Treasure Island* and *Huckleberry Finn*.

Then with the old man urging him to splurge, the boy added *Robinson Crusoe, Gulliver's Travels,* and *Twenty Thousand Leagues* to his collection.

Those five books became a major focus of their lives. Every evening they would read together. Always for an hour. Sometimes for more than two. They read everything twice. The boy would lead off. Concentrating on rhythm and expression. Honing his word-attack skills. Pausing to inquire about novel lexicon items. Absorbing the gist of the tale. Then the old man would repeat the same pages, while the boy sat back, savoring every word.

The final pages of a book frequently produced a great distress in the lad. As if he were mourning the passing of a friend. He would force the final words through his tears. Then he would slowly pass the book to the old man and ask, "Why does it have to end, Grandpa?"

The old man would smile. To be loved by the boy was gratifying. To be honored by inclusion in his ancestry was positively heartwarming. "All things end, Tocayo. It's just the way of things. Everything that begins has to end."

"I know about that, Grandpa. But I mean the story. Why does the writer stop? Why can't he just make the story go on and on?"

"Maybe it just seems like the right place to end, Tocayo. Or maybe the writer wants to start a new story. Or maybe he just gets tired."

"I guess so." The boy remained unconvinced. But he could relate to the part about getting tired. During the evening sessions he often had to pretend not to notice that the old man was nodding off.

What with his bookish inclination and his almost exclusive association with adults, it perhaps was understandable that he was marked by many as a strange child. A common phenomenon you say. Most kids have an axon awry or a dendrite askew. But no. His was a broader range of strange. He seemed to lack many of the standard cerebral synapses.

Picture him at ten. His fifth grade teacher has a girlfriend who is studying psychology. The teacher recommends the boy as the subject for a research project. As an icebreaker, the amateur psychologist assays a free-association exercise. By way of example, she states that the word "egg" might suggest the word "chicken." Or "dinosaur," her subject counters. She reminds herself that not all fish swim with the current and proceeds. The word "game" evokes "chess" and "chess" evokes "strategy." So far so good. The word "run" suggests "energy" and the word "energy" suggests "food." A bit precocious. But hardly alarming. The word "food" suggests "family." That's great. Let's explore that. Alas! The word "mother" incongruously elicits "river." The student of psychology inspects her subject's body language for signs of repressed mirth. Not a hint. All right. One last attempt. The word "house" very properly connects with "home." A sigh of relief. But not enduring. The word "home" quirkily connects with "Milky Way." Pause for clarification. A candy bar? Explosion of glee. Of course not. The galaxy. Hmm. Yes. Well. Perhaps another day we can try this again.

At thirteen he went off to study with the Jesuits. The academy was both a junior and senior high. It was short on sports and science equipment and long on classical languages and hazing.

Most of the hazing, of course, was directed at the newcomers. At a meager eighty-five pounds and less than five feet tall, Librado was an obvious target. But in this instance, the obvious did not occur. Thanks to his bilingual upbringing. Before his very first class on his very first day, the strapping juvenile at the next desk stood and asked, "¿Nadie habla español?" Librado politely allowed his companions to volunteer first. No one spoke. "Condenado estoy," announced the tall youth. It was time to intervene. "Yo sí hablo español." The other lad looked him over doubtfully. "¿De dónde eres?" Librado considered Reynosa and McAllen and rejected both. "Yo soy de Texas. Me llamo Librado." The tall youth responded with a bear hug and, "Librado, mi salvador." Then more calmly, "Yo soy Perfecto Limón."

Yes indeed. He was the son of a Bolivian billionaire. From four to fourteen, he had attended a private institute in La Paz. The school specialized in English and martial arts. Early on, Perfecto had perceived that he would not do well at both. But which to choose? He studied his environment. No one remotely close to him spoke English. There were, however, hostile ninjas lurking everywhere.

His mother had deemed his admission to the Los Angeles academy a miracle. Certainly her prayers to Saint Jude had aided the cause. Her husband's hint of a sizable endowment for the school had also helped. But the Jesuits had posited a condition. The parents must hire someone to tutor their son in English. Ecce Librado. Perfecto pronounced him the savior. Having already cashed the first check of the endowment, the Jesuits agreed.

It was Librado's first job. But he received no actual wages. Instead Señor Limón paid for the tutoring directly to the school. Then the bursar credited Librado's tuition account. For the next two years, ten hours each week, he labored at Perfecto's improvement.

With the muscular Bolivian hanging around, Librado had nary a worry about hazing. Tutoring Perfecto was something else again. When it came to learning, Perfecto was an indolence of fecklessness and sloth. He would demand that Librado do his homework. Then he would whine at the injustice of having to copy the work in his own hand. Ignatius Loyola would have declared him a caso perdido.

There was more. Perfecto enjoyed inflicting pain. When he discovered a classmate with a speech problem, he mimicked. When he identified another with epilepsy, he aped his behavior during a seizure. He once inquired of a hemophiliac lad whether it was true that he menstruated. In short, Perfecto was a prick. Following his second summer vacation, he did not return to school. When it became clear that his absence was permanent, even the Jesuits acknowledged that they had been holding their breath.

Before he left, however, he helped Librado acquire a nickname.

It happened in an English class. The Jesuit scholastic was lecturing on Swift's *Modest Proposal*. "Swift is suggesting that if children are to be raised to a life of hopelessness in any event, would it not be more efficient to cannibalize them as children?"

Librado raised his hand. The instructor paused and recognized him.

"You mean effective," Librado said.

The instructor did not follow. "Effective what?"

"You used the word efficient. But you should have said "effective." "Efficient" describes a process. "Effective" describes a result. Swift is talking about a result. So the better choice of adjective is "effective" rather than "efficient.""

The scholastic was baffled. All that occurred to him was to ask, "What is your name, young man?"

"Librado Lee, Sir."

"Well, Mister Lee, you are the most loquacious young man that I have encountered in some time."

Perfecto Limón joined the fray. "Te dijo 'loco,' hombre. No te dejes. El no puede decir eso."

Librado responded mildly. "I'm sorry, Sir. I won't interrupt again."

The apology was accepted. The scholastic's feathers came unruffled. But the nickname stuck. From that day forward, Librado Mario Lee would be known as Loco Lee.

At about that time, he started what he called a journal. A rather odd piece of work. Such documents usually begin with a preface in which the writer explains his motive and mission. Loco leads off with an aphorism. *In order to stand, you must first arrive at an understanding with the ground.*

The body of the work is largely what he himself would one day call "verbalized navel-gazing." Page one contains the following: *For complex life forms, balance is everything. Balance results from the*

BOOK TWO, CHAPTER ELEVEN

harmony of horizontal and vertical. Where the horizontal and vertical meet they form a center. In self-conscious life forms, that center is the locus of the Self.

And then just when the reader is concluding that the dubious gruel is warmed-over Whitman, page two stuns with, *There is a lot of talk about a movement. But it's all just talk. Nobody is really doing anything. Ideas are powerful. But their power is released only in the area of action. Wigging out on a joint and whispering the word "movement" every few seconds accomplishes nothing.*

Aha, the reader reacts. Reheated existentialism. He's searching for a project. Maybe. Page three says, *All creative energy flows from the center. Energy flowing from the center is intentional, that is to say, directed toward a purpose.*

Then, without so much as a conjunction, he leaps back to the other polarity. *How can we keep insisting that we are part of a movement, when we don't move? All this interior crap is really beginning to gall. The war gets bigger and crazier, and we sit around discussing the coming of the Age of Aquarius. More like the age of acquiescence, if you ask me.*

The summer he turned sixteen, Librado went out to Delano to join the farmworkers' march to Sacramento. At first a huge high. Finally he was doing something. But soon reality brought him up short. The farmworkers were a family. Some were actually blood relatives. Some were related by marriage. Many shared a place of origin. All were connected by a common experience. He was an outsider.

No one discouraged his presence. No one disparaged his participation. He marched along. When he knew the words, he joined in the song. But he could not lose the feeling of being out of place. He simply did not belong.

On the third day, he was adopted by a long-haired, stringbean girl who shared his feeling of isolation. That evening she talked him into "bugging out for San Francisco." She even allowed him to loan her the bus fare. Arriving in the city, she stationed him on a park bench while she went to the bank to withdraw some money. Two hours passed before he accepted the fact that he had been stiffed.

Back in Los Angeles, he found a job at a golf course. A most fortuitous event. A week later Uncle Librado suffered another heart attack. From then on, most of his income went for medical expenses. Loco would have to see to his own education.

He was an honor student. The Jesuits wanted to help. For the next two years, in lieu of tuition, he tutored three Chilean students. From an additional part-time job, he contributed to the household expenses.

He qualified as the salutatorian of his class, an honor he declined. He was disgusted with his classmates. All their talk was of getting into college to avoid the draft. Graduation was a sham.

He took his diploma. He reported for his physical. He decided that San Francisco would be a better place to wait for the axe to fall. There, in November, his cousin Noise caught up with him.

He answered the knock on his sleeping room door and asked, "Can I help you?"

"Hey Primo," was the reply, "¿Cómo estás?"

It was the boxer. From about twelve years earlier. In Corpus Christi, Texas. The eyes gave him away. A shade of grey that he had seen only once. It was definitely the boxer.

As if to confirm his recollection, Noise punched him on the shoulder. "¿Cómo estás, Primo? ¿Te acuerdas de mí?"

"Sí, me acuerdo. Everybody calls you Noise."

"You got the right guy. How about you? Do they still call you Librado?"

"Actually they started calling me Loco a few years back."

"Loco. No kidding." There was a pause for some restrained bobbing and weaving. Then, "Anyway, Primo Loco, aquí estoy. Are you going to invite me in or what?"

"Actually, this place is too depressing. Let's go somewhere."

They walked to Golden Gate Park. On the way, Loco asked about Isabel and her siblings and Margarita and Noise's parents. The boxer answered, but he seemed preoccupied. A little too intense. As if he had signed for a title match with the outcome very much in doubt.

They found a shady piece of park and stretched out.

"So how's your mom?" Noise asked.

"She's okay."

"She sent me a letter a couple weeks ago."

Loco laughed. "You mean this isn't just a friendly visit."

"Yes and no."

"Well, let's get it over with. I'm about to be drafted. I'm making a big mistake. I'll be shipped off to Vietnam where I'll be killed three or four times. So I should seriously consider going back to Mexico." He paused. "Is that about right?"

The sarcasm was ignored. Instead, Noise began making his case against the war. He argued that the military did not know what they were doing in Vietnam. They had always defined success in war as the taking and holding of territory. That did not work in Vietnam. So they had resorted to a body count as a means of measuring progress. But that didn't work either. There was no way to know when you had killed enough to declare a victory. So they were floundering. They could no longer define a mission. The troops picked up on that. They were getting restless. In some cases, they were fragging their own officers. His conclusion was that only an idiot would allow himself to be duped into participation in such a disaster.

Loco had expected a set piece. But nothing like what he got. His cousin, it turned out, was not the lightweight he had anticipated.

"You've obviously thought about this a lot."

"Not that much," Noise answered. "But I've talked to four or five guys who were there, and they all say the same thing."

"I appreciate that. But it doesn't really get to the problem as I see it."

"Don't tell me," Noise interrupted. "You owe it to yourself. You have to prove your manhood."

"Not even close."

"¿Entonces qué?"

Loco shook his head. "I don't know if anyone else would take this seriously."

"Try me."

"Okay. Let's suppose I don't go. Somebody else will have to go in my place. That's not right." Noise did not react. Loco took that as a cue to continue. "This started back in high school. Graduation was getting close. Guys were talking about colleges. And a lot of them really wanted to continue their education. But some guys didn't. They were planning to enroll just to avoid the draft. They would make jokes about the poor bastards who would be drafted because they didn't have the money or the connections. It was disgusting."

"So this is about haves and have-nots?"

Loco thought for a second. "I suppose that's one way to put it."

"And you think you might be one of the haves?"

"No, but . . ."

"Find your ass." Noise interrupted. He wasn't bobbing and weaving now. He was throwing combinations.

"Find what?" Loco asked lamely.

"Find your ass. When you don't know where you are, find your ass. The rest of you will be somewhere in the area. You don't have money, right?"

"No."

BOOK TWO, CHAPTER ELEVEN

"You don't have connections, right?"

"No."

"You see? There's your ass. You are one of the have-nots, Primo. Those smug bastards at your high school weren't laughing at some dudes from the boonies. They were laughing at you."

The logic was hardly elegant. Nor was it overwhelming. But it did present a perspective that he had not appraised. He would have to reconsider his position. But not at that precise moment. Not with the boxer jabbing and feinting.

The next day, Noise picked him up from work and took him to Fisherman's Wharf for dinner. Loco ordered for both. Noise began talking about cars. Loco began yawning. The bouillabaisse arrived. Loco recommended some museum-hopping for the next day.

"You like art, Primo?"

"Of course."

"Then you have to see Florence. Someday if you can afford to visit one city in the world, but only one, make sure it's Firenze." Loco's jaw began to sag, and for the next half hour it just kept dropping. Not only did Noise remember. He appeared to be actually revisiting the sites and scenes that he was describing. The Piazza della Signoria. The Ponte Vecchio. Santa Croce. The Uffizi. Michelangelo. Giotto. Botticelli. Leonardo. It all spilled forth with the freshness and intensity of first love.

"Incredible," said Loco. "You are one big packet of surprises."

That wasn't the end. The next night, as he was leaving for Los Angeles, Noise slipped an envelope into Loco's jacket. A polite thanks. "A couple twenties. Or maybe a fifty," Loco told himself. But later he discovered eight crisp one-hundred-dollar bills. A whole year of college.

The following week he enrolled for the January semester. He put his nose to the grindstone and maintained that posture for the next four months. With impressive high school transcripts and admirable scores on the placement tests, he was able to enter with advanced standing in Spanish, English, and history. When he successfully completed courses in those subjects, he was then permitted to pay for the retrocredits. He also took courses in biology, math, and economics. In May, when he took stock, he could pridefully state that he had accumulated forty-two credits with one semester's labor. On the down side, he was exhausted, depressed, and broke.

The depression hurt the most. The war had expanded into most of Southeast Asia. Many veterans of the movement had ceased believing that the government could be influenced by peaceful means. Some of these folks had begun to advocate violence. Others had opted for Krishna. Still others had adopted acid.

With his earnings from a summer job, he paid off the last of a college loan. That allowed him to acquire a transcript of the course work he had done. A classmate told him of a relative in Canada who owned a bookstore and might have a job for a knowledgeable draft resister. Loco feigned disinterest, but he wrote down the name and address of the bookstore. And so it came to pass that in September, Ho Chi Minh joined the ancestors, and Loco Lee the expatriates.

It was the worst of times. Other than his mother, he trusted almost no one. He spread the word that he was outbound for Vancouver but went instead to Winnipeg. The bookstore owner there was very friendly but could offer him only part-time employment. Later that fall, he stumbled onto another part-time job teaching Spanish in a private school. And that led to some tutoring. By the following summer, he could afford a small apartment.

In July a letter from his mother said that his Grandmother Gómez had died. Concha had gone to the funeral. She had looked forward to a deliciously gossipy visit with Cousin Andrea. But in the intervening years, the doctor had acquired a beau. With a roving

BOOK TWO, CHAPTER ELEVEN

eye. At least it soon started roving in Concha's direction. She stayed only one day after the funeral.

Stuff kept happening. In October, Uncle Librado died in his sleep. His son Alvaro made the funeral arrangements. Few attended. The obituary failed to mention his participation in the revolution. Sic transit and all that.

A month later, Loco received another letter from his mother. She was seriously considering a move to Milwaukee. Margarita was there. Isabel was there. She would be closer to Winnipeg. Cousin Noise had offered to sell her a house on a land contract. What did her son think of the plan? Loco rushed off a response giving every encouragement.

Winnipeg winters stimulated journal entries. By this time, Loco was analyzing his role as a dissenter. That led to some generalizations about dissent in a society. Here's a sampling:

Every society is hell-bent on self-preservation. Boundaries must be fixed, so that order can be conserved. In a healthy society, this is done inefficiently. Limits are defined fuzzily. Nonconformity is allowed at the margins. In fact, in a healthy society, the nonconformists not only reside on the margin. They constitute the margin. They collectively comprise the fuzzy border between order and chaos. As such, they perform an essential function for the society. They mediate the interchanges between order and chaos, which assure the continuity and health of the society.

The nonconformists nibble away at the edges of chaos. In doing so, they push the frontiers of order into the undefined and undared. In these novel regions, they encounter pristine but perilous intellectual nutrients which they ingest and digest and thereby render safe for assimilation by society at large. At the same time, they release into chaos the destructive energy, which is a by-product of their activities in pursuit of purposes nonconvergent with those of the society.

But all this is said of the peripheral characters. This is just part of their ongoing argument with the majority about what constitutes a healthy society and how it should function. The resulting disruption is minimal and low-key and predictable.

But what if the dissent arises not from the periphery but from the center? What if a group of solid citizens begins to see that the purpose and policies of their government are at variance with the fundamental principles of the society? And what if the number of these solid citizen dissenters continues to grow? What happens then?

Since the dissent is at the center, there is no mediation by the non-conformists. Emotion dominates. Intensity builds. Disruption is maximized. Institutions designed to conserve order start to come apart. Society lashes out at itself. If nothing intervenes to slow or halt the process, meltdown eventually occurs. Order begins to create chaos.

And off on the periphery, an ancient anarchist watches and whispers to himself, "Goddamn! And these fuckers used to say we were crazy."

Loco wrote those words less than a year after the Kent State killings. It was still early to be waxing philosophical about dissent. But, of course, he had distanced himself from events psychologically as well as geographically.

About that time, he met the woman who was to become his wife. It was mid-April. Still winter in Winnipeg. Snow had fallen in the early morning. The front steps were still slippery as he exited the apartment building. On the third from last step, his feet went out from under him, and he slid onto the sidewalk, knocking down a young woman who was about to enter the building. She landed on top of him, in what the two would one day dub the inverted missionary position. A scramble followed as both began a rush to reacquire their dignity. But they had not failed to note the other's facial features. They paused in their battle to regain their feet and looked more intently at each other. Then, as if on cue, they simultaneously asked, "Are you Chinese?"

They giggled as they got to their feet. He answered, "No, not really," then, "I'm late. I have to run." He started down the walk, turned, said, "I'm sorry I ran into you," started off again, turned back again, said, "I didn't mean that the way it sounded. I mean . . ." then in total confusion, "I'm really late." The flight response kicked in.

Their next meeting was not until June. And then quite by accident. He was working the register at the bookstore. He had just concluded a sale. The next customer set a book on the counter. He glanced at the title. *On Aggression* by Konrad Lorenz. He looked up. "One of my favorite books." The young woman was not a regular customer. But he had seen her somewhere. "I'm doing a paper on displacement behavior," she said. "For a behavioral psychology class." Their eyes engaged for a few seconds. Recognition. Then laughter, as each pointed at the other and asked, "Are you Chinese?"

He immediately began to apologize. "I'm sorry. I should have stayed to find out if you were all right. But I was really really late."

"Oh, no problem. I was fine. Do you live in that apartment building?" She laughed nervously. By education and example, she had become Westernized. But there were neuropathways which were still severely stressed whenever she boldly approached a man.

"Yes, I do. Do you live there?"

"I just moved in. In March." She handed him a ten-dollar bill. He made change and handed her the receipt. The silence became mildly awkward.

"Well I guess I'll see you around then."

"Sure. Take care."

It was a commonplace exchange. But in the following days, he discovered that she had insinuated herself into his consciousness. Not yet a pervasive but already a predictable presence. Occasionally he would pass by a mirror, pause, point to his image, and ask, "Are you Chinese?"

But he was much too busy to cultivate a social life. By then he was working full time at the bookstore. He continued to give private Spanish lessons. He had started taking classes at the university. Twice that summer, he saw her from his apartment window as she was leaving the building. On a day when he was not scheduled, she asked for him at the bookstore. It was snowing again before they finally got together.

A Sunday afternoon. Ordinarily he would have gone out to tutor and then to the library to cram for a math quiz. But Monday was a national holiday, and his students were off on a long weekend. A knock at the door. There she was, holding out a dish and saying, "I made egg rolls. Do you like egg rolls?"

"Is the pope Catholic?" he responded automatically, then became flustered as he considered the possibility that he had offended.

She understood. "No problem. I'm Buddhist."

They laughed together. He realized that she was still standing in the doorway. "Come in," he said too loudly. She entered. "How did you find my apartment?"

"A couple months ago, I asked the maintenance man if he knew where the young man with the Chinese eyes lived. He gave me your apartment number. Twice I tried to bring you egg rolls, but you are never home."

"That's true. I'm usually not here. But I'm glad you kept trying. And you couldn't have picked a better day. I have nowhere to go. I have nothing to do. And now I can sit and munch egg rolls all day."

They shared a smile. "Should I make some coffee?" he asked.

"I brought some tea. Do you drink tea?"

He started to chuckle. She caught the vibe. In unison they questioned, "Is the pope Catholic?"

BOOK TWO, CHAPTER ELEVEN

He found a pot and started to draw some water. Only then did the obvious occur to him. "I'm sorry. I should have introduced myself. My name is Librado Lee."

"I am Mai Lu Lor."

"Mai Lu," he repeated. "That's beautiful. It sounds like the name of a flower."

"Now the big question," she said. "Are you really Chinese or just your eyes?"

"The honest answer is just my eyes. The family name is Chinese. So I probably have a few Chinese ancestors. But my family is mostly Mexican, and that's the way I was raised."

"Now you have to ask me," she said.

"Of course. Here it comes," He did an imitation clarion call. Then, "Are you Chinese?"

"No, I am not Chinese. Everyone thinks so, but I am Hmong."

She was about to continue, but he interrupted. "Hmong! You're kidding. I was just reading about this a few days ago." He accessed a data file in his brain, assumed the voice of a museum guide, and proceeded to reel off a list of facts about the Hmong. "The Hmong are ethnic highlanders. They inhabit the mountains of southern China as well as Vietnam, Laos, and Thailand. Their religion is Animism with a smattering of Buddhist practices. They sustain themselves by slash-and-burn agriculture. Their principal crops are corn and dryland rice. They are organized socially into extended families and clans under the direction of male elders. Linguistically they have strong oral traditions but no written language until recently." He paused. "That's what the books say. Is it fairly accurate?"

She laughed. "I guess so. How do you remember all that?"

"I really don't know. Stuff just sticks in my brain. But how did you get here? I mean how did Mai Lu get to Winnipeg? You are a long way from those mountains."

"I am from Laos. My biological parents died when I was about six. An epidemic of some kind. Maybe typhoid. Another family took care of me for awhile. Then one day a rich man offered to buy me. He wanted me for a slave. But then a missionary couple in our village heard about it. They offered a few dollars more. So I ended up with these missionaries. They didn't have any children. So they adopted me. They took good care of me. They taught me English. I had books to read. I had a nice home with plenty of clothes and good food. But they were very cold people. Very rigid. Very Calvinist. I ran away twice, but my people always sent me back because the missionaries had paid for me. Then one day, my missionary mother got cancer. She died when I was ten. My missionary father moved back to Canada. We lived in Vancouver. He sent me to a girls' school. I did cleaning and cooking so that I could stay there at the school during the summers. I only went home at Christmas. When I graduated, he sent me here to the university. He has a sister here. I lived with her for a year. But she didn't want me to have friends. So I moved out. And here I am."

He shook his head in obvious admiration. "You were very brave."

"I guess I was. Sometimes. But you don't think about it when it's happening. You notice the bravery in the remembering." She paused. "How about you? How did you get to Winnipeg?"

"I'll tell you about that. But first things first." While she steeped the tea, he started sampling the egg rolls. "Mmm. Pork. And bean sprouts and bok choy and scallions and what else."

"An ancient Chinese secret ingredient."

He laughed. "Called soy sauce."

Soon the tea was ready. Mai Lu served it and again requested a nutshell biography. Loco refused to begin. Until he had devoured four egg rolls. Finally with exaggerated care, he picked a few crumbs off his plate, smacked his lips, assumed an extravagantly avuncular pose, and announced, "Once upon a time, there was a small boy named Librado Lee." She giggled. He stopped and scolded, "I will not be made sport of, young lady." She giggled harder. "My dear girl, I am at a total loss to discover the object of your merriment." She doubled over and rolled off her chair. It seemed a sensible way to express enjoyment. So he joined her on the floor. Slowly, shyly, their hands met, and then a minute later, their lips. A tentative, hurried kiss from which both quickly retreated. He got up and pulled her to her feet. "Let's go for a walk."

"Good idea. I'll get my coat and meet you in front."

They strolled north from the campus area. A brisk wind in their faces discouraged conversation but did not prevent their holding hands.

Dinner at her apartment. Traditional roles. She with a stirring performance at the wok. He with what began as a scintillating narrative display. Much ado about his early life and times. Doña Concha resplendent in every scene.

He had not intended to color his mother so heroic. But the details had configured themselves so in memory. He started with recollections of McAllen. Concha understandably was the star. Then and through the trek to Corpus Christi for the rescue of Cousin Isabel. And on through the move to Los Angeles to aid Uncle Librado. And on and on.

Mai Lu interrupted with an inept attempt at humor. "Are you trying to tell me that I don't have a chance?"

Loco was confounded. "You don't have a chance? What does that mean?"

Trying for clarification, Mai Lu instead achieved additional excavation. "What I'm saying is, how can I compete with superwoman? You make her sound like a combination of Florence Nightingale and Eleanor Roosevelt."

Loco laughed. "I see what you're saying. But I didn't mean it like that." Quagmire Creek loomed just ahead, but he blundered fearlessly on. "Maybe you're starting to take your psychology books too seriously."

The room temperature fell by several degrees Celsius. They ate their rice and Cantonese pork. Loco managed to sustain his tale. But with more determination than verve. By meal's end, he had stooped to anecdotes of his days with the Jesuits. Mai Lu began to yawn. Frankly and frequently. He soon took his leave.

From his window the following morning, he watched her go out with girlfriends. He felt rejected. Illogically. Absurdly. But yes, rejected. All day the feeling endured. When he tried to read, she was a distraction. When he went for a walk, she became an obsession. In the evening he knocked at her apartment, only to be disappointed again.

Tuesday it was back to the grind. Work study sleep. Work study sleep. Weeks passed. From time to time, he slipped a note under her door. And got a note in return. Finally the Christmas holiday. She was off to Vancouver. Would he have time to accompany her to the airport? Yes he would. An edgy, clock-watching hour before departure. Fretful farewells. He should not expect her back before the middle of January. New Year's morning, she knocked on his door.

"I'm sorry. I know this is all wrong. I'll come back later if you want."

On the eve of the holiday he had over-imbibed and under-slept. But he sensed her desperation. "No. No. Come in. I'm sorry I look so awful. The neighbors had a party." He paused. "Can you make coffee while I shower?"

In the kitchen a half hour later he asked, "So what happened?"

"I went home." She paused to suppress her grief. "It was the usual routine. Until the second day after Christmas. Then my missionary father drops a bomb. He announces that he's having heart problems.

He's going to retire. He wants someone to become his full-time care provider. A combination nurse-housekeeper-cook. He wants me to quit school and take the job. In return, he will leave me an inheritance, so that when he's dead, I'll be financially independent." She paused, but Loco was too dumbfounded to speak. "I don't have to feel obligated. I can say no. But in that case he will have to make other arrangements. He will still pay for my last year of college. But after that, I'm on my own. I won't be able to expect his help from then on. Not with anything. His home will no longer be my home."

Loco was astounded. "My god! That's incredible. I know you said that the two of you weren't close. But he adopted you. And now he's telling you to get lost. He's disowning you. It's unheard of."

She began to sob. "Remember I told you that he had paid for me? Maybe he really thought of me as a slave." At that point she began to cry uncontrollably.

Loco embraced her, and stroked her, and murmured bits of soft nonsense into her ear, until the shudders subsided. Then she continued, "The next day I had a talk with his niece who had moved in with him. She just recently got divorced. She has a small child. So she needs a place to stay and a job." She paused for a deep breath. "It turns out that he had already made her the same offer. And get this! She had already said yes. Do you see what that means? It means that he had already decided that I would say no to his offer. And that he wanted me to say no. When he asked me, he was only doing what he felt obligated to do. In order to have a clear conscience." She surrendered again to grief. Then, through the tears, "I always tried to believe that they had really accepted me. I always tried to believe that they really loved me. But it wasn't true. They were just doing their Christian duty. Their religion said that they should love me. So they pretended. They gave me things. They took care of me. But they kept me at a distance. Because they didn't really feel it. I wasn't really their child. I wasn't even one of them. I was a stupid little Hmong girl who needed their pity."

Eventually the mundane prevailed. He toasted some bread and scrambled some eggs. After considerable coaxing, she ate a little. The food seemed to have a calming effect. But there was one additional thorn to extract.

Loco asked, "The airline let you change the date for your return?"

"No, I took the train. I wanted to get away as fast as possible," she explained. "At the end it all turned into a nightmare. He called me into his study. He was sitting at his desk. He handed me three checks. He said goodbye. But he kept staring straight ahead at the wall. He wouldn't even look at me. I took the checks and ran."

She paused and met his gaze across the breakfast table. There were no more sobs, but her eyes were again moist. "I'm all alone now. I have no one."

Quickly he got up and went to her. He dropped to his knees and gathered her legs into his arms. Then he looked up at her, and with only a tiny twinkle in his eye, said, "I'm not much. But you can have me."

She grasped his head between her hands and searched his eyes with hers for a long, long minute. Finally she answered, "Yes, I will have you, Librado Lee."

When at last she released him, he said, "Hurry. There's a hundred things to do."

He marched her to the bedroom. Inside she turned to him, expecting a kiss. Instead he pointed to a closet. "There's a carpet sweeper in there. You clean. I'll wash." He collected the soiled sheets and pillowcases and headed for the basement laundry. She was too bewildered to object.

Two hours later, he was back. With the clean bedding and some Chinese food. First they made up the bed. Then he hustled her into the kitchen. He found a bottle of wine and poured generously into a wide bowl. "We will drink together," he pronounced. "The depth of your thirst demonstrates the strength of your commitment." They drank. Enthusiastically. He surrendered the dish to her to finish the last drops. By then she understood that he was fabricating a ceremony to formalize their bonding. But she was not quite prepared for what happened next. He opened the carton of pork fried rice and began feeding her.

She stayed his hand for a second. "You know that this is what my people do."

"Yes, I know," he answered.

"But how do you know?"

"I am a citizen of the planet. It's my job to know."

She laughed, squeezed some rice between her fingers, and started feeding him. "Nothing will surprise me after this."

But there was one more marvel in his medley. After the meal, he led her to a nearby park. There he found a patch of untrampled snow. Moving his feet, heel to toe to heel, through the snow he marked out the figure of an ankh. Then he lifted Mai Lu and carried her to the point where the tau cross intersected the loop. He set her down and announced, "Here we will make our vows."

"Vows?" she questioned.

"You know. Promises. You want to promise me something, don't you?"

She protested, "I don't know what to say."

"Just say what seems right for you. And don't promise anything that you can't or won't do. It's easy. I'll go first." He paused to allow some solemnity to settle over the scene. Then taking her hands in his he declared, "I promise to love and respect you. I promise to help when you want help. I promise to share with you the much or the little that I have. I promise to stay with you for as long as you want me."

After some urging, she vowed a like troth.

It was a high-sky evening. The crisp January air was exhilarating. But only briefly. Soon Mai Lu was trembling. Loco quickly heaped up the snow from the ankh so that it would not be desecrated. Then, hand in hand, the two raced for the warm apartment and the clean sheets.

In the bedroom it was her turn to lead. They embraced. Mouths joined. Her tongue slithered between his lips, parted his incisors, and darted inside. Tongues touched. Rockets glared. Lightning flared. A huge feeling of relief. It was going to happen. He might perform badly. He might even perpetrate a disaster. But the gnawing ambiguity of the last few months was finally going to end. It was going to happen.

Her tongue retreated and his own chased it across the border into her mouth. She lifted hers to let him enjoy the soft underside. He groaned softly as his penis got stiffer and stiffer. She gently eased him away and removed her blouse and bra saying, "Let's do a shower to warm us up." He caught himself staring and gulped, "Good . . . good idea." Her breasts were rather small. But perfect. Perfect. He quickly peeled off his sweatshirt. A pause. Who should do what next? Not to worry. It took her all of ten seconds to slip out of her jeans and step out of her step-ins.

He gawked at her magnificent bush. He had never fantasized about anything as lush. Whoops. It was his turn. By then his penis was full and taut. He carefully lowered his jeans and removed his shorts. He straightened up awkwardly. In a moment, she was kissing him again and guiding his penis between her legs. He moaned. "Did I hurt you?" "No, I just . . . it feels so good." She giggled. "It's supposed to." They reconvened their game of tongue tennis. Then she eased herself away and started for the bathroom. Exposing a pert little butt. Irresistible. He caught her from behind and thrust his penis against her. Then foolishly apologized. She turned her head,

"Whatever feels good to you and doesn't hurt me is okay." Reassured, he enthused. She lifted her right leg in a sort of diminished arabesque. He pushed forward. She lowered her leg. He enthused some more. Finally there was one last thrust which lifted her to her toes. He groaned as the semen spurted twice and then oozed.

A few minutes later he was sitting on the toilet seat watching her shower. When she got around to cleansing her genitalia, she turned modestly away from him. There was that pert little butt again. And still inspirational. He joined her in the shower. She turned to him. He began to taste her. Fiercely. Indiscriminately. Earlobes. Cheeks. Throat. Shoulders. Much attention to those perfect breasts. He sank to his knees and stuck his tongue into her navel. And continued on down her belly, until he was sitting with his face pressed to her stupendous bush. He adjusted her legs so as to give better access to his mouth. His tongue moved around the labia. And then inside. To the clitoris. She grasped his head with both hands and moaned. Again he enthused. She began to pant. Her buttocks began to twitch. Again and again she thrust herself against his tongue. He grasped her flanks, hung on, and continued to stroke. Finally she doubled forward, panting and groaning, and was still.

When she had recovered somewhat, she tried to pull him to his feet. But he would not be moved. Until he had helped her to another climax. Then he rose. She scrubbed his back. He scrubbed hers. And then to bed.

She wanted to talk, but in less than a quarter hour, he was cheerfully snoring.

They spent the remainder of their days in Winnipeg in a warm dreamy swoon. Time intruded. But only for the essentials. They marked their marriage with a civil ceremony. They combined a summer holiday and honeymoon hiking in the Rockies. They began to experiment with the inverted missionary position.

CONTINENTAL NEXUS

For their New Year's anniversary, Doña Concha accepted an invitation. Mai Lu was a bit uptight. But without cause. After some minimal observation and some considerable conversation, Concha declared her son blessed in his choice of spouse. In her words, "It's not my place to approve or not, pero esta muchacha me cae a todo dar." Concha also sang the praises of the family in Milwaukee and urged the lovebirds to consider joining her there. "La casa que tengo es grande. Y vacía."

A few weeks after Concha's visit, the conscription law south of the border was suspended. A return move might still be hazardous, but over time, the risks should diminish. Mai Lu and Loco began to make plans. In the spring, she completed the requirements for her degree. He gave notice at the bookstore. Both spread the word that they would soon be off to California. That summer they slipped across the border and headed for Milwaukee.

CHAPTER TWELVE

Marta maintained what she hoped was a safe distance while Noise manhandled their luggage. He crunched two valises under the hood of his VW Beetle, and jammed two more into the rear seat alongside her brother Toño. Then he ushered her into the front passenger seat, trotted around to the driver's side, jumped in, and chugged away from the airport.

More than four years had passed since he had left Milwaukee and come to Puebla. Marta was understandably eager to initiate the news exchange. But Noise restrained her. "Hold on. We'll have lots of time for that. First I have to get this insect onto the autopista. And for that, I need to deal with this pandilla de locos. Back in the sixties, an old-timer told me that you can divide all the people in the world into two groups: cowards and suicide troops. But he never had to drive in Mexico City. Take my word for it. These guys are way past suicide troops."

The traffic moved in spasms. As each light went green, full throttle was essential to avoid being overrun. Then halfway down the block, furious braking erupted as the next light went red. Herking and jerking along, Noise made his way to the Zaragoza. Once on the boulevard, there were fewer traffic lights, and the pace became a little less choppy.

As they moved along the Zaragoza, Marta noticed how Noise

maneuvered the Beetle into the center of a cluster of vehicles and struggled to hold that position. She asked why.

He laughed nervously. "You know about the mordida?"

She nodded.

"Well, this boulevard is a favorite of the chotas. Especially like right now in the evening. If you can stay in the middle of a pack, you have a better chance of not getting picked off."

Nervous silence continued. Time dragged. Finally they arrived at the entrance to the Puebla tollroad. Once on the highway, the hypervigilance eased, and Marta began to talk.

"Getting here was a real mess. Almost everybody wanted to come. But Mamá Margarita had surgery on both feet about a week ago. She can barely walk. Papá Miguel is taking care of her. Concha is trying to help Isabel with the kids. But Concha works full time. So only Toño and I could get away."

"But my sister is okay?"

"She's fine. I mean she will be soon. She had ingrown toenails. On both feet. The surgery went perfectly. She'll never have that problem again. But for right now, walking isn't much fun."

"I remember a letter saying that she was having trouble with her feet. But that was months ago."

"It started months ago. But you know my mom. First try every home remedy. Then you call the doctor. By the time she finally made an appointment, her toes were infected. She was on antibiotics for a week before they could do the surgery."

"And nobody could convince her to go to the doctor sooner?"

"Everybody tried. But Uncle Noise," she put her hand on his shoulder, "she's an Alvarez. You know about that. We're all hardheaded. Even the women." She paused and reconsidered. "No. I take that back. Especially the women." She paused while Noise passed a convoy of overloaded trucks. "Concha is another case.

BOOK TWO, CHAPTER TWELVE

Probably worse. A couple months after she got to Milwaukee, she started a job as a cook's helper. It's a private bilingual school. They call it Aztlán." She paused while he passed another overloaded vehicle. "Anyway, the lunch program was going broke. They were talking about discontinuing it, and having the students bring lunch from home. Concha said no. A hot lunch was important. She told them how they could make changes and save the program. A lot of the parents agreed with Concha. But the head cook didn't like the plan. Too much work. She quit. So they gave the job to Concha. And she did it. She started using her own recipes. And making her own bread. And doing her accounting on weekends. By the end of the school year, the lunch program had stopped losing money."

Noise gave Marta an appreciative glance. "I'm really glad you told me that. When Concha wrote to me about buying the house, I said, 'yes.' Like that." He snapped his fingers. "But afterwards I started wondering how she was going to make it in Milwaukee."

Marta nodded. "I think I know what you mean. You look at Concha, and you see small, and you start thinking soft. And you probably keep thinking soft. And then one day, something gets her all stirred up, and she shows you that stainless steel backbone." Noise laughed. "About a month ago, they had a day off from school. Concha was outside puttering in the garden when the garbage collectors showed up. They didn't notice her. One of them spilled something when he was emptying her garbage bin. I guess he was going to walk away and leave it there in the alley. I was in the kitchen at Isabel's house. I couldn't tell for sure what happened. But the man must have tried to defend himself by saying that he didn't know he was being observed. Anyway the next thing I heard was what Toño and I call 'The Voice!'" Marta stopped and assumed the intonation of a regal pronouncement. "A decent person does not do his job well because someone is watching. A decent person does his job well because he respects himself."

Noise chuckled and pounded the steering wheel. "That's a great story. And I guess you're right about most of the Alvarez women. But then there's Isabel. How's she doing with her army of kids?"

"She's surviving. A lot better now than when she first got there. For a while we had three kids in diapers. Three! And sometimes they would synchronize their diaper messing. Whew! Give me a break! You don't know how bad a house can smell until you've been in one where there are three kids in diapers. I used to tell Isabel to give them away and get a cat. And I hate cats." Noise roared his appreciation. "Anyway, that's behind us now. No more diapers. In fact they will all be in school this coming fall. Nico in first grade. Eddie in full-day kinder and Frances in half-day kinder."

For a few seconds Noise was in shock. "That's incredible. They're already in school?"

"Figure it out. How long ago did you come to Puebla?"

"I guess so. But the kids are doing fine?"

"They're adorable, Noise. You would love them. The baby Frances is at that perfect age for frilly dresses. Concha buys her things, and Mom makes her outfits, and everybody goes ooh and aah. And Frances poses and preens and struts like a little princess."

"How about the two boys?"

"They're okay. But they're just boys. They hate to take a bath. They won't play tea party. The only thing they're good for is being boys." Noise punched her on the arm. "And they're constantly punching you on the arm." Even dour Toño laughed then.

"And how goes it with my brother-in-law Miguel?"

"Papá Miguel has never been better. The best decision he ever made was to quit his job and start the remodeling business. Now he makes his own work schedule. He comes home for lunch. When he works on Saturday, it's because he wants to." She paused to reflect.

BOOK TWO, CHAPTER TWELVE

"Of course, he still gets up at six o'clock in the morning to make everybody breakfast."

"And gets you up at seven to eat."

"Exactly. Some things don't change." There was a warm, comfortable silence for a minute or two. Marta decided to wait no longer. "You haven't asked about us."

"You're right. Silly me." He turned toward the back seat. "So how are you doing, Toño?"

"Real good. I'm working. They wanted me to go to college, but I decided I'd rather have a job."

That seemed transparent enough to Noise, but Marta saw the need for some embellishment. "My brother is not academically inclined. I think we should accept and respect that."

Noise answered "Definitely," as he swallowed a chuckle. She ignored the repressed mirth and began, "Now about me. I just completed my first year at the university. I'm going to major in sociology for sure. And maybe history. I'll probably go to school year-round. That way I can finish in three years."

She paused to allow for inquiries, but Noise was directing his undivided attention to the road. They were beginning the climb out of the valley, a long series of upward runs, each including at least one hairpin curve. These were followed by brief intervals of flat road where some speed could be recouped. The traffic pattern became bizarre. Overloaded trucks struggled along at five kilometers per hour in the right emergency lane. Supercharged buses cruised along at fifty in the far left lane. The one lane between soon was being utilized as two, in order to accommodate the varying speeds of the bulk of the traffic.

Here and there a vehicle, usually a truck, would break down or overheat. Frequently the driver had no opportunity to pull over onto the emergency lane. He would stop wherever he could. Then he would set out a line of stones stretching back from his truck. That was supposed to alert the oncoming drivers to the vehicle parked on the highway.

Noise rounded a curve and swerved violently to the left to avoid one of the stones. Marta screamed. "My god! You could get killed here."

"Not if you stay awake."

"Is that legal? Stones on the road?"

"If legal is what people agree to do, then I guess it's legal."

"It's crazy. Don't they have flares?"

"Most of the truck drivers are owner operators. Flares are not high on their list of needs."

"But stones? Give me a break. That's just grabbing whatever is handy. Don't they try to prepare before they leave on a trip?"

"Prepare for what?"

"An emergency."

"How do they know what the emergency is about until it happens?"

"I mean prepare in general."

"They do prepare in general. They pray to their favorite saint to bring them luck."

"Luck! Luck doesn't come from praying."

"Of course it does. If that's what you believe. Besides, when you prepare for an emergency, you're asking for one to happen."

She shook her head. "They told me it would be different here, and believe me, they weren't kidding."

Noise tried to caution. "Just try to ease into it. Take things in for a few days before you decide that we're all crazy."

He maneuvered around more stranded vehicles, groped his way through occasional patches of fog, and managed a standoff with the ultra-suicidal drivers who shared the road. Eventually he reached

BOOK TWO, CHAPTER TWELVE

the summit. Ahead was the sinuous glide down to Puebla. Vigilance again abated. Marta asked, "How about you, Uncle Noise? You seem to be very happy."

He pondered his answer. "I guess I am. I don't really think about happy. But the family here is great. They take care of each other. They share what they have. You're really going to love these people. Just be yourselves. They don't like people who pretend. Les gusta la franqueza. Y el relajo. Don't take yourselves too seriously and you'll be fine."

Another silence followed as she tried to phrase the question she had been avoiding. Finally the need to express it overcame the need for felicitous phrasing. "Y este hombre que fue nuestro padre biológico, ¿cómo se murió?"

Noise took his time. "Nadie sabe. Rogelio, el primo que vive en la siguiente casa, me contaba esto. Dice que mi tío estaba enflacando mucho en las últimas semanas. Parece que tenía problema con el estómago. De por sí comía como pájaro. Pero el sábado pasado no quiso comer nada. El domingo no se presentó para almorzar y Rogelio fue a buscarlo. Lo encontró en la cama. Ya muerto. Seguro que se murió en la noche. El que era su doctor dijo que se trataba del hígado. ¿Quién sabe?"

She took a deep breath and said, "He was an alcoholic, wasn't he?"

"Maybe. Probably. What difference does it make now? He's dead. En paz descanse."

She became silent. Noise patted her arm and said, "I know. Too many things are happening. And you've never been here before. So at first you're going to feel out of place. But just go with it. Let it happen. You'll be fine. Everybody here wants to help you get through this. So let them help. That's what they're supposed to do. They're your family."

Marta pondered the words and nodded her head. "I understand what you're saying. But there's something else. This man was my father. I thought I would feel something. And I don't."

Noise became impatient. "Can you control your feelings?"

"Of course not."

"Then what are you talking about? Do you have any memory of this man?"

"None at all."

"Exactly. You were about three when he walked out on you. That was seventeen years ago. In all those years, he never tried to contact you. He never bothered to say he was sorry. He never even made any excuse. He just finished the rest of his life alone. That was his choice." Noise paused to catch his breath. "Now he's dead. You and Toño came to the funeral. Out of respect for a fact. He was your father. That's great. Everyone here will think that's terrific. But nobody expects you to act like this was some great tragedy."

She stared straight ahead for a few seconds, then turned and touched his arm. "Thanks. That's exactly what I was thinking. And it's exactly right. But I needed to hear it from somebody."

He punched her on the shoulder again. "You're going to be fine." Then, remembering Toño in back, "Both of you. Everybody here knows the story. Nobody expects you to act like you just lost a parent. So don't even think about pretending. You don't have anything to prove."

She agreed. She probably should have said so and let it go at that. But there was one more sliver she wanted to extract. "We've had a really good life, Uncle Noise. Mom and Dad have given us everything. A good home. Good nutrition. Good nurturing. Affection. Education." She paused. "We probably wouldn't have had all that if our biological father had raised us." Another pause. "Sometimes I think about that, and I'm glad Mom and Dad took us. But then I feel

BOOK TWO, CHAPTER TWELVE

guilty about our biological father." Another pause. "Is this making any sense?"

"Bad sense, if any," Noise responded. "You're checking their teeth."

She started to interrupt, but he quickly added, "I'll explain that." After a pause. "I know I read this story in Germany, so I guess it's German. Anyway, in the story there's a guy who's feeling guilty because he had some luck. An old man tells him, 'When the gods smile on you, smile back. Don't start checking their teeth.'"

Marta laughed. "I guess I was doing that." There was silence for a few minutes. The remainder of the highway down to Puebla was a long straightaway. Little by little, their concentration on the road began to dwindle. Suddenly an ambulance overtook them and screamed past in the left lane. Marta pulled her head down between her shoulders. Then she glanced at Noise. He was chuckling again.

"Didn't that startle you?" she asked.

"I flinched. But you get used to that sort of thing. Actually that was pretty tame. Some of the Cruz Roja drivers like to get right behind you before they start their sirens. That'll clear your cobwebs."

"But you think it's funny."

"It's a different kind of funny. Life is harder here in the South. So humor has a harder edge. Almost cruel sometimes."

Marta gave him an appraising look. "That's very interesting. You are becoming an idea person."

This time he roared. "Hilarious, isn't it? And there might even be some truth in it. My cousin Arturo says that everybody here is an idea person. But custom and tradition dominate the way we live. Ideas have no way of becoming reality. So our ideas become toys. We use them the way kids use a ball. We juggle them. We bounce them around and kick them. But there's no seriousness. It's all just a game."

"That happens to people everywhere. Not just here."

"Maybe. But cousin Arturo says that he sees a difference when he goes north to Houston. He's a doctor. Some kind of cardiac specialist. There's a hospital in Houston where he's a consultant. Anyway, he says people in the North use ideas as tools instead of toys. They shape them and sharpen them and put them to work."

She started to comment but he interrupted. "Arturo and I have a running argument. He says that when people from the South go North, they find opportunities to finally use their ideas as tools rather than toys. According to him, that's why they like it there. That's why they stay." He paused. "I say he might be right about the professional people that he meets in his work. But for most of the people who go North, it's still toys. The difference is that they make a few dollars and start buying grown-up toys like refrigerators and pickup trucks. Those things gradually replace their ideas. Life becomes easier but not as interesting."

"So who's winning the argument?"

"I don't think anybody is trying to win. We just like knocking heads. He pulls rank on me with his superior education. But then I rank him, because I know more about what it's like en el norte." He paused thoughtfully. "But the best part is that he takes me seriously. That's a good feeling."

She stared at him for several moments. "You have changed, haven't you?"

"Not that much. I still chase skirts."

"Shame on you." This time she punched him on the shoulder.

Near the bright lights of Puebla, they stopped for gas, then drove on to San Isidro and Jachalco. They arrived around midnight. Rogelio received them warmly. His wife, Leticia, made them a late supper and sent them off to bed.

The following day, the Alvarez and Robles families buried Antonio Alvarez Senior. There was a church service, then the procession to the community panteón, then a meal for the relatives

BOOK TWO, CHAPTER TWELVE

and other mourners. Bleary-eyed and frazzled from their journey and the overwhelming novelty of their environment, Toño and Marta exchanged condolences with several dozen people, none of whom they had previously met, and most of whom they would never see again.

Some relatives from Puebla including the Garcías stayed overnight and well on into the next day. But by the third day, the family had been reduced to the local group, and Marta began to sort things out. Rogelio Robles was her biological father's first cousin. He was married to Leticia Bravo. These two had a pair of sons, Raul and Oscar, who were married to the García twins, Laura and Hilda. They also had a daughter, eighteen-year-old Victoria.

It was Victoria who took on the role of hostess for her northern cousins. The third day after the funeral, she hurried them through brunch and away for a tour of Jachalco's extinct volcano. Single file, they descended to the floor of the crater. Near the bottom, the trail became wider and the slope more gradual. Victoria let her body go limp, so that her weight carried her headlong down the final twenty meters. She had performed this feat often and was easily able to maintain her equilibrium. Not so cousin Toño, who, sensing a challenge, attempted to emulate her. He lost his balance, executed a remarkable, albeit unintended, double somersault, and tumbled to a stop as Victoria's giggles turned to groans, "Ay Dios mio, te lastimaste."

It was soon determined that most of Toño's injuries were in the area of his pride. Nevertheless, a rest seemed in order. The three found a shade tree, scared off a pair of mating lizards, and settled down to a rather disjointed conversation.

As usual when meeting new people, Victoria was a font of viviality. "Ustedes no saben el gusto que me da tenerlos acá. Siempre me ha gustado conocer a gente que viene de lejos. Y más ustedes, que son familiares, y que son de la tierra de mi primo, Noise." She paused for a resupply of oxygen. "¡Pero pobrecitos! Han de estar bien aburridos ya con este pueblito."

As usual when confronting new people, Marta was an affectation of insouciance. "¿Aburridos? ¿Por qué? Para nosotros todo esto es nuevo." Internally she shuddered, remembering the day after the funeral when she had finally braved the wall lizards in order to take a bath. "Por eso, todo es muy interesante."

"A mí no me engañan. Ustedes están aguantándose. Y yo entiendo. Vienen de la ciudad para pasar una semana completa en este rancho.¡ Qué error! Han de sentirse como presos."

"Presos, no," Marta answered. "Pero sí me siento rara cuando no me dejan ayudar en nada. Ayer en la tarde, estaba yo en la cocina. Tus cuñadas estaban pelando papa. Yo intentaba ayudar y me quitaron el cuchillo."

"Bueno. De eso tienes que entender, Marta. Ustedes están de visita. Mi Mamá no va a dejarte trabajar en la cocina. ¡Cómo crees!"

"Comprendo que así tenía que ser al principio. Pero ya tenemos varios días aquí. Y ustedes siguen tratándonos como invitados. ¿Hasta cuándo van a tomarnos como parte de la familia?"

"Está bien. De eso puedo hablarle a mi Mamá. Pero a la vez, insisto. Parte del problema viene de que ustedes se encuentran en un ambiente muy reducido." She paused and redirected the premise at Marta's brother. "¿Tú qué dices, Toño? ¿A poco no te sientes raro en este pueblito?"

Toño aimed to please. "Yo digo que todos los lugares tienen algo. Aquí como que está muy calmado. Eso también vale . . ."

Marta tuned him out and took note of her surroundings. At the far end of the crater, a farmer and his mule were patiently tilling the milpa. Somewhat closer on their left, a herd of sheep cropped the sparse vegetation. Above on the rim of the crater, a boy bounced along on a donkey. Marta was fairly indifferent to these bucolic snapshots. But Victoria's insistence that she and her brother were entirely out of their element was beginning to irk. A counterthrust suggested itself. "Anoche mi hermano y yo estábamos hablando con tu Papá. Para él, este pueblo es todo su mundo."

Victoria concurred. "Para mi pobre Viejo, sí. Este pueblo es su mundo. Le gusta el silencio. Le encantan los campos. Su pueblito es todo. Se molesta cuando tiene que salir." She paused. "Pero yo, no. Yo necesito más aire, más libertad. Este pueblo me hace sentir muy cohibida. No puedo respirar. No puedo estirarme. No. No. No. ¿Conformarme con esto? ¡Qué error! Yo tengo que viajar. Y lo voy a hacer. Voy a conocer otros lugares. Voy a encontrar a gente de otros ambientes. Algún día, voy a escapar." She stopped then and laughed in apparent recognition that she was overdramatizing.

Marta joined in the laughter. Then, "¿Qué estudias en la universidad, Victoria?"

"Enfermería."

"¿Y te gusta?"

"Sí. Mucho. Me encanta la ciencia. Y es un estudio que se puede utilizar en todas partes del mundo."

"Pues sí. Dondequiera hay enfermos."

"Y las mismas enfermedades. Pulmonía es pulmonía. En Puebla. En Londres. En Tokio. En Chicago."

Marta nodded agreement. "Tú de verdad tienes ganas de viajar."

"Es lo que más deseo. Es la ilusión más grande que tengo." She paused, took a deep breath, and said, "One day I will visit you in Milwaukee."

Marta was delighted. "You are learning English."

"I try. I don't have sufficient opportunity to practice."

"Really? That shouldn't be a problem. Noise is here. Doesn't he help you?"

"Yes, he help sometimes. My friends come to study. He put more attention to them."

Marta quickly changed both the language and the subject. "Hablas bastante bien, Victoria. El día que llegues a Milwaukee, no vas a tener ningún problema."

"¿Me lo dices en serio?"

"En serio. Además, enfermeras bilingües hacen falta en muchas partes. Hay bastantes oportunidades."

"En ese caso voy a comenzar con mis planes para visitarlos allá."

There was a pause. Then Victoria asked, "¿Tú también estudias, Toño?"

The young man tossed a stone at the lizards which were attempting to reunite. "Yo, no. Me querían mandar a la universidad. Pero les dije que no. Tengo otros planes. Prefiero trabajar. Así tengo mi propio dinero y no tengo que pedirle a nadie."

"¿Y conseguiste empleo?"

"Sí, estoy trabajando. Ahora en una tienda de hardware. Pero voy a buscar chamba en los autobuses del condado. Mi plan es de entrar en eso dentro de dos años. Ahí tienen todo. Buen salario. Buenos beneficios. Aseguranza. Pensión. Todo. Una vez que estoy adentro, me compro una casa y tengo la vida hecha."

"No creo. Siempre te va a faltar algo."

"¿De qué estás hablando? ¿Qué me va a faltar?"

"Una compañera con quien puedes compartir tu suerte. Y con quien puedes disfrutar de la vida."

"¡Nombre! Con buena chamba y casa, ¿cuándo me van a faltar mujeres?"

That was too much for Marta, "Hablas demasiado, Tonto. ¿Qué sabes tú de mujeres?"

Alarmingly, Victoria rose to the defense. "El hombre no necesita tanta experiencia para saber que la casa atrae a la mujer."

Marta was so distraught that she very nearly responded with an insult. Instead she swallowed her words, arose, and said, "Vamos a caminar mejor."

They started across the floor of the crater. Victoria warned about the sheep, "Los machos topan," and they gave the herd a wide berth. This necessitated passing near a clump of scruffy conifers, from which they spooked a large canine. The animal made its escape into a cornfield as Toño asked hopefully, "¿Un perro, verdad?"

"Coyote," answered Victoria. "Pero no hacen nada."

Toño was not reassured, "¿Son como lobos, no?"

"Acá no hay lobos. No sé como son."

Toño probably knew even less about wolves. But his imagination had been stirred. Soon he began complaining about a sore ankle. As they approached the cornfield, his condition worsened. He quickly agreed to Victoria's suggestion that they return to the village. In fact he set a rather lively pace on the way back.

In the Robles kitchen, they found Rogelio and Noise sampling the juice of the maguey.

"¿No quieren probar esto?" Noise invited.

"No, gracias," Toño answered.

"¿Qué cosa es?" asked Marta.

"Pulque. Es el jugo fermentado del maguey."

Marta sipped from Noise's glass. "Qué curioso sabor." She turned to Toño, "¿No quieres probar?"

"No. Yo sé que no me va a gustar," he answered.

An awkward moment. Then, Victoria to the rescue. "Ven, Toño. Voy a revisar ese tobillo." The two departed. Marta joined the tipplers. "¿De qué están hablando?"

Rogelio answered. "Tu primo me estaba preguntando de tu tío Ramón. Le digo que Ramón se fue de la casa cuando yo tenía como doce años. Por eso, mis recuerdos son los de un chamaco. Y aún así, tengo la impresión muy fuerte de un hombre ya bastante amargado. El no tenía ni veinticinco años cuando se fue, y ya se portaba como viejo afligido por la vida. De verdad, una cosa triste."

"¿Pero, por qué?" Marta asked.

"No sé. Como que tenía rencor con la vida. Pero, si me preguntan de los golpes que había aguantado, no les puedo contestar nada."

"Una mujer lo decepcionó," Marta guessed.

"Posiblemente. Siempre andaba muy nervioso. Tenía reacciones muy fuertes. Hasta violentas a veces."

"A lo mejor por eso se fue," Noise speculated. "El sentía que nunca iba a estar bien en su casa y, antes de cometer una cochinada, se fue."

Rogelio smiled broadly. "Estás acercándote a un concepto que yo he tenido por mucho tiempo acerca de la gente vagabunda. Yo digo que la persona amargada se vuelve vagabunda. Anda por muchas partes. Conoce muchos lugares. Pero no se halla en ninguna parte. ¿Y por qué? Porque el lugar de uno, o sea el pueblo de uno, es el espejo en que nos reflejamos. Yo me encuentro en mi pueblo, por que este lugar me refleja. Como si fuera espejo. Cuando voy a mis campos, me encuentro. Allí me hallo. Cuando vengo otra vez a mi casa, me encuentro. Aquí me hallo." He paused briefly. "Pero la gente amargada no se encuentra en ninguna parte. Y por eso, siguen viajando y siguen buscando."

Into the following pause Marta pushed her question of greatest import. "¿Mi Papá era uno de esos individuos?"

The answer came immediately and forthrightly. "No. Tu Papá, en paz descanse, nunca se amargaba. Sí, se atontó. Los golpes de la vida lo habían dejado débil y el alcohol lo acabó. Pero hasta el fin, él era una persona de buen corazón. Yo he conocido a varias personas que tenía problema con el alcohol. La mayoría es gente de pleito y pelea. Y tu Papá, no. Nada de aquello. Siempre muy respetuoso. Siempre muy pacífico. Y lo que más me gustaba de ese hombre fue la calma que mantenía. Nunca se quejaba de su suerte ni su destino. Su palabra

BOOK TWO, CHAPTER TWELVE

en todo caso fue, 'Son cosas de la vida. ¿Qué se puede hacer?'"

More talk of Alvarez ancestors. Then Rogelio went off to tend to some animals. Noise studied Marta's face. "You look better today," he concluded. "The first few days, you looked like leftover guacamole."

"This is really hard for me," Marta answered.

"You mean the funeral?"

"Actually, that was the easy part. But since then, I just feel completely out of place."

"Like how?"

"It's hard to explain. Everything is so different here. I never imagined it would be so dry and dusty. There's dust on everything. At night I set out the clothes I'm going to wear the next day, and in the morning they're covered with dust." She caught her breath. "It's all over the house. On the people too. Don't you feel gritty all the time?"

"I guess I'm not that sensitive."

"And the cats," Marta ignored him. "There are cats all over the place. And they get into the house, and sleep on the beds, and spread their fleas. Now tell me that's not disgusting."

"What else? Get it all out."

"There's never enough privacy. Yesterday I walked through the bedroom next to mine and walked in on your cousin. I think it was Laura. I can't really tell them apart. Anyway, she was changing her clothes. Well, not everything, but she had her blouse off. So I excuse myself and go on through. I walk outside, and there I catch this little boy who's spying on your cousin while she has her blouse off."

"I know that kid. He works for the Jachalco mafia."

"And the flies. They're incredible. I've never seen so many in one place. Where do they all come from?"

"It's the animals," Noise tried to be serious for a moment. "If you have chickens and horses and pigs around, you're going to have flies too."

"And the water," Marta ignored his explanation. "There's never enough water for anything. Before I take a bath, I have to ask if it's okay." She lowered her voice. "Sometimes there isn't enough water to flush the toilet."

"Okay. So what's the bad stuff?" Noise joked.

Marta nodded. "Believe me. It gets worse. Rogelio's family is really nice. Everybody. They all try to be so helpful. But they don't know me. So we keep getting into these awkward situations."

"Like what?"

"Like they offer me something to eat that I never ever eat. But I want to be polite. So I try it. And they expect me to like it. So I pretend that I like it. So what happens? They run to get some more."

"They want you to feel at home. The old estás-en-tu-casa routine. That shouldn't surprise you."

"At home, nobody bugs me about eating things that I don't like."

"So tell them you don't like it."

"It's not that simple. I didn't come here to offend people."

Noise was silent.

"I don't understand what's happening," Marta confessed. "Everything all of a sudden is totally unpredictable. When we left Milwaukee, I was actually excited. I thought I would love traveling. Visiting new places. Seeing new things. Meeting new people. But it's nothing like what I was expecting. Now I just feel strange. Like I'm out of place. Like maybe I'm not even me. I'm serious. There are moments when I actually feel like I'm losing my identity."

Noise refused to commiserate. "Maybe you need to wear a wristband with your name on it."

Marta ignored him. "Another thing is the time. There's a lot of time every day when I don't have anything to do. So I go to the kitchen to see what the women are doing. And maybe they're cooking. Or washing dishes. But they won't let me help. So then I find a book and a place to read. And I'm just getting started when someone comes in and decides that I'm reading because I'm bored. So they join me. Then they try to stimulate some really lively conversation by asking me about the weather in Milwaukee."

"That sounds like an easy one."

"Right. After two minutes of that, I really am bored." She paused to reflect. "Have you ever thought about how important other people are for our identity?"

"Not lately."

"Well, I've decided that it's really important. The people around us interact with us in predictable ways and that reassures us that we are who we are. And this all just happens. We don't think about it. We don't even notice really. It just happens. But then we go to a new place. Now the people don't act in predictable ways. And so we begin to look at ourselves differently. We begin to see ourselves the way these new people see us. And it's upsetting. Even unnerving. We begin to have doubts about who we really are."

At that point Noise did something immensely predictable. He offered her a glass of pulque.

"No, thank you. It tastes like sour milk," Marta answered. Then, "There. You see what I mean? If Rogelio had offered me a glass, I probably would have said yes, and forced myself to drink the disgusting stuff."

Noise again studied her face. "So when are you leaving?"

"I wanted to talk to you about that. Our plane tickets are for next Saturday. I was hoping you could help me cash in my return ticket and get a bus ticket instead. That way I could see a little of the country."

"And have a good reason to leave a few days earlier."

"That too. I was hoping to get away next Tuesday."

"I'll take care of it," he answered rather grimly.

She could see that she had disappointed him. But better him than Rogelio or one of his family. And besides, what was Noise getting all righteous and uppity about? He was the one who had told her she didn't have to prove anything to any of these people. She excused herself and went to look for her brother.

That afternoon, she washed her hair. But at the clothes-washing sink in the patio, thereby avoiding the traffic to the lizard-infested bathroom.

On Sunday afternoon she staged her second and final bath of the visit. First a washtub and stool were placed in the bathing area. Hot water was poured into the tub. Next Toño entered the area and shooed away the lagartijas. Then, with her hair protected by a plastic cover, and with Toño standing sentinel at the door, Marta entered the bathroom. She hastily removed her clothes, lathered her body, scooped and splashed the water from tub to body in a less-than-thorough rinse, wrapped herself in an oversized bath towel, and ran for her bedroom.

"¡Payasa!" was Noise's terse reaction.

"Pobrecita," Victoria responded. "Ella nunca imaginaba que se iba a encontrar en un ambiente tan rústico."

On Monday evening there was a special meal for Marta's despedida. Caldo de habas and mole de espinazo. With the help of a little brandy provided by Noise, Marta smiled her way through the meal and the storytelling that followed. She even managed a few tears at the farewell abrazos the following morning. Then it was back to the capital in the VW Beetle. Her goodbye to Noise was almost stonily cold.

On the bus, she tried to concentrate on what was ahead. Away in the North, people were awaiting her. Mamá Margarita warm and caring. Stalwart Papá Miguel. Isabel and the kids. Soon this whole misadventure in the South would be nothing but an annoying recollection. Still . . . the people left behind did tug at her consciousness. She could not lose them so easily. And the memory would sting a little. She had disappointed them. No, it was more than that. She had disappointed herself. She tried to push the memory away, then gave in and let the welter of emotion wash over her. She closed her eyes. She wept. But without a struggle. Soundlessly.

The road north was mostly a visual desolation. Later she would remember the savage sameness of the semi-desert between Huizache and Matehuala. And the mounds of rubble around Monterrey, passing themselves off as mountains. And, of course, she would always remember the boy.

The bus station in San Antonio. Seated in the waiting area. Eyelids drooping. Legs chastely crossed. A faint tap on her raised shoe.

"Peseta para comer," he mumbled.

She opened one eye. He was about seven or eight. Standing straight but head turned away. Gaze fixed firmly on the floor. Hand outstretched. Palm upward.

"Peseta para comer," he mumbled again.

The words were barely audible, but the gesture was universal.

"¿Dónde está tu Mamá?" Marta demanded.

"Se quedo allá," he answered.

"¿Allá dónde?"

"Allá en el pueblo."

A woman mopping the floor nearby intervened.

"Perdone, Señorita. El niño no quería molestarte. Tiene hambre. Es todo."

"¿Usted es la Mamá?" Marta demanded.

The woman smiled. "Ni lo conozco. Alguien lo dejó aquí como

ocho dias atrás."

"¿Lo dejó? ¿Como sabe usted?"

"Yo trabajo lunes a sábado. Aquí está toda la semana. Yo quería llevármelo a la casa. Pero mi esposo me dijo que no." She gave a shrug of resignation. "Ni modo. Ya tenemos tres."

Marta turned to the boy. "¿Con quién viniste?"

"Con un muchacho del pueblo."

Numerous questions followed regarding the boy's home and family. Two things soon became clear. He had no clue as to how to return and, more disturbingly, no inclination to do so.

"Entonces estabas escapando," Marta accused.

"Sí."

"Y el otro muchacho también."

"Sí."

Marta shook her head. "¿Cómo llegaron aquí?"

"No sé. Primero vinimos en tren. Luego caminamos mucho. Luego subimos a una troca cuando no estaba mirando el chofer. Luego caminamos mucho otra vez. Luego subimos a la troca de un Señor. Mi amigo se fue con él. Me dejaron aquí. El Señor me dio unos centavos pero ya se acabaron. Y tengo hambre."

"Sí. Sí. Ahorita vas a comer. Pero primero me tienes que decir como te llamas."

"Quince."

"¡Quince! Quince no es nombre. Es número."

"Pero así me dicen."

"¿Y por qué quince?"

"Porque soy el número quince de mi Mamá."

"¿Tu Mamá tuvo quince hijos?"

"Ya son más. Pero yo soy Quince."

"¿Y tu nombre cristiano?" she asked.

"Soy Juan. Pero no me gusta el nombre."

BOOK TWO, CHAPTER TWELVE

"Bueno, Juan. Te voy a llevar a comer."

He was adamant. "Si me dices Quince, voy. Si no, no."

Marta recognized the impending contest of wills. She could also foresee the hollowness of victory. "Quince," she mused. "Hmm. Quince. Sí, se presta para nombre, ¿verdad? Bien. Vamos a comer, Quince. ¿Ya has probado las hamburguesas?"

"Sí. Me gustan con queso. Pero con cebolla, no."

"Wouldn't you know it," Marta editorialized. "Already he's a greasy-finger gourmet."

The boy showed the way to the nearest fast-food joint. Marta sipped a soda while he put away two cheeseburgers and a large order of fries.

"De verdad tenías hambre," she commented as he finished the last of his burger.

"Comí muy poquito en la mañana."

She stared at him thoughtfully. He became nervous. "¿Por qué me miras así? ¿Qué te pasa?"

"Estoy pensando en tu futuro."

"Yo no tengo futuro. ¿Qué es futuro?"

"¿Nunca has ido a la escuela?"

"No. Pero puedo firmar."

Again she attempted to organize her thoughts. It occurred to her that she was playing at the inquisitor so as to more effectively procrastinate. She simply had to do something about this child. But what? She could report him to the authorities. That would achieve nothing more than the need for another escape by the boy. She could just leave him to fend for himself. But since she was returning from the funeral of her father, and since they had already shared food, that was out of the question. She could take him to Milwaukee. That was probably the least legal and the most moral option.

Meanwhile the boy kept busy by cracking his knuckles. "No hagas eso," she ordered.

"Pues tú, no te pongas así de callada."

"Perdón. Ya me dijiste que te pongo de nervios." She paused briefly. "¿Te gustaria ir más al norte conmigo?"

"No sé. No conozco por allá. ¿Tienen hamburguesas?"

"Muchas. Y mejor que aquí."

"¿Y me vas a poner a trabajar?"

"Claro que no. Te voy a mandar a la escuela."

"¿Con los otros niños?"

"Claro. ¿Por qué?"

"No sé leer. Se van a reir de mí."

"Bueno. Primero te enseñamos a leer. Y después puedes ir a la escuela con mis sobrinos. Son tres sobrinos. El mayor se llama Nicolás y tiene casi la misma edad que tú."

He rolled that thought around for a moment. Apparently it pleased him. He began to grin. Then a shadow crossed his face. "Pero tienes que decirles a la gente allá que me llamo Quince."

The shadow had forecast far worse. "Sí. Claro. Yo les digo. Es muy importante eso. Y hay otra cosa importante. Al rato cuando estamos en el autobús. Si alguien te pregunta, tienes que decirle que eres mi hermano."

Again he became thoughtful. "No sé. Mi Mamá siempre me dijo que las mentiras son malas."

"No es mentira. Es engaño," she quibbled. He stared at his hands while she searched for a means of upgrading her casuistry. "Mira, Quince, allí en tu casa, ¿te llevaron a misa?"

"Sí, cuando llegaba el padre."

"Bien. Entonces te enseñaron que Dios es el Papá de todos. De toda la gente."

"Dios hizo todo. Así nos dijo el padre."

BOOK TWO, CHAPTER TWELVE

"Bien. Y Dios es el Papá de todos."

"Sí, de todos."

"Es tu Papá y mi Papá."

"Sí, de todos."

"Entonces tú y yo somos hermanos."

For an instant, the boy's face showed nothing. Then the blank became a vision of guileful comprehension. In a hushed conspiratorial tone, he answered, "Así vamos a engañar a la gente, ¿verdad? Ellos van a pensar que somos hermanos de de veras. Pero es de mentiritas. De la iglesia no más."

She shrugged. "Algo por el estilo." His conversion clearly would be neither swift nor easy.

Back at the bus station, Marta bought a second ticket for Milwaukee. A cash flow problem was imminent. But if she fasted for a day, she could feed the boy perhaps twice. If he slept a lot, that might be enough.

On the bus between San Antonio and Dallas, Quince asked to see his ticket. Marta showed it to him. He asked if he could hold it. She first threatened him with the dire consequences of losing it, but then agreed. He studied the ticket for a long time. Eventually Marta dozed off. Quince eased the ticket into a pants pocket.

In Dallas, they had to transfer to a bus going east to St. Louis. Marta tried to keep an eye on the luggage. Quince headed for the bathroom. He never came back.

At the first boarding call for St. Louis, Marta began a frantic search for him. In desperation she stopped a man who was about to enter the bathroom and asked him to look for the boy inside. "He's wearing jeans and a blue shirt. About eight years old."

"Spanish-speaking?" the man asked. Marta nodded. "He went out that door to the street a half hour ago. Seemed to be in a hurry. The reason I remember him is because he tried to sell me a bus ticket. At least I think that's what he was trying to do. He wasn't a relative of yours, was he?"

"No. Just somebody I met," she answered.

Late Friday night, Marta got out of a taxi in front of her house in Milwaukee. She paid the driver, stared distractedly at the departing cab, and paused in the middle of the street to take stock of her emotional state. Something was stirring inside. Possibly prompted by the long, cramped hours on the bus. Probably abetted by the fretful sleep of the last few days. Or maybe not. Maybe it was just the feel of finally having her feet on the ground after all that riding. Whatever. Two rather vague sensations were tugging for her attention. One was the nagging impression that she had left something undone. The other was the disturbing intimation that her life was about to embark in a new direction.

She looked around. At Concha's bungalow, only a night light flickered. Isabel's house was also dark. No matter. It would keep. She could sort it out the next day. For the moment there was but one enormously consoling and sufficient reality. She was home.

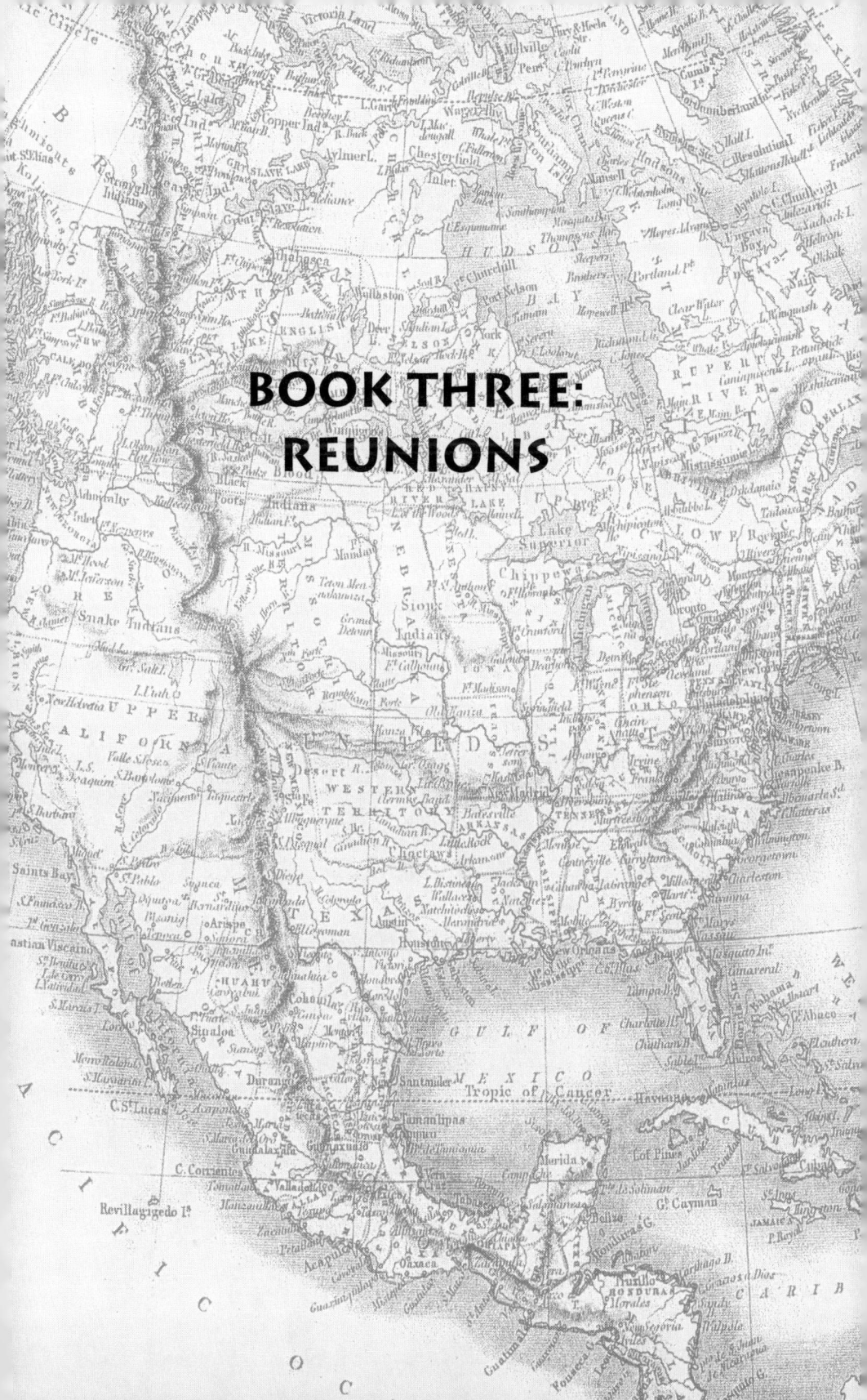

BOOK THREE: REUNIONS

CHAPTER THIRTEEN

It was a day like any day. Call it a Tuesday. Partly sunny. Wind out of the southwest. A day closer to the fall than the vernal equinox. Hot. Sticky hot. Milwaukee tropical.

The universe muddled along. In its quanta mode, photons, quarks, and sundry other oddities and entities rushed about their indeterminate business. Particles and antiparticles met and mutually annihilated, leaving but flashpoints as evidence of their sometime existence. In its magna mode, suns sprang from the wreck and dreck of earlier stars. Giant maws devoured everything in their neighborhoods, including the neighborhoods. The cluster of galaxies known to Earthlings as the Local Group plunged through space. The galaxy known as the Milky Way spiraled along within that cluster. The planet known as Earth maintained its petty pace within that galaxy. And in a tiny locus of that planet, in the yard behind the house where he lived with his mother and wife and daughter, Loco Lee soaked his feet and took stock of his cosmos.

Eventually there might be an entry in his journal. But for the moment he was brainstorming. Nimble knowing. Cerebral cut and paste. Fuzzy think. To his way of reckoning, there was no other activity even remotely as entertaining. He wrote: *Chaos and Order are the two Guises that Energy assumes as the Universe unfolds.*

He read the sentence aloud and scowled at the empty chair facing him. It was a fair approximation of the lure he had intended. He decided to pursue. He wrote: *Chaos is the ordinary Guise of Energy, since much of the stuff in the Universe has not decelerated sufficiently to allow for the emergence of order. Order is the Guise that Energy assumes as sufficient deceleration occurs. With Order in the ascendancy, Energy generates forms that are further and further decelerated. In time there are packets of Energy sufficiently decelerated to allow for individuation. In some of those packets, Energy is reduced to a velocity that allows for self-awareness.*

He put down the steno pad. He put down the pen. He shifted his attention to his feet. The water in the hot basin had cooled. The water in the cold basin had warmed. Time for a change. He lifted his left foot from the hot basin, dried it, and slid it into a huarache. He lifted his right foot from the cold basin, dried it, and slid it into a huarache. Then he stooped and emptied the basins. From two hoses he did a refill. One with water as hot as he could endure. The other with water as cold as he could endure. He reseated himself, but this time in the north-facing chair. He removed his huaraches and lowered the left foot toward the cold basin and the right toward the hot. Then, using a breathing technique to get past the shock, he resettled his feet in the water. He recalled the first time his mother had discovered him performing the rite.

"Are you trying to hurt yourself?" she had asked.

"Of course not. It's a ritual."

"For what?"

"The goal is to bring the yin and yang first into focus and then into balance."

"And what do you get out of that?"

"The wisdom beyond categories."

"You know you're talking nonsense."

He had decided to tweak gently her nose. "You profess membership in a church that teaches a doctrine called transubstantiation, and you say I'm talking nonsense."

"I don't pretend to understand these things," she had thrown back at him as she marched away.

He picked up his stenopad and pen and wrote: *Self-conscious individuation is not a painless process. The result is an "I" in isolation. Ouch! The Self has second thoughts. Return to the herd. Hide in a nation or a congregation. Lose yourself in the struggle for accumulation or accomplishment.*

He paused for a readback. Even for a fuzzy-thinker, the change in perspective was disturbing. In a single paragraph he had gone from amateur cosmologist to pseudo sociologist. Verbalized navel-gazing was lurking in the wings. He dropped his pen. Nighttime was the right time for cosmology.

He yawned mightily and began to massage his neck muscles. Then he let his head loll back and watched the cumulonimbi approach through the blue. The early afternoon heat was making him woozy. He surrendered to his drooping eyelids and drifted toward sleep. Within three winks of the wisdom beyond categories, he was suddenly jarred back to full alert. From behind, two hands closed over his eyes, and a husky female voice intoned, "Adivina. ¿Quién soy?"

"The bilingual beauty of Brew City," he answered as he turned to grab for Isabel's daughter, Frances.

She danced away from him. "How did you know?"

"An extremely lucky guess. There are at least ten or twelve nubile nymphs in this town who attack me in precisely the same manner." As he spoke, he noticed Illinois Alvarez standing behind the nymph.

"Hola, Primo." They had not met since the funeral in Chicago a month earlier. "¿Cuándo llegaste?"

"Temprano. I had breakfast with Isabel and spent the morning getting acquainted with this young lady."

"I'll leave you guys alone," said the young lady. Then to Loco, "Can I look at your art books?"

"As long as your mother isn't around," Loco answered. Isabel disapproved of even the most cautious representation of a naked body. Frances skipped into the house as Noise whistled, "She's really something."

"Maybe the healthiest person I know," agreed Loco.

There was a long pause. Then, "So. Are you here to stay?"

"I'm not sure. I'll try it for a while." Noise pointed to the twelve-pack he had brought along. "Too early for a beer?"

"Not if it's wet and cold."

They each opened a can, said "Salud," and drank. Noise stretched out on the grass, and Loco joined him. "How long has it been?"

"About fifteen years. A lot of mud down the river. You've got a wife and a little girl now."

"I have. I met Mai Lu in Canada. Our little girl, Juana, was born here. She's six."

"You look good. I mean, you look like you're doing okay."

"I guess I am. I've been working days with Miguel since I got here. Rehabbing houses. And in the evening, I teach English as a Second Language. The day work is whenever he needs me. The evening job is three nights a week. So I have time to be lazy and cook and write." He shrugged. "What else is there?"

Noise laughed. "I'd need a couple cars to tinker with. And a good woman. Or two."

They laughed together. "You never married."

"They keep getting away." Noise ignored Loco's chuckle and continued. "I'm serious. The same thing keeps happening. I meet her. I spend six months teaching her to make love. She goes off and marries another guy."

BOOK THREE, CHAPTER THIRTEEN

"Maybe you need to be a little less effective as a teacher."

"Maybe. Anyway, now that we're talking about teaching. My cousins are going to need some English lessons."

"The two young men who came with you from Puebla?"

"Those two. They're my Aunt Pilar's grandsons. I'm supposed to help them get started. Another case of the blind leading the blind."

"I haven't seen them around."

"No, they've been helping Margarita move my mom and her things from Chicago. That should be finished this week. Then we'll all be here."

"I could start the classes next week if they want."

"Sounds good. I'll let them know it's a done deal."

"It'll be good to have some new faces around."

"Speaking of faces. All the old faces seem to be treating me a little special. Is that my imagination, or is everybody overdoing it a little?"

"Well, I suppose your father's death has everyone trying to be a little extra cheerful around you."

"Isabel is the worst."

"Probably true. But that's not a passing fancy. According to her, you saved her life. Her gratitude is systemic. You'll have to put up with that."

The direction of the conversation was evidently uncongenial to Noise. "Her kids seem to be doing okay."

"Frances, yes. The guys, maybe."

"Nico is the oldest, right?"

"Right. He's fairly standard issue. Spends most of his time combing his hair and striking poses. Eddie is a different story. He has developed some curious habits. To put it delicately, he seems to be rather fond of his sister's undergarments."

"That could be standard issue. As you put it."

"Carries it to the point of doing fittings."

"That might be a bit much. Who told you about the crossdressing?"

"Frances. She's cool. But there might be some votes for crucifixion when the feces and the fan collide."

"His mother."

"And others. His Aunt Marta might be the most vocal."

Noise shook his head. "Adolescence sucks."

"Hey, don't go getting profound on me," Loco admonished with mock severity. Then, adjusting his tone, "My guess is that this is for real. Not just some adolescent experimentation."

"And you're suggesting that we should do . . . ?"

"Nothing. Son cosas de la vida. But I might need an ally sometime down the road."

"Count on it." Noise opened another beer and drank deeply. Then, "I got a chance to talk to your mom in Chicago. She's thriving."

"You could say that. The only strain for Doña Concha is that she's armed for dragons, and there just aren't enough of them around these days."

Noise laughed. "No offense, Primo, but she is still an eye-grabber."

"Are you kidding? My mother is the foxiest fifty-year-old on the planet."

"Come on. She can't be fifty."

"Figure it out. I'm thirty-three."

Noise pondered a moment. "I guess that's right. I've got just one speed bump left between me and forty." He shook his head. "Anyway, she's a cook at a school, right?"

Again Loco assumed a tone of mock severity, "Please. Stint not your words. She is Food Service Manager at Aztlán Alternative Bilingual Community Elementary School. You would be unwise to forget that fact."

BOOK THREE, CHAPTER THIRTEEN

Noise chuckled for a half minute. "Okay. Now I've got a tough one for you. Is your mom the number one female in the group here?"

It was Loco's turn to ponder. "That's a very interesting question. I've never really thought about it." He considered the idea from various perspectives.

Noise became impatient. "Let me try it a different way. If you were taking a picture of the whole Milwaukee group, who would be in the center of the picture?"

"That's an easy one. Margarita and Miguel."

"Okay. That's a respect thing. But take my sister and Miguel out of the picture. Now who's in the center?"

Loco procrastinated. "Did you ask my mom about this?"

"She said Victoria."

"Hmm. I guess I agree with Mom. Victoria is in the center. But Doña Concha is right next to her. Probably upstaging her ever so slightly."

Noise grinned. "One shaky vote for Victoria."

Loco, after a moment of thought, "Let me qualify that a little more. Everybody here contributes something. But because of the nursing skills, Victoria has chances to contribute more often."

"That makes sense. But this isn't Jachalco. You don't have to go twenty kilometers to find a doctor."

"Sure. But there are times when extra attention makes all the difference. A couple of years ago, Miguel fell off a ladder and broke his arm. When the cast came off, he needed physical therapy. The doctor said he probably wouldn't recover completely. Victoria went to therapy with him and made notes on the exercises. Then she started working with him. She'd fuss and bother, and finally he'd go along, just to get her to leave him alone. After three or four months, Miguel had recovered completely. The doctor couldn't believe it, until he met Victoria. Miguel took her along to his last appointment. He introduced her as Florence Nightingale von Bismarck."

Noise grinned again. "That sounds like Miguel."

"Exactly. The long reach for the laugh. Classic Donovan. But Victoria does some funny stuff too."

"She married Toño, for one."

Loco stifled a chuckle. "Aside from that." He paused for a transition. "This happened when our little girl Juana was about four. One night she started showing signs of fever. Victoria came over to see what was wrong. She did an examination and announced that she was taking Juana to spend the night at her house. My wife told her that wasn't necessary. Her answer was that Juana had chicken pox. She wanted her kids to get it at the same time. She was sure that would happen if they slept together."

Noise asked the obvious. "Why would she want her kids to get chicken pox?"

"Two reasons, according to Victoria. First they would have it, and be done with it, and put it behind them. That made sense to me. But the second reason knocked my socks off. She said that sharing the illness would provide a bonding experience for the kids."

"Did it work?"

"You mean did they bond?"

"Well, that too. But did her kids get sick?"

"Right on schedule. About fifteen days later, they had the same rash and fever. As far as bonding is concerned, the three kids are very close. But who knows how to sort out all that causality?"

As the afternoon heat waxed, the twelve-pack waned. The conversation did both. Prompted by a profusion of inquiry from Loco, Noise held forth on his years in the South. About Puebla. About Tía Pilar and her famous common sense. About the tragic death of cousin Arturo and his wife and daughter. About Uncle Chucho, who had led Noise to an understanding that regular work and the good life need not be incompatible. About Chucho's twin daughters, Laura and Hilda, who had married the Robles cousins in Jachalco. And finally about how "family" had come to mean so much more than an agglomeration of accidental kin.

In the late afternoon, Frances reappeared along with Victoria's daughter, Alicia. They escorted Noise to Victoria's house for dinner. Loco would have been astounded to learn that the principal item on Noise's agenda that day had been an inquiry regarding the cerebral health of cousin Marta.

A month earlier, Marta had cornered Noise in Chicago two days after his father's funeral. She was a paragon of courteous inquiry. Initially. Ostensibly. What was the likelihood of his remaining in the North? What had set off the economic crisis in the South? How was the family in Jachalco dealing with the crisis?

Noise answered the first question with a shrug. To the second, he responded by expounding on the lunacy of attempting to erect an entire national economy on anticipated revenue from petroleum exports. Then he began on the family question and quickly, predictably, became wildly anecdotal.

The stories lengthened. Marta's patience shortened. Soon she was interrupting with, "Yes, of course," and "I understand that," and other ill-concealed attempts to hurry him along. But Noise had mounted a favorite hobbyhorse and would not easily be headed. Sagas scintillated. Epics proliferated. Fabulous fables frothed and flowed. Marta, however, was not about to be outpersisted. Into one of his breathing pauses, she squeezed, "You haven't asked how I've been doing."

Stunned. Stammering. Stopped. Stupefied for a moment. Finally he grasped that his Jachalco family narrative was not a major item on her agenda. She noted his stifled grin as he answered, "Sorry. I guess I was getting a little long-winded." Then, "How have you been doing."

"I have to tell you about something," she said.

"Somehow I suspected that."

"Don't be a wise guy," she snapped. And was instantly repentant, and said so. But she did have his full attention.

"What's this all about?"

"It's about something that happened to me. Maybe three years ago." Recall was not without pain. She took a deep breath and pushed ahead. "There was this guy. I met him at the university. We dated a couple times. After maybe the third date, I asked him to stop calling. I did not want to pursue the relationship." She paused to check for attention deficit. "At the time I thought he was too shallow. Now I guess I'd say he was just another creep."

"He didn't improve with age?" Noise interjected.

She smiled in spite of herself. "No, he didn't. Anyway, that should have been the end of it. But about six months later, I went to a party at a friend's house, and there's the guy again."

"Your friend was matchmaking."

"Not at all. She had no idea that we knew each other. Anyway, we talked for a while. The usual stuff. What have you been doing? Do you happen to know so-and-so? Nothing even remotely personal. But when I was getting ready to leave, he kissed me. I didn't object, but I certainly didn't give him any encouragement either. I said my goodbyes and left."

"Expecting that to be the end of it."

"Exactly." She collected her thoughts for a moment. "My girlfriend lives on the second floor of a duplex. From the entry there's a long straight stairs up to her front door with a small landing at the top. As I was leaving, I stopped on the landing to check my things, and I discovered that I was missing a glove. So there I was, deciding whether to go back or not. The guy, incredibly, followed me out, and without any preliminaries, put his arms around me from behind, and started pushing himself against me." She took another deep breath. "I went ballistic. I whirled around and jabbed him as hard as I could with my elbow. He lost his balance and fell head-over-heels down the stairs. I guess I surprised him."

"That's probably a safe assumption."

"Actually he was hurt pretty badly. They called an ambulance to take him to emergency. He had a concussion, and some cracked ribs, and a couple other problems. Fortunately, my girlfriend had found my missing glove just after I left. She came running out to see if she could still catch me. So she saw exactly what happened and could vouch for the fact that I had been assaulted."

Noise shook his head sadly. "But that didn't change what had happened to you."

She gave him an appreciative glance. "That's very perceptive of you."

"So how did you come out of it?" he asked softly.

"Physically, I didn't have a scratch on me. Every other way I was a mess. I was crying and shaking and I couldn't stop. Then the ambulance was screaming. Then some police officer was asking me a million questions, and the only thing I could answer was that it had all happened so fast. Then my friend took me home. Papá Miguel gave me some brandy, and Mamá Margarita sat with me until I fell asleep."

Noise shook his head in commiseration.

"I had a restless night. I was up really early. There was nobody in the kitchen. I remember pouring myself a glass of orange juice." She paused and pressed her eyelids together in an effort to improve recall. When she resumed, it was with an air of weary resignation. "The kitchen was warm enough. And I was wearing a jogging suit. But I was still shivering. And the glass I was holding was so cold. And it felt on my hand like it was getting colder and colder. And harder too. The glass felt incredibly hard. Then I noticed why. My hand was squeezing the glass. Tighter and tighter. I started shaking again. Uncontrollably. Just like the night before." Marta paused and looked around, as if searching for the next words. Then, "I forced myself to walk to the kitchen sink. I poured the juice down the drain. I went back to bed. I didn't get up for two days."

She noted Noise's reaction. He started to reach out to her. Then he pulled back. No surprise there. She had almost come to expect it. The gesture begun. The gesture curtailed. What was astonishing was her own ambivalence. One part of her pleaded for an embrace. Another part simultaneously sent a stronger message to back off.

She watched him resolve the conflict in displacement behavior. He got up. He picked up his chair and turned it one hundred eighty degrees. Then he straddled it and rested his arms on the back support. "We don't have to continue this," he said softly.

"I know," she answered. "It's okay."

He stared at the floor for a moment and then at her. "Afterwards . . ." He cleared his throat. "Afterwards, were you able to . . ."

" . . .have a relationship with somebody else?" She finished his question impatiently.

"I guess that's what I mean."

"Since then, there have been two guys. The same thing happened both times. We started out fine. But as soon as they tried to get close, I had a flashback. Then I just went cold."

"You don't blame yourself, do you?"

"Of course not. But not blaming myself doesn't change anything."

He was silent for a long minute. Then, "Why was it so important to tell me this today?"

"So that you would hear it first from me."

"You mean other people will have a different version of the story."

"Maybe not. But they'll try to put their own spin on it. They might even try to make me look bad. And that's not right. I was there. It happened to me. I'm the only one who knows how it feels."

"So you think you're being misunderstood."

"No. I don't care about that anymore. In fact I wish they'd all quit trying to understand and just leave me alone. Is that asking too much? Just stop with the concern. And the analysis. And the advice. And the condolences. Just stop."

Noise looked puzzled. "So you feel like the family is getting into your business too much."

"Not directly. But yes. I still get these looks like I'm some kind of Pobrecita. And I still walk in on conversations and notice that there's a sudden change of topic."

"That shouldn't come as a shock. We're talking about your family. Expecting them not to be concerned about you is like expecting a rabbit to stop eating carrots." He paused. "Actually I've never seen a rabbit eat a carrot. Have you?"

She ignored his attempt at humor. "I can't be like everyone else. I'm not going to marry, and have a family, and dwindle happily into a housewife like the rest of them. And I don't see why I should have to apologize for that. It's not like they're right and I'm wrong. I'm just different. That's not a crime."

Noise nodded agreeably, and she continued. "It's not like I'd mind having a child of my own. And I think I'd probably be an excellent mother. But it's not going to happen. That's not the end of the world. There are lots of single people who lead very rewarding lives."

Noise concurred. "Look at me."

For some reason that remark reactivated Marta's tears. This time Noise did reach out to hold her. The embrace was exactly what she had expected. She sensed his reaction. "I know," she sniffed. "It's like hugging an ironing board."

He tried to make light of it. "I really don't have that much experience with ironing boards. Maybe you just need more practice."

The two separated and faced each other awkwardly. A rather grim silence. Marta left. A few moments later, Concha entered.

Concha had gone to the kitchen with the innocent intention of getting a glass of ice water. But when she found Noise alone, and a cursory perusal of the refrigerator turned up a six-pack of lager, she experienced a sudden change of thirst.

"Good time for a beer?" she asked.

"Brandy after dinner, but beer when it's near."

"That's a fresh one."

"It should be. I just made it up."

They said "Salud" and drank.

"So. How does it feel to be back?"

"Strange. All the old gang is too busy for me. They're all rushing to be on time for something. If you get in the way, they just run over you. I have to go. That's all I hear. I have to go. How about lunch? Sorry, I have to go. What about a ball game? I'd really like that. But I have to go. So when can we get together for some lies about the good old days? Hey, that's a great idea. We'll have to do that. But right now I have to go." He cast her a devilishly baleful look. "You don't have to go, do you?"

Concha returned his look. "Not till next week. Unless we run out of beer." Then after a pause, "How was the crossing?"

BOOK THREE, CHAPTER THIRTEEN

"No problem. A little visit to the fish. Then a small bird to San Antonio. Miguel picked us up there."

"You brought some cousins with you."

"Ellos me dicen Tío. Soy primo de su Papá. En paz descanse."

"Todavía vive la abuelita de ellos, ¿verdad?"

"Sí. Mi Tía Pilar. La mujer mas hermosa del mundo entero."

"Te cuidaba mucho."

"Me daba de comer. Me aconsejaba. Me protegía. Me regañaba. Todo."

"Con razón la quieres tanto. But these two cousins. Shouldn't they be at home helping their Abuelita?"

"That's the plan. After they find work, they're supposed to start sending her money. But that's mostly a pretexto. According to Tía Pilar, ellos tenían que venir conmigo porque se estaban maleando."

"Meaning?"

"They were students at the university. After their parents died in the accident, they were handling it okay. At first. But little by little, they started losing it. Instead of going to class, they started screwing around with pot. And hanging out with a gang that did harder stuff. When we got the call about my father's heart attack, and I decided to come back, Tía Pilar said they were coming along."

"Willingly?"

"Oh sure. They wanted to get away. I know what that's like. The feeling you get when you know you're screwing up. Especially when you don't know how to stop. You jump at a chance to get away from it all. I did the same thing when I ran off to join the army."

"And you're supposed to straighten them out."

"I know. That's got some humor in it."

"Everybody will help," Concha reassured. "You'll all be in Milwaukee, right?"

"I guess so. Margarita says she's going to move my mom. If Mom goes, there's nothing to keep me here."

"Good. We'll see some new faces. That hasn't happened since Librado and Mai Lu came from Canada. And that was about ten years ago."

"Your son and his wife. How are they doing?"

"Really good. Librado teaches part-time and does remodeling with Miguel. Mai Lu works for the public schools. She's a community outreach person for the Southeast Asian families. She's also our chief gardener. I have one grandchild, Juana, who will be six this year."

"So that's the four at your house."

"That's right. Isabel has four also. She and her three children. Although Frances spends as much time with me as she does with her mother. And there are four at Victoria's house. She and Toño and the two children. And when your mom gets there, Margarita will have four at her house."

"Marta lives there."

"Right. But we'll fit you and your cousins in somewhere."

"So, who's the queen bee in Milwaukee?"

"Queen bee?"

"You know what I mean. Big families usually have a female that everybody sort of orbits around. In Puebla it was mi Tía Pilar."

Concha was thoughtful for a moment. Then she objected, "Wait a minute. The only job of a queen bee is reproduction."

Noise laughed. "You're right. I definitely didn't mean that. But you get the idea. Who holds it together? Who do people look to when there's a family crisis?"

"Margarita, I guess."

"Can't be. My sister has trouble deciding which shoe to put on first."

"I guess it's Victoria then."

"She's too young."

"But she's the witch doctor. People take her their aches and pains. That's how these things start."

"I was hoping you'd nominate yourself."

"Me?" Concha chuckled. "I'm much too frank. Too direct. I go right for the chin. Most people don't appreciate that. When people ask you for advice, what they really want is to hear that you think they're okay. Victoria is good at that. The gentle touch. She's like a powder puff." After some reflection, "I'm more like a piece of sandpaper."

Noise laughed. "You're exaggerating."

"Maybe a little. I never really thought about any of this. It all just happens."

Noise took a long meditative pull on his beer. "They remember you in Jachalco. From the visit when Victoria and Toño got married."

"That's hard to believe."

"They still talk about the horseback riding. The day Rogelio put you on that lazy old mare, and you asked for something livelier."

"I wanted something that could run. That poor old yegua couldn't even walk very fast."

"So Raul put you on his stallion. Rogelio started yelling, '¡No! ¡No! ¡La vas a matar!' You just went ahead like it was all in a day's work. That's what blew them away."

"The stallion was okay. When I was a girl, yo montaba caballos cuando apenas los estaban amansando."

"But nobody in Jachalco knew that. So there you go. Racing out of town. Everybody thinks the stallion is in control. But you run him for a half kilometer, and rein him in, and come galloping back. Raul yelled, '¿Qué tal?' and you sort of shrugged and said, 'Está mejor que la yegua.'"

Concha emptied her can of beer. Noise popped the lids on another pair. Concha continued the reminiscence. "The thing I loved about Jachalco was Rogelio's family. They are so sincere. All of them. But especially his wife, Leticia. When that woman tells you, 'Estás en tu casa,' she really means it."

"I know. And they're always the same. Every time you go there. Rogelio is as close as you can get to the perfect man. If I ever have to grow up, I want to be like him."

Concha studied Noise for a long minute and nodded. "You really like it there, don't you? You'd like to go back."

"I'd leave tomorrow if I didn't have these cousins to look after. But Tía Pilar is counting on me. I owe it to her."

"Primo, you're making a big deal about this. It's not that hard. There's a house on the west end of our block that belongs to Miguel. He and Librado are remodeling it. The downstairs is finished. The cousins can move in there. Librado can teach them English. If they need jobs right away, Isabel has a friend who runs a temp agency."

"Then I can go back tomorrow."

"Not so fast. The part about owing your Tía Pilar is still there. You have to keep your cousins out of trouble until they land on their feet."

"You could do that for me."

"I could. But I won't."

"You're a hard woman, Concha Alvarez."

"I guess I am." She laughed.

Noise let a minute pass. Then with feigned indifference, he asked, "So what's going on with Marta?"

Concha refused to pussyfoot. "She told you about the famous attack."

"Well, yeah. That was part of the conversation. You don't think it happened?"

"I know it happened. But it was not the big deal she makes of it. Marta has trouble connecting with males. She probably always will."

"Why it that?"

"A lot of reasons. Regardless of what she says, she remembers being abandoned by her father. Then she watched what happened to Isabel. Then her brother goes off and marries without even consulting her. On top of all that, she went to school with a bunch of nuns. They filled her head with a lot of nonsense about offering our desires like a sacrifice to God." She finally paused for a breath.

Noise said, "I take it you're not into sacrifice."

The only effect of that ironic inquiry was to raise the volume of Concha's response by a few decibels. "If God wanted us to be nuns and hermits, he would have made us without desires. But he didn't. He gave us desires. He gave us bodies to satisfy those desires. Think about it. What kind of God would make people with bodies to feel and enjoy passion, and then tell us not to use those bodies. That's crazy. But that's what the nuns preach to these teenage girls. Con razón estamos en lo que estamos."

"Wait a minute. Nobody takes that stuff seriously anymore."

"Marta does. For her that attack was like a test. And she passed the test. So she has a crazy feeling that she can be proud of that. But there's more. Now she has a personal experience to justify how she feels about men. Now when she argues that men are all out for just one thing, she can use that experience for evidence. And then she becomes even more convinced that the best thing for her is to live alone."

"Maybe in her case it is. What's wrong with that?"

"There's nothing wrong. But it is really sad."

Noise was ever uncomfortable with pessimism. "She'll probably turn it around."

"Amen," Concha answered. "We all want her to start liking herself again. Then maybe she can connect with somebody. Otherwise, life is extremely long."

The talk continued. One by one, they worked their way through the clan, eventually coming to Isabel's daughter Frances. Concha grew unrestrained in her praise. Finally Noise interrupted. "Are you sure this Frances is not your child?"

Concha responded fervently, "Anyone you ask will tell you the same thing. If they had a daughter, they would want her to be like Frances."

Frances made it a point to be at home on the morning that Noise visited her mother. Her motivation was a mix of courtesy and curiosity, and rather more of the latter. Several relatives spoke of Noise as the enfant terrible of the family. Her mother, on the other hand, mentioned his name with a reverence generally reserved for Saint Jude and the Guardian Angels.

As fourteen-year-old Frances descended to the kitchen, her two brothers were leaving for their summertime jobs. She ran to the door and yelled a goodbye to each. Eddie waved. But Nico had already assumed his guise as senior gainfully-employed-male of the family and could not be bothered. That was standard early-morning behavior. The preparations for their guest were otherwise. The kitchen reeked of bacon, a food customarily consumed only at Christmas morning breakfast. The sound issuing from the tape player was even less explicable. Instead of the usual annoying raucous rancheras, they were being subjected to something that Frances immediately dubbed Mexican elevator music.

"Aren't we overdoing it just a little?" she asked her mother.

Isabel was flustered but purposeful. "Ayúdame con la mesa. Pick up the plates. Wipe the table. Get some more orange juice. What are we forgetting?"

"Maybe who we are," Frances editorialized sotto voce. Then with increased volume, "Can I ask you again why we're doing all this?"

"Porque mi primo Noise is the one who saved this family. That's not enough?"

"Mother. He bought this house for you. Then he went away. You did all the rest."

"I did what I had to do for my children. But he gave us a chance. Without this house, we're a welfare family in a slum in Chicago."

Frances pulled a long-suffering face and went about her assigned tasks. She cleared and wiped the breakfast table. She reset it for three. She mixed another pitcher of orange juice. She looked up. There he was. Already inside the screen door. With an index finger over his lips, signaling silence. No doubt about his identity. She had been hearing about those eyes since she could hear. She watched as he crept up behind her mother. Then from each side he jabbed a finger into Isabel's ribs. A scream as her mother turned, voice raised in anger at Frances. Then she saw who it was. Her attack nearly took him to the floor. He spread his legs for balance as she clung to him. Tears came. Glandsful. Then cupsful. Then bucketsful. As the display continued, Frances gave Noise the "Está loca" gesture. But her own eyes were also a little misty. Which was rather odd. Never before had she been affected by emotional spillover.

For a long minute, Isabel maintained her bear hug. Over her shoulder, Noise mouthed the words, "What's happening?"

Frances answered, "Hi. I'm Frances. Fourteen. Five-two. Naturally wavy hair. And bilingual."

Noise took the extended hand and pressed it to his lips. "Encantado, Señorita. Many have praised you, but no one has done you justice."

She was about to respond that she had also heard much of him. Then stopped. From his expression, she realized that he had intended more than a standard compliment. She smiled, basking in the glow of his open admiration. This was more intriguing than she had anticipated. Now if her mother could regain some control.

Eventually Isabel's tears subsided. Reluctantly she released her cousin. But only to become compulsive about his breakfast. "I've got bacon and eggs. I've got toast and coffee." She tried to leap in several directions simultaneously. "A lo mejor ni comes de estas cosas."

"Yo como de todo," Noise declared as he seated himself at the table. He drank a glass of juice and turned to Frances. "You're in high school?"

"I start in September."

"First year. Wow! How I remember! Feeling what? Excited? Eager? Indifferent?"

"Actually a little apprehensive."

"Apprehensive?" Noise rolled the word around in his brain. "Sure. There has to be at least a little of that. And when you're all done studying, you will be a doctor. Or a lawyer."

"Actually I'd like to be a songwriter," she answered. This was getting truly weird. She had never revealed that to any other family member. Not even to Concha. And she told Concha everything.

"A songwriter. Sure. Why not? As we used to say in the sixties, you've got it together."

Frances understood the idiom, but she rejected the hypothesis. "Not really. Actually I'm a mess. At least psychologically. And I have only my bilingual upbringing to blame."

Noise restrained his mirth.

"That was intended to be humorous," she reassured. "But not everybody gets the joke. There are people working for the English-only mob who actually preach that crap."

"No seas vulgar, Hija," her mother scolded.

"Sorry," she answered. "I should have said excrement."

Noise bit his lip.

BOOK THREE, CHAPTER THIRTEEN

"Tell us about Puebla," Isabel said. "How's the family there?"

Noise took a deep breath. "Uncle Chucho's gang is fine. That's the good news. You already know that there's not much left of Aunt Pilar's family. I brought her two remaining grandchildren with me."

"Dante and Daniel."

"That's right. The rest of the family was killed in a car accident about a year-and-a-half ago."

"I remember," Isabel answered. "You called Margarita. Something about an ice storm?"

"They were driving home from the capital. The highway runs up into the mountains. The road gets really slippery up around the tree line. Especially on very cold nights."

"Freezing condensation," said Frances, thereby earning a stern look from her mother and an appreciative one from Noise.

"Exactly. According to the highway patrol report, they slid into the rear end of a slow truck, bounced off a guard rail, and flipped over several times. Arturo and Ramona were killed in the crash. Their little girl, Dora, died later in the hospital."

Isabel said, "Explain to Frances how these people are related to her. If I do it, I'll just confuse her."

"Sure. Your Grandma, Eva García, was a sister to my mother María and Aunt Pilar. Tía Pilar had just one son, Arturo. So Arturo was a cousin to me and your mother. Arturo and his wife Ramona had three kids: Dante and Daniel, who came to Milwaukee with me, and the girl, Dora, who died in the accident."

"Pobre Tía Pilar," lamented Isabel.

"So Dante and Daniel are my second cousins," said Frances.

"Así dicen acá en el norte. En el sur son primos no más. One more thing. They call me Tío. And they'll call your mother Tía. That's because we're in their father's generation. It's the custom down there."

The talk circled the family. Noise did a listing of Uncle Chucho's offspring with a capsule biocharacterization of each. Next the Jachalco relatives were tallied and sketched. Then, closer to home, Isabel began a litany of the faults and lapses of her children. Nico was much too sure of himself. Some day he would find himself in a predicament that he could not control. Eddie was quite the opposite. He had no notion of what he wanted. Other people led him around by the nose. And then there was Frances.

"Who is too stubborn and too independent and too spontaneous," Frances interrupted. "And those are her good points. She's also a loudmouth and a tomboy. Not to mention being sinfully bilingual."

"Well, it's true," agreed her mother. "You are too independent. You do talk too much. You are stubborn."

"And I am too bilingual."

"I never said that. All I said was, English is more important." She turned to Noise. "Isn't that right?"

In Puebla, Noise had extricated himself from mother-daughter contentions often enough to have learned the blessings of indecision. "English is pretty important here en el norte."

"Is there anything wrong with my English?" Frances demanded.

"Nobody said that," her mother responded defensively.

"So why are we saying English is more important? Why can't I speak English well, and Spanish well, and say that both are important?"

"Okay. That's fine," her mother conceded. "But do you have to go showing off with words that other people don't use and don't understand?" Isabel again turned to Noise. "The other day she comes out with this word that nobody ever heard of. What was it?" She looked helplessly at Frances.

"Chantaje," said Frances.

"Blackmail," said Noise.

BOOK THREE, CHAPTER THIRTEEN

"Exactly," said Frances.

"What?" said Isabel looking from one to the other.

"Blackmail," said Noise. "Chantaje means blackmail."

"You know that?" Isabel was incredulous.

"Only because of a girlfriend I had in Puebla. She was studying psychology at the university, and she used to throw stuff at me that she was picking up in her classes. Including something called chantaje emocional. The trouble was, she used it for everything. If I sneezed, it was because I was looking to get some sympathy. It didn't take long for me to develop a serious dislike for psychology."

A vindicated Frances could not resist a, "You see, Mother?"

Isabel was not yet vanquished. "Well, I just don't think it's polite to use words that most people don't understand."

Noise the peacemaker. "As a general rule, I agree with that." Then to Frances, "Where did you pick up that word?"

"Nico brings me books in Spanish from his school library. It was in a detective story."

Encouraged by Noise's eager questioning, Frances held forth on bilingual reading and her favorite books. She studied his reaction, gradually becoming more convinced that he was paying her what she considered to be the ultimate compliment. He was interested in her opinions, not just because they were interesting, but because they were interesting and hers. She was an interesting person. Or was she? Maybe this was another exercise in wishful thinking. Like the day her mother's compañera de trabajo had listened for several minutes in apparent fascination, then turned to Isabel and said, "What a lovely daughter you have. Do you remember the hat I wore to Silvia's wedding?" Ice chips in your bra. That's what that was like. But maybe not this time. There was an acid test. Should she dare? Of course she would. So. Apropos of nothing, she asked, "Do you believe in God?"

Noise reacted as if he had been expecting that very question. "I never know how to answer that. There are good reasons for saying yes, and good reasons for saying no."

"I think everybody believes," Frances stated her own opinion. "It's just that everybody has their own idea of what it means. Like we say in Spanish. Cada cabeza un mundo."

"That could be."

"My mother believes that God is a big person who lives in the sky and helps people who pray to him."

"A lot of people believe something like that."

"Not me. I think God is inside me. God is the part of me that tries to do good. My mother says that's not correct. What do you think?"

"I like it. If it helps you make sense of things, then it's right for you. God is big enough to be different things for different people. And whatever you believe, it should help you understand how things fit together. If God has a job to do, that should be the job. Helping people make sense of things." He paused to catch his breath. "Anyway. You still have to respect your mother's way of believing."

"I do," she beamed. He was for real. One of the elect. One who could doubt. One who could dialog. One who didn't think everything was already decided, and all you had to do was memorize the correct answers.

The amateur theologizing continued through the table-clearing and dishwashing. Soon it was time for Isabel to leave for work. On her way, she dropped Frances and Noise at a neighborhood store where he bought some beer. Then Frances escorted him to Concha's house and turned him over to Loco. But not without a reminder. "Don't forget. We're having dinner with mi Tía Victoria."

BOOK THREE, CHAPTER THIRTEEN

Victoria had already begun her dinner preparation. She had emptied about two pounds of pinto beans onto the kitchen table. Now she was using the flat of her hand to pull the beans, a few at a time, over the edge of the table and into a pot. Inspecting, meanwhile, for small stones that might have been bagged with the beans, and which could leave an unsuspecting chewer in orgies of pain, and reconsidering his opinion of dentists.

The beans would be the last food eaten, of course, but cooking time required that they be first on the stove. She would also serve a sopa de fideo. And a rice dish. But what of the entree? Since her arrival in Milwaukee, Victoria had learned various ways of preparing pork chops and spare ribs and meatloaf and pot roast. But she knew her cousin Noise would already be missing the Southern cuisine. It was only a question of what.

She filled the bean pot to three-quarters full of water, added a little salt, and put it atop a burner on her range. She opened her freezer and perused the contents. Beef and chicken. Consider the beef. How about a mole rojo. She had the dried chile. In the family garden, there were potatoes, tomatoes, zucchini, corn, and green beans. Noise would love it. But her kids would use the chile as an excuse not to eat any vegetables. Consider the chicken. How about asado de pollo. The very dish her mother had made on the day when Victoria had first encountered cousin Noise. Perfect.

She opened her herb and spice cabinet. Yes, there were oregano, tomillo, cloves, and cinnamon. In another cabinet, she located a bottle of vinegar. She was sure of the onion and garlic, and just the previous day she had picked some tomatoes. She returned to the freezer, pulled out a chicken, and popped it into the microwave oven to defrost.

Bringing on a wave of recall. On her visit to Jachalco two years earlier, her mother had rebuffed the offer of such an oven. "No,

Hija. En la casa de mi comadre en San Isidro, ya probé la comida que sale de esos hornos. Es comida de flojas. A mí me daría mucha vergüenza servirle una comida así a tu Papá." Victoria had objected mildly that the unit would be helpful for reheating. That had only served to bring on an extended lecture.

"Las parrillas de mi estufita me sirven bastante bien para recalentar, Hija. Eso es lo de menos. Lo mas importante es saber apreciar lo que nos ha dado la vida. Una comida bien preparada y compartida con la familia es uno de los principales gustos. Por eso, si hay suficiente, hay que festejarlo." She had paused to shake her head sadly. "Pobres que no tienen suficiente. Pero pobres de verdad los que tienen suficiente y no quieren tomar el tiempo para prepararlo bien."

Victoria sighed. "Mi Mamá," she said aloud. "Nunca va a cambiar." And then a more endearing thought. "Y a una distancia de más de tres mil kilómetros, me sigue vigilando."

Soon the chicken had thawed sufficiently for cutting. She browned the pieces thoroughly in a frying pan and transferred them to an earthenware cazuela. In an iron skillet, she seared an onion and several tomatoes. Next she blended them along with the oregano, tomillo, cloves, and cinnamon. She poured this sauce over the meat and added a little vinegar and a pair of bay leaves. When the sauce began to simmer, she tasted it and added another touch of vinegar and a dash of salt. She stirred the sauce, again tasted, and pronounced it satisfactory.

On to the rice. In a blender, she combined a large slice of onion, two cloves of garlic, a teaspoon of salt, two tomatoes, and a cup of chicken broth. That ready, she browned three cups of rice, poured the sauce over the rice, and allowed the mixture to cook for a minute. She added about five cups of water, brought the mixture to a boil, covered the pot, and reduced the flame to a mere flicker. Twenty minutes later, the rice was done. She fluffed it briefly, set it

BOOK THREE, CHAPTER THIRTEEN

aside, and started the soup.

About five o'clock, Victoria's daughter Alicia and her cousin Frances pushed Noise through the front entrance, he pretending mightily to be the reluctant guest.

"Primo," Victoria greeted him. "¿Cómo estás?"

"Prima," he responded. "Aquí no más." They laughed and embraced.

"¿Cuánto tiempo tiene?" he asked.

"Apenas dos años. No te acuerdas que yo estaba en Jachalco cuando bautizaron al niño de Raul y Laura. ¿Cómo se llama? Andrés, ¿no?"

"Sí, Andrés. Y sí me acuerdo del bautizo. Fue el mismo día que te disgustaste con tus cuñadas."

"¿Fue ese dia?" she reflected for a second. "De verdad, así fue. ¡Que error! ¡Que borlote! Y por unos cuantos dulces. Pero cuando se me calienta la sangre, a mí se me olvida hasta mi nombre."

"¿Qué pasó?" Frances demanded. "Cuenten."

"En la fiesta," Noise explained, "quebraron una piñata. Como los niños de allí no tienen dulces todo el tiempo, tienen que aprovechar las pocas oportunidades. Atacan y agarran los dulces como pueden."

"Yo me acuerdo," said Alicia. "Mi hermano Tony quería entrar. Pero yo no. A mí me daban miedo esos niños."

"¿Pero qué pasó?" Frances insisted.

"Lo que pasó es que Tony sí entró," continued Noise. "Y al principio se puso bueno. Ya había juntado unos dulces. Pero él no entendió que tenía que guardarlos. El los dejo en el piso a un lado. Se dieron cuenta los canijos primos y se los quitaron."

"That's not fair," said Frances.

"That's exactly what Tony yelled," Noise remembered. "And he was raised here en el norte, so that's understandable. People here believe in fair. But his mother didn't have that excuse. She was raised in Jachalco."

Victoria nodded. "Yo iba a quitarles los dulces de mis sobrinos. Pero mis cuñadas Hilda y Laura no me dejaron. Peor. Me regañaron."

"¿Pero, por qué?" Frances was incredulous.

Victoria heard the question. But she was too busy with her own thoughts to answer. "Hasta aquel día, yo pensaba que mis hijos se estaban educando aquí, igual como si estuviéramos viviendo en Jachalco. Y con aquella experiencia, me di cuenta que no es así. Mis cuñadas tenían razón. Yo estaba confundiendolos a mis sobrinos. Ellos siempre están oyendo el dicho de sus padres. Ponte abusado, Hijo, ponte abusado. Cuando le quitaron los dulces a mi Tony, ellos estaban siguiendo aquella palabra."

Frances looked helplessly from Noise to Victoria and back to Noise. "Wait a minute. Those kids took Tony's candy. And you're saying that was okay?"

Noise started to answer, but Victoria interrupted. "Lo que los niños aprenden allá con la piñata es muy importante. Porque la ley de la piñata es la ley de la vida. El más abusado siempre va a quedar con los dulces. Mis cuñadas me estaban recordando que mi hijo también tenía que aprenderselo."

"I don't get it," Frances challenged. "¿Qué es lo que tenía que aprender Tony?"

"A ponerse más abusado."

"Abusado," Frances mouthed the word as if it were some horrible-tasting medicine. "We don't use that word around here. At least I don't remember hearing it."

"The word means alert or ready," Noise explained. "A person who is abusado is always on the lookout for opportunity. And when he finds one, he goes for it."

BOOK THREE, CHAPTER THIRTEEN

"Even if it isn't fair," Frances objected.

Noise made another attempt. "We're talking about a measuring stick here, right? We want a way to judge what people do. Fair is one kind of measuring stick. It's a good one. And if enough people agree to be fair, and if there's enough candy for everybody, it works. But it doesn't work in Jachalco. Not enough people know about fair. And there isn't enough candy for everybody. So we need a different measuring stick. That's where abusado comes in."

"And you're saying that abusado is right?"

"No, I'm not. I'm saying it's different. Fair is a good measuring stick. So is abusado. Neither one is right or wrong. They're just different. But if Tony is in Jachalco, he has to get used to the measuring stick that they use there. He has to learn about abusado." Noise paused to allow Frances time for another protest. When it didn't come, he said, "I don't know about the rest of you, but I'm starving."

"Good," said Victoria. "Vamos a comer."

"¿Toño?" Noise inquired as he seated himself at the kitchen table.

"Trabajando. Llega después de las diez," Victoria answered as she served the soup.

Alicia had been sent to the Donovans to bring her brother home for dinner. Now she called from next door to say that she and Tony had accepted an invitation from Mamá Margarita to eat pizza.

"Aprovechan," chuckled Victoria. "Como tú estás aquí, ellos saben que no voy a decirles nada."

Noise had started on the sopa de fideo, but he paused to express his appreciation. "Como si estuviera yo en Jachalco, Prima."

The dinner talk was full of names from the South. Frances asked a few questions and took a few cerebral notes, but by the time the beans were served, she was experiencing circuit overload. She finished eating, cleared the table, washed some dishes, and went off to see what Concha was doing.

Noise sat back, nodded approvingly at the table, and said, "Tu comida me da a entender que estás contenta, Prima."

"Estoy muy contenta. La familia aquí me ha demostrado cariño desde el primer día. Me respetan. Me toman en cuenta. A veces me traen sus problemitas. Hemos convivido muy bien."

"¿Y tu matrimonio?"

That provoked a long, studious pause. Finally she answered. "Voy a ser sincera. Mejor dicho, te voy a confesar. Yo no estaba preparada para casarme." She took a deep breath.

"¿En qué sentido?"

"Tenía yo muchas ilusiones. Veía yo las cosas, como dicen acá, con lentes color de rosa."

"Apenas tenías veinte años. ¿Qué esperabas?"

"Efectivamente. Me faltaba madurez. Vivía yo creyendo en milagros. Para darte una idea. Estaba yo convencida de que algún día mi esposo se iba a volver romántico." She paused for a laugh, longer on self-disdain than mirth. "Imagínate. Toño y yo. La pareja más romántica y más feliz del siglo. ¡Qué error! ¡Que tontería tan más grande!"

"Pero dices que estás contenta."

"Porque con el tiempo, empecé a abrir los ojos. Vi a otras mujeres. Aguantando golpes. Aguantando borracheras. Ignorando engaños. Luego veo a Toño. Fiel. Trabajador. Atento a sus hijos. Mis sueños de antes se evaporan. Pero lo que me queda es mucho. Estoy conforme. El me ayuda con el quehacer de la casa. El me apoya con mis planes para seguir estudiando. No nos falta nada."

For some time, she continued to laud her spouse. Her listener displayed rapt attention. Or so she thought. Until he began to yawn.

"I'm boring you."

BOOK THREE, CHAPTER THIRTEEN

"No, I'm just tired. First Isabel, then Loco, then this. My ears need a break."

It was a little after ten, and, faithful as advertised, Toño walked in. Just in time to say hello and goodbye to Noise.

Noise was soon experiencing his own romantic snags and hitches as he eased into a new environment. Following his usual habit, he began hanging out around the local university. But it was summer. Very few of the students were impressionable recent graduates of all-girl academies, vulnerable to tales of dalliance on the Danube or a tallying of the treasures of Firenze.

There was one abortive episode in August. A myopic matron, who had attended her philosophy class only twice during the eight-week session, accosted Noise in a bar. Mistaking him for her professor, she introduced herself, and began to ply him with drinks and hints of additional delights, which might induce him to consider issuing her a passing grade in the philosophy course. The offer was beguiling. The woman was not unattractive. But Noise could not bear the thought of performing as anyone other than himself. So. He confessed to not being the professor. She reacted first with incredulity, then with anger, then with indignation. She ended by accusing him of impersonating a professor, and stormed out of the bar, stiffing him with the bill. It was not an auspicious entrance onto the Milwaukee scene.

As the fall semester approached, his isolation continued. Desolation ensued. He even took to studying his image in the mirror. What was wrong? His hairline was intact. His cheeks were firm. His posture was acceptable. His pectorals and belly were still hard. His cheeks were firm. What was wrong? What were they seeing that he couldn't see?

In desperation, he enrolled in an evening class. Two nights a week, for an hour and a half, he would acquire an appreciation for

Shakespeare. And meet some eligible females. During the first week, he did induce a smile from the thirtyish woman in the next seat. But then she spoke, and her first paragraph contained nineteen references to her husband. Noise got the message.

Disheartened and despondent, he entered the third session fifteen minutes late. And immediately discovered that the teacher, a blond woman of ample, albeit well-proportioned figure concealed in impeccably tailored suits, had decided to make an object lesson of his tardiness. As he seated himself, she asked, "What would be some early examples of artistic works that demonstrate how Renaissance man is redefining himself?" She looked down at her seating chart and called his name, clearly relishing his anticipated bewilderment.

"Donatello," he said. He had run up the stairs and was still catching his breath.

Graciously she pointed out the obvious. "You've given us only a name. Perhaps you'd like to elaborate."

"In Firenze. In the Museo Nazionale (a tour guide would not have better rendered the Italian) there are two sculptures of King David. One as a youth. One as a boy. The youth is a marble (he was about to say 'fully clothed' when Greta Heilsam whispered in his ear) in classical drapery." He paused and in his imagination blew Greta a kiss as he savored the phrase. "The boy is a bronze, nude, except for a hat and boots. Both show the human body as an object of interest and admiration. That's pretty typical of Renaissance man."

He studied her reaction. She was grudgingly impressed, but very cool. "You have seen these works?"

"It's been a while. Fifteen or sixteen years."

"But why Donatello? There are several Florentine artists more famous than he."

"You asked for early examples. Donatello was a whole generation

BOOK THREE, CHAPTER THIRTEEN

before Leonardo and Michelangelo."

"Yes of course," she answered lamely. Then, noting that the rest of the group was decidedly indifferent to Florentine art, she added, "Perhaps we can continue this after class." Which in fact occurred. Noise outdawdled the stragglers, then quickly suggested a drink somewhere. She started to say yes, remembered a commitment, and proposed instead a Friday dinner date. Noise agreed. She scribbled an address on the back of a business card. "I'll be waiting in the lounge at six o'clock."

Noise arrived at the not-quite-luxurious, lower east side, monthly-rate hotel a little after six. When the lounge clock chimed six-thirty, he got up to leave. Just as she entered.

"There you are, Miss Thompson," he said with more relief than enthusiasm.

"Please. No need for that. We're not in class. Call me Hannah. Sorry I'm late. My mother on the phone. As soon as she heard that a man was waiting downstairs to take me to dinner, she determined to make me late. Nothing personal of course. She doesn't know you. It's just that she's very fond of my ex-husband."

Noise sorted through that barrage. "Hannah," he said. "What a nice name." Then, "You're divorced."

"Women with ex-husbands frequently are," she joked.

He chose to see the humor rather than the sarcasm. "I'll try to remember that." Then, as long as they were winging it, "Children?"

"None. And thank you for asking. That's always one of those pussyfoot issues that are best disposed of immediately. How about you?"

"Wifeless. Childless."

"Good. Well begun, half done."

Noise was familiar with the old saw and was tempted to speculate about the other half. But he checked himself. It was early. And he was more than a little off balance. Ordinarily he was able to dictate the pace and tone of a developing relationship. But in this instance, he was being outquicked and outfranked from the start. It was unnerving. And unremitting. She recommended a restaurant. He agreed. She proposed that they walk. He agreed.

On the way, they did a review of the recent weather. Once there and better armed, she with a martini, and he with a double scotch, they took on the heavier lifting.

"So. You're an artist of some kind."

"Mechanic."

She studied his face for a long minute. "You're not . . . no . . . you really are serious." Then, "How foolish of me." Then, "And Donatello?"

"Probably would have made a good mechanic himself. He definitely understood how things fit together."

"So how did you . . ."

" . . . get to Florence?" he completed her thought. "I was in the army in Europe. There was a chance to travel. So I did. Most of Bavaria. Some of Austria. Some of Italy. Florence is numero uno."

"What a wonderful opportunity."

"Europe was nice."

"Where did you go to school?"

"Chicago."

"The University of Chicago?"

"I'm a dropout," Noise bluffed.

"And when did you get interested in Shakespeare?"

"Many years ago. But that's not the main reason why I signed up for the class. I wanted to meet some girls."

"Refreshingly honest," she editorialized. "But what's the problem? You're certainly not shy."

"I just moved here."

"From Chicago?"

"Actually from Puebla."

"Pueblo, Colorado?" assuming she had misheard.

"Puebla, Mexico."

"You lived in Mexico? For how long?"

"Almost fifteen years."

"You were sent there by the company you work for?"

"Actually I went to visit my relatives in Puebla, and I decided to stay."

"Wifeless. Childless. Why not?"

He decided that it was his turn. "How about you?" It turned out that she was short on travel but long on schooling. Including a doctorate in English literature. Noise was impressed but not abashed. "So. Is Shakespeare really the best? Or is he overrated?"

"It depends. As a dramatist, he's the best. As a poet, he certainly has his equals. As a portrayer of character, Chaucer is much more subtle." She paused. "But that's my opinion. You're a reader too. What do you think?"

"I think he does one thing better than any other writer."

"Really? What's that?"

"All the good writers try to show us the way we are. Shakespeare shows us how we might pretend to be better."

"I'm not sure I'm following you."

"I mean the way his people talk. And the style they give to what they're trying to do. Everything seems grander than what our lives really are. But that doesn't bother us. We like that. We like his people. We like their style. They make us think that we could be like that. Grander. Better than we are. Even if it's only sometimes. Even if it's only pretend."

She analyzed his words for a minute. Then, "You have a great feel for literature. That's a real gift. I have to think my way into the work,

CONTINENTAL NEXUS

but apparently you just read and sense the intent of the writer. That must give you a good feeling."

There was genuine admiration in her voice. The scotch became lighter. The conversation more inspired. Soon he was discoursing on the majesty of Alpine Europe and the wonders of old reliable Florence. Miss Thompson had read about most of what he had seen. She questioned and quizzed intensely, improving his recall. Memories freshened. Detail began to abound. The mood expanded. They ordered, ate, and were sated. While narrative flavored the meal like some rarefied condiment.

They departed the restaurant with joined hands, but soon realized that sweaty palms were not enhancing the romantic glow. Near the hotel she paused, visibly agitated. "I want to invite you up for a drink." She paused again, this time for a profuse blush. "But I'm really horny." Emotionally choked, she pushed ahead. "I really want to screw." She tried unsuccessfully for a deep breath, then blurted, "I just want you to know what you're getting into, if you come up."

"No problem," Noise swallowed hard and managed a jaunty, "I always like to get into something when I come up."

A raunchy, nervous, belly laugh rewarded the obvious wordplay. They entered the building and raced for the elevator. An elderly man joined them on the ride up, and they restrained themselves for his sake. But once inside the apartment, a bedlam of coition ensued.

With minimal fuss, she kicked off her shoes and shed her skirt and blouse. Then backing him against the door, she attacked his mouth. First with her own, and then with a pair of amazingly aggressive breasts. Soon she dropped to her knees, clawed off his jeans and shorts, and went down on him. As he came, she brought her breasts back into play, and then with her hands, she anointed her belly and his thighs with the semen. Like a lamb he followed her to the bedroom. She pushed him onto the bed, turned him over, and, using his tailbone as a stimulus, brought herself to orgasm. Then she headed for the shower.

Ten minutes later she was back. Once more the aggressive breasts aroused him. She mounted, and capturing his penis with her vagina, she again brought herself to orgasm. Once. Twice. Thrice. Each time falling forward over him, burying her tongue in his mouth as she writhed and moaned and panted. On the third coming, he also exploded, and she eased herself down onto him so that he could feel the teasing pulses of her vagina. Finally, the two lay side by side, sweating and spent.

There was no question of his not spending the night. An hour passed before he had regained sufficient energy to push himself into the shower. A cursory wash and he was back in bed. Lying there, ventral to dorsal, he reviewed his performance and reflected idly that never before in his life had he achieved so much by doing so little. He considered sharing that thought but changed his mind. It would start another conversation. He was much too indolent for that.

Had they conversed, Noise would have learned that the evening had also been a somewhat breakthrough event for his partner. For Hannah Thompson, professor of literature, and devotee of the Greek ideal of all in moderation, was awash in the evening's orgy, and slowly reaching the conclusion that there might just be something to be said for the unexamined life.

CHAPTER FOURTEEN

It was a day like any day. The sun, which had just appeared above an Atlantic-bound front, was pleasantly warm. The breeze blowing down from the Canadian prairie was cool and fresh. It was a Saturday. The last one of June. The day of the Alvarez annual weed pull.

Loco had just awakened. A scratch. A stretch. Another scratch. Something was up. There was something he was supposed to be doing. The music. That awful chumpa chumpa. Attacking through the east window. Rancheras. Isabel's rancheras. Summoning all to a day of communal gardening. And he was late. How late? He got up to check the clock in the cage. Almost ten. Indisputably almost ten. The ancient timepiece was always accurate.

As to the cage, that was a touch of Mai Lu's whimsy. Several years before, she had purchased a canary. Hence the cage. A month later, the bird had died. Hence the empty cage. One day while cleaning house, she had serendipitously set the clock down in the cage. Later, about to remove it, she had stopped to reflect. To a lover of the odd and the incongruous, this arrangement was a masterpiece. A visual editorial on human exertion. A droll metaphor for human existence. She nodded her approval. The clock had inhabited the cage from that day forward.

Loco eased into his jeans, slipped into his sandals, and bounded down the stairs. The house was cool. He closed the back door to

BOOK THREE, CHAPTER FOURTEEN

lower the music volume. On to the bathroom. Standard morning hygiene. Once more to the kitchen. Cereal would be the quickest. A box of cornflakes on the table. And next to it the notepad he had been using the night before. Recall ensued as he found a bowl and some milk.

Daniel and Dante Palafox had come for their English class. Both had been tired. The lesson had dragged. Afterward, much talk about the accident that had resulted in the deaths of their parents and sister. Distanced from the event by more than two years and several thousand kilometers, the young men now accepted their loss fatalistically. Predictably. Loco had known dozens of people from the South. Virtually everyone believed in destiny. Son cosas de la vida was one statement of that faith. A mature creed. Derived from generations upon generations of badly nourished but madly fertile masses. Resigned to the rule of an elite. Whose faces changed from era to era. But whose motto was invariably: "The exertion of the many for the ease of the few." And these masses rarely revolted. Why would they? It was all destiny. Perhaps it was ordained that one day their offspring would join the elite. Then they too could laze and loll, impervious to the laments of the multitude. That accounted for their perennial prayer, "Ojalá."

Loco picked up the notepad and deciphered his scribbles from the previous night. Starting with the epigramatic analogy that had haunted his musings for months. To wit: *As meat is to lions, so is meaning to humans. We must have meaning to go forward. Art is a source of meaning, and one art form that we find especially congenial is the story. We want our lives to also have a beginning, a middle, and an end. That in place, we tend to accept the finality of death, even while we lament its inevitability.*

The converse is also revealing. We rail against an early or premature death. Irrationally to be sure. For we observe that in other species, many individuals die before they reproduce. So we know that nothing is assured. Nothing was ever promised. Nevertheless, when a human dies before procreating, or before having the opportunity to consciously decide not to procreate, we feel that this individual has somehow been cheated.

But we go much beyond even that. We assert that life beyond procreation is not only beneficial but even essential for the full maturity of the individual. We are convinced that individuals should reach their three score and ten or four score or even a century. And having advanced to such an age, they should still possess enough health, enough leisure, and enough wealth to be capable of occasionally kicking back and reflecting, "It is good to have lived."

In the margin next to the last paragraph Loco had written "Great Expectations." He smiled wryly at the words, then spooned some more cornflakes into his mouth, and went on to an earlier page of notes. To wit: *Just as the people of the southern regions of the continent are unmitigated fatalists, the folks of el norte are thoroughgoing meliorists. They are often mistakenly labeled optimists, but this fails to give them their due. For, yes, they believe that things can get better. But their faith goes well beyond that. They believe that they themselves can make things better. By applying sufficient effort and the appropriate technology. Infertility? Just say the word and nine months later we can have the little lady popping septuplets. Impotence? Speak up and in no time we can have the poor guy lifting weights with his donniker. Poverty? It's only a question of time before the market itself solves that one.*

He finished the cereal and lifted the bowl to drain off the milk. "And now to horticulture," he yelled as he exited the house. He looked toward the garden. No one there. The music had calmed, and from beyond the fence that separated Isabel's lot from the garden came the sound of human converse. He walked down the alley and

BOOK THREE, CHAPTER FOURTEEN

entered her yard. Everyone was there, consuming coffee and enchiladas.

"Thanks a lot for inviting me," he attempted to play the Pobrecito.

"Entre menos burros más zacate," said Noise.

"Nobody tied you to the bed," Concha volunteered.

"Ya sabes del pájaro madrugador," added Victoria.

Loco switched to a peevish pose, "So where's my breakfast?"

Isabel was unreservedly indifferent. "Sorry. The food is all gone. But we still have coffee."

Loco accepted a cup. "What time did you get here?" he asked Noise.

"About an hour ago," Noise lied, and immediately everyone turned on him.

"Yeah, right," huffed Isabel. "Try fifteen minutes."

"Apenas pudiste escapar de La Rubia," Victoria contributed.

"¿Cuál Rubia?" Noise played the inocente.

"La que bajaba de tu casa con la mano todavía metida en tus calzones," Concha responded.

"Man, this group is hostile," Loco complained. "Somebody put one too many chiles in the hot sauce."

Everyone roared their approval. Concha went for the topper. "¿Qué dice La Rubia de tu salsa, Noise? ¿Un chilito demás? A mí se me hace que no. Yo creo que La Rubia es de mucha resistencia."

Noise and Loco exchanged a meaningful glance. Their choices were simple. They could yield at once and go away mauled but still ambulatory. Or they could stay and be annihilated. Together they arose and walked toward the garden, their crests drooping noticeably.

"That was vicious enough," said Noise. "Now I know how the coyote felt when the wolves invited him to dinner."

More familiar with the ways of the womenfolk, Loco gave it a different spin. "They probably wanted to discuss something, and we were in the way."

A row of marigolds bordered the west side of the garden. Near the flowers, Mai Lu had left several hoes.

"This is a first for me," said Noise. "You'll have to show me what to do."

"First you decide whether you want to hoe or pull weeds or both."

"What are you going to do?"

"I like to weed. It requires only minimal brain function, and you can get as dirty as you want."

"Sounds perfect to me."

Loco dropped to his knees between two rows of potatoes. Noise did likewise.

"You recognize the potato plants?" Loco asked. He awaited and got a nod from Noise. "Good. It's that simple. Everything else is a weed."

The two began to work. They tugged and lugged at crabgrass, thistle, velvet weed, purslane, and an occasional dandelion. Having extracted the plants, they shook off the dirt clinging to the roots and stacked the weeds in small piles, to be carried later to the compost heap. "They won't all come out clean," advised Loco, "but even damaging them gives a relative advantage to the potato plants."

Halfway down the row, Noise looked up and said, "I wanted to ask you how the English classes are going with Daniel and Dante."

Loco laughed. "That's exactly what I was just thinking about. We had a session last night. We spent most of the time discussing family stuff." He paused. "Which wasn't all bad. We need to get past the teacher-student thing. They haven't connected very well with the family."

"But are they learning anything? I can't get them to say a word in English."

"Don't expect that to change. Why should they speak English with you?"

"Why not? Just to practice."

"That's probably not going to happen. There are a lot of factors that complicate language learning. But aside from age and past education, the most important variable is the relative willingness of the learners to open themselves to risk."

"You're talking about people who take chances. People who try to talk, even if they make fools of themselves."

"That's exactly what I mean. Now. Think about it. On a scale of one to five. If the fives are the biggest risk-takers, where would you put your cousins?"

Noise tried a stall. "Five is the best?"

"Five is for the people most willing to risk."

"I don't know. I guess the cousins are about average. Maybe a three."

"Not even close. I'm a three. Mai Lu is a four. You and Victoria are fives. Your cousin Dante is a two. At best. And Daniel is about a one and a half."

Noise thought about that. "Okay. Let's suppose the numbers are right. But getting back to that other thing. Some people aren't afraid to make mistakes. I don't see how that makes it easier for them to learn."

Loco awarded him an appreciative glance. "There are a couple of reasons. The first is pretty obvious. People who aren't afraid to make mistakes practice more. They walk straight into language situations that other people try to avoid."

"You make us sound like pendejos."

"Not at all. People actually envy risk-takers. Maybe not openly. But secretly, we all wish we could be like that." Noise did not respond. Loco continued, "The second reason why people like you are better learners is because you make more mistakes."

Noise stopped weeding and favored Loco with a long, dubious stare, but all he said was, "Yeah. Right."

"Really. Two terrific things happen when you make a mistake. People rush to help. They correct you. Immediate feedback. That's one good thing." He paused. "But something even more important happens. Little by little you discover that communication can occur without perfectly constructed sentences. As long as you have the correct words, you can get across, even if your accent is bad and your syntax is a mess."

Noise was still at a stop. "So you're saying that the best learners are the people who make the most mistakes."

"If you can isolate that variable, yes."

"You mean leaving out age and education and stuff like that."

"Exactly."

Noise shook his head. "I guess it's crazy enough to be true." After a pause. "So what about my cousins? You're saying they're never going to learn?"

"They're plodders. But as long as they keep trying to learn, I'll keep trying to help them."

"Where do you get the patience? When I try to help them practice by saying 'Good morning,' and they answer in Spanish, I get pissed."

Loco laughed. "I guess language teachers develop linguistic calluses over the years."

They returned to their task. A few minutes later, the women entered the garden. There was some predictable banter. To Isabel's, "Good to see you guys working for a change," Noise responded, "Yeah. Yeah. We can get cheerleaders at ten cents a herd. What we need is weeders."

Loco noted the presence of Mai Lu and Concha and Victoria. That left a significant absence, about which he immediately inquired. "What happened to Marta?"

BOOK THREE, CHAPTER FOURTEEN

Marta had left the Donovan house before nine o'clock. She wanted to avoid the annual June weed pull. She also wanted to forestall the need to explain her absence. Let them surmise. Let them theorize. They all knew so much about how she felt. They were all experts on why she hurt. They all had guaranteed remedies for her pain. Let them have a field day. Let them conjecture. Let them speculate. Let them talk.

First some errands. A letter mailed at the post office. A book dropped off at the library. A coat picked up at the dry cleaners. A check cashed at the bank. It was a delight to maneuver her three-month-old Buick through the nearly empty streets.

Noise had tried to discourage her from buying the car. Maybe he had been right. From his self-serving viewpoint. He had started doing the service work on her old Chevy, and it had been running like never before. But it was still an old car. It looked old. Some small dents. Some scratches and scrapes. A bit of rust here and there. More importantly, the styling was embarrassingly outdated. The vehicle was post-obsolescent. Noise had argued that she was wasting her money. He had insisted that he could keep the Chevy going for another three years. "¡Cállate ya!" she had finally yelled at him. She wanted the Buick. She had the money to pay for it. It was her money. If she was wasting it, that was her business.

He had kept his distance after that. Good riddance. Who did he think he was anyway? Nobody told him how to spend his money. Nobody told him to stop throwing it away on that tramp that everybody called La Rubia. That whore with the inflated tits. Who would drop her pantyhose for him any time he whistled. Who called herself a professor no less. At a supposedly Catholic university. Screw Noise.

Marta had anticipated killing about two hours on her errands. But hardly an hour had passed and they were all done. It was going to be a long day. She pulled into the parking lot of a diner that advertised breakfast specials. Inside she slid into a booth and checked the silverware. It did not inspire confidence. Just a roll and coffee then. She ordered. A cheerless waitress complied almost immediately.

Marta stared at the Danish. Either it was vintage yesterday, or it had aged very gracelessly. She sampled the coffee. ¡Madre Santa! Where had she tasted something that bad? No, the question was not rhetorical. There had been an actual occasion. Toño's face was squarely in the middle of the experience. It was a restaurant. Not this one, but very much like it. She was with Toño. After a movie. The year before he had married Victoria. What was the name of that movie? Toño had taken her. Sometime in the fall. The same year that he had returned to Jachalco to romance Victoria. Those two creeps had made wedding plans for the following year. Then back in Milwaukee, Toño had remained faithful to his goody-goody fiancée by inviting his sister when he wanted to see a movie. The jerk! Only in hindsight had she understood that she had been a stand-in for Victoria. Yuck!

"When was the last time you cleaned your coffeepot?" Marta inquired as she was paying her bill.

"I just give people what they ask for," answered the cheerless waitress. "I don't make the coffee. And I certainly wouldn't drink it."

In the Buick again. A check of her watch. Not much after eleven. Another ten hours to kill. She had planned some shopping and a movie. But that was for late afternoon and early evening. What now? She noted her location. Jackson Park was in the area. That would fill some time.

The park reminded her of other summer Saturdays. Often she had gone there with Isabel's children. They would take bread for the waterfowl. The boys favored squishing the slices into pellets and throwing the bits as high as possible for the gulls to grab in midair. Frances preferred letting the geese snap the bread directly from her extended fingers.

That, of course, was the relatively docile Frances of yore. Not the rebellious hoyden she had become. With little respect for her mother. Even less for her aunt. And no regard whatsoever for tradition.

Strong-willed even as a toddler, she had grown into a typically contrary adolescent. There had been spats and bickering over the years. But nothing had prepared Marta for the scene at the breakfast table two months back.

It had been a Saturday morning. Marta had accepted Isabel's invitation to brunch. Frances had listened as her mother and aunt discussed her fifteenth birthday. Marta had proposed a large event. She would sponsor the hall and music. Perhaps Concha would provide the food. It could be big. Very big. Between them, Mamá Margarita and Papá Miguel knew most of the Milwaukee Hispanic community. They could have the event announced at three or four parishes. This might be the biggest quinceañera ever.

Marta had interpreted her niece's obvious growing agitation as a sign of excited anticipation. Consequently, she was completely taken aback when Frances interrupted with, "I don't want a quinceañera. I hate the idea. It's a silly tradition. I detest the concept. Why are we even talking about this?"

Isabel had reacted as if her daughter were disparaging only the size of the proposed celebration. "No, Hija. We don't have to make it such a big deal if you don't want."

"That's not it, Mother. I don't want a quinceañera of any size. Period."

"You're upset because we didn't ask you first," her mother attempted to mollify.

"Mother, I am not upset. I am angry. And not because I wasn't asked first. Although, now that you mention it, that would have been nice. But I am angry because you are trying to push me into this.

And I hate it. It's so sexist."

"No digas eso, Hija. Think about what you're saying. My mother wasn't there to give me a quinceañera, but I would have loved it. Now it's your turn, and I can't afford it. But your Tía here is offering to be your Madrina and pay for everything. And instead of being glad and grateful, you start telling her you hate it."

"Why do you say it's sexist?" Marta had asked.

"Why don't they do it for the boys?" Frances had countered.

"It's a tradition that honors the special place that the woman has in Hispanic culture," Marta had argued.

"That's exactly my point," Frances had blazed. "It's another way to put the woman on a pedestal, where she can be honored and admired and controlled. In her place."

"Why is that bad?" Marta had insisted. "Everyone has a place. The woman, the man, the child. I don't see the problem."

At that point she was talking to her niece's back. As she exited, Frances had not allowed the front door to come within a yard of her fanny.

"I'm really sorry," Isabel had whined.

"It's not your fault," Marta had consoled. But she hadn't really meant it. It was Isabel's fault. She had never disciplined her kids como Dios manda. No wonder they were a pandilla de descarados.

Marta had not, however, gracefully acknowledged defeat. It was not her style. And there were still options. She would enlist the aid of her sister-in-law. If Victoria would argue the case for a fiesta, Frances would at least have to listen.

No need for much ado about how to ply her cuñada. Tradition. Conservation of the cultural. Replication of the ritual. Cinco de mayo. Diesiseis de septiembre. Las mañanitas for the Virgen en diciembre. Those were community-wide events. But families had to do their part too. The Baptisms and First Communions had to be celebrated en grande. And the quinceañeras. Another opportunity for a special display. Demonstrating how the family was at the center of the culture, and how the woman was at the center of the family.

"You see my point, Victoria?"

"Claro que sí."

"You agree that every family should participate in this effort, as far as their economic situation will allow?"

"Por supuesto. But what are you saying? Toño and I are not doing enough?"

"No. No. I'm talking about Isabel." She paused and sighed. "Actually I'm talking about Frances."

"What about Frances?"

"She says she doesn't want a quinceañera."

Victoria reflected for a moment. "Probably she's thinking about her mother. She knows it's expensive, and Isabel doesn't have the money."

"I offered to pay for the hall and the music. If Concha does the food, and you and Mom do the dresses, and Noise and Loco do the drinks, that's ninety percent of the cost."

"But Frances says no?" Victoria quizzed.

"She still says no. She says that it's sexist. It's a tradition that helps keep the woman in her place."

"I agree with that. It is sexist."

"But you told me you had a quinceañera."

"Es cierto. Siempre me han gustado las fiestas. Y los quince años en Puebla es una superfiesta."

"You had a party, but you didn't approve of the tradition."

"Lo estás complicando mucho. I had a party because it was my turn. And I like parties."

"Then you will help me with this?"

"With the dresses? Of course."

"I mean, will you talk to Frances?"

"I will talk to Frances. I will tell her what I think. But she will decide."

That was all she could get from Victoria. And of course it would not be enough. But there was one other person who could help. Frances respected Concha more than her own mother. If Concha would say that the quinceañera tradition was a good one, Frances might still be rendered compliant, even if unconvinced.

The flaw in that scheme was that Frances had stolen a march on her. Concha was forewarned, forearmed, and formidable. Marta walked into a buzz saw.

"You and Isabel are pretending that you want to do something for this poor child. What a pair of egoistas. You don't want a fiesta for Frances. You want a fiesta for you. You didn't even bother to ask her before you started making plans." With a deep breath, Concha achieved an actual as well as symbolic second wind. "And what is this supposed to prove anyway? That the Alvarez are rich now? That we really know how to throw a party? If that's your motive, okay. Do what you want. But don't put Frances in the middle. She doesn't want it, and I'm going to make sure that nobody forces her to participate."

And the word of the preachy bitch had prevailed. Soon, even spineless Isabel had stopped pressuring her daughter. But where did the witch come off? Why did everybody defer to her? She was not the family spokesperson. She was a nobody. A cook, for god's sake. She hadn't even finished high school. And yet everybody kowtowed. But no. Not everybody. Not this one. Not Marta. There were any number of people on the planet that Marta could live without, and Concha was right near the top of the topmost quartile. Screw Concha.

BOOK THREE, CHAPTER FOURTEEN

Concha, meanwhile, was hoeing and hilling the jalapeño plants, blissfully oblivious of her cousin's execrations. She was, however, hyperaware of the presence of Noise. For one obvious and one less evident reason. The obvious was . . . well . . . obvious. As she hoed and hilled, her torso bent forward, her shapely derriere soon attracted his admiring attention. She straightened and turned to catch his stare.

"Looking good, Prima," he nodded with an ear-to-ear grin.

"Just concentrate on those weeds," she scolded.

"I'm trying. But it ain't easy," he drooled.

She positioned herself in what she calculated to be a less inspiring attitude and returned her attention to the peppers. The less evident reason for her unease could not be as easily dispelled. Earlier that year, Noise had stumbled onto the secret of her Friday night trysts.

Not that there was anything to hide. They were all consenting adults. Exactly. They were all . . . of course they were. Why even mention that? It implied that there was something about the relationship that needed defending. And that was just plain silly.

It was also very old news. Years ago after taking the job as Food Service Manager at Aztalán school, Concha had hired an assistant. Lucy Santos. Pobrecita. A single woman who had left the better part of her eyesight in a clothing factory, where for twenty years she had labored over an industrial sewing machine. As a kitchen helper, Lucy was more enthusiastic than skillful. On a good day she could boil water without scorching the pot. Initially. But she was a willing worker and a quick study. Concha encouraged her effort and admired her energy. A close friendship ensued.

One Friday after work. An invitation to the Santos home. For dinner and a game of cards. Accepted with some trepidation. Was she being invited to cook her own dinner? Not to worry. There was a brother, Diego. Who just happened to be the chef at a moderately renowned establishment, rather preposterously named Renacimiento. Lucy had carefully failed to mention him. The fourth person present was introduced as Lucy's friend, George Salazar.

The dinner menu. Nopales navegantes, a cactus broth derived from the buds of the prickly pear. Followed by the nearly inevitable rice. Followed by chiles rellenos, or stuffed hot peppers. Followed by the inevitable beans. The soup was an enormous success. Gastronomically and conversationally. Concha had tasted nopales only in salads. She rhapsodized, then requested the recipe. Diego agreed to share. Tan amable. Gracias. No hay de qué. They discussed seasonings, discovering a number of common predilections. Chile powder was an invention of the devil. Except for its possible effect on vampires, too much garlic was worse than too much chile. Recipes were to be honored more in the breach than in the observance.

The evening of cards began on a less harmonious note. The three Milwaukee natives all wanted to play the locally famous schafskopf or sheepshead. Concha resisted. The game was a tangle of technicalities and tactics. Points had to be counted as the hand was played. Partnerships between players formed with each new deal and then dissolved. Adepts adored the intricacies. Concha found them boring. Instead of aiding sociability, the game usually became annoyingly, cloyingly intense. Especially for the males. Didn't anyone play poker? Of course they did. Humor the newcomer. Seven card stud? Why not.

Settled then. And productive of a much friendlier ambience. Each player analyzed her own cards and made of them what she could. If they merited an ante, she could play. If not, she could fold. If something in the conversational flow held her attention, she could elect to chuck in even her meritorious cards. And follow the flow.

BOOK THREE, CHAPTER FOURTEEN

Bouncing along to the gentle jostle of the loser's quibble and the winner's crow. Wrapped in the warmth of the careless moment and the caring friends.

Late night coffee and sweet bread. Shortly thereafter, Lucy announced that she and George were going to bed. "Diego te puede llevar a casa, Concha. O como sea." Concha was not at all prepared for "como sea." Diego drove her home. The conversation was very polite.

During the following months, there were several more Friday dinners at the Santos home. Then the foursome began to venture out. Timidly at first. A fish fry. A movie. Finally, at Lucy's instigation, they attended a festival at one of the predominantly Latino churches. And Concha made a delightful discovery. Diego could dance.

He could really dance. Not like the strutters, who partnered with the most smartly dressed women, but always appeared to be paired with a mirror. Nor like the sweaters, who never missed a beat but always looked like they were in the eleventh of a twelve-hour shift. No. Diego was smooth. But not pompous. Competent but not compulsive. And when the piece ended, he would raise his hands in a self-deprecating gesture and say, "Algo por el estilo." It was but a short time later that the late night rides home stopped, and the "como sea" started.

Years passed. The Friday evenings became a part of Concha's weekly rhythm. So much so that her son once declared, "Mi Mamá se vuelve muy cristiana el viernes. Ella pasa toda la noche con los Santos."

Eventually Noise returned from the southern reaches of the continent. Since he also had a weakness for the cumbia and the danzón, it was merely a question of time before he and Concha stumbled into each other on the dance floor.

The collision occurred at a Valentine's Day affair. In fine fettle, but with all his attention directed toward Ms. Thompson, Noise was oblivious to Concha's presence. She, however, had spotted him earlier and was more prepared for the fact, if not the force, of the encounter. "Are you spying on me?" she challenged.

"Of course not," he defended himself as he recovered his equilibrium. Then regaining the sly glint in his eye. "But I can. If you're doing something really wicked."

Introductions were done. Hands were pressed. "We're with some people," she explained. "Otherwise I'd invite you to join us."

"No problem," he answered. Pleasantries were exchanged. Polite separation was effected. So much for that.

Well, maybe not quite. In the following weeks, she would sometimes find him staring. With that waggish knowing grin. He was wearing it even now. Even pulling weeds. ¡Carajo!

"Would you stop that!" she scolded.

Evidently he would. The grin faded, and the next thing out of his mouth was an innocent question. "So what happens with all this stuff?" He spread his hands to indicate the garden.

She gave the stock answer. "We eat what we can, and what we can't, we can." She let him puzzle over that for a minute, then went to the rescue. "It's not that mysterious. Some of it we eat right away. Some of it we put in the freezer or in canning jars to eat in the fall and winter."

He continued to mull over the mellifluous phrase. "We eat what we can. And what we can't, we can." He mumbled it a second time. "Who came up with that?"

"It's from an old joke. I think Miguel is the only one who remembers the story."

They rededicated themselves to their tasks. But soon Noise had another question. "Does this garden really save you money?"

Isabel was the first to respond. "In my case, for sure. With three kids to feed, it's a big deal for me."

"Everybody saves a little," Concha continued. "But it's more than that. I agree with my son. Everybody should raise some of their own food."

"So they know how much work it takes," Noise supposed.

"Not only that. It's important to maintain contact with the earth. To understand our dependence. And to learn how things grow," added the practical Mai Lu.

"When you grow your own food, you know what you are eating," Victoria joined the chorus.

Concha summarized, "You see? There are more reasons for doing this than there are people. But everybody agrees on one thing. It's a good excuse for a family get-together."

Noise had a few less-theoretical doubts. "But how do you decide who gets what? When the stuff is ready to eat."

"That usually isn't a problem," Concha explained. "When the vegetables are ready, everybody just comes to pick the lettuce or spinach or whatever they can use."

"First come first served."

"Pretty much like that."

"So what if I want some lettuce, and I go to the garden and find out that you just took it all."

"En ese caso te invito a comer."

"Me fregaste," Noise admitted.

She laughed and continued her explanation. "Some things like green beans and tomatoes are special. They get ripe faster than we can eat them. So we usually have a couple of bean-snapping days in July and August. And a couple of tomato-canning days in September."

"And you have enough for everybody?"

"Sometimes more than enough. Last year the tomatoes were sensational. We might still have fifty jars left when the new crop is ready this year."

"What about those jalapeños? Do you have a way to keep them?"

"They'll keep in the refrigerator for weeks. But not indefinitely. That was a problem. Until two years ago. Then somebody told me how to toast them on the outdoor grill and then freeze them. That works great."

"You've got it all down to a system."

"Not really. Every year is a little different. But we keep working. We keep learning."

Noise got to his feet, stretched, and gave the garden an appraising, end-to-end review. "This is really something." Then after a pause, "Who eats the marigolds?"

"The bees and other insects come for the pollen. And while they're here, they help to pollinate the other plants." She paused. "Your sister plants the flowers. And every year she reminds us of what her mother-in-law told her years ago. That you can't eat them, but when you see how beautiful they are, part of you doesn't feel so hungry."

"Maria Guadalupe," Noise intoned in a voice awash with reverence.

Concha noted his shift in mood and ceased her chatter. Soon she too was cultivating introspection. What a grand day! Her body warmed to the sun-bathed rhythm of the work. The munch munch munch of the hoe began to comfort. Skin moistened. Muscles loosened. Tendons flexed. Dendrites dozed. Axons nodded. Neurons napped.

Time passed. The munch munch munch continued. Concha had nearly finished the fifth and final row of peppers when the neighborhood erupted with a banshee shriek from across the street. What! Instant alert. Every nerve and sinew at the ready. Confusion lasted but a second. Then she recognized the source of the screams. It was the children racing to join the gardeners. Victoria's Tony and Alicia. Her own granddaughter Juana. And the ever irrepressible Frances.

BOOK THREE, CHAPTER FOURTEEN

Frances had taken the younger children for some splashing and thrashing at one of the county park swimming pools. Now they were back and eager to help in the garden. First the matter of greetings. Buenas tardes. Buenas tardes. Tía. Tío. Et cetera. Et cetera. Self-consciously proffered by the youngsters. They, convinced that adult preoccupation with forms signaled a mild derangement. Approvingly acknowledged by the adults. They, convinced that forms were the very mortar of civilized society.

"You're late," Noise joshingly accused. "We've been out here sweating for hours."

With a shrug, Frances gave her standard response. "What do you expect from bilinguals? We're totally unreliable. ¿Qué se puede hacer?"

"There's room for another weeder in the potatoes," he invited.

"No thanks. I can't trust these guys with anything as complicated as a potato. If I'm lucky, they can still tell a cabbage from a weed."

Then, employing her best rendition of Sylvester the cat, "Let's go, you despicable little rodents."

The rodents, who loved her deliriously, each displayed an ear-to-ear grin. Basking in the warmth of her pretended disdain, they followed her to the assigned task. On each of the previous June weekends, Frances had been working in the cabbage patch. So. Within a half hour the few remaining weeds were dispatched. It was time to begin the garden geography class.

Cabbage was one of the vegetables that the Alvarez family shared with their neighbors. For that reason, it was abundant. Five rows in fact. With twenty plants in each row. From the eastern border of the garden, Frances marched down the middle row to the seventh plant. There she stopped, pointed to a small pile of stakes that were used to mark rows, and said to Tony, "Bring me one of those, please." He complied. She pushed the sharp end into the ground near her left foot. "Now," she intoned, spreading her arms to the north and south, "this is North America." A pause. "Not the whole garden," she amended. "Just the potatoes and cabbage and peppers. ¿Entendido?" Alicia and Juana nodded. Tony was enormously pleased that he had been able to help, and he just continued to beam without responding. "I'll take that as two affirmative and one blissfully indifferent," summarized Frances. Then, "The stake that I just planted marks the location of a city. It's the place where two very important rivers of North America come together. The name of the city is two words. The first word is 'Saint.'"

"Saint Anthony," Tony guessed.

"Good guess, but wrong saint," said Frances.

"St. Louis," said Alicia.

"Very good," said Frances. "Now tell me the names of the two rivers."

"The Mississippi," said Juana.

"Oh man! I knew that one," Tony complained. "They're not giving me a chance. Everybody knows the Mississippi. It's the biggest river in the world."

"I'm glad you know the answer, Tony. But the Mississippi isn't the longest river in the world. Not even close," said Frances.

"It is the longest," Tony insisted and appealed to a higher authority. "Uncle Noise, tell her it's the longest."

"I'm not sure," Noise hedged, "but there's a river in Africa called the Nile. That might be the longest. Is that right, Teacher?"

"That's correct," said Frances. "But what's the other river that enters the Mississippi in St. Louis?"

"The Missouri River," said Alicia.

"That's the one," Frances praised. "Now we have to stop and locate the rivers. Tony, you do the Mississippi. Alicia, you do the

Missouri. Juana, you write St. Louis on one of our markers and stick it on the stake."

The children had cut long strips from plastic grocery bags. These were used to represent the rivers. Tony tied the end of his to the St. Louis stake and started south. "That's not right," Juana told him.

"Yes it is. It goes south. Isn't that right, Frances?"

"Actually it goes north and south," Frances intervened. "So you were half right."

"You see? I was half right," crowed Tony.

In the interest of precision, Juana pointed out the obvious. "Half right isn't the same as all right."

"So what," was his rebuttal. But he let his cousin wrap the middle of the plastic strip around the St. Louis stake. Then she walked north with one end of the strip while he went south with the other. Alicia, meanwhile, tied the end of her strip to the same stake and started walking northwest.

"Wait a minute," Tony yelled at her. "You can't do it on the end. Frances said that's wrong."

"Wrong for you," his sister countered. "You're doing the Mississippi. I'm doing the Missouri."

"That's right," Frances concurred. "Remember, we said the two rivers come together. So when it gets to St. Louis, that's the end of the Missouri."

"I don't know where to go with this," said Alicia.

"In what state does the Missouri originate?" Frances asked.

"Montana, I think."

"Very good. For the starting point, put a stake in the ground just south of the potatoes, at about the third cabbage from the end," Frances said and went to help. She maneuvered the plastic strip around cabbages so that it followed a more westerly movement from St. Louis to Kansas, then north-northwest up into North Dakota, then almost straight west to its origin. "There. That's pretty much what the Missouri does. Now for the Mississippi." She pushed two stakes into the ground about an inch apart where Juana was standing. "These are for the twin cities that are just a little south of where the Mississippi begins. Who can tell me their names? One starts with the word 'Saint.'"

"This time I'm not guessing Saint Anthony," Tony grumbled. Then after searching the teacher's face for a second, "It isn't Saint Anthony, is it?"

"No, it's not," said Frances.

"I told you it wasn't," Tony yelled. "I knew that wasn't the right answer."

"Is it St. Paul?" asked Alicia.

"Yes. And the other city?"

"It sounds like mini apples," said Juana.

"Mini apples!" hooted Tony. "Boy! Is that lame!"

"Actually it's very close," said Frances. "The name is Minneapolis. Now, about your end of the river, Tony. There's a city down there too. It starts with the word new."

"New York. New Mexico. New Orleans. New . . . " He ran out of gas. "It isn't any of those, is it?"

"Yes it is," assured Frances. "It's New Orleans."

"It is? New Orleans. Wow! I did it. I got it on the first try."

Juana giggled and Alicia said, "That's right. You got it on the fourth guess of your first try."

They placed a stake above the mouth of the Mississippi and labeled it New Orleans. Then they backed off into the pepper patch for a review. Tony rattled off the names and locations of the rivers and three of the four cities, needing help only with St. Paul.

"Do you feel your feet getting wet?" asked Frances.

"I do," said Juana. "And I know why. It's because we're standing

BOOK THREE, CHAPTER FOURTEEN

in the Gulf of Mexico."

"Mexico," said Tony. "That's where my Abuelitos are. What's the name of el pueblito, Alicia?"

"Se llama Jachalco," answered his sister.

"Jachalco. Jachalco." Tony practiced. "I always forget Jachalco." Then, "Let's put a stick where Jachalco is."

"Good idea," said Frances. "But I'm going to need help with this one." She did a quick survey of the possible consultants. Then, "Uncle Noise, where do we put a marker for Jachalco?"

Noise slowly raised himself to his knees, grinned, cleared his throat, and began scratching his head. From years of observing classroom behavior, Frances recognized the telltale signs. He hadn't a clue. Now what? For a second she held her breath. Then, miraculously, he spoke. "Mi primo, Arturo, me dijo muchas veces que Houston queda mero al norte de Veracruz."

Loco to the rescue. "Houston would be about two cabbages west of New Orleans."

"And Puebla is maybe one cabbage west of Veracruz," added Frances.

"There you go," Noise summarized. "Down there in that last row of peppers."

Frances planted the stake.

"That doesn't look right," said Concha. "I thought Puebla was straight south from Milwaukee. Why don't you check with Victoria. She should know."

Victoria was in the tomato patch north of the potatoes, but she had heard. "A mí no me pregunten. Yo compro mi boleto y me subo al avión."

Again Loco intervened. "Think about it. New Orleans is east of Veracruz, and Milwaukee is east of New Orleans. If you fly straight south from Milwaukee, you end up in Yucatán. So I think Noise is close enough. At least for a pepper-patch map."

Frances laughed. "That's settled then. Let's put a label on it."

"Let me do it," pleaded Tony.

"Fine," said Frances. "Alicia can tell you the letters."

"I can do it by myself," Tony insisted. "I know my letters."

"Okay. What's the first letter?" Alicia challenged.

Tony sounded out the first syllable. "*H*," he declared. "Just like hop."

"Wrong," said Alicia. "It's Spanish. The *h* sound in English is the letter *j* in Spanish."

"Is that right?" Tony asked Frances.

"She's right, Tony. This is a perfect example of why all of us bilinguals are such a mess."

"I'm not a mess," Tony contradicted, "and I know my letters. I just need a little help with Jachalco."

"So what comes after the *j*?" Alicia challenged again.

"Let me do it by myself." He concentrated for a few minutes and came up with Jachalko.

"Very good," Frances praised. "Just change the *k* to a *c* and you've got it."

Tony made the correction and stuck the label on the stake. "Aquí viven mis Abuelos," Tony declared proudly. "I have Abuelos in Jachalco and Milwaukee. Juana doesn't. She just has Abuelos in Milwaukee."

"Tony, that's not nice," scolded Concha. "You said that just to hurt your cousin."

Tony was an expert at repentance. "Sorry, Tía Concha. I didn't mean it."

Juana went to her grandmother and gave her a hug. "It's okay," she reassured. "I know I have the best grandma anywhere."

"Frances, take these children inside," Concha ordered. "Get

them some juice. There are oatmeal cookies in the refrigerator."

Frances again assumed the cartoon character voice. "Come on you despicable creatures. Let's get you some rodent nutrition. I know you've been wondering why you have this uncontrollable attraction to cheese. I can help you understand that."

Inside, the children gobbled their snack and disappeared into Juana's playroom. Leaving Frances alone at the kitchen table. With a vague empty feeling. Well, maybe not so vague. Aunt Marta had been inexplicably absent from the family gardening. Frances had hoped to use the occasion for peacemaking. Thwarted plan, empty feeling.

Not that she had any regrets about squelching the proposed quinceañera bash. She did, however, recognize that her rejection of the proffered fiesta constituted unorthodox behavior. But so what. What did they expect. From weird you get weird. "And I am for sure weird," she mused aloud.

"Y así te queremos," responded a voice from behind. Frances emitted a small yelp and whirled to face the intruder. Beaming at her was an astonishingly stealthy Aunt Victoria.

Victoria had entered the kitchen not to spy on a niece but to dice a pork roast. That being the first step in the preparation of the evening meal. A gardening day tradition. A minor communal feast on the Alvarez calendar. Distinctive fare for famished weeders. Known to the children as Chinese tacos. Most folks called them egg rolls.

The origin of the tradition corresponded to the arrival of Mai Lu and Loco in Milwaukee. In the course of their first participation in gardening day, Mai Lu had mentioned to her husband that the new-crop onions would be just right for egg rolls. The rest, as they say, was history.

As Victoria was beginning with the meat, Mai Lu came in from the garden. Deference entered with her. "Are these pieces small enough?" Victoria asked.

"About one cubic centimeter," Mai Lu answered as she inspected. "That's fine."

Frances volunteered and was assigned the task of chopping the scallions. Mai Lu started a search for a pot sizable enough to contain the meat and the considerable volume of vegetables. Eventually she located a large earthenware cazuela. Which Victoria had brought back from Jachalco some years before. Which had recently been used to transport some food to Concha's house. Which, like many food-bearing dishes, was slow to return to its house of origin. The sight of which now triggered some tender memories.

"I remember the day I got that cazuela from my mother," Victoria smiled. "First she gave it to me. Then she took it back and packed it in a box with about five kilos of newspaper. Then she gave it back to me. Then, when we got on the bus to Puebla, she took it away and held it on her lap. She was convinced that I was going to break it. I had two pieces of luggage to worry about and two toddlers to watch, but my mother wanted me to put all my attention on that cazuela."

"There must have been something special about it," said Frances.

"Very special. Her mother-in-law, Sacramento, gave it to her as a present."

"Sacramento. That's my bisabuela."

"La misma."

Frances put her hand on the cazuela. "Isn't this amazing? I'm touching something that my bisabuela touched a long time ago."

"And your bisabuela was a great lady. Even if only half of the stories are true."

BOOK THREE, CHAPTER FOURTEEN

"You told me once that she raised two families," Mai Lu interjected.

"Tell about that," pleaded Frances. "I love stories about the family in the old days. When I listen, it's like I'm in the story too."

"When my father was still a baby," Victoria began, "there was a big disaster in the family. Two of his brothers and a cousin died in a swimming accident."

Frances could not restrain an interruption. "Mamá Margarita told me that something pulled the boys under the water."

"Nobody knows what really happened," Victoria cautioned. "But anyway, that was the start of a series of disasters. First my abuelita, Ana, went a little crazy and stopped taking care of my father, who was still a baby. Then my abuelito, Gilberto, died. A lot of bad things happened at about that same time."

"And my bisabuelita, Sacramento, kept the family together," Frances stated proudly.

"That's what they say. She took care of her three children and two nephews. Plus a sick brother, and a disturbed sister-in-law, and her father who was retired. They say that sometimes she would finish her housework and go to help the men in the fields."

"Mamá Margarita told me that my bisabuela could hoe corn better than a man," declared Frances.

"Maybe she could," Victoria smiled at her niece's enthusiasm. "One thing she didn't do. She didn't sell the land. My father and my brothers work the same forty hectáreas that she and her sons worked."

"Tell a story about Sacramento, Tía. Tell your all-time favorite story about her."

Victoria reflected for a long moment. Then, "Okay. My favorite story about Sacramento. But you have to help me at the end."

"How do you mean help you?"

"When I get to the last line, you have to translate for me."

"Okay. Sure. But what's the line?"

"No. You have to wait until we get there. Then I want you to translate."

Frances assumed the pose of the rapt listener.

"I heard this story from my mother," Victoria began. "It happened when Sacramento was about fifty years old. One night after work, a man named Ricardo came to talk to her. He worked the field next to one of hers. The corn in the fields was just about ready to pick. Ricardo said that someone was stealing his corn."

"Stealing corn?" Frances questioned. "Do people really do that?"

"Actually it happens a lot. Anyway, this man Ricardo said that his sons had gone to watch the field for three nights. Every night they came back with the same story. About midnight a donkey walked down the road next to the field. When he got to the field, the donkey changed into a man. He went into the field and filled a sack with corn. He carried the sack to the road. He tied it to his back. Then he changed into a donkey again and walked back to town."

"Spooky!" said Frances.

"How do you say nagual in English?"

"I don't know that word," Frances admitted. "What is it?"

"Algo como brujo."

"Witch."

"No. El macho de la witch."

"Warlock."

"Something like that. But a nagual can change from a man to an animal and back again. That's what some people believe."

"This is some great stuff," Frances enthused. "What did you call this thing?"

"El nagual. It's just a superstition, of course, but people in the small towns still believe in things like this."

"But not my bisabuela," conjectured Frances.

"Eso vas a ver ahorita," said Victoria. "Anyway, this Ricardo was convinced that the nagual was stealing his corn. He wanted to know if the nagual was stealing from Sacramento too. And if he wasn't, what was Sacramento doing to protect her field. Sacramento told Ricardo that she would investigate." Victoria paused. "So that night, Sacramento got her shotgun and went to hide in her field. About eleven o'clock, Ricardo's two sons came down the road with a donkey. One of the sons had a sack. They went into their father's field and filled the sack with corn. Then they put the sack on the donkey and walked back to town. In the first house on the edge of the town lived a man who had a store. He bought small quantities of corn from the people of the town when they needed money. Ricardo's sons went into the backyard of this man's house. A little later they came back out, jingling some pesos."

"Incredible," said Frances.

"Anyway, the next morning Ricardo went to talk to Sacramento. He asked if she had seen the nagual. And Sacramento answered . . . here is where you have to help me, Frances . . . 'Que nagual, ni que la fregada. Tus propios hijos te están robando, Pendejo.'"

Frances was more than up to the task. "Don't tell me about some silly nagual," she translated. "Your own sons are stealing your corn, you jackass."

Uproarious hilarity ensued. Enduring for several moments. Then some eyes had to be wiped.

Mai Lu was the first to recover. "You can say that word, Victoria. Nobody will be offended."

"That isn't the problem," Victoria answered. "I know you aren't offended. But when I try to say words like that, they come out funny. I don't sound right."

"How do you want to sound?" Mai Lu asked.

"Like Frances. When she says a word like that, it sounds natural. When I say it, it sounds too polite."

"It's because you try to tiptoe around the word," Frances theorized. "So you sound careful, when you want to sound just the opposite. But that's okay. I liked helping with the story. My bisabuela Sacramento was so cool."

Another collective chuckle. Then back to the task at hand. Mai Lu browned the meat and seasoned it with moderate amounts of salt, pepper, and garlic. Plus a dash of ginger and a generous gush of soy sauce. Next she added the scallions. Meanwhile, Victoria and Frances were slicing the cabbage. When that was ready, Mai Lu folded it into the meat mixture and did the same with the bean sprouts.

"Is there any trick to that?" Frances asked.

"Just one," answered Mai Lu. "Don't cook the vegetables too much."

"What's the proportion of meat and vegetables?" Victoria asked.

"I don't really have a recipe," Mai Lu admitted. "But I guess this is about four pounds of meat, four pounds of cabbage, and four pounds of bean sprouts. That will make about sixty or seventy egg rolls."

When the meat-vegetable mixture was ready, they spread it out in a wide tray to cool. In a deep skillet, oil was heated for frying. Then production began.

One by one the egg roll wrappers were filled with a scoop of pork-cabbage-bean sprout. The wrappers were rolled until closed, then sealed by daubing the edges with beaten egg. Victoria rolled, Frances sealed, Mai Lu fried. About an hour later there were sixty-seven egg rolls gracing the kitchen table. It was time for a sample. Mai Lu mixed some sweet-and-sour sauce with a dash of soy sauce and a dollop of hot mustard. Then she dipped an egg roll into the sauce and handed it to Frances, who bit, chewed, savored, and pronounced, "My Aunt Marta says that sex is overrated. After

BOOK THREE, CHAPTER FOURTEEN

a bite of one of these, I think she's probably right."

After that commercial, how could Victoria resist? She also dipped, savored, and concurred, "Maybe nothing is perfect, but these are very close." Then she excused herself and went across the street for a pot of vegetable soup which she had prepared the previous evening. When that had been reheated on Concha's stove, it was time to eat. The children were sent to fetch the Palafox brothers and the folks at Mamá Margarita's house. Then dinner was announced to the gardeners.

The meal was a contentious affair. Much posturing and boasting about whose labor had been most efficacious. Noise alleged that on size alone, the potato patch qualified as the most onerous task. Concha countered that his choice of assignment had been most fortuitous, since the potato patch was where he could do the least damage.

Victoria served the soup, then stationed herself advantageously for monitoring the endearing and predictable foibles of her family. Someone would fuss with the children to get them to eat their soup. That would be Mamá Margarita. Someone would wolf his food, the more quickly to escape to the arms of his teenage goddess. That would be Isabel's oldest son, Nico. Someone would nibble apprehensively into an egg roll for the very first time, eyeball an inoffensive bean sprout, and surreptitiously slide the novel concoction under his napkin. That would be the Palafox brothers. Someone would note their distress and rush to warm some rice and beans and tortillas for them. That would be Mai Lu. Someone would jibe at their discomfort, while simultaneously devouring his own and their share of the egg rolls. That would be Noise.

Noise had done well by his pledge to Aunt Pilar to put her grandsons on the path to righteousness and wealth. "De pura chiripa" she might have editorialized. "Sheer serendipity," is an adequate translation, but "clan collusion" would have been more faithful to the facts.

Through Isabel's intervention, Daniel and Dante found employment at a leather manufacturing plant. Loco taught them English. Marta introduced them to the people at the parish rectory. Margarita taught them to launder their clothes. Miguel provided housing in a half-refurbished duplex at the west end of the Alvarez block. Victoria, Mai Lu, and Concha conspired to "fatten them up."

But Noise had been no idle spectator during this period of adjustment. On the contrary. He was quite zealous for the welfare of his sobrinos. It was just that his talents inclined toward the less prosaic exigencies of life. Such as transportation. A multifaceted need. Requiring a correspondingly varied response. For dancing and dining out, a fifty-six Continental would do quite nicely. For employment, an ancient clunker of a pickup would suffice. No, the antiquity of the vehicles would be no cause for alarm. Replacement parts would be a mere nuisance. Especially after he had located every junk and salvage yard in the county, and come to know the monikers of most of the resident grease monkeys.

An outsider would have been quite baffled as to the ownership of the vehicles. At their uncle's urging, the Palafox brothers had made the purchases. But both the pickup and the Continental were registered to Illinois Alvarez. The nephews performed standard maintenance. Their tío provided repairs and replacement parts. Noise also infrequently used one of the vehicles, but, when doing so, unfailingly asked their permission. To all concerned, this arrangement made eminent good sense.

His mechanical flair assured that Noise would not want for transport. Some evening after work, Miguel would drop by and begin grousing about the transmission on his green van. Or on his day off, Toño would show up and start wondering aloud why the brakes on his station wagon were making funny noises. All received the standard reply. "I can probably sniff out the problem, but you'll have to let me drive it for a few days. It's up to you."

Then the keys would be left with him, and he would execute a few errands as he did his test-drives. In the course of which, he would also identify the source of the problem and later make the indicated repairs. And then, because Miguel was practically his father, and too busy with rehabbing to adequately care for his vehicles, and because Toño's wife Victoria was practically his favorite cousin, and Toño was a consummate dunce when it came to car service, Noise would throw in a few freebies. Like an oil change and a tune-up. And later Miguel would comment to his wife, "It's amazing how my cuñado can just put his hand on an engine and like that, it's got more zip." All of which explained only partially why Miguel had just dropped an envelope onto Noise's plate as the latter was swallowing the last bite of his eighth egg roll. So Noise quite understandably asked, "What's this?"

"Open it. See what you think," suggested Miguel.

The envelope contained a legal form of some kind. Unfamiliar with such documents, Noise perused the front side, noticed his name next to the word "buyer," turned to the back side, and saw his name printed below a space marked for a signature. "Is this some kind of contract or what?" he asked.

"It's an offer to purchase," Miguel explained.

"Why does it have my name on it?"

"You're making the offer."

"How could that be? This is the first I've heard about it."

"What I mean is, if you agree to sign, then you're making an offer."

"Offer to purchase?" When Miguel nodded, Noise asked, "Purchase what?"

"A car service shop on the south side."

"A car service shop," Noise repeated.

"On the south side," Miguel repeated.

"It's a joke." Noise paused. "It's got to be a joke, but I don't get it."

"It's not a joke. There's a building for sale. It used to be a service center. Some of the equipment is still there. I know the owner. Un Tejano. Se apellida Estrada. He's in some financial trouble. That's why he wants to sell. The property is probably worth fifty. But he'll take thirty. If we give him a third up front in cash. That way he can liquidate his debt and give you a clear title."

Noise locked onto Miguel's gaze in what Hispanic children once called "jugando un serio." "Me estás vacilando," he accused, but his brother-in-law denied the charge. Noise shook his head. "You mean . . ." he started, then paused and shook his head some more. "This paper says that I am offering to purchase a property. For thirty thousand dollars. And ten of that will be paid up front in cash."

"That's exactly what it says."

"Miguel. This is a joke. Why are we discussing this?"

"Because the money is in the bank."

"Are you kidding? There isn't a bank anywhere that would loan me a Kleenex. Not if my nose was dripping on their floor."

"Maybe not. But if you hand them a paper saying that it's your money, they have to give it to you."

"Right. If I'm pointing a thirty-eight special at a bank teller."

Margarita intervened. "Ya, Miguel. Dile. ¿Qué estas esperando?"

"Okay. Okay. Here's the deal, cuñado. Fifteen years ago, you bought these two houses and the garden from me. Margarita and I decided to divide the money into three parts. We used one part to pay off my debt. We put one part into a retirement fund. The third part we put into a savings certificate for you." He paused and added, "So you'd have something to start with when you came back north. Are you following me?"

"Following, yes. Making sense of this, not really."

"Let me finish. What happened is that you got incredibly lucky. All that time you were chasing skirts en el sur, interest rates were going through the roof acá. And the rates stayed sky-high. Your money actually doubled twice while you were in Puebla."

"And that means what?"

"It means you have the money to buy that service shop. For cash. And still have a couple thousand to invest in equipment."

Noise objected that the money was not really his. Then he protested that, even if it were, he knew nothing about running a business. Finally, beaten down more by loquacity than logic, he consented to "at least check out the place."

So he and Miguel and Loco and the Palafox brothers drove to the south side to do precisely that. Almost in spite of himself, Noise was impressed. The location was about three blocks from a freeway exit, in a light industrial area, surrounded by an effusion of predominantly Hispanic neighborhoods. The building was about twenty feet by fifty-something. It had two service bays, adequate storage space, a small office, and a miniature parking lot for vehicles awaiting service.

"This might work," Noise admitted, "if the money really is in the bank."

"Trust me," Miguel reassured.

"I'd need a bookkeeper."

"Your sister will do it for three percent of the gross."

"I'd probably want a helper, too."

"Allí está," Miguel pointed toward Dante.

"You already asked him, didn't you?" Noise accused.

The grinning response was completely unabashed. "As a matter of fact, I did. And he said yes. The plan is for him to help part time at the start. Then if he likes it, you can teach him the trade."

Noise cast his brother-in-law a reproachful glare. "Do I get to say yes to this? Or is that already a given?"

"Actually there's one more egg to crack before we serve this omelet." Miguel cleared his throat. "When you say yes, I want it to be yes for five years."

Noise voiced his predictable objection. "You're saying that you expect me to agree to do this for the next five years?"

"I'm not asking for a guarantee. Just your best shot. But yes, for five years. Then if you want to call it quits, Dante and I should be able to buy you out."

Noise hemmed and hawed and harumphed for a good minute. Then, "That's your only condition?"

"That's it."

"And by when do I have to decide?"

"I'm a reasonable individual. Take a half hour if you need it." The grin exploded into a chuckle, and soon Noise was overcome by the contagious merriment. Then, "Actually I don't have to give Estrada an answer until late next week."

Eventually the group returned to Concha's house. Noise stayed only long enough to laud the cooks for the egg rolls. Then he excused himself and went home to shower. La Rubia arrived shortly after nine.

"How was gardening day?"

"Crazy. But fun." He told about the weeding. And the geography lesson. And the egg rolls.

"I don't want to nag," she reprised what was by now a familiar plaint, "but I would really like to meet these people. I remember Concha from that dance. And sometimes I say hi to the brothers who live downstairs and call you Tío. But there are at least another dozen

BOOK THREE, CHAPTER FOURTEEN

relatives you talk about that I don't know. And they all live right on this block."

"I promise, Hannah. That's all going to change this summer. When my father has been dead a year, the family will start celebrating things again."

On his good days, he was a bad liar. The truth was that he had consciously shielded her from his clan. From their openness. From their candor. From their disquieting habit of ingenuousness.

Picture it. Stage it. The smiles. The warmth. The handshakes. Maybe even an abrazo or two. Come and join us. We've heard so much about you. Come and be a part of the group. Some shared talk. Some shared food. All the time taking her measure. In more ways than one. Well. So. Time to go. Polite valedictions. Kissy farewells. Curtain. Mild applause. Then the carping would start. Her clothes were too ostentatious. Her vocabulary too pretentious. Her manner too haughty. Hosted. Toasted. Roasted. All in a day's work. But that was not the worst. The whole truth was that, before long, their perceptions and projections would begin to undermine his own. Insidiously, invidiously, the image that he held dear would be altered. At certain moments, he would see her with the eyes of the clan. Everything would change. She would mistake his reappraisal for rejection. Eventually she would be gone. Like all the others.

But what was he to do? For a long time she had resisted and was now resenting the imposed isolation. And then there was the small matter of Miguel's proposal. Five years in Milwaukee. As an entrepreneur. And of course, he would say yes. Because Miguel was asking. And because training Dante was one more way to repay Tía Pilar for fifteen years of caring. And because, what the hell, it would probably be fun. Especially if there was someone to share the adventure.

There he was. Full circle. Back to La Rubia. Turning away from the window, where he had been staring out at the early dark, he flashed her a devilish grin and said, "Come on. It's time you met my sister."

CHAPTER FIFTEEN

It was a day like any day. An unusually warm, late fall, early morning breeze, moving over the relatively cooler water of Lake Michigan, had cloaked the city in fog as far west as the Alvarez enclave and beyond. It was a day for blurring distinctions. A day for fuzzing perceptions. Anyone inclined to fudge the lines that defined his existence would have found this Thursday much to his liking.

Loco had bumbled through another early morning kitchen routine. Toast and coffee for Mai Lu. Pack her a lunch while she munched. A bleary farewell kiss as she went off to work. Juice and cereal for Juana. A dawdling daughter this day. Not at all her style. Commanding call up the stairs. Response: "Dad, there's no classes today. I told you that last night." Oh. Right. Of course. I knew that. That's why Miguel isn't expecting me at work.

So. Coffee. Heavy on the leisure. Knock on the kitchen door. Frances, what a nice surprise, come in. No, thanks. Victoria wants me to watch Alicia and Tony. Juana can come too. Good thought, but Juana is still . . . In one nimble nanosecond, his daughter was at his side. "Can I Dad?" Sure. Come for lunch. All of you. Give me a call when you get hungry.

Back to the java. Very heavy on the leisure. His mother exited the upstairs bath. Went directly to the basement. Started the laundry. Another ten minutes and she would be in the kitchen. With at least one query, and possibly an entire agenda. He grabbed his toast and coffee and hurried to the den. Carpe that diem.

He had written nothing since the previous Sunday night. And then, a mere handful of paragraphs. All more or less brave starts at what might evolve into a theatrical piece. Regarding what had lately become a nearly manic fascination. Borders. Borders in all their guises. Borders as perceived by Noise: a minor irritant to travelers. Borders as perceived by the Palafox brothers: occasions for affronts to their patria. Borders as boundaries. Borders as conjunctions. Borders as projections of collective phobias. Borders as schemes for the rational orchestration of essentially irrational forces. Borders as obsessions.

Sample one. *Property rights derive from the recognition and acceptance of a successful sometime theft. When a group, calling itself a tribe or a nation, perpetrates the successful theft, a border results. Presumably the thieving nation has been satisfied that the extent of the theft has been adequate. Presumably the victim nation consoles itself with the bromide that the larceny could have been worse. Anyway, what we have is a border. That's yours. This is mine.*

Sample two. *The question remains as to how the border will be construed. Will it be a barrier? Sternly separating. Coldly prohibiting. Or will it be a membrane? Mildly mediating. Moderately accommodating. (Continental Europe has exaggerated examples of each. The massively forbidding Berlin wall and the superpermeable boundaries of the European Union countries.)*

He read the two paragraphs aloud and editorialized, "Elliptical brains will ever engage in elliptical thought." But he was drawn to the images of wall and membrane. Evidently he had also found them to his liking on Sunday.

Sample three. *Historical evidence, from Hadrian's British construction to the more recent Siegfried Line, indicates that the wall is at best a short-term option. The nation's leaders explain to the people that the wall is there to protect them. The people reasonably conclude that if they need to be shielded, then something is out there. Something big. Something bad. In time it becomes very big and very bad. The people are left to imagine just how bad. So they do. They fantasize about what is out there. Soon what is out there begins to grow. It becomes the cause of earthquakes, crop failures, and things that go bump in the night. But this state of alert cannot be maintained. In the long run, people will become fatalistic. The day will come when a leader will stand and shout, "Remember the wall. Remember that we built the wall to protect you." But the people will shrug and turn away with a, "Who cares?"*

The next two pages of his notebook were filled with scrawled numbers and skewed triangles. Frances frequently came by for assistance with her geometry homework. She had been assigned to a class section whose teacher took the cavalier stance that, "Some people just can't get geometry. Especially girls. Do the best you can. If you work hard, you'll get a passing grade." The "some people" might have generated a grudging resignation. But the "especially girls" produced a fierce determination. Loco questioned the teacher's motivational technique, but he agreed to tutor. With only moderate success. There were nights when he found himself uttering a silent, "Holy Pythagoras, give me patience."

He made a face at the triangles and paged ahead to the following paragraph.

Sample four. *The membrane model is friendlier but freighted with complexities. One has to do with the twin towns that are typical of borders. Clearly the people of these municipalities will want access to employment, commerce, and social events in the other town. Of course this access will be confined. A more bothersome complexity has to do with the access of people residing farther inland. This access will be distinctly defined and encompass greater restrictions. In both cases, the limitation of access will depend on political winds, which are always variable and often vicious. Policy may ebb and flow with the whims of demagogues.*

He reacted to the paragraph with a disparaging scowl. There was nothing wrong with it. Except that it missed the mark by a mile. Here was the beast. Here was the monster. Here in his grasp. Here was opportunity. To rend and tear until he had reached its very innards and eviscerated the brute. Instead he was proceeding as if his intent was to tickle it to death. He was serenely portraying the folly of past and present, when what was called for was an assault on the future, including proposals for a true continental congress and North American citizenship.

He read on. The paragraph that followed was more to the point.

Sample five. *In the case of North America, the border between the plentitudinous nation to the north and the multitudinous nation to the south is an especially contentious issue. It features a free flow of tourists north to south, and a prohibited but stubbornly persistent flow of job-seekers south to north. The Palafox brothers and many others from the south view this arrangement as illogical and unfair. To them, it constitutes a denial of reciprocity. And any such denial is a heavy-handed reminder as to which of the two nations was the successful thief. Given that scenario, a smoldering resentment is not only likely. It is to be expected.*

There now. That had some bite to it. Or at least a bit of bark. But reading on, he soon noted that he had abandoned the personal and retreated into the gloom of economics.

Sample six. *Lately there is much talk about a continental free-trade zone. But here, too, the people of the southern nation feel that their interests are being ignored. The model most often proposed for the trade zone includes uninhibited movement of goods and services.*

BOOK THREE, CHAPTER FIFTEEN

It includes uninhibited movement of capital. It includes the uninhibited movement of all the services ancillary to the application of capital to production. But then it excludes the uninhibited movement of labor. Simply stated, at the caprice of the holders and investors of capital, the jobs can migrate to the workers, but the workers cannot migrate to the jobs. This is a market economy? Adam Smith would have scorned such a proposal.

Loco shook his head. The paragraph made a good point. But much too abstractly. Hunger was not abstract. He got up and began to pace. North to south to north. Everything he had written was on background. To focus the picture, he needed some people. And a confrontation. Something dramatic. Something to concentrate the tensions that constituted an actual rather than a theoretical border. He paused. Maybe some music. Occasionally Vivaldi helped. He put on a recording of Le Quattro Stagioni. Back at his desk, he hummed along. His writing did not.

Minutes passed. The strings and woodwinds darted to and fro. Assuaging the axons. Distracting the dendrites. Soothing the synapses. Plucking the stresses from his brain. He eased back into the chair, slipped his feet from his sandals, closed his eyes. Soon he was heeding his breathing. In, two, three, four. Out, two, three, four. Space faded. Time ceased. A gentle mist settled over the scene. And ever so slowly, a figure emerged from the haze. Then a second figure. The first a small fearful youth. Indocumentado. In the very maw of the migra. Undergoing interrogation. The second a tall, brawny inquisitor. Asking over and over, "Why do you return to where you are not wanted?" And the encroacher responding, "Because we are hungry."

It was a negligible nugget, but he had often started with less. He locked the characters into freeze-frame and began an analysis. Each would have a personal and a national history. Which would blind him to the motivation of the other. The inquisitor would stand ramrod straight with the force of the law in his spine. The encroacher would sit slouched in defeat but still convinced that the law of hunger should be preemptive. Drama would ensue if each could be prevailed upon to convincingly stumble toward a recognition of the other's humanity. An aching task. The interrogation room would be too cramped to allow for much action. Dialog would have to carry the burden.

He grabbed a pen and began to scribble. Character quirks. Random stage directions. Dashes of dialog. Then further reflection. And again to the scribbles. By lunchtime, the floor of the den had been resurfaced with a sprawl of notes and notions.

Shortly after noon came a call from Frances. By then he was not only talking to himself; he was actually arguing aloud. This was obsession. The arrival of the children brought genuine relief.

While Frances served the juice and warmed the tortillas, Loco reheated rice and beans left over from the previous day's dinner. On each of four plates, he served a small mound of rice topped by a sunny-side up egg. On three of the plates, he added a dollop of frijoles planchados, exempting that of Alicia who was a nonbeaner.

He had intended to return to his den but decided instead to join the lunch group. Juana had been watching a program about Australia the night before and wanted to know more about marsupials. Tony nearly rolled off his chair when Loco introduced the word "wombat."

Then it was time for a kitchen cleanup. Bringing on a dispute as to the division of labor. Amid the bickering, Frances let out a scream. Everyone followed her gaze to the doorway. Entering was her brother Eddie, wearing a very sallow countenance and an extremely bloody jacket. Behind him, with a face almost as ashen, was his Aunt Marta.

BOOK THREE, CHAPTER FIFTEEN

Marta's day had begun typically enough. Following the mandatory "Buenos dias" at the breakfast table, Mamá Margarita and Papá Miguel typically had ignored her as she drank her usual glass of boring grapefruit juice and ate her usual two pieces of boring rye toast with her usual cup of boring instant coffee.

Her parents were discussing Daniel Palafox. Who was now working part time with the rehabbers. Several days earlier, the young man had neglected to gather all his tools before leaving the work site. A circular saw had been left behind, and that night it had been stolen.

"I told him," her father was saying, "when you're collecting the tools, you have to check every room. Not just the last room where you were working."

"He's just starting, Miguel," her mother defended the culprit. "He's still learning."

"I just hope we don't run out of tools while he learns," her father countered, giving his wife a violent wink.

Marta cringed. Not at her father's attempt at humor. But at the sheer predictability of the whole scene. It was by now so routine. So ordinary. So common. This was what passed for conversation in her house. She heard it every day. But on days like this, it tested the very limits of her tolerance.

It was so dull. It was all so hopelessly dull. Didn't they hear themselves? Didn't they realize how tedious their lives had become? There was this huge world out there. Everything was changing. There was a revolution going on. The industrial age was giving way to the information age. Computers were everywhere. Everybody was talking about the future. You heard words like cyberspace and superchips and worldwide electronic networking. It was a wave. It was irresistible. The future was here. The future was now. And how did her parents react to all this? They were sitting at the breakfast table discussing circular saws.

She gave each of her irrelevant darlings the customary peck on the cheek and went off to work. But the mood persisted. Even at her desk in the human resources department of a major insurance provider, she continued the verbal flagellation of her benighted clan.

They were all irrelevant when you thought about it. Well, maybe not all. Her brother was heavily into the stock market and slowly accumulating a fortune. At least that was forward-looking. And Isabel's oldest son, Nico, seemed determined to pursue a career in journalism. That at least was exciting, if not exactly new-wave.

But then there were people like Concha. A middle-aged metiche. A first-class, menopausal meddler. She knew what everybody was doing. She knew what everybody was supposed to be doing. She had all the answers. And she was not at all shy about giving advice. Everybody in the family except Marta seemed to be convinced that she was some kind of female Solomon.

What a crapulous crock! Who gave this witch the idea that she was some kind of estrogenized Einstein? Look at the job the woman had. This model of all earthly wisdom was not an advisor to heads of state nor a consultant to multinational corporations. No. She was a cook. She earned her daily bread by seasoning ground beef. And chopping tomatoes and lettuce. And shredding cheese. And stuffing taco shells. And then feeding a gang of Milwaukee's grossest mocosos. Oh sure, she had a fancy title. Coordinator or manager or something. But when you cut away the crap, she was just a cook.

Marta paused to savor the dregs of her spite. Her family. What a pack of irrelevants. She could care less what they did. They could ignore her. They could marginalize her. They could even snub her. This was her payback. Right here. Sitting in her cushy chair at her cushy desk doing her cushy job for a cushy paycheck. If they were so inclined, they could kiss her decorous derriere. In the meantime, she would continue to spill her caustic vituperations.

BOOK THREE, CHAPTER FIFTEEN

Who else deserved a little special attention? What about Concha's genius of a son, Loco. Now there was a real forward-looking, get-ahead guy. His idea of a hard day was to get up about ten, poke his nose into a book for two or three hours, and then enjoy a leisurely lunch. In the afternoon, he would marinate a few artichokes and spend the rest of his day thinking environmentally pure thoughts. But cut him some slack. At least he had some education and lived in a little larger world than his mother. But he was so out of it. He was supposed to be a writer. But he worked like some kind of monk from the Middle Ages. He didn't have a word processor. He didn't own a computer. No. He wrote with a pen. With a pen! The third millenium of the Christian era was about to commence, and this guy was still writing with a pen. Give me a break.

The supervisor walked by, and Marta shuffled some papers to indicate that she was busy. She had a report to submit by eleven. But she had already gathered all the data. What remained was to structure the information, and her spreadsheet would do most of that task. There was no point in finishing early. That would only result in an additional assignment. Besides, she had not released this much venom in months, and it felt exhilarating. Poor Marta, they all lamented. Well, screw them. Poor Marta was doing just fine. She squirmed her butt into an even more precise accommodation with her cushy chair.

Victoria. Now there was a deliciously easy target. There was no need to look beyond her clothes. Unless you were looking for some justification. Sure, the kids were in a private school. And yes, she and Toño were each paying for a car. And her nurse practitioner training was expensive. But come on. She had a job. Her husband not only had a job. He had money to play the stock market. And the woman dressed . . . no, you could not say dressed. The woman appeared in public looking like a dowdy, nineteenth-century country-school mistress. And that wasn't even the worst. The woman . . . no let's tell it like it is . . . the sinvergüenza shopped at secondhand stores. You had to blush just thinking about it. Her sister-in-law bought and wore clothes that somebody else had worn and discarded. Where was her head? Didn't she think that people noticed such things? Was she blind or stupid or both?

She checked the clock. Time to start on that report. For the next two hours, she juggled numbers into the requisite semblance of order. Next she spent a quarter hour in the restroom messing with her hair. Back at her desk, she reread the report. The numbers held little significance for her, nor did she know their use within the company. Maybe they had no use. She could care less. She made a phone call, fussed with some papers, and watched the clock. Finally it was eleven-thirty. Her hope was that the supervisor would note the proximity to noon and not assign her to a new project until after lunch. "Competence blended with deference," Marta reminded herself as she approached the supervisor's work station. Then, "I'm really sorry this is late, Mrs. Phelps," she gushed her rehearsed apology. "I had a problem with the data. There appears to be an anomaly in the numbers for the third quarter of last year. But maybe not. It might be within the standard deviation. You know more about that than I do."

Mrs. Phelps scanned the report and reacted as predicted. "Very nice work, Marta." She checked her watch. "Take an extra fifteen minutes for lunch." Smiles all around. Exit.

For lunch, Marta had agreed to meet a friend at a restaurant just south of Lincoln. She started for the freeway, reconsidered, and maneuvered the Buick onto the Sixth Street viaduct. At Lapham she stopped for a red light. A young man crossed in front. Running. Supporting one arm with the other, as if he had injured it. He bore a disturbing resemblance to . . . no . . . he was in fact her nephew Eddie. She watched as he headed north and darted into an alley. All very suspicious.

When she had assured herself that no one was following him, she turned left onto Lapham. Two more lefts brought her into the alley that he had entered. There he was, leaning against a garage. She pulled up next to him, looked at the arm, and nearly fainted. The entire right sleeve of his jacket was stained with blood.

"My god, Eddie! What happened? Get in. Let me take you to the hospital."

"No hospital," he hissed through gritted teeth.

"Okay. Okay. What happened?"

"I hurt my arm," he answered with exaggerated calm. "I just hurt my arm. I'm okay." He nearly choked on the word okay.

"Were you fighting?"

"Tía," he pleaded, "stop with the questions. I just need to . . ."

"Get in," she ordered. "Don't argue with me, Eddie. Just get in the damn car."

Reluctantly he obeyed.

"Now. We are going to an emergency room. Help me think. Thirteenth and State is the closest, right?"

"No hospital, Tía. Help me. But no hospital. Please."

"Eddie, don't be dumb. You need a doctor to check that arm. Now be quiet and let me concentrate."

"No hospital. I can't go. If you try to take me there, I'll jump out of the car."

"Eddie, what is wrong with you? You are bleeding. You need a doctor."

"Isn't Tía Victoria at home? She can look at my arm. Just take me home. I'll be okay."

Meanwhile, Marta was recrossing the viaduct with every intent of transporting him to an emergency room. When she got to State Street, she pulled into the left-turn lane.

"Not here!" he yelled. "Not here! If you turn here, I know you're going to the hospital. If you do that, I'll jump out."

He already had his hand on the door release. One glance at his face convinced her that he meant every word. She pulled back into the northbound traffic and went on to Walnut. There she turned left.

"I don't know if Victoria is home, Eddie. Even if she is, I'm sure she'll take you to the doctor."

"No, she won't! I mean she can't! I can't go to the doctor." He was near hysteria.

"Okay. Fine. Just tell me what happened."

"I got hurt. That's all. It's not that bad. Victoria can take care of me."

In a few more minutes, they were parked in front of Victoria's house. As Marta had anticipated and warned, there was no one home. Slowly she returned to the car and eyeballed her nephew. "Orale, Eddie. Ya basta con las chingaderas. Ahorita me vas a decir lo que te pasó o te voy a arrimar unos cuantos encima de lo que traes."

It was the voice of command, in the language of command, and he responded predictably. "Okay, Tía. Te voy a decir." He took a deep breath and said, "I got shot."

"Shot!" she almost jumped off the planet. "Who shot you? Why?"

"Some guy. I don't know why," he whined. "Now do you get it? That's why I can't go to the hospital."

"Okay. I get it. But where then?"

"Mejor llévame con mi Tía Concha."

Concha had just come up from the basement with a basket full of socks, which the children were going to sort and pair. She fixed first Eddie and then Marta with a steely stare. She sighed. So much for getting the jump on the weekend laundry.

"Tía Concha . . . " Eddie began.

"Sit down, Eddie. And be quiet for a second." She shifted her gaze to her granddaughter. "Juana, you and Alicia and Tony go to your Tía Margarita's house. Dile a tu Tía que necesito una rama de tenme acá." Juana started to respond, but Concha placed her index finger over her lips. There would be no discussion. As the little ones moved toward the door, she added, "Frances, see that they get there. Then go to Victoria's house and bring me a first-aid kit. Mine is at work."

"What . . . what should I do?" Marta stammered.

"You know the clinic where Victoria works. Go there. Talk to her. Personally. Don't leave a message. Tell her four things. Her kids are fine. Eddie is hurt. She should try to leave early. Come to Concha's house."

Marta repeated the instructions.

"The important thing is the first," Concha emphasized. "Be sure that the first thing she hears is that her kids are okay. If she knows that, then she'll be able to think and form a plan. So be sure to mention the kids right away."

"I could go to the clinic," Loco volunteered.

"No, I need you here. Find me a scissors."

"Should I come back?" Marta asked.

"If Victoria is coming, then you go back to work. Don't talk to anybody about this. Act like nothing happened."

Marta left.

Concha instructed Eddie to place the injured arm on the kitchen table. Then with the scissors, she cut away the sleeve of his jacket, exposing the wound.

"Warm water, washcloths, hand towels," she instructed Loco. As he went to collect the items, she peered closely at the crease in Eddie's arm. "This was made by a bullet, Eddie."

"I guess so," he answered.

"No, you know so," she corrected firmly.

"Am I going to be all right?" he asked.

"Good as new. But not for a few days." She smiled reassuringly, nearly as relieved as he that the wound was only superficial.

"So it's not that bad."

"It's okay to be scared. It looks like lots of blood. But it was almost a miss. We'll get the bleeding stopped. Then you'll have to take it easy for a while. Do you remember the last time you had a tetanus shot?"

"Last summer. Remember? I cut myself when I was helping Papá Miguel with some drywall."

Concha did a preliminary cleaning, then applied gentle pressure with a towel wrap to absorb the last of the blood loss. Frances returned. Concha winked her into a chair directly across from Eddie.

"We need to know what happened, Eddie. You have a right to your privacy. But this is family business now. Can you understand that a little?"

He nodded.

"Okay then. Where were you? What were you doing there? How did this happen? And if you think you know why, tell us that too."

Eddie stared at the table and began. "I went to Felipe's house."

"And Felipe is?"

"Felipe is my friend. I mean . . . yeah, he's my friend." He nodded at Frances. "Does she have to be here?"

"I want all of us to hear this. Then, if there's an investigation, the four of us will all be telling the same story. Does that make sense?"

Eddie shrugged and repeated, "I went to Felipe's house. But he wasn't there. I rang the doorbell twice. After the second time, I waited, and then I started to leave. A car came down the street with

BOOK THREE, CHAPTER FIFTEEN

two guys inside. The guy in the passenger seat had a gun. He shot twice and they took off. I guess the second bullet hit me."

"They didn't say anything?" Loco asked.

"They yelled some stuff."

"Like what?"

"Maricón. Punk. Take that, Rico."

"Rico?"

"Yeah. They must have thought I was somebody else."

"Do you know somebody named Rico?"

"Nope."

"Do you know the guys in the car?"

"Nope."

"How do you know this Felipe?" Concha asked.

"He went to my school last year."

"And now?"

"Nowhere. As far as I know."

"And you went to his house at lunchtime?"

"Yeah, about lunchtime."

"Why did you want to talk to Felipe?"

"No special reason. Just to talk."

"Okay. What happened after you got shot?"

"I ran. Aunt Marta saw me. She picked me up. She brought me here."

There were queries aplenty but little else was learned. Eddie was a font of quibbles and evasions. But he was consistent. That would be useful, in the event that detectives started sniffing around.

Victoria arrived. It was not difficult to discern that the crisis had passed. She asked a few questions. Then, "Me lo voy a llevar a mi casa. Allí tengo todo. Vamos Eddie." And an afterthought, "Tú Frances, ven a ayudarme."

When they had gone, Concha turned to her son. "Now you tell

me what really happened."

"Who knows?"

"Was he telling any of the truth?"

"I don't think he was trying to deceive us. But he wasn't telling everything, either."

"Exactly my impression. He's hiding something."

"This Felipe character. Sounds like a gangbanger to me. Why else does somebody get shot in front of his house?"

"Or he's selling drugs. That's just as scary."

Both became pensive for a minute. Concha suspected that her son was also being less than forthright. She decided to test that hypothesis.

"Eddie is . . . different, isn't he?"

"How do you mean?" he answered blandly.

"You know. People talk about sexual orientation. That's the way I mean different."

"What you're trying not to ask is if he's gay. And the answer is yes. He's gay."

"Exactly," she answered in a voice bathed in forbearance. "But what I want to know is if he's practicing."

"You mean is he a practicing gay, the same way people talk about someone being a practicing Catholic."

There. She had him. "Are we discussing this seriously, or are you demonstrating how witty you can be?"

"I'm sorry. I will forego the wit. What you're really asking is: Do I think he has been practicing with Felipe?"

"The thought occurred to me."

"Suppose he has. So what?"

"You approve of such behavior?"

"What's to approve? That's for Eddie to decide."

"But you don't disapprove."

"Look. Let's say there's a person born deaf. He can't learn to speak, so he learns sign language. Is it my place to approve or disapprove of his using sign language?"

"What does that have to do with being gay?"

"To me it's the same thing. If you're born different, you have to learn to deal with that."

"It isn't the same thing at all. We all have to communicate. So the deaf person has to use sign language. But if you're born gay, you don't have to practice."

"Maybe you do. Maybe the need is even stronger than the need to communicate verbally. Or maybe it's the same need. Or a different aspect of the same need."

There it was. He was doing it again. He had this horrible, annoying habit. Right in the middle of an ordinary conversation, he would stop talking to her and start a discussion with himself inside his head. But aloud. A stupid soliloquy. Which she supposedly should consider herself privileged to observe. At times he nearly drove her to rage. Well, not today. Today she would learn what he really thought. She still had a trick or two in her bag.

"It just isn't natural," she pronounced.

Almost immediately, he ceased his rambling monologue and favored her with a twinkling eye and slightly raised eyebrow that seemed to say: I'm not sure what you're doing, but it's cute. "Explain natural," he said.

"Natural. Male and female. That's the way reproduction is done. And if there's no more reproduction, that's the end of us humans."

"I don't disagree with any of that. But what's your point?"

"Gay is not natural."

"Why not?"

"Sex is for reproduction. Gay is not for reproduction. So it's not natural."

"I'm confused. Not everybody is gay."

"That's my point. If everybody was, that would be the end of us."

She watched him raise both hands, place them over his ears, then slowly move them down the sides of his face until they met in a prayerful intertwining below his jaw. It was what his wife had named his "patience overload response." The next words out of his mouth would be, "Wait a mite."

"Wait a mite," he agonized. "Not everyone is gay. There are plenty of people to reproduce and maintain the gene pool. Besides, just because something isn't standard doesn't mean that it isn't natural. Whatever natural is."

That was another of his annoying little quirks. He would sometimes pretend that he didn't know the meaning of a perfectly ordinary word. Like natural.

"Natural is what happens spontaneously," she lectured. "If you want to understand natural, just look at the animals."

"You think animal behavior is natural?" he asked in a tone which promised that you were about to be skewered.

"Of course," she answered a little too loudly.

"Even when it comes to sex?"

"Sure. Why not?"

"Okay. Animals mate during a season. When they finish, that's the end of sex. Until the next mating season. Is that natural?"

"Sure. For them."

"So why do humans continue to mate, even after the female has conceived, or even when it is certain that she cannot possibly conceive?"

"Because that's natural for people. They have a need to bond, even when they aren't reproducing."

"They need to bond."

"Exactly."

"And people who are attracted to others of the same sex. They would feel this same need, wouldn't they?"

"I suppose they would," she admitted.

"So maybe if they decide to practice that kind of bonding, we should just stay out of the way."

She had one more trump. "But Eddie is still legally a minor."

He scratched his head. "That's the sticky part of this, isn't it?"

"Somebody has to talk to him."

"About being gay?"

"About all of this. We should at least try to get him to stop seeing this Felipe. That boy is obviously dangerous."

"Maybe that bullet will send him a message."

"That's probably right. But talk to him. Maybe you can help him sort this out. Anyway, he needs to know that his family is there for him."

"What about his mom?"

Concha looked pained. "I'm trying not to think about that."

"She'll be home from work in a few hours. It's either you or Victoria."

Concha covered her eyes with one hand. "I can't dump that on Victoria. But Madre Santa! I wish there was somebody else. The woman will go crazy with guilt."

"Just tell her straight out, and then close your ears and let her whine."

"That's easy for you to say. You won't be listening to the litany. About how the kids were too close together. And that was all her fault. And she didn't have money for diapers. And that was all her fault. And her breast milk was no good. And that was really her fault. And now her son is gay. And guess whose fault this will be!"

Again they were pensive for a minute. Then Concha asked, "Did it seem like Frances was awfully quiet while Eddie was telling his story?"

"A little."

"No. A lot. She always has plenty to say. But today it was like . . . like she already knew the whole story."

Loco shrugged.

Concha nodded to herself. "She knows something." She paused but continued to nod. Then, "So. You go get the kids. They're probably driving Margarita crazy. I'm going to wash another load or two. But before Isabel gets home, I'm going to have a little talk with Miss Frances."

Frances was also eager to have a little talk. But with her brother. While his wound was being sanitized and bandaged, she had impatiently assisted and gnawed at her lip. But now, with Eddie resting on the sofa in Uncle Toño's den, and Victoria back in the kitchen starting dinner, she lashed out in a husky whisper, "You think you're slick, don't you?"

"What did I do?" he grumbled defensively.

She shook her head in disbelief. "My own brother. A total jerk!"

"What are you talking about?" he whined.

"And innocent!" She raked him from top to bottom with a scathing glare. "Oh yes. Poor Eddie. He's hurt. Quick. Drop everything. Run to help. What can we do for poor Eddie?"

This time he did not protest.

"You think you can get away with this?"

"What?"

"Eddie. Everybody is trying to help. The least you can do is be honest."

"I didn't lie," he defended himself.

"You let everybody believe that you've been going to school."

"I didn't say I was going to school. They didn't ask me that."

BOOK THREE, CHAPTER FIFTEEN

"They had to ask you?"

For a few seconds he showed some spunk. "Why should I get myself in more trouble, if nobody asks?"

"Okay, I'm asking. When did you stop going to school, Eddie?"

The spunk quickly disintegrated. "I only went a couple of weeks in September."

"Why?"

"Lots of reasons. They were calling me stuff. You know. Names. Fag. Maricón. It started last spring. But not so bad. I finished the year. But when we went back to school in the fall, it got a lot worse. That's when I stopped going."

"And started hanging out at Felipe's?"

He nodded.

"Why?"

"I had to go somewhere. I couldn't go home."

"So you go to Felipe? Get real! The guy is a gang-banger, Eddie. The only thing you could expect to get from him was trouble."

"He was nice to me. I thought he could protect me."

She shook her head in disbelief and disappointment. "Why didn't you try to talk to somebody in the family?"

"I tried with Nico. He told me he was ashamed of me."

"Nico is a teenager just like you. I'm talking about somebody older."

"Like who? Loco?"

"Why not?"

"The only thing he knows about is books."

"You never gave him a chance. At least he could have helped you talk to Mom. Or did you want her to find out about it on the ten o'clock news?"

Eddie winced. And not from the pain in his arm. Good. She would have his undivided attention now. "So. What's the plan from here on?"

He shook his head. "Can you help me, Frances?"

"Not if you're going to play games."

"Okay. No more games. I'll be honest. I mean I'll try."

"The first thing is no more Felipe."

Eddie snorted. "You think I want to go back there after what happened today?"

"Don't jive me around, Eddie. A dog will go back to where it puked."

He reassumed the docile mode. "Okay. I promise. No more Felipe."

"Would he look for you here?"

"I told him I lived in Bay View."

For a few seconds she regarded him with undisguised approval. "So. You were hedging your bet right from day one. There's hope for you yet, my brother."

"I won't go back to school," he challenged.

She was thoughtful for several moments.

"I won't go back," he repeated.

"I heard you the first time. Be quiet for a second." She got up and paced the room. Then, "Last summer you worked with Papá Miguel. Did you like that?"

"It was okay. I'd rather do outdoor construction. But rehabbing is fun too."

"So. Why can't you go to work for him again?"

"He won't let me till I finish high school."

"Do you know what a GED is?"

"Sure. It's like a . . . oh, I get it. I could drop out and study for the equivalency diploma."

Frances was unrelenting. "You could drop out! Like somehow this is new! But yeah, that would be a plan. And Uncle Loco who doesn't know about anything but books could help you."

"Maybe he would. I could ask him."

Again she waxed incredulous. "Eddie Alvarez, you are some kind of dumb. Even for a bilingual you are dense. Don't you get it? We are your family. We want to help. We want you to do well."

He was not listening. "You know what? This might just work. If we could get Mom to go along."

"Let me worry about Mom. But you have to talk to Uncle Loco. And take him along when you go to talk to Papá Miguel."

There were some minor adjustments and additions to the plan. Then Frances went to volunteer her services in the kitchen. Victoria sent her to get the children. Which led to a little strategic planning with Loco and his mother. And so it came to pass that when Isabel arrived that evening, she encountered her daughter and cousin Concha at her kitchen table, casually sharing a pot of coffee.

When Frances asked, "How was your day?" Isabel began to suspect that all was not well. She searched their faces for a clue and found dedicated unconcern. Something terrible had happened.

"Eddie's in jail," she guessed.

"No, he's not," said Frances, "but he is at Victoria's house."

"Why?"

"He's fine," Concha answered. "But he did have a little accident. Victoria wants to keep him at her house tonight. In case he has trouble sleeping."

"I better get over there." Isabel started for the door.

"He's fine, Mom. He's resting. Probably even sleeping by now," Frances consoled. As her mother hesitated, she added, "Anyway, we need to talk. Before you barge in on him."

"Why?"

"Some stuff has been happening. Around Eddie's school. You probably know that there are gangs around there."

"¡Dios mio! You mean he's in a gang?"

"No, but those people do crazy stuff. And today Eddie just happened to be in the wrong place at the wrong time. He got shot."

"¡Madre Santa!"

"He's okay, Mom. Really he is. The bullet just nicked his arm. It's like a deep scratch. He just needs to rest."

"I checked it myself," Concha added. "There was some bleeding. That scared him. But it isn't anything serious."

Isabel sat down and said, "Nico. He's okay?"

"He wasn't there," Frances reassured. "He's upstairs studying."

"Were the police there?"

"No. Eddie came home with Aunt Marta. I guess she just happened to be in the area."

"So he won't have a record?"

"Mom! Why would he have a record? Eddie wasn't doing anything bad. Somebody shot him. That's all."

"But why would anybody want to shoot Eddie?"

"We don't think anybody wanted to shoot him. Those people are crazy. They just start shooting. He happened to be in the wrong place."

"So it was a gang thing. And Eddie got caught in the middle." Isabel clearly wanted to believe.

"That's what we think," Frances rushed to confirm. She paused to permit a transition. "But there is one problem. Eddie doesn't want to go back."

"Who would? We'll have to find a different school for him."

"No, Mom. What I mean is, he doesn't want to go back to any school."

There was an intense hiatus in the talk. Frances felt her mother's stare. She concentrated her own gaze on a stain in the table cloth. It was an irregular spot. Not a circle. Nor a triangle. Nor a square.

BOOK THREE, CHAPTER FIFTEEN

Even geometry might not have a formula to calculate such an area.

After a while Isabel began nodding, as if in agreement with some inner voice. "It's the sissy thing again, ain't it?"

No one responded.

"I knew this would happen. I was hoping it wouldn't get out of hand before he finished high school. Poor Eddie. It's my fault really. He needed a man to look up to. I should have found some way to give him a father. But it never worked out. The same thing kept happening over and over. I'd make a nice start with a guy. Then I'd bring him home. He'd notice the three children, and I'd never see him again." She reflected for a moment. "I never could find a way around that. You can't hide three kids."

"Mom!" Frances pronounced the monosyllable with a triple vowel sound between muted consonants. "That doesn't make any sense. If that's the way it happened, then how do you explain Nico? With his hormone overload and his superstud complex."

"Don't you see? Nico was the first. He was the only one. So he probably got enough attention. When Eddie came along, it was too much for me. I was exhausted. And depressed. I didn't give him the same attention. I probably even neglected him."

"I don't believe that. Maybe Nico did get some extra attention. That doesn't explain the difference between him and Eddie. No way. Nico is who he was always going to be. And Eddie is who he was always going to be. And nothing you did could have changed that."

Isabel heeded not. "When Eddie was small, maybe about four or five, he'd dress up in my clothes. Like little girls do. He'd come and show me how nice he looked. I never knew how to react. Part of me wanted to warn him that he was doing something weird. But another part of me wanted to hug him and tell him it was okay. Usually I didn't decide. I just stared at him. Like he was somebody I didn't recognize. Then he'd look hurt and go away."

Frances was tethered out. "Mother. Come back, Mother. This is not about you. This is about Eddie. We need to agree on a plan."

Concha intervened. She talked about how busy Miguel was. How he needed to hire another full-time rehabber. How Eddie could be that person. How her own son could help Eddie with studies for the equivalency diploma. Finally, Isabel grasped that her daughter and her cousin were there for more than commiseration.

"Somebody will have to discuss this with Eddie," Isabel cautioned.

Frances and Concha exchanged a smug glance, and the latter answered, "We thought that would be your job."

It was Isabel's turn to preen. "Have you talked to Miguel?"

"We think Eddie should do that," Frances answered. "You know. Sort of man-to-man. It might help him feel a little better about himself."

The plan was expanded, clarified, reviewed, and pronounced satisfactory. Isabel went forth to recommend the scheme to her son. Concha went along to nudge and prod as needed. Frances emptied the coffee from her cup and served herself some grape juice. Then she climbed the stairs to her room, stretched out on her bed, and rewarded herself with a huge cerebral hug.

Luck. Undiluted luck. But then, maybe luck was just the residue of effort, as some folks believed. The gods could testify that she had done her Sisyphean best to wrest something positive from this potential fiasco. And Eddie out of the closet would be a relief. For everyone. Even Eddie. At least in the long run. In the short run, it would probably be puro infierno. Thanks in part to that pendejo, Nico. Eddie's big brother. Eddie's big hero. And now Nico was ashamed of him. Which to Eddie meant that everybody in the family was ashamed of him. It would take time to dispel that demon. But for the moment, she was content. She had schemed. She had enlisted the cooperation of the family heavyweights. She had done her part.

Now she wanted some rest. Let someone else push the rock for a while.

As it turned out, someone did. The very next morning, Eddie was forced to confront his formidable Aunt Victoria.

Victoria had the healing touch. She was blessed with an abundance of contagious vitality. She possessed the competence that inspires confidence in the patient. She carried herself with a minimum of pretense, thereby easing communication between care receiver and caregiver.

Eddie experienced the full force of her efficacy on the morning following his mishap.

"Buenos días. ¿Cómo está el paciente?"

"Buenos días," he answered. "I'm sorry you had to miss work because of me, Tía."

"Don't give yourself illusions," she corrected. "I wasn't scheduled today." Then, "I need to change that bandage. ¿Dormiste un poco?"

"Un poco. I was restless. I kept moving around and bumping the arm." Then, after a considerable silence, "Don't you want to know what happened?"

"I know what happened. Somebody shot you."

"I mean what really happened."

"If you want to tell me." She recalled her own adolescence. Misadventure always produced an urge to confess. Even when the confession bore only the most tenuous causal connection to the mishap. As apparently it did in this instance.

"I'm gay," he announced and attempted a dramatic pause.

Victoria met his gaze with transparent insouciance. "And?"

"You're not shocked?"

"You said that to shock me?"

"No . . . I mean . . . I don't know what . . ."

She interrupted. "I want you to understand me, Eddie. I don't pretend to know what that feels like for you. If you want to tell me, fine. But don't tell me just to shock me."

"I'm sorry, Tía. It's hard." Eddie rattled off a version of the previous day's events.

"I don't believe you started this conversation just to tell me a lot of facts, Eddie."

"No entiendo, Tía."

"Tell me about the feelings. Everything you said makes it seem like you are defending yourself. Como que alguien te está acusando. So I know you are angry. Yo entiendo eso. We all feel angry when people attack us."

"I don't want to be angry, Tía."

"Comprendo. But you don't stop the feelings by saying you don't want them. Who are you angry at?"

"Everybody."

"That's too many. Give me a name."

"Nico."

"That's better. Why Nico?"

"He's so . . . so . . ."

"Macho," Victoria guessed correctly. "I know. He's big. And strong. And he has all the sensitivity of a tostada."

Eddie laughed.

"At your age it's natural to be envious of other people. But open your eyes, Eddie. Nico is a big strong guy. But really, your brother scores zero for sensitivity."

"Who wants to be sensitive?" Eddie whined.

"You're right. Not teenage males. But someday that will be important. And then, who knows. Maybe Nico will be envious of you."

He maintained his skeptical air until she challenged. "Okay.

Another name. Who else makes you angry?"

"Frances. She's always in my business."

"Maybe she cares about you."

"She acts like she's my mother."

"No she doesn't. She tries to protect you from your mother."

"That's what I mean. It's like having two mothers."

Victoria laughed. "So you're angry at both your mothers."

"They blame me for being gay," he accused.

"No es cierto. Frances never blames anybody. And your mother blames herself for everything."

Unable to sustain the specific accusations, he retreated to the generic. "They all pretend that my being gay doesn't bother them. But they're all faking it. Nobody has accepted me the way I am."

"Maybe not even you." She watched him struggle with that possibility.

Then he reacted with an adolescent pout. "I never asked to be born."

"Do you know somebody who did ask to be born?" She was sorry to flatten his balloon so brusquely, but he could not be allowed to pass off such trivialities as real thought.

When he attempted a, "No, but . . . " she began to lose patience. "Do you think your mother asked to be born?"

He shook his head sullenly.

"Nico? Frances? Anybody?"

Again he shook his head.

"Then you are not really a special case, verdad?"

"But why do they have us? Why do people have kids?"

Was he clairvoyant? For the last several days that very query had been flitting about the borders of her awareness. "Buena pregunta, Eddie. I think we have kids to connect the generations. Our kids connect us to our grandchildren. That's easy enough to see. But our kids also connect us to our parents in a strange way. When I look back and see the mistakes that I made with my own kids, then it's easier to forgive the mistakes that my parents made with me."

The connection hypothesis did not satisfy. "Maybe that explains something for the parents. But not the kids," he objected. "I want to be more than just a connection between generations."

"And of course you are," she agreed.

"I understand that I'm not a special case. But why is it so hard for me? Why do I have to hurt so much?"

In her own adolescence, she had asked, "¿Por qué me duele tanto?" And people had assured her that they too felt her pain. In retrospect, she had never believed any of them. But now? Now she was thirty. Now she saw it distinctly. Maybe this was the wisdom of the ancients. That life could be encompassed only after multiple perspectives had been achieved. But hold that thought. Right now Eddie's need was more urgent.

"I think we hurt so much because we have such powerful imaginations. We can see ourselves as much more than we are, and doing much more than we actually do."

He mulled that over, then tried the teenager's favorite ploy. "I don't get it."

"When I was your age, I was completely unhappy with my life. The world was so big. It had so many opportunities. And I was trapped in a little town called Jachalco. It had nothing I wanted."

"You felt boxed in."

"Yes. That's perfect. I felt like I was living inside a closed box."

"But you knew there was more."

"I was sure there was more."

"But it was out of your reach. And people wouldn't let you get to it."

"Exactly."

"That's how I feel," Eddie agreed. "But I don't think it starts when we're teenagers. I remember stuff like this from the time I was a little kid."

"Tienes mucha razón. Probably from the time we start to imagine, we start to hurt too."

"I wanted to be a princess. But nobody would let me. Frances was the princess. Everybody said so. They even called her princess. I hated my sister. But of course it wasn't her fault."

Victoria had finished rebandaging the arm. Now she reached out and stroked his thick black hair. "Eddie. Eddie. What am I going to do with my beautiful Eddie?"

"Don't say stuff like that." He squirmed away from her hand. "I don't want people feeling sorry for me."

"It isn't that, Eddie. I just want you to understand that other people feel the same pain."

A leaden silence ensued. She studied her hands while his resentment receded. And he had plenty of reasons to be resentful. All the males like Nico. All the females like Frances. And never being this or that. Always needing to create a third way of being in the world. With a whole different set of choices. A whole alternative range of experience. A whole new array of issues. There was more than enough to resent. But he must avoid the trap of believing that he was a special case. There were no special cases. If anything held up her world, it was that conviction. No special cases.

Perhaps it was time for some cajolery. "Te voy a contar una historia de mi hijo. Tony was about five when this happened. He liked to play on the swings that Papá Miguel built in the backyard. Tony was really good on the swings. He could swing by himself. He was very proud of that."

"I remember," Eddie agreed.

"One day, I was over there talking to Mamá Margarita. Tony and Alicia were swinging. Tony was going faster and higher and faster and higher. I started watching him. Like I was hypnotized. He was getting more and more excited. Then his eyes went all buggy. Like he was having a vision. And he was. He was watching himself turn into a bird. He was going to fly. I jumped up. But it was too late. He let go of the ropes and right at the top of his forward swing, he leaped. And he really did fly. But just for a second. When he hit the ground, he was knocked out. Then he started breathing again. But he didn't cry. He was hurt and bruised. But he didn't cry."

"He was being brave," Eddie suggested.

"I think it was more than that. You have to understand that he was completely convinced that he was going to fly. And he couldn't understand why it didn't work. He looked and looked and looked at the swing. What was the problem with his vision? Why didn't it happen like the picture in his brain? He just could not believe it."

"So what's the point?" Having lost the center stage spotlight, Eddie showed petulance.

Victoria laughed. "There are many many points. The first is that we can't do all the things that we can imagine."

"You mean like Tony trying to fly."

"Precisamente. And when we try something that is out of our reach, we usually end up falling very hard."

"Tony hitting the ground."

"Exactly. But even when we fall very hard, the Earth will be there to catch us."

Eddie pondered. "That I don't get."

"It isn't very complicated. Tony fell. He didn't fly. But he didn't go off into another dimension either. The Earth caught him. He was still there to try something else that he imagined."

"What does that have to do with me?"

"You can't fly, Eddie. You can't be a princess. You can't be a macho type. But yesterday when you fell, the Earth caught you.

BOOK THREE, CHAPTER FIFTEEN

You're still here. You can try something else that you imagine."

"Like what?"

"What do you want to do?"

"Build things. Like Frank Lloyd Wright."

"Then do it. Build things."

"How? He was an architect."

"He wasn't born an architect. You can study. You can learn. Work with Papá Miguel. Learn everything he knows. Go to night school. Read books. Try, Eddie. And believe me. The Earth will catch you if you fall." She took his good arm and pulled him to his feet. "Now that's it. No more lazy time. Get out of here so I can get some work done." She eased him out the front door and watched as he reluctantly crossed the street and entered his house. Back in the kitchen, she poured herself a cup of coffee and slumped into a chair. Suddenly she was overwhelmed by physical and moral fatigue. A memory assailed her. From her childhood in Jachalco. Her father's enormous sow had produced a litter of twelve piglets. They were so perfect, the babies. So sleek and round and voracious. And they each had a nipple on the sow's belly. And they all ate together. All continually pulling at her. Simultaneously. Ravenously. And they thrived. Every day they got fatter and fatter. And every day the sow got thinner and thinner. Victoria had fantasized that one day the sow would be gone. Vanished. Totally consumed by the needs of others. And sanctioned by the law of necessity.

She took a deep breath. Another. There. A little better. But still there was frustration. She wanted to share the pig story. With someone who would help her laugh. Not because the story was silly. But because it was unassailably true. Someone strong enough to recognize the absurd for what it was. Absurd.

She paused. Yes. He was exactly the right person. She blushed violently. The man she was picturing was not her husband. He was her cousin, Noise.

Noise, by the most outlandish coincidence, was in fact on his way. Ordinarily he opened the shop about ten o'clock. But on this day, the barking of his neighbor's dog had rousted him from bed at eight. He had gone to work without breakfast, and now in the late morning his thoughts understandably turned to Victoria and enchiladas.

He was primed to impose, but a cursory review of her aura indicated a radical change in plan. "When was the last time you treated yourself to a liquid lunch?"

"Ni sé de que me estás hablando."

"¿Tus hijos?"

"Con Mai Lu. ¿Por qué?"

"Hecho. Vamos a almorzar."

"No puedo, Primo. Tengo un millón de cosas que hacer."

"Con más razón."

She feigned reluctance. He threatened force. She capitulated. A half hour later, they were seated across from each other in a booth at a grog and grub on the south side. He ordered a pitcher of beer and enchiladas.

"Yo no tomo cerveza," she protested as the drink arrived.

"Ha llegado la hora de aprender," he remonstrated.

"Salud." They clinked glasses and he chugged a quarter liter. She began with a simpering sip. He set down his glass, the better to assail her. "Señorita, por favor. No estás tomando vino. Con esa actitud, me ofendes a mí, al cantinero, a la distinguida asamblea presente, y más que nada, a la pobre bebida que nunca te ha hecho nada."

He paused to observe the effect of his sermon. It proved to be momentous. She stood, raised her glass and declared, "Como dice la gente de acá, Why the hell not!" She quaffed. Righteously. Steadily. To the very bottom. For a second he feared that she would hurl the empty glass at the wall. Instead she resumed her seat, teased a small foam moustache off her upper lip with her tongue, and announced, "You're behind."

He drained his glass and poured another round. When the enchiladas arrived, the pitcher was nearly empty. Making the food just barely eatable. Victoria garnished the meal with her tale of the dozen piglets and the vanishing sow. Noise was astounded.

"How did you remember that? You never paid any attention to the animals."

"Me impresionaba mucho, yo creo."

"¿Y de verdad, se murió la cochina?"

"¡Nombre! Creo que les dio todavía dos crías."

He roared. "She was a real comeback mama."

After another brave attempt to finish at least one of the enchiladas, Victoria put down her fork. "Estoy muy agradecida," she announced.

"¿Por qué?"

"Porque la gente que fabricaba la cerveza no fue la misma que hacía las enchiladas."

Again he roared. "Estoy de acuerdo, Prima. Vamos."

He bought a six pack, and they drove to the lake. There she downed another beer as if in desperation, wiped her mouth with the back of her hand, giggled for a minute, and then started to cry.

"¿Qué te pasa, Prima?"

"A lo mejor estoy borracha," she sniffed, then reconsidered. "No. No es eso. No sé. Tengo mucho sentimiento." She slid toward him on the seat. He raised his arm to accommodate. She snuggled against his chest. "Gracias, Primo."

"Hey, what are cousins for? But you have to tell me what's going on."

"I'm a mess." She switched languages and explained, "No hay manera de traducir, 'I'm a mess.'"

"Okay, you're a mess. Why?"

"Ya no vivo por mí misma. Soy títere de todo el mundo. Me mandan acá y allá a su capricho. En serio. Ya no cumplo mis gustos. Ya no hago caso a mis deseos. Vivo por los demás. Soy enfermera, lavandera, cocinera, consejera. ¿Me comprendes? Ya no soy persona. Soy una serie de funciones." She paused and reprised her theme, "Soy títere de todos."

The moment called for a benign inquiry, but Noise was both uncomfortable and confused. He opted for a wording of his discomfort. "Maybe you should be telling this to your husband."

"Lo he intentado," she defended herself. "¿Sabes como me contestó? Que son los años que estoy sintiendo. ¡Menso! Apenas tengo treinta. Mis cuñadas en Jachalco ya cumplieron cuarenta y me escriben de fiestas y visitas. Si ellas todavía pueden brincar y bailar, ¿por qué no puedo yo?"

"Me dejaste en la terminal," he tried to express his confusion, but she interrupted.

"Ya ves. Es como te dije. I'm a mess. Hace diez años yo tenía montones de ilusiones. Y sí," she interjected a derisive laugh, "se trataban de noches sin dormir. Pero por andar de callejera chiflada. No por estar desvelándome con mocudos."

That, he decided, might be worth a guess. "Somebody in the family dumped on you." He stopped to consider the suspects.

"It's Eddie," she acknowledged. "He's out of the closet, as they say."

"Eddie is . . . Oh! Right. That closet. But how did you get mixed up in it?"

Victoria recounted a version of the events of the previous twenty-four hours.

"Pero él está bien," Noise concluded.

BOOK THREE, CHAPTER FIFTEEN

"¿Quién sabe? El brazo está bien. Más adentro, no sé."

With his right arm he hugged her more closely, and with the left he began to stroke her hair. "Relax, Prima. You did everything you could. It's up to Eddie now. And he'll be okay. Besides, he isn't a different person than he was two days ago. Nothing really changed yesterday. Except maybe now people can stop pretending."

"But he's so helpless."

"Not any more than another seventeen-year-old. Adolescence is crappy for everybody."

"No digo que no. Pero por lo pronto, Eddie necesita un cambio de ambiente. No sé. Tal vez trabajando con Papá Miguel."

"¡Nombre! Eso le va a caer de maravilla. Pero estábamos hablando de ti, Señorita. Y tú me haces recordar una frase de mi Tía Pilar cuando veía a alguien sacrificándose sin necesidad. Decía 'Aquella no es tu cruz.' Y la frase te queda a ti en este caso de Eddie y su futuro. Aquella no es tu cruz, Prima."

"Quiero ayudarle."

"Quién no quisiera. Pero no puedes vivir por él. Es la lucha de Eddie." He reflected for a moment. Then, "Besides, you're a nurse. You should understand about staying close to the person, but keeping your distance from the person's problem."

She nodded emphatically into his chest.

"I've been thinking about that lately," he continued. "Not just with Eddie. With all the teenagers. We should try to stay close to the person but separate them from the problems. That way we won't drive them crazy, and they won't drive us crazy."

Again she nodded vigorously into his chest.

"My parents used to drive me crazy. It was like they were always holding their breath. Waiting for me to screw up. So I'd feel the tension and screw up even more. If they just would have let it happen, life would have been better for everybody. I mean, teenagers are always going to screw up. So relax. When they fall, pick them up. But don't stand around watching them and holding your breath."

And on he carried. Blissfully unaware that he had redirected the tenor of the dialogue. Shortly he began recalling the adventures of his misspent youth. One involved a would-be tryst with a lass of uncertain virtue. To gain entrance to her bower, Noise had shimmied up a pine, sidled precariously along a branch, slithered onto a window ledge, jimmied the sash, eased himself inside, groped for the bed, contacted flesh and, as the bedroom light went on, discovered that he was about to embrace the young woman's father. His exit understandably took on a certain urgency.

One anecdote led to another. The tales of callow dissipation burgeoned. Laughter abounded. As the lazy afternoon wound down, so also did Victoria's tensions. Noise sensed the increased spontaneity. He recalled the girl he had known in Jachalco. All romance and rhapsody. Exuding dreams and schemes.

"Vamos a caminar," she suggested. They walked south to the marina and back. The wind off the lake pierced and chilled, and they raced the last twenty meters to the car. "Ahora sí, tengo que buscar a mis hijos," she pronounced.

There was little talk on the way home. But as she was leaving, she favored him with a radiant smile. "Gracias, Primo. Me hacía mucha falta el relajo."

Noise drove to the shop and for an hour mucked about with a transmission. But it was Friday. The phone was blessedly silent. And he sensed a vague, lecherous stirring within. The image of mellifluous Ms. Thompson soon began whispering sweet nothings in his ear. An hour later he was standing inside her apartment.

She was about to greet him with a kiss but quickly pulled away. "What's going on?"

"What do you mean?"

BOOK THREE, CHAPTER FIFTEEN

"You smell like a woman," she accused.

"What are you talking about? I just came from the . . ." then he remembered. "Oh, that. I had lunch with my cousin."

"Really! Did she eat off your shirt?"

"What's that supposed to mean? She's my cousin for Christsake."

"You don't get that smell by sitting across the table from someone. Who was it?"

"I told you. My cousin. Victoria. The one who lives next to my sister."

"The one who stepped out of the nineteenth century photo? You just might be telling the truth. That's the kind of scent she would use."

"Might be telling the truth?" That was all he needed to hear. Before he had met Hannah, he had bothered but little about fidelity. But this time was different. He had told her so. He had promised. How could she possibly mistrust? Did she think that he made such promises on a whim? An even better question: did she believe that he would attempt to justify himself? Never. He turned on his heel and was gone.

He started down the interstate toward Chicago. It was a high-sky evening. Already dozens of stars were visible, with the promise of more. He remembered the times as a boy when his father would drive to Aurora on a Sunday afternoon to visit a compadre. Noise would go along to keep his father awake on the late drive home. Away from the city, the night sky would be overrun by stars. From his earthbound point of view, they seemed to be piled atop one another competing for space. And now they were calling again.

He took the bypass west and then the southwest road toward Rockford. Ahead was a rest area, far from the city. A numinous, luminous cosmos was summoning him to worship. With frankincense memories fogging his brain, he drove to the spot and parked.

Vast was such a tiny word. Apt perhaps, therefore, for a meager achiever facing such majesty. Here was the galaxy gathered in one great swath across the sky. The Via Lactea. The creamy road to where? The neighboring galaxy. And then? More of the same. The Universe creating space as it expanded. Make way. Make way for the universe. Except that there was nothing there to make way. In fact there was no "there" until the universe arrived. And there was so much of it already. You can't imagine. Only this time it was true. You really couldn't imagine.

And where did that leave him? A little off balance. But other than that, okay. He knew his place. A puny member of a petty species on a paltry planet orbiting an insignificant star. And yet, when all that was said, this wee wisp of a human could stand before immensity and whisper Wow. And feel Wow. From hair roots to toenails, he tingled with Wow. The Wow was real. Validated by a glob of organic self-conscious matter. So. When you thought about it, this dumpy lump of matter really mattered. Because the Wow was important.

Only, of course, because he said so. And he did.

CHAPTER SIXTEEN

It was a day like any day. Perhaps a Wednesday. Summer in Jachalco. Altiplano rhythms. Energy in. Energy out. High sky by day meant heat. The sun seared the igneous gravel until the air baked to a dry twenty-seven degrees Celsius. High sky by night meant radiation. The earth yielded up the day's warmth until the air chilled to a mere twelve degrees. Broad-brimmed hats by day. Sweaters and jackets for nightware. All rather standard for the locals.

For a novice such as Loco, it was all rather novel. A minute ago he had been standing in the open with the sun burning his neck. He had stepped into the shade of a capulín, and within seconds, his body had reacted with a shiver. This was the tropics?

He shooed away one of the small lizards called lagartijas and seated himself against the wall of the Jachalco cemetery. He had just spent more than an hour walking among the dead, searching out grave markers bearing the surnames Robles or Alvarez. He had made notes. A jumble of data. He needed to sort and order while it was still fresh. More importantly, while he could go back to double-check.

Two individuals were of special interest. Sacramento Robles and Natalia Alvarez. These two were unquestionably the most redoubtable of the female ancestors. Loco wanted to preserve at least a sketch of each for his daughter Juana.

The current scion of the Jachalco clan, cousin Rogelio, had been raised by Sacramento. For that reason, the anecdotes about her abounded. But Natalia, Juana's great-great-great-great-grandmother, had been nearly begloomed by the murk of time. Sacramento had recounted a brief biography of the older woman to Rogelio, who in turn had related it to Concha, who had retold it to Loco.

To wit. As a young woman during the French occupation, Natalia had taken up with a French officer and by him had birthed a child. When the boy had reached school age, the father had insisted that he be educated in France. But Natalia would not hear of such a separation from her son. By night she spirited him away. She mounted her burro and journeyed until she reached a station of a stagecoach line. There she sold the burro and purchased a ticket for the farthest town known to her.

Which just happened to be Jachalco.

At the hacienda of Jachalco, she started to work as a cook. But soon her talents were recognized by the majordomo, who became her mentor. He taught her, among other things, mathematics. Eventually she learned enough to occupy the position of bookkeeper for the hacienda. She prospered and in time became the owner of twenty hectares of land.

Alas! Her son did not fare as well. Evidently he could not forget his French sire. As a young man, he left home in search of his father. Never to return. But not before he had fathered a boy who was named Rodolfo Alvarez. Who, as an adult, wedded the renowned Sacramento Robles. Who in time begot a son, Ramón. Who begot a daughter, Concha. Who was, of course, Loco's very own mother.

It was a good enough tale. A nugget of history. A touch of romance. A cornucopia of courage. But some of the details would withstand very little scrutiny. Such as the disappearance of Natalia's son. The French occupation had endured for less than a decade. By

BOOK THREE, CHAPTER SIXTEEN

the time the boy had reached manhood, his father would have long since departed for France. Was it credible that the son would have the resources to follow him there? And, leaving aside the question of the boat passage, how would he have proceeded in a foreign land with no more than the name of his parent? Bravely imaginative. But not exactly glowing with verisimilitude.

One detail of the story was thoroughly substantiated. Natalia Alvarez had acquired twenty hectares of land. Her descendants could speculate about the wiles and guiles employed to achieve the acquisition. But the land had been transferred with title to her grandson, Rodolfo. So it was unquestionably hers. ¡Y que milagro! A female from nowhere, becoming a proprietor, during the Porfiriato. That alone established her reputation as an uncommon woman.

Loco attempted to organize a chronology of the ancestors but soon gave up. There were just too many names that he didn't recognize. Besides, his cerebral circuits were fizzling out. He had left the Robles house that morning wearing a sombrero borrowed from Rogelio. But it had quickly become a hindrance. The sweat dripping from the hat onto his notepad had hampered data collection. So he had cast the sombrero aside. With the result that the sun had addled his brain to a point of near dysfunction. "You can have your wall back," he nodded at the lagartija. "I'm out of here."

He retrieved the hat and started back toward the village. With each step, a powdery dust rose from the trail to cover his clothes and stuff up his nose. Lethargy quickly assailed him. Lassitude soon prevailed. His shoulders sagged. His footsteps dragged. In the shade of another capulín, he paused. Balancing himself with one hand on the tree trunk, he stared at what appeared to be a fallow field. But no. A closer review identified a sparse crop of beans. The plants drooped in the shimmering heat. Dust devils whirled down the rows like furious fledgling tornados. Suddenly he remembered what Marta had told him when he had asked her about her experience in the South. "You will hate it," she had assured him. "All of life's irritants regarding food, drink, and every form of hygiene have been magnified and brought together in one place on the planet. And that place is Jachalco."

That was back in June, when Victoria had announced that she and Alicia and Tony would be vacationing in the South. Would anyone like to join them? Concha would. And she would take Frances. Loco wanted to go, but he had received an assignment to teach a summer course, which would not conclude before the end of July. Perhaps Concha would like to take granddaughter Juana. Indeed she would.

So. During the first week of July, Victoria, Concha, and the four minors headed south. The report of their safe arrival included a bad news postscript. Aunt Pilar was not at all well. And as the season advanced, her health continued to deteriorate. At the beginning of August, her condition had become critical. A few days later she died. Noise immediately closed up his shop and caught a plane for Puebla. Loco tagged along.

Since then, a week had passed. Following the funeral, Loco had joined the group returning to Jachalco. On his third day there, he had decided to begin his research in the cemetery. Which had brought him to his present position. Swaying beneath a capulín. Waiting for his pulse to slow. Wondering when he might resume his normal respiration.

About a hundred meters ahead, the road became rockier and less dusty. He set that point as an objective and again put his feet to the trail. Then he fixed on a stone fence in the distance and made that his next target. And then another tree, and then a bend in the road, and finally a building. And so, by cerebrally amenable stages, eventually he reached the town.

BOOK THREE, CHAPTER SIXTEEN

Once more he was panting. His thirst was thunderous. On the very outskirts, he staggered into a small store and greeted the proprietor. "Buenas tardes. Cerveza. Dos Equis."

The woman responded to his greeting as she did his bidding. He waved off the proffered glass and raised the bottle to his lips. The top had a gritty feel. He heeded not. A half dozen swallows and done. He put some money on the counter and signaled for another. A second purchase evidently obligated the proprietor to initiate some dialogue. "Usted no es de acá, ¿verdad?"

"No. Yo vengo del norte."

"Ah. Del norte." And then again, "Del norte."

"Sí. Vinimos a visitar a Don Rogelio Robles."

"Ah. A Don Rogelio. Venían de visita."

"Sí. Soy pariente de Don Rogelio."

"Ah. Pariente de él. Qué bueno."

There was a substantial pause. The woman seemed to be deciding whether or not to risk further inquisition. In the end she opted for the safer alternative of reworking the already established data. "Entonces venían a visitar a Don Rogelio."

"Sí. A eso vinimos."

"Entonces Don Rogelio es pariente de usted."

"Sí. Mi abuelito era primo de él."

"Ah. Primos. Qué bueno." Then after some reflection. "Su abuelo no era Don Antonio Alvarez."

"No. Mi abuelito era su hermano Ramón Alvarez."

She did not disguise her disappointment. "No. No me acuerdo de Ramón Alvarez. ¿Por qué voy a mentir? No lo conocí. Pero Don Antonio, como no. Un Señor muy amable." She paused and measured Loco's need. "¿Otra?"

"Una más y ya." That apparently was what she too had calculated. She brought the beer, collected for the three drinks, and disappeared into the living quarters behind the store.

Loco finished his third and sauntered on to the Robles home. On the patio, Victoria was braiding her daughter's hair. "Buenas tardes. ¿Dónde andabas?"

"Fui al panteón."

"¿Me puedes ayudar un rato?"

"Claro que sí. ¿Qué hago?"

"Límpiame los chicharos, por favor. Mi Mamá me dejó con la comida hoy. Quiero hacer un mole de espinazo. Pero estoy atrasada." She finished the braiding and sent Alicia off to play.

Loco pointed to the bag of pea pods. "¿Qué tanto?"

"La mitad. Voy a poner la carne." She went into the kitchen.

Loco loved the simplicity of tasks such as pea shelling. After some initial concentration, the hands moved almost without cerebral intervention. The brain was free to roam where it would.

Within a few minutes, he was back in a high school classroom. They were discussing group dynamics. The Jesuit teacher was discoursing on a phenomenon that occurred in close communities, where the members were hyper-atuned to each others' needs. People showed up where and when they were needed. But without being called. They arrived. They helped out. They left. But they could not explain how or why they knew they were needed. It just felt right. "Maybe that's why I'm here shelling peas," he concluded.

He dawdled along. The pile of peas in the pot inched upward. The mound of pods at his feet deepened. Just as he was concluding his labor, Rogelio appeared with two glasses and a bottle of mescal.

"Señor Librado. Usted trabajando. Eso no tiene perdón. Vamos a tomar una copa."

Victoria was five paces behind him. "¡Qué! ¿Qué van a hacer con mi trabajador?"

Her father fixed her with a stern glare. "No, Hija. Eso no está

BOOK THREE, CHAPTER SIXTEEN

bien. ¿Cómo vas a decir que este Señor es tu trabajador? La amistad es buena. Pero no hay nada mas importante que el respeto."

"Sí, Papá," she responded, winking at Loco when she was sure that her father was not observing. "Ya que me regañaste, me tienes que servir una copa." With a hug she completed his discomfiting.

"Bien. Trae otro vaso." As she released him and went to obey, he recovered his self-possession.

They drank. Victoria returned to her mole. A second time they drank. Rogelio began to talk. Of his village. Of his land. Of his ancestors. Once more they drank. The talk continued. Loco again recalled Marta's badmouthing of Jachalco. Clearly based on a faulty analysis. Jachalco was ever so right. Therefore, there must be something amiss with Marta.

Marta was busy about her business in Milwaukee. Or, rather, what she had subsumed as her business. Caring for her brother, Toño. Whose uncaring wife had abandoned him for more than a month already. And who now was availing herself of the death of Mamá Margarita's aunt as a pretext for lengthening her absence.

But that was not the worst. Even more infuriating than her sister-in-law's neglect was her brother's unnatural resignation. Not only was he uncomplaining about the forced resumption of his bachelor status. He never mentioned it. He plodded through the daily routine with the same phlegmatic unconcern as always. He went to work. He drove his bus. He came back home. He ate some food. He drank some beer. He watched the news. He went to bed. Madre Santisima! Where were his cojones?

Determined to jerk or jolt him from that rut, Marta attempted a culinary assault. A special dinner. Enchiladas verdes. His favorite. Fortuitously, since it was the only spicy dish that Marta knew how to prepare. In fact, she had already made the enchiladas twice during Victoria's extended vacation. Would her brother notice that she was again recycling her restricted repertoire? Probably not. That was part of Toño's charm as a diner. He had the palate of a ravenous wolfhound.

The filling for the enchiladas was a mixture of shredded chicken breast, chopped onion, grated cheese, and sour cream. When that was ready, she warmed some tortillas so as to make them more pliable for the wrapping process. Then she spooned a generous scoop of the mixture into each of eighteen tortillas and packed them closely into a cake pan.

The sauce for the enchiladas was a blend of cream of celery soup, two cups of chicken broth, and a half cup of salsa verde. Marta poured the sauce over the wrapped tortillas and baked the dish for a half hour. Topped with chopped tomato and lettuce, it made a balanced meal. A point of concern only to Marta. With or without nutritional equilibrium, Toño would dispatch eight enchiladas.

Which he was now doing. Merrily munching along until he noticed his sister's plate, where one lonely enchilada had nearly vanished beneath a blanket of lettuce. "That's all you're going to eat?"

"I'm not that hungry," she answered. Then, "What do you hear from Victoria?"

He ignored her question and continued with one of his own. "How much do you know about mutual funds, Marta?"

"Nothing. I mean I know what they are. But what does that have to do with your wife and kids and when they're coming back?"

"This is where it's at, Marta. Mutual funds. You've got to start learning about this. It's really important to get into one of these early. Everybody is going to make money. But the people who get in when the funds are new are going to make the megabucks."

"Victoria hasn't even called?"

BOOK THREE, CHAPTER SIXTEEN

"She called two days ago. But you're not paying attention. I'm talking about growth funds. Do you know what they are?"

"So when is she coming back?"

"Probably next week. She didn't say for sure. Do you know where the really smart investor is putting his money these days? Not just any growth fund. The guys who know where it's at are into international growth funds now."

"Doesn't it bother you that she's refusing to say exactly when she's coming home?"

"Why should it bother me? When they get here, they get here. International growth funds are the investment of choice because . . . pay attention now . . . most investors still don't trust them. When you mention international, they get all suspicious. Too far. Too foreign. Too many unknowns. But they don't stop to think. It's the fund manager's job to sort all that out. Just like for a domestic fund. The difference is that an international fund has more upward potential because there are fewer hogs at the trough."

Marta shuddered. He was doing it again. Repeating those disgusting phrases that he learned from a passenger on his bus route who was a transplanted hillbilly. This required sterner measures. "Excuse me. Maybe I need my ears checked. I thought I heard somebody say that Victoria was your wife."

Alas! Sarcasm was wasted on Toño. "Here's a little secret, Marta. People who are not into a mutual fund by the end of the year can forget it. The train, as they say, is getting ready to leave the station."

She attempted a derail. "Okay. I can understand your cavalier attitude toward your wife. But you have to miss the kids. At least a little."

"What does this have to do with my kids? We're talking about your economic future. Marta, you have to start thinking about these things. Your pension isn't going to be enough. Social Security probably won't even exist. You have to start planning for your retirement."

"Toño! I'm still in my early thirties."

"Exactly. It's not too late to start." He looked left and right as if checking for eavesdroppers. "Less than two years ago, I salted away ten grand in an international growth fund. Guess how much that ten is worth today?" He paused. It took a few seconds for her to realize that he wanted her to make an actual guess.

"Twelve," she blurted.

"Try sixteen," he corrected.

"Sixteen!" In spite of herself, she was impressed. But then alarmed. "Toño, that's sixty percent. In two years. Are you sure you're not mixed up in something illegal?"

"It should be illegal," he guffawed. "But no. It's just a lucky hit. Anyway, with inflation factored in, it's not all that incredible." He launched another attack on the enchiladas.

She took advantage of his renewed appetite. "Why don't you just tell your wife that you expect her home by a specific date?"

He stopped chewing. "Why would I do that?"

"Toño, don't be dense. To show her that you are still in charge."

He swallowed twice, then delivered a patient lecture. "Marta, I am probably dense. But I am not blind. Women are always in charge when it's a tradition thing. And that's not bad. Traditions are important. They make things change slower." He paused and shifted to a more personal tone. "Anyway, that's what Victoria tries to do with the kids when she takes them to Jachalco. She wants to teach them stuff. You know. About the family. Why we talk a certain way. Why we eat a certain way. All that stuff. And women do that better than men. So they should be in charge." He forked in the next mouthful and paused to editorialize, "These are really good."

"Tradition!" she snorted. "After the last time they came back, I caught Tony peeing against a tree. I asked him what he was doing.

He said that's the way the boys did it in Jachalco." She paused to soak her follow-up question in acid, "Is that what you have in mind when you start spouting off about tradition?"

He ceased chewing only long enough to repeat, "These are really good."

"Tradition is just your wife's excuse to get away from you. And those poor children. I can just imagine. Running all over that village like a couple of orphans."

That was too much. Even for imperturbable Toño. "That's just not fair, Marta. You and I were adults when we went there. We saw mostly the downside. In my case, the big thing was too many people for one bathroom. There were always five people ahead of me in line. But for the kids, it's great. They have lots of cousins to play with. When they play in the street, there's no traffic to worry about. And they have neat experiences. On the phone the other night, Tony was telling me about a calf that was born. And he was there when it happened. My Tony. He was so excited that he got me excited. What a terrific experience for a city kid. That was really great."

"That's what you mean by tradition? Watching the birth of a calf? That's disgusting, Toño."

"No, it's not. And anyway, it isn't just that. Their Spanish is always better after a vacation down there."

"You could send them to summer school for Spanish."

"It's not the same thing. It's that whole family thing in Jachalco. You know what I mean."

"Family!" she scoffed. "What is this sudden obsession with family? And in Jachalco! What about right here? What does your family right here ever do for you?"

"Not that much. But it feels good to know they're around."

"It feels good!" she mocked. "Terco! They make jokes about you."

He studied her face for a second. "You mean when they call me

Mr. Stock? Stuff like that?"

"That doesn't bother you? It's like saying you're one-dimensional. The only thing you know about is money."

"So? Where's the problem? The same people that make the jokes come to me when they need a loan."

That was possibly the most intriguing statement he had ever made in her presence. It took all her self-control not to blurt out, "Who?" But she caught herself, took a deep breath, and reined in her curiosity. Then, with exquisitely disingenuous modulation, "You mean the loan to Papá Miguel for the truck he bought last year?"

"That too. But I was thinking more about when Noise needed some equipment for his shop."

"Noise came to you for a loan?"

"Sort of. He was doing some work on my car. We got talking about stuff he was going to install when he could afford it. One thing led to another."

"But he didn't come to you and ask."

"Not really. But Concha did."

Had her brother just announced that he was pregnant, he could hardly have rendered her more speechless. Fortunately, Toño gave her time to dissemble and then reassemble her emotions as he rattled on with his narrative. "Sure. Last year. When she needed a new roof for her house. She came to me for the loan. Where else could she go? I don't want to badmouth her son, but he isn't exactly the most ambitious guy around."

"That's interesting," Marta squeezed through clenched teeth, then quickly arose to start the dishes. Years before, when she had purchased her new car, she had gone to a bank for a loan. Not wanting to be a burden to her brother. And now she was discovering that her cousins were lining up to put the touch on him. Not that he was all that blameless. In fact, all the big talk about his precious investments practically made him a mark. So yes. He was guilty. He had committed several deadly sins. But the least forgivable by far was the loan to Concha.

Concha had gone south with great expectations. For many years, she had foregone a real vacation in order to provide food service for the children attending the Aztlán summer session. But not this year. Already in April she had notified the administration that she would not be available for the summer program. Then in May, Victoria had surprised with the invitation to Jachalco. Serendipity abounded.

Until their arrival in the South. There they were greeted with the news of the waning health of Pilar García. Who was, of course, Tía Pilar to Noise and Margarita. But also to Rogelio's daughters-in-law, the García twins, Laura and Hilda, who were caring for their aunt. Concha, with her nursing experience, and Victoria, with her training, were immediately pressed into service. Each of the visitors was paired with one of the twins. One week, Victoria and Hilda would attend to the patient in Puebla, while Concha and Laura looked after the family in Jachalco. The following week, the pairs would exchange assignments.

The Puebla rotation was the more stressful. Pilar's last weeks were a rhythm of daze and doze. Her nurses assisted her from a chair on the balcony overlooking the street, to a chair in the living room facing a wall of family photos, to a chair at the kitchen table confronting a plate of food. In the first chair, she grumbled weakly at the traffic. In the second, she mumbled cheerfully at the relatives. In the third, she nibbled indifferently at the food.

There were two such daily sequences. One in the late morning. One in the late afternoon. The interval between was dedicated, at the patient's demand, to telenovela viewing. Which usually became, in Concha's phrase, "more siesta than soaps."

Nighttime was the most stressful. From ten o'clock until daybreak, Pilar lay in a semi-reclining posture battling apnea. Continual monitoring was required. One caregiver slept while the other kept vigil.

In the daily routine, there was, however, one period of reduced anxiety. From about eight in the evening until ten, Pilar was able to sustain a moderately sound repose. The caregivers had their one opportunity for some serious schmooze. Had they been so inclined. But Laura often seemed more disposed toward dispute. As now, when she began a discussion with an accusatory, "Todas las mujeres del norte son muy atrevidas, ¿verdad?"

Concha noted the tone and adopted a conciliatory response. "Yo sí soy culpable. Pero no creo que conozcas a muchas mujeres de allá."

"Es que veo a mi cuñada Victoria muy cambiada desde que fue a vivir con ustedes."

"¿Cambiada? ¿En que sentido?"

"En todo. Más que nada en su concepto de ella misma."

"¿Es más pretenciosa?"

Laura blushed, as if she had in fact suggested such a conclusion.

"No. Lo que quiero decir es que ella es más independiente. Más libre."

Concha smiled. "Se me hace que tu cuñada era bastante independiente mucho antes de llegar a Milwaukee."

Laura was not to be put off with humor. "Puede ser. Pero insisto. Allí encontraba campo para estirarse más."

"Allí es otra onda. Eso sí es cierto. Y sí, hay más campo para la mujer, como tú dices. Pero también, hay algo mas. Allá es la tierra del individuo. Para entender a la gente del norte, hay que entender eso." She reflected for a moment. Then, "Acá en el sur, la familia tiene mucha importancia. La persona cuenta con su familia. La persona siempre se mira como parte de la familia. Tú, por ejemplo, eres de los García de Puebla. Tu esposo es de los Robles de Jachalco. Cuando tú quieres hacer algo, tus familiares te van a ayudar. Te van a empujar. O como decimos en Texas, te van a puchar. Supongamos por ejemplo que tú quieres conseguir un puesto con una compañía. Tu familia te va a ayudar. Si alguien de tu familia conoce a alguien de la compañía, esa persona va a hacer todo lo posible para facilitar tu entrada. Todo eso es bastante común y muy normal acá." She paused and then with emphasis repeated, "Acá." Another brief pause. Then, "Allá es otro cantar. No quiero decir que la familia se descuenta completamente. Pero la persona tiene que hacer su lucha como individuo. O sea, en el caso de Victoria, lo que ella ha logrado, lo ha hecho por su propio esfuerzo. Tal vez por eso anda con la nariz alzada un centímetro demás."

"Comprendo," Laura responded. "La persona tiene que hacer su lucha. Pero eso no es motivo para despreciar la ayuda de la familia. Vamos a tomar el ejemplo que tú sacaste. Yo estoy buscando una posición. Encuentro algo que me gusta. Ahora por qué no voy a ocupar todas las mañas que tengo para conseguir el puesto que quiero."

"Suponiendo que estás calificada."

"Hasta eso, si quieres. Vamos a decir que estoy super calificada. Ahora contéstame. ¿Por qué no voy a usar todas mis armas para ganar la batalla?"

"¿Incluso la influencia de tu familia?"

"Eso incluso. ¿Por qué no?"

"¿Y si otra persona busca el puesto. Calificada también. Pero de familia sin conexiones?"

"¡Qué lastima! ¿Pero de que tengo la culpa yo? Como dice mi Tía Pilar, 'Siendo buenos cristianos, luchamos para mejorar el mundo. Pero tenemos que vivir mientras en el mundo que hay.'"

Concha nodded. Not so much in agreement, as in recognition of the wisdom of the South. It was a tougher environment, and its denizens had tougher rules for survival. Finally she responded, "No estoy alegando. Sólo quiero decir que allá no es así. Hasta podría yo contarte de casos en que la persona escondía sus conexiones familiares para estar segura de que la decisión fuera por sus calificaciones y no sus conexiones."

Laura shook her head. "Eso para mí no tiene sentido. Para luchar, tenemos dos brazos. Las cosas que sabemos y las personas que conocemos. Y si tenemos dos, ¿por qué no vamos a ayudarnos con los dos?"

"Y para la otra persona calificada, mala suerte."

"Jamás voy a decirle mala suerte. Pero son cosas de la vida. Aquella persona va a comprender el caso igual que yo. Y me va a tomar como tonta si, teniendo la capacidad para desempeñar el trabajo, no hago todo lo posible para conseguírmelo."

Concha sensed the rising emotion but decided to press the issue a little harder. "Pero sí, han de existir casos en que alguien sin calificaciones gana el puesto por sus conexiones familiares."

"¡Juta! Miles de casos. Pero aún así. ¿Cómo vamos a decirles a los familiares de tal persona que no la apoyen? Ni por ser muy santos, se van a detener."

Concha laughed. "¡La famosa franqueza poblana! Cómo me cae de agrado."

Laura bristled slightly but then resumed the offensive. "A poco me vas a decir que el nepotismo no existe allá."

"Sí, existe. Pero debajo de la mesa. Allá nadie respeta a una que gana su posición de tal manera. Allá la persona tiene que demostrar que merece el puesto."

"¿Y a ti te agrada aquel sistema?"

"Me parece mas justo."

"¡Justo!" Laura scoffed. "Justo cuelga su sombrero en el más allá. En esta vida la corona va a la más mañosa."

BOOK THREE, CHAPTER SIXTEEN

Concha maintained her courteous bearing. "No tiene que ser así."

"Quizás allá, no. Ustedes tienen suficiente. Hasta para compartir con otros pueblos. Pero espera el día en que las cosas empiecen a faltar. Entonces sí, ven a cantarme la canción de justo."

Concha studied the other woman for a moment. Except for a handful of circumstances, they could be sisters. "En eso, tienes razón," she voiced her concordance. "Donde hay suficiente, es más fácil creer en la justicia."

But Laura would not be so easily appeased. "Pues allá ustedes. Si con el simple hecho de demostrar sus méritos, el individuo puede triunfar, qué bueno. Yo nunca he vivido allá. ¿Qué voy a saber yo? Pero a mí me parece mentira." She paused for a deep breath. "Además me parece que ustedes viven en un ambiente bastante frío."

Concha continued to stroke with a lighter touch. "Se supone que no te estás refiriendo a la temperatura en enero."

Laura ignored the levity. "Pues sí. Me das a entender que el individuo es todo. Y que todos compiten sin el apoyo de nadien. Cada quién busca su suerte. Sin contar con la familia. Todo eso ha de resultar en un ambiente muy frío."

"Puede resultar así," Concha conceded. "Pero no tiene que resultar así. En Milwaukee, yo y mi familia y tu cuñada Victoria y tus primas Isabel y Margarita y las familias de ellas y tus primos Noise y Daniel y Dante, todos convivimos, compartiendo ayuda y trabajo. A veces hay desacuerdos y disgustos pero mayormente nos llevamos bien." She paused. "Pero eso sí, cuando vamos a buscar empleo, se trata de cada quién."

Perhaps the enumeration of the northern relatives had mollified her. Or perhaps the vindication of her southern traditions had now been achieved. Or perhaps Concha's unbridled charm had finally worked its magic. Whatever the case, Laura's demeanor gradually softened and the conversation took a turn for the trifling.

"¡De verdad! Ustedes ya son muchos en Milwaukee. Aquí estamos quedando muy pocos. En la casa de mi Papá son nueve. En Jachalco somos once. Y nada más."

"En Milwaukee somos veinte contando a la mujer de Daniel," said Concha. "Parece que ella va a quedar con él."

"¿Ya tiene mujer mi primo? Pero dime. ¿Cómo es ella? ¿Cómo se llama?"

"Se llama Lupe Silvas. Es de Durango. Es una persona muy sencilla pero muy simpática. Y trabajadora como pocas. Tiene suerte tu primo."

"¿Y el otro? ¿Dante?"

Concha chuckled. "No, ese joven es como el primo Noise. Pescando por todo el mar. Pero no te preocupes. Un día de estos va a dar con un pez que no lo soltará."

"De veras. No he preguntado por mi primo Noise. Sigue de soltero."

"Por lo pronto. Pero ya tiene un rato largo con una de allá. Ella es profesora de la universidad. Y sí, se quieren bastante. Pero a la vez son como el tiempo de allá. Siempre variable."

"¿Y cómo es ella? ¿Está bonita?"

"No sé contestarte. Es de cuerpo regular pero grande."

"Quieres decir que es una gorda."

"No. Tiene el cuerpo como una sueca o alemana. ¿Me entiendes?"

"¿Así? Cae de sorpresa. Acá él buscaba a pura mujer delgada."

Again Concha chuckled. "Bueno. Tal vez por los años que ya lleva, necesita a una más maciza para detenerse."

Laura laughed her appreciation. But then, "Lástima que no pueda encontrar a alguien. El pobre tiene la misma edad que yo."

"No te preocupes por tu primo," Concha answered. "Ese hombre sigue gozando de la vida como nadie." She went on to explain about the service shop and how quickly the business was growing.

"¿Y la prima que nunca sale de viaje?" Laura asked at the next pause.

"Isabel," said Concha. "Está bien. Estando en su casa. Ella es la mejor comprobante que no todas las mujeres de allá son atrevidas. Esa pobre tiene miedo de su propia sombra."

"Tiene varios hijos, ¿verdad?"

"Tres. El mayor, Nico, ya está en la universidad. Parece que va a estudiar periodismo. El segundo, Eddie, trabaja con Miguel, el esposo de tu prima, Margarita."

"Y la otra es la muchacha que vino con ustedes esta vez."

"La misma. Espero que tengas tiempo para conocerla un poco. Es una muchacha encantadora. Inteligente. Amable. Para mí, es muy especial, mi Frances."

Frances was feeling anything but special. Unless you counted especially unsettled. She was lying among the northern visitors on a mattress on the floor of a bedroom in the Robles home in Jachalco. Hoping for sleep and meanwhile sorting out reactions to the new environment. The jumble of novel experiences hardly constituted cultural shock. But life in the South was definitely different.

There was nothing odd about being in bed. The bell in the hacienda chapel had just sounded midnight. And the mattress on the floor was eminently explainable. The six visitors from Milwaukee had been assigned one bedroom. With one full-size bed. But two mattresses and double bedding. Even a northern bilingual could figure that one out.

Bedtime did, however, have its curious aspects. The rigid scheduling for one. Every evening at about ten o'clock, all household activity came to a screeching halt. Most of the family gathered in the kitchen for what was called la cena. The children had a glass of warm milk and a piece of sweetbread. After which they recited their formal valedictions and were shooed off to bed. The adults drank coffee. Some ate tacos made from the leftovers of that day's dinner. The morrow's work was discussed. Plans were elaborated or modified or confirmed or postponed or dropped. Occasionally, some disagreement would extend the talk. But on most nights, lights were out by eleven. Any subsequent commotion, especially from a minor, had better be legitimized by a bellyache.

The one night on which the schedule varied was Saturday. Work ended earlier. Following dinner, the family took long leisurely baths. The older people singly. The youngsters in pairs or even small groups. Afterwards, the women and girls might engage in some mutual grooming. The men might extend their evening talk beyond eleven o'clock, especially if someone had sprung for a bottle of brandy. At the margin of the male group, the freshly bathed boys would dawdle and yawn, looking uncharacteristically scrubbed in their spotless clothes.

Bathing was also necessary, of course, during the week. But then it was purposeful and quick. Whenever it occurred, Frances found the method enormously fascinating but also just a little daunting. A perennial scarcity of water dictated the procedure. A tub, ordinarily used for washing clothes, was filled with warm water. The bather removed her clothing and, using a minimum of water, soaped and scrubbed her body and shampooed her hair. For scrubbing, the bather employed a sort of sponge called estropajo. This sponge was made from the fiber of a luffa gourd, and, what it lacked in delicacy, it easily made up for in thoroughness. After scrubbing, the bather seated herself on a short stool and, using a large dipper, rinsed her head and body as best she could. Frances quickly discovered that thick hair such as hers never got quite clean.

The dearth of water affected most aspects of hygiene. A glassful could be used for brushing teeth. A liter was considered sufficient for ablutions preceding meals. To the children's delight, handwashing after snacking was not even encouraged. The toilet was not flushed after urination, only after defecation. Then, four or five liters were drawn from the reservoir or fuente and, after being used for a handwash, were poured directly into the toilet bowl. Water from the scrubbing of floors was also subsequently utilized for flushing.

Drinking water was brought from San Isidro in demijohns called garrafones. If this ran out, water from the fuente was boiled. After observing Hilda and Laura for two weeks, Frances was as water-conscious as any Jachalco native.

The chapel bell sounded the half hour. Frances hardly noticed. Slowly, quietly, ever so calmly, she had gently drifted off into a smooth, soft, ever so soothing . . . "Ouch!" she yelped as her bed partner, cousin Juana, jabbed a severely pointed elbow into her defenseless ribs.

Wide awake again, with Juana now in the cerebral mix, Frances began replaying a scene from a month earlier in Milwaukee. She had been helping Concha in the garden. It had rained earlier in the day, and her sneakers had each accumulated about five pounds of garden soil. When they finished, she had removed her shoes and gone into Concha's kitchen to get a knife to clean them. Inside, she had encountered Uncle Loco and his daughter Juana deep in discourse on the subject of culture.

"I expect that you will get me up to go to school tomorrow morning," Juana was saying.

"Fine. That's an excellent example. You understand what expectation means." For a few seconds, Loco had stared at Frances and her bare feet. "Now, let's suppose that a friend invited you to dinner, and you accepted. When you got to your friend's house, would you take off your shoes before you went inside?"

"Maybe. If I was in Japan," Frances kibitzed.

"We're talking about here. Right, Dad?"

"Right," Loco grinned. "Here you would expect to keep your shoes on." A transitional pause. "Now. When it was time to eat, would you expect to sit on a chair or on the floor?"

Juana favored him with a long-suffering look and sighed, "On a chair."

"Not if you were in Japan," Frances interposed.

Juana scolded. "Aren't you listening? We're talking about here."

"Correct." agreed Loco. "But Frances is reminding us that our expectations would be different if we lived in a different place." Another transitional pause. "Now, what would you expect to use in order to get the food from your plate to your mouth?"

"Maybe a fork," Juana answered. Then after further consideration. "Or maybe a tortilla. Hey, this is getting interesting. All of a sudden, I have two expectations. That's an example of the two cultures. Isn't it, Dad?"

"That's exactly right," her father agreed. "And that's exactly what I want you to understand. Culture is about expectations. When you can predict how things will happen, it means that you know the culture."

Frances decided to stir the pot. "What if you were in a place where people were eating but they didn't use plates? Instead, they had a huge bowl of food in the middle of the table. Everybody used their hands to take food from the big bowl and put it directly into their mouths."

"I would know that I was in a different place," Juana answered and then thoughtfully added, "Or maybe a different time."

Her father nodded. "That's a good point. The expectations of people change from one place to another. But they can change from one time to another too. Did your teacher talk about that?"

"A little bit. But I wanted to ask you about something else. The teacher keeps saying that culture is our way of seeing the world. I don't really get what she means by that. What does it mean that culture is our way of seeing the world?"

Frances looked at Loco and said, "Let me try this one." Then, addressing Juana, "Let's go back to my example. All the people that were dipping their hands into one big bowl of food—let's call these people the Sharing People. And you, Juana, are observing the Sharing People. Somebody asks you why they aren't using plates. How would you answer?"

"Do I have to do this?" asked a resentful Juana.

"Why not try it," her father cajoled.

"Just give me one possible explanation," said Frances.

"Okay. They don't have money to buy plates."

"Good hypothesis. But you, Juana, are rich. You buy plates for all the Sharing People. But when the plates arrive, they refuse to use them. Now, how do you explain the fact that they aren't using the plates?"

"It's probably because they just don't want to change."

"But why? Why do they refuse to change?"

"They got used to eating like that."

"That is an incredibly accurate answer, Juana. The Sharing People all eat from one big bowl because they are the Sharing People. Their way of eating shows how everything belongs to everybody, and everybody has an equal share."

"I just think it would be better if they all had their own plates."

"Why do you think that?"

"It would be healthier, right? Because if everybody eats out of the same bowl, and one of them is sick, pretty soon everybody will be sick."

"Another excellent observation," Frances praised. "In our culture, hygiene is really important when it comes to food. That affects the way we see the Sharing People. We look at them, and we say they don't know how to handle food properly. And I bet if the Sharing People would see us eating, they would say we don't know how to share food properly."

Juana did her own summation. "I get it. We're part of a certain group. The group teaches us how to see the world. So we learn to see the world a certain way. And the way we learn, that's our culture."

"I couldn't have said it better," her father concurred.

Juana beamed for a few seconds. Then, "And when we go somewhere, we take along our culture because it's inside us. It's our way of seeing the world."

"That's exactly right."

She beamed again. Then another doubt. "But isn't there something wrong? It sounds like we're all prejudiced."

"We are all prejudiced," Frances answered. "In favor of our own culture."

Juana appealed to her father. "Is that right, Dad? I mean, is it okay to think our way is the best way?"

"The best for us. Sure. That's okay."

Juana reflected, then took on the air of the cat who had just supped on an especially savory canary.

"What?" her father asked.

"No. I was just thinking that social studies class is going to be a lot more fun tomorrow."

He laughed. "I was hoping that you were thinking about the trip with your grandma to Jachalco."

"I forgot about that. But that's right. In Jachalco, I'll be able to see how this stuff really works. This trip is going to be fun."

Back on the mattress on the floor of the bedroom, Frances massaged her offended ribs and mumbled, "Fun for you and your elbows." Then she slipped out from under the covers and went to the window. She eased back a corner of the curtain. There it was. The same fabulous vision as last night and the night before. The Milky Way. Spectacularly stretched above the darkened village. There were no words for it. You could say immense or magnificent. But if you used those words for anything else, then they were just not enough to describe the galaxy.

Then another thought. This road of stars spanning the night sky was shining for everyone. In Japan, China, India, Iran, Egypt, Angola, England. In each of these, there was probably a girl her own age who sometimes experienced this same vision. And all equally awestruck. Cultures might distinguish. Cultures might divide. But this was there for everyone. All were equally part of this. For everyone this was home.

A voice from the bed jarred her back to Jachalco reality. "There's no sleeping in tomorrow morning. When it's time to get up, you get up. Ready or not."

The warning came from her suddenly very practical Aunt Victoria.

Victoria had also been a little unsettled by her return to the ancestral village. Not, of course, because of the water shortage. That vexation went back to her childhood. Nor because of the rigidity of the daily schedule. That was no more annoying than putting on an old coat. Nor even because of coming once more under her mother's sway. That, in fact, even had its upside. Now and then she could harbor the illusion that someone else was in charge.

No. None of the above. But something was awry. Her parents seemed strangely resigned and withdrawn. Her brothers treated her with entirely too much deference. Her sisters-in-law exhibited an ill-concealed edginess. There was a veritable aura of intrigue about the household.

She had mentioned her misgivings to Concha when the two exchanged information in Puebla at the start of Victoria's second rotation with Aunt Pilar. To forestall eavesdroppers, the two were conversing in English.

"Something is wrong. Definitely. Everybody is acting like they're expecting an earthquake."

"I'm feeling the same thing," Concha had agreed. "But I thought maybe it was just me. Anyway, I'll be in Jachalco this next week. I'll find out what's going on."

"How? I don't want to offend people with a lot of questions."

"Trust me. It won't take a lot of questions."

"So how then?"

Concha arched an eyebrow. "Well, it's either sex or money, right?"

In spite of herself Victoria had laughed. "But how do you tell which?"

"Los niños y los borrachos dicen la verdad," Concha had responded. And during the following week, she had proceeded to prove the veracity of the ancient adage.

When the two were together again the next Sunday, she had announced, "It's money."

"What's money?"

"What we talked about hace ocho días. It's money."

"Oh, that! So it's money. What does that mean?"

"The Robles family has had some money problems that they didn't tell us about."

"When?"

"Last winter. Laura's daughter, Ofelia, had an emergency appendectomy. Then she caught a staph germ and had to stay in the hospital for another two weeks. I guess they would have managed, except that the corn crop was so bad last year."

"How did you find out about this?"

"I started with that woman who runs the chángarro two blocks down. Everybody calls her Doña Petra."

"Doña Petra! You talked about the family with that woman? Concha! She's the town newspaper."

"Exactly. I had a beer with her one afternoon, and she told me about the appendectomy and the bad crops. The children filled in the rest of the story."

"Which is?"

"That they've been living mostly on beans and tortillas. Then you show up with your kids. Plus three more mouths that they weren't even expecting. As my Uncle Librado used to say, 'El charco ya se convirtió en mar.'"

"¡Madre Santa! ¿Qué podemos hacer?"

"I know. I feel awful. They don't have money to buy meat for themselves, and they're buying meat for us. Anyway, that's one thing I took care of. I found the butcher and paid him off. Plus two weeks in advance. Then, on Thursday I took the children shopping."

"Shopping? Where? How?"

"In San Isidro. Thursday is market day. Frances and I made a picnic lunch. We told your parents that we wanted to take the children to the hoyo grande. So Rogelio hitched a team, and everybody piled onto the remolque. Then instead of the hoyo, we went to market day."

"You drove the horses to San Isidro!"

"Why not? It's all dirt side roads until you get to town. Anyway, we went shopping. The boys got new shoes and jeans. Ofelia got new shoes. Then, in the market we bought kilos and kilos of tomatoes and onions and potatoes and chiles and bananas and oranges and mangoes and all that stuff. Then, at a grocery we bought a case of pasta and twenty kilos of rice and a case of oil and some more stuff. The children helped carry it all to the remolque and we drove home."

"What did my parents say?"

"Your mother cried a little. I got a bottle of brandy for your father. He was okay. After he explained to me about twenty times that women didn't do such things."

"So what else do you think we can do?"

"You need to find out more about the medical bills that they still owe."

"Okay. I'll work on that. What else?"

"There is one more thing. Start working on a plan for a bank robbery. I'm almost broke."

That was almost not funny. If, as it now appeared, the visitors would be staying some additional weeks, routine expenses would surpass what had been projected. And clearly Victoria would have to help with the accumulated medical debt. A not insignificant burden. As she discovered while extracting data from her sister-in-law, Hilda.

"¿Qué pasó con la cosecha del año pasado? Mi Papá me contaba que levantaron muy poco."

"Casi nada," corrected Hilda. "Fue por las heladas. Se dañan las plantas y luego se secan. Es lo que me dicen. Hasta la fecha, no sé mucho del campo."

"¿Y de qué comían ustedes todo el invierno?"

"De mi sueldo."

"¿De tu sueldo de maestra? ¿Nada más eso?"

"Bueno. Levantaron suficiente maíz para tortillas. Y la cosecha del frijol estuvo regular. Pero sí, mayormente de mi sueldo."

"¿Y la cirugía, cuando la hija de Laura se enfermo?"

"Tu Papá pagó las cuentas. Pero sí, se trataba de un préstamo. Consiguió el dinero de un compadre en San Isidro."

"¿Y por qué no nos avisaron?"

"Tu Papá no quiso. No nos explicaba claramente. Pero digo yo que estaba sentido por tu reacción a la llamada en Año Nuevo."

"¿Cuál llamada?"

"¡Pues, cuál otra! ¿No te acuerdas? El día primero. Ya en la noche. Como a las once me parece. Todos hablábamos. Tus padres. Tus hermanos. Yo. Laura. Hasta los niños. Mucha alegría. Todos contentos. En ese momento. Luego recibimos la carta en qué nos decías que la llamada te había salido muy cara. Y en el futuro, por qué no escribiéramos mejor una carta cuando no se trataba de emergencia." She paused and editorialized, "Una regañada muy bonita."

"Estás exagerando mucho, cuñada. Yo nada más les dije que les pude haber mandado el dinero que gastamos en la llamada."

"Eso dirás ahora. Pero tu Papá estaba bastante sentido. Pregúntale. Si no me quieres creer."

"Sí, le voy a preguntar. Y le voy a dar otra regañada, aún más bonita por no habernos escrito lo que estaba pasando aquí."

They were determinedly silent for several minutes. Finally Victoria surrendered. But she turned the talk to a new theme. "Quiero preguntarle algo, Hilda. Nunca platican tú y Laura de lo que sacrificaron cuando se casaron y se fueron a vivir en el pueblito."

"¿Y por qué dices que sacrificamos? Fuimos a vivir con nuestros esposos. Es todo. Lo mismo hiciste tú."

"Pero mi esposo trabaja en la ciudad. Sol o lluvia, buen tiempo o mal tiempo, él va a tener su cheque cada semana. En cambio, mis hermanos viven del campo. Año tras año ustedes sufren los caprichos del tiempo. Y de vez en cuando, les falla. Como el año pasado. A eso me estaba yo refiriendo."

Hilda attempted one further dodge. "Es igual, cuñada. Tu esposo es chofer. En cualquier momento le puede pasar un accidente. Así es la vida en todas partes."

"No es igual," Victoria countered. "Si a mi esposo le pasa algo, el seguro paga los gastos médicos. Y hasta su sueldo está garantizado durante la rehabilitación."

"¡El sueldo también!" Hilda was genuinely impressed.

"La mayor parte."

Hilda nodded in admiration. "Los gringos piensan en todo, ¿verdad?"

"Los gringos piensan en mucho, porque tienen el conqué," Victoria agreed. Then returning to her agenda. "¿De veras nunca hablan tú y Laura de estas cosas?"

"Sí. Hemos hablado," Hilda admitted. "Pero yo nunca he tenido miedo por mí misma. Pase lo que pase, yo me quedo al lado de mi esposo. Pero por mis hijos, sí. A veces me pongo a pensar que si por vivir en un pueblito, no estamos negándoles oportunidades."

"¿Y nunca han hablado con mis hermanos de un cambio de ambiente? Ellos tienen suficiente educación para ganarse la vida en la ciudad."

"De tal propósito jamás vamos a hablar."

Victoria was taken aback by the earnestness. "¿Pero por qué dices jamás?"

"Porque tus hermanos son del campo. Igual que tu Papá. Son profundamente del campo. Y con el tiempo, algo le pasa a esa gente. No entiendo exactamente de lo que se trata. Pero parece que, por tanto pisar las tierras, con el tiempo ya no se puede distinguir precisamente donde termina el campesino y donde comienza el campo. Son inseparables." Victoria wanted to respond, but Hilda raised a hand to detain her. "Déjame contarte algo de tu Papá. Cuando mi suegro completaba los sesenta y cinco años, sus hijos lo animaron a no molestarse más con el campo. Y sí, les hizo caso. Unas semanas se quedaba en la casa, haciendo cualquier cosita para pasar el tiempo."

BOOK THREE, CHAPTER SIXTEEN

"Le caía mal," Victoria guessed.

"Malísimo. En poquito tiempo se volvió ancianito. Hasta jorobado. Bueno, no me vas a creer, pero hizo una cita con el médico. Imagínate. Tu Papá. El hombre que jamás consultaba ni al curandero."

Victoria laughed. "De verdad, andaba desesperado."

"Pero, como siempre dice él, ahorita vas a ver. El doctor le dio la receta para curarse."

"¿Medicina?"

"No. El doctor le preguntó en qué trabajaba. Mi suegro le contestó que por los años que tenía ya había dejado de trabajar. El médico se hizo como alarmado. '¡Años! ¡Cuales años!' gritaba. 'Usted todavía tiene el cuerpo de un hombre de cincuenta.' El siguiente día tu Papá regresó al campo y empezó a componerse." She paused for a summary. "Es como te digo. El y el campo son inseparables. Y así es con tus hermanos también."

They talked on. But Victoria had nothing to rebut Hilda's reasoning. And, as the days passed, opportunities for conversation became fewer. Their patient's health continued to decline, taking a sudden downturn toward the end of July. Pilar's appetite for food dwindled daily. There were signs of impending kidney failure. Cerebral function diminished. She slowly withdrew into her memories.

Occasionally, recall would become lucid, her voice weak but surprisingly clear. The listener would be treated to a brief sermon. Usually directed at her son, Arturo. A sample. "¿Qué esperas, hijo? El niño no tiene color. No está comiendo bien. Te digo que necesita una purga. Tu esposa dice lo mismo. Hazle caso. A veces la Mamá sabe más que el doctor."

Recollections stirred most frequently when she was in her living room, surrounded by her family photos. And there, seated in her favorite chair, one morning in early August, Pilar García died. With no complaint. With no dramatics. She silently slipped away.

It had been a long, restless, worrisome night. Todas desveladas. In the morning, Victoria had gone to the pharmacy to refill a prescription. On her return, she found Pilar and Hilda, side by side, both apparently asleep. Except that in the case of the Tía, she was already partaking of her descanso eterno.

There was nothing more to be done for Pilar. But Hilda might be spared some additional grief. So for one hour more, Victoria kept vigil. When her sister-in-law awoke, she whispered, "Ya se fue. Esta vez no podía despertarla." Then, leaving Hilda to the details, Victoria stumbled to her bedroom and collapsed. Not to stir until the wee hours of the following morning.

She arose with an odd compulsion to clean. She began by mopping floors. First the bedroom. Then the living room. In the bathroom, she scrubbed everything she could reach, including the walls. Finally, in the kitchen, she scoured some pots from the previous day's meal and washed and dried the dishes. She returned to the living room feeling calm and relaxed. She picked up the phone and dialed her number in Milwaukee. When it rang five times, she concluded that her husband had already gone to work. So. Second option. She flipped a cerebral coin. It landed on Noise.

Noise had pointed his nose south from the moment that Victoria had announced her vacation plans. Miguel had objected that Dante was ill-prepared to assume full responsibility for the shop. After a token rebuttal, Noise had conceded as much. But then came word of Tía Pilar's death. Certainly he would attend the funeral.

Would others? Isabel credibly could not afford the airfare. Margarita pleaded arthritic knees, her usual subterfuge when facing the terror of flying. Daniel and Dante, Pilar's grandsons, were willing.

BOOK THREE, CHAPTER SIXTEEN

But both wanted to return to Milwaukee and they were daunted by the cost and hassle of a border crossing. Everyone contributed for the funeral, but in the end, the only additional mourners from the North were Noise and Loco.

On the plane ride south, Noise shared some recollections of Aunt Pilar. "Everybody who knew her would tell you that she was a sweet old lady. But she could be tough, too. Especially when it came to getting her money's worth. She told me she got that from her grandmother, Asunción, who raised her. I don't know about that. But she was tough. I remember when my Aunt Josefa would come home with some mangos or aguacates that she bought from some kid on the street. There would be a few good ones on top, and the rest would be garbage. Aunt Pilar would pitch a fit. 'Otra vez te dieron gato por liebre, Josefa. ¿Cómo voy a creer que un mocudo te puede lavar el coco con tanta facilidad?'"

"Was she like anybody from the family in Milwaukee?" Loco asked.

Noise considered. "No, not really. She believed in all those old-fashioned virtues. And she could preach. Man! She could really get on my case. 'Ili! Ili!' she would groan. '¿Qué podemos hacer contigo? Andas como gato callejero. Tantito las hembras alzan la colita y ahí estas de un brinco.'" He paused to award the remembrance an appreciative chuckle. "But I guess my favorite sermon was about la mujer débil. She could really do a number on that. And she never got the joke. She could stagger a man with a backhand up the side of his head and then preach him a sermon about la mujer débil."

Again the appreciative chuckle. Then, "She'd tell me about how I was a man. And the man is strong. So it's his responsibility to control his urges. He can't expect any help from the woman . . ."

" . . . because, as we well know, the woman is weak." Loco finished the sentence and this time joined in the laughter.

"But I wasn't the only one to catch hell from her," Noise continued. "Sometimes her son, Arturo, would stay out partying with some people. Then he'd be slow getting started the next morning. And Tía Pilar would be knocking on his door. The man was forty years old and a doctor. And his mother was still rousting him out of bed."

"A tough lady," Loco concurred.

"And tough with her words," Noise paused for a transition. "She had all these old sayings, dichos or proverbs, for just about every occasion. My favorite was the one she used when I'd come up with some lame excuse for something I did. She'd say, 'Pues sí, cuando comenzaron los pretextos, se acabaron los pendejos.' And she wouldn't be laughing."

Loco shook his head. "But you make it sound like everybody loved her."

"Everybody did. She never stayed mad at anybody. She'd get on your case about something one minute, and the next minute she'd be feeding you."

Loco was thoughtful for a minute. Then, "There are a bunch of strong women in the Alvarez and García clan."

"Let me throw one at you that might be a surprise. Cousin Isabel."

"No. I agree. She's a very good example. And it doesn't come easy for her. She has to push herself to be strong. That's what I mean. It must be something in the genes."

"It sure missed me."

"Might be specific to the X chromosome."

"If they ever start cloning themselves, we're in a lot of trouble."

"Maybe not. We're talking strength here. That's not the same as muscle. They'll still keep us around to change tires and move the refrigerator."

Noise laughed. "You know who was another good example of

what we're talking about? But not from the Alvarez or García clan."

"Somebody I know?"

"No. I guess you're right. You didn't know her. Miguel's mother. Maria Guadalupe something. Rodriguez, I think. Anyway, she married Miguel's father and came to live in Milwaukee. She didn't know how to cook or shop or anything. I guess they had servants for that. But she pushed herself. And she learned. She must have. After Miguel's father died, she and Miguel survived the Depression." He reflected for a moment. Then, "Now that took some cojones. A kid and his mother who could barely tie her own shoes getting through something like that."

"This is the first time I heard you mention her. Were you close?"

"She died when I was about ten. But before that we used to hang out together. I remember she would read me stories. Then she'd give me money to sneak out and buy ice cream, which I guess she wasn't supposed to eat."

"Miguel hardly mentions her."

"I know. He gets all emotional when he remembers her. Then he gets embarrassed about the tears. So usually he keeps his memories inside. But once in a while he'll come out with something. Like when he's eating. You know how he is about smells."

"Wood smells. I know about that."

"He's that way with food too. Oranges remind him of his mother. When he peels an orange, watch how he takes a deep breath to catch the scent of the fruit. He's thinking about her. And pot roast. I guess it was one dish she learned how to cook. So when Margarita makes pot roast, he remembers his mother. But it's the smell of the carrots that triggers the memory." He paused and attempted to backtrack. "How did I get started on Maria Guadalupe?"

"We were talking about strong women," Loco said. "I think you wanted to get back to your Tía Pilar."

Noise refocused. "She was special. One time I asked her how I could tell what a woman was really feeling. Her answer was, 'Pregúntale, Hijo. Pregúntale. No siempre te van a decir la verdad. Pero siempre te van a decir algo. Y ese algo puedes usar para saber lo demás.' And she was right. You may not get what you want. But you always get something. Women can't resist a question about feelings."

"You've been lucky with women."

"I've been lucky, period. I was thinking about that a couple of days ago. I even came up with a little theory. Luck can be vertical or horizontal, and horizontal is better." He maintained a serious exterior, but a riotous grin lurked behind his lips.

Loco favored him with a questioning glance and answered, "You lost me there."

"A piece of vertical luck would be a one-time stop on the road. It would change your life. There would be a before and an after, and they would be very different."

"Like winning the lottery."

"Yeah. That's perfect. Before you win, it's all hard work and pain. Then comes the vertical event. You win. Everything changes. Now it's all fun and games. A complete turnaround."

"So what's the horizontal?"

"It's like driving on a newly paved road. It just goes on and on. It's pure smooth all the way. No one big event. But a whole series of small, lucky happenings. And always right on time. Just when you need a small break, you get a small break. That's horizontal luck."

"But wait a minute. You had a piece of vertical luck. That time you found the money."

"You're right. That could have been vertical luck. But I didn't let it happen. I smoothed it out. I spread it around, so that a bunch of people got a small blip, but nobody got a big one."

"Not even Isabel."

"She probably thinks so. But really, it wasn't a big blip for her either. Everything she has, she had to work for."

"Wait a minute," Loco objected suddenly. "Are you saying you thought this through and made a conscious decision to spread out the luck so that it would be a horizontal and not a vertical event?"

"No. I'm saying just the opposite of that. I'm saying that I smoothed it out without even knowing what I was doing. I just did it. That's what horizontal luck is all about. You do the right thing at the right time. You meet the right people at the right time. Without planning any of it. It just happens. Smooth. Horizontal."

Loco shook his head. "You really believe this."

"What's not to believe? Look at the stuff that's happened to me. Crazy stuff. Wonderful stuff. Take the repair shop for example. Suppose I would've started the business when I first found the money. Before I went to Puebla. It would have been a total disaster. I would have pissed away thousands of dollars for nothing. Isabel would be on welfare with ten kids, and I'd be a bum."

"But you didn't even think about starting a business until a couple of years ago, when Miguel found that vacant building."

"That's right. I didn't. But if Miguel had pushed me back then, I probably would have done it. That's another example of what I'm talking about. The right people point me in the right direction at the right time."

"And the right direction was Puebla."

"You got that right. Uncle Chucho taught me about working, and Aunt Pilar taught me about living. Otherwise, ¿quién sabe?"

"Do you feel bad that you didn't get to see her once more before she died?"

"Not really. We said goodbye. When I left Puebla three years ago."

"You mean like a final goodbye?"

"I didn't think about it at the time. But now I see that it was. She even gave me her blessing."

"No kidding."

"For real. She put her hands on my head and said a little prayer."

"Like what?"

"Like, 'Dios te bendiga, Hijo.' And then she said something really nice. She said, 'En realidad tú no necesitas estas palabras, M'hijo. Para ti, la vida ya es una bendición.'"

CHAPTER SEVENTEEN

It was a day like any day. A Monday to be precise. Vintage late December. Eight inches of lake-effect fluff had fallen during the afternoon. Now, in the glow of the streetlights, all that glitter could not be shielded. Even by the heavy drapes closed over the bay window of Concha's living room, where the tenson was about to be staged.

Not that Loco, who had written the tenson, and had now assumed the role and position of stage director, was unduly worried about the lighting. The spots were there simply to differentiate the two characters. The off-on switch served only to mark the transitions. No. Loco's major concern was for ten-year-old Tony and the disaster that he might perpetrate on the paragraphs he was about to render as an introduction to the piece.

It was evening. A week past the winter solstice. The third day after Christmas. Innocents' Day on the Christian calendar. The day that the Alvarez children traditionally entertained their elders. And this year Loco had written a tenson for them to perform.

Two rooms of the lower floor of Concha's home constituted the theater. The dining room and living room together formed an inverted uppercase L. The vertical post that was the dining room served as auditorium. The area where the vertical post met the horizontal bar in the living room was the stage. The extreme end of the crossbar was the offstage area where Tony now fretted and tugged at his suddenly too-warm turtleneck sweater.

"Let's get started," Tony grumbled.

"Not yet. Give them a chance to get settled. Let the anticipation build a little." Loco patted the boy on the back. "You'll be fine. Just read it the way you did last night. Slowly. Your Aunt Concha was very proud of you."

Concha had attended the dress rehearsal the previous evening and, as per Loco's instructions, had heaped encomia on Tony's performance. Which had helped. A little. The boy was slightly less downcast about being cast as the announcer.

The problem was inherent, of course, in the tenson itself, written for two characters. Alicia, Tony's sister, and Juana, their cousin, had seniority by one calendar year and an eon of maturity. What remained was the role of announcer. Which Tony eventually had accepted. But with very bad grace.

"Girls get to do everything," he had objected.

"Girls who are older," Loco had corrected.

"It still isn't fair."

"Actually, you've got the most important part," Loco had cajoled. "The people who will be watching have never seen anything like this. So your job is to explain to them what they're going to see. If you do a good job, they'll understand. If you don't, they won't."

Finally the boy had agreed to participate. And he had learned his part, lollygagging and foot-dragging all the way.

And now he was on.

Loco cut the house lights and eased Tony into position on stage. Then back at his offstage vantage point, he hit a spot. Tony blinked twice, welcomed the audience, and began to read. "What you are about to see is called a tenson. In English it is also called a flyting. It is sort of a poem. But it's really more like a battle of words. There

BOOK THREE, CHAPTER SEVENTEEN

are two characters in the tenson. One is called the south wind. One is called the north wind. They are opposites. The south wind speaks Spanish. The north wind speaks English. The two are arguing or disputing. That's what makes this a tenson."

He paused. Except for the self-congratulatory grin, following the successful enunciation of the word "disputing," he had done well. Now he took a deep breath and read the Spanish version of the introduction. Then he exited to polite applause. Loco wanted to hug him, but there wasn't time. Instead, he darkened the stage and waited as Alicia and Juana found their marks. Pause, two three four. Deep breath. Hit the switch. A spot circled each of the girls and they began to recite.

South Wind (Juana)	North Wind (Alicia)
Yo soy la voz del viento	*I am the voice of the wind*
Yo soy la voz del viento del sur	*I am the voice of the north wind*
Anhelo amparar el instinto	*I rise in defense of restraint*
Yo soy la voz del viento del sur	*I am the voice of the north wind*
Yo soy la voz del viento	*I am the voice of the wind*

Blackout for transition. If the audience had been paying attention, the roles would be established. The satin costumes (Juana in red and Alicia in green) reinforced the distinction. The girls had projected energy and seriousness. They were ready. Now the punch-counterpunch could begin in earnest. Loco forced himself to finish his count. Eighteen, nineteen, twenty, lights, action.

South Wind (Juana)	North Wind (Alicia)
Yo soy la voz del viento del sur	*I am the voice of the north wind*
Yo soy la voz del instinto	*You are the voice of excess*
Me atrae lo extravagante	*You've more than that to confess*

CONTINENTAL NEXUS

Me alegra lo espontáneo So you get drunk every Sunday
Me encantan los días festivos You even celebrate Monday
Me fascinan los atrevidos Blissful they rush to their doom
Arriba los arriesgados Fools in a race to the tomb
Vivan los despreocupados Clowns trying hard to amuse
Brindo por el vagabundo A scoundrel with nothing to lose
Felicito a los enamorados Straining to keep their hormones hot
Me enfiesto con los poetas When was your last hepatitis shot
Comparto mi don con los pobres Fifty percent of nothing no less
Yo soy la voz del instinto You are the voice of excess
Yo soy la voz del viento del sur I am the voice of the north wind

Blackout for transition. Now it was the north wind's turn to flaunt its stuff while the south wind counterpunched. Again Loco forced himself to finish his count. Finally. Twenty. Lights. Action.

North Wind (Alicia) **South Wind (Juana)**
I am the voice of the north wind *Yo soy la voz del viento del sur*
I am the voice of restraint *Eres la voz represiva*
I celebrate the quiet deed *La sepultura festiva*
I follow the path of prudence *Con tanta cautela me cansas*
I venerate moderation *Modera tus alabanzas*
I cherish the rational life *Congelada y sin sabor*
I sing the praises of common sense *El burro canta mejor*
Here's to the faithful worker *Que siga fiel y tonto*
Cheers to the one who endures *Se morirá muy pronto*
I honor the rule of law *Defensor de los poderosos*
I laud the blindness of justice *Matador de los desdichosos*
My friends are those who obey *Conformidad opresiva*
I am the voice of restraint *Eres la voz represiva*
I am the voice of the north wind *Yo soy la voz del viento del sur*

BOOK THREE, CHAPTER SEVENTEEN

Blackout for the briefest of transitions to the conclusion. Which was simply a reprise of the opening. And . . . lights.

South Wind (Juana)	North Wind (Alicia)
Yo soy la voz del viento	*I am the voice of the wind*
Yo soy la voz del viento del sur	*I am the voice of the north wind*
Anhelo amparar el instinto	*I rise in defense of restraint*
Yo soy la voz del viento del sur	*I am the voice of the north wind*
Yo soy la voz del viento	*I am the voice of the wind*

The actresses had been directed to strongly project the third line of the conclusion. Then they were to gradually lower the volume level. The final line was to be spoken in a near whisper.

Juana and Alicia followed their instructions to the letter. This had the predictable effect of hyper-focusing the attention of the audience. The effect was . . . well . . . dramatic. Loco signaled the end of the piece with a five-second blackout which also allowed the announcer to join the actresses on stage for a bow. He hit the switch. The house lights came on. Nothing happened. For a long, long second.

Then Tony took over. "You're supposed to clap if you liked it."

Belatedly the applause exploded. Then the voices began to work.

"That was really something, Primo," Noise praised.

"The best thing you ever did," Isabel agreed.

"The children were great," Mai Lu added.

But no one could out-enthuse La Rubia. "That's exactly right. The kids made it work. But how do you get them to perform like that?"

"They're special kids," Loco explained. "I got them by special order from the special kids factory."

"Seriously though," Hannah pressed the point.

"Seriously, they work hard," Loco responded. "And we've been doing this for a bunch of years. So even though they're ten and eleven, they're veterans." He turned to his daughter. "How long have you been doing this, Juana?"

"Since I was five. Before that Nico and Eddie and Frances got all the parts."

"We were the best," Nico boomed. "Remember the year we did the Albee play? *The Zoo Story*. Remember that, Eddie? We were superstars, man."

"You were very good," Loco agreed. "But you copped out on me."

"I guess we got too old," Nico rationalized.

"So how long has this been happening?" Hannah asked.

"About a dozen years. At first the kids just wanted to recite poems. Then we started trying plays and stories. And here we are."

"Well, all of you should be proud," Hannah continued. "I understand about ten words of Spanish. And I was absolutely hypnotized. But why a flyting?"

"I was trying to write a play," Loco answered. "With a similar theme, north and south. And it wasn't going anywhere. There was no action in the play. So the characters had to carry the load and they just weren't up to it." He paused. "Anyway I like the way it worked out."

"So how did that turn into a flyting?"

"One day I was doodling on a piece of paper and I wrote, 'The north wind cold and the south wind hot.' I read the words a couple of times and added, 'The north wind's cool is the south wind's not.' The rest, as they say, is history."

"But those verses don't show up in the flyting."

"I know. That's how these things work. You cross the water, burn your boats, and leave everybody wondering how you arrived."

"Well, I think the whole performance was outstanding. And the costumes were fantastic. Where did they come from?"

"Noise's sister, Margarita, made them. With some help from

BOOK THREE, CHAPTER SEVENTEEN

Victoria. And I agree. They were fantastic."

"So some people write and some perform and some sew. This is like a real community theater," Hannah gushed.

Loco laughed. "You're making it sound much too serious. We just try to have some fun." He paused briefly. "What I hope to create for the kids are some good childhood memories. And if we spin off some good family vibes for the adults, I can live with that."

"Well, I didn't like it at all," came a judgment from the far north end of the dinner table. Everyone turned to look. It was, of course, the voice of the chronically contrary Marta.

Marta had spent the last night of her long holiday weekend sharing some savory gossip and three piña coladas with her sister, Isabel. The three drinks were precisely two beyond her usual intake. Consequently, the drive to work on Monday morning was one great vague. Her brain a condensed version of the mounds of cloud moving in from the lake.

At lunchtime, she dialed Isabel's number. No answer. She wanted confirmation. Had she heard correctly? Or had her avid brain dream-created the tasty tidbit? La Rubia is pregnant. No. She was sure. Isabel had said it. In those very words. La Rubia is pregnant. What a nugget. If it were true. But why would it not be true? Isabel had overheard Concha telling Mai Lu about a phone call to Noise. While they were talking, he had carried the phone into the bathroom in order to check on La Rubia. Who was busy barfing. Concha had heard the retching in the background. In fact, Noise had confirmed as much. No. Not the pregnancy. But he had told Concha that Hannah was being sick. What other explanation could there be? Nobody in the family had the flu. La Rubia is pregnant. As Loco would say: the feces and the fan have intersected. Now the fun will really begin. The fearless fornicator will now become the terrified terminator. The genteel university professor will find herself in line behind some adolescent ninny at an abortion factory.

Actually, that was not very likely. She would have connections. She would know a doctor who would know a doctor. Discreet. Reliable. Avaricious. Maybe someone whose services she had used before.

Too bad about Noise though. He would never know a thing. Probably wouldn't even be consulted. And he was such a dunce. On his own he would never figure out what was happening.

Marta muddled through the snowy afternoon in a mild haze. Back at the Donovan house after work, she found a note from Mamá Margarita. "Dinner at Concha's. Bring two folding chairs." She complied. She was standing in Concha's kitchen before she remembered that it was Innocents' Day. She had intended to absent herself, and now she had walked right into it. Dumb! Really dumb! Now she was fairly caught. She could leave as soon as dinner concluded. But meanwhile she was stuck.

And "meanwhile" would include enduring the ridiculous theater piece that Loco had concocted. Which was not a play. And not a poem. Not anything really identifiable. Unless you called it a bilingual bore. And then, to really pop a brassiere strap, there was horny Hannah gushing all over Loco like he was the greatest thing to pick up a pen since John Keats.

"I didn't like it at all," Marta challenged. "It's silly. The south wind. The north wind. There's nothing to it. It's just like the snow we had this afternoon. Bofo. Nothing to it."

Loco ever the gentleman. "Maybe you could be a little more specific, Marta. What exactly didn't you like?"

"Well. First of all, what are you trying to say? That all the people from the South are free and uninhibited and all the people from the

BOOK THREE, CHAPTER SEVENTEEN

North are rigid and inhibited? Even as a stereotype, that's crazy."

"I don't think he meant . . . " Hannah began to respond.

"I didn't ask you," Marta sniped. "Let Loco answer for himself."

"I forgot the question," Loco said.

"The question was if you really expect us to accept your premise that all the Spanish-speakers are liberated and all the English-speakers are control freaks."

"Well, first of all, the tenson is not about two groups of people. It's about two themes."

"Wait a minute," Marta interrupted. "If it's not about northern people and southern people, then why are you using English and Spanish? Why not Russian and Japanese?"

She realized that she was flailing wildly, and she expected Loco to respond in kind. Instead he went pensive for a few seconds. Then he surprised with, "That's an excellent suggestion. Let's pursue that. Russian and Japanese. If those were our options to represent the two winds, which would be the voice of restraint?"

Marta said, "The Japanese, I suppose."

Hannah interjected, "Except that they would be the east wind."

Marta favored her with a withering glare and added, "The Russians would be the defenders of instinct."

"Good," said Loco. "We all agree. But now ask yourselves why we agree. Why do we see the Japanese as restrained and the Russians as instinctive? Common sense tells us that there must be some Japanese who are very instinctive and some Russians who are very rational."

"Of course," Marta agreed.

"But popular perception would not allow the Japanese to be depicted as spontaneous."

"What's your point?"

"My point is that the south wind has to be associated with the

379

Spanish-speaking character, or instinct. And the north wind has to be associated with the English-speaking character, or restraint. Just to be believable. Because of popular perception."

Marta got the point, of course, but she was conceding nothing. Instead she returned her attack to her original target. "Anyway, you seem to be associating the spontaneous with everything you believe is good and restraint with everything you believe is bad. And that's just plain ridiculous."

"I don't see why you have to analyze everything," Noise grumbled. "Why can't you just enjoy it and let it go at that?"

Everyone ignored his outburst. So he went off to the kitchen to talk shop with Miguel.

"The two themes got equal play," Loco defended his craft. "For every thrust, there's a counterthrust. Neither theme is favored."

"Then what are you saying? The balanced life is the good life. That's as old as the Greeks," Marta scoffed.

"Actually, it's a little more complex," responded a still-unruffled Loco. "It's sort of a reminder that we are both instinctive and rational and that we need to find a place for both in our lives."

"And you think that concept came across in your piece?" Marta waxed incredulous. "I didn't hear anything even remotely like that."

"Art always carries that message," Hannah asserted.

"Art!" Marta stormed. "Now we're supposed to believe that this collection of cliches is art!"

"I think we're getting carried away," Loco cautioned. "Let me tell you a little bit about how I work. Something starts bothering me. I usually ignore it at first. Then maybe it starts getting insistent. So I decide to work with it. I start trying to find its energy. If I succeed, then I have a theme. Next I look for a form. Something that will contain and focus the energy of the theme. And that's it. That's all I'm trying to do with the north wind and the south wind."

BOOK THREE, CHAPTER SEVENTEEN

"Well, fine." For the moment, Marta pretended to be mollified. "But where do you come down? Which side of the fence are you on?"

"You mean north wind or south wind?"

"Exactly."

"Hmm. Let me phrase this as carefully as I can. A reasonable individual would want some joy in his life. So we need instinct. But instinct is unable to defend itself. So we need reason, too."

"You're saying that we should use our reason to defend instinct!" Marta jeered.

"Yes, I'm saying that. One of the functions of reason is to defend instinct. It's not the only one. But it's an important one."

"¡Estás más loco que tu nombre!" Marta crowed.

Loco placed his hands over his ears and slowly moved them down each side of his face until they met in a prayerful intertwining below his jaw. "Wait a mite," he cautioned. "We're getting way too theoretical. Let's get back to the real world. In the real world, reason and instinct don't fight. They cooperate. They do it all the time. Take pair-bonding for example. It would never happen if reason and instinct weren't in collusion. Reason by itself would always come up with another rationale for not proceeding. And instinct by itself would be happy with sex only."

Marta perceived Loco's example as a personal affront. "Two people rubbing their bodies together is pure instinct. You can call it sex. Or you can call it pair-bonding. But you can't call it rational."

"I agree," he surprised her again. "The body-rubbing is instinct. At least when it's done well. But pair-bonding, at least in humans, is a lot more complicated than just body-rubbing." Loco paused, stared at her for a few moments, then seemed to come to some resolve. "Anyway, the tenson does not prefer instinct to reason nor reason to instinct. It tries to establish a tension between the two with the hope that some sparks will be produced when the two confront each other."

"If the sparks happened, I missed them." Marta was determined to have the last word.

Isabel said, "What's for dinner?"

Loco said, "Mother made barbacoa."

Hannah said, "The sparks happened for me."

Marta said, "I thought you didn't speak Spanish."

Hannah said, "I don't. But I still . . . "

Marta said, "Then you missed half of it. But I suppose half a spark is enough for you instinctive types."

Loco asked Isabel, "Did you have to work today?"

Hannah said, "The energy comes across even if you don't know the precise meaning of the words."

Isabel said, "I'm taking some vacation days."

Marta said, "Energy is what we used to get from Nico and Eddie. Back in the days before my cousin here decided that he was a writer. Right, Nico?"

Nico said, "The kids do a nice job. But I think we were better."

Loco said, "How much vacation time do you have?"

Hannah said, "You and your brother did an Albee play?"

Isabel said, "We get two weeks a year plus two personal days."

Nico said, "We did other stuff too. Scenes from Chekhov and Beckett. But Albee was our number one guy." He struck a pose and recited, "'Mister, I've been to the zoo!' Remember that, Eddie?"

Eddie said, "I wish I could forget. In the play, I had to use a knife. And I don't even like to slice bread."

Hannah said, "I like Chekhov. And Albee is okay. But how could you prefer that to doing original work by somebody you know? And a flyting no less. One of the oldest literary forms that we know about."

Marta said, "We're supposed to be impressed by the fact that it's old? In that case, why not go all the way? Back to squeals and grunts and chest-thumping. That would be even greater art. Not to mention more instinctive."

Eddie said, "I don't know why that is. Guns don't scare me at all. But show me a knife and I start shaking."

Loco said, "Excuse me," and went to the bathroom.

Marta fixed Hannah with an intense stare. The moment had arrived. It was time to stop all the jabbing and sparring and cut to the knockout. It was time to pop the question. "Is it true . . . ?"

It was not to be. The door between the kitchen and dining room opened. The intrusive interrogative was skewered in mid-flight as dinner was announced by Concha.

Concha was a poacher of recipes. Unregenerate and indiscriminate. She scrounged the nooks and crannies of the planet in search of new ideas for soups, salads, breads, meats, and desserts. She filched from every region. No ethnic cuisine was beyond her reach. At various times and from various books and cooks she had pilfered ways of preparing everything from bouillabaisse to pig in a basket.

And nothing was sacred. Every recipe could be improved. And even if it couldn't, trying was fun. "You keep reinventing the wheel," Mai Lu sometimes complained.

"Maybe so," Concha conceded, "but when I finish, then it's my wheel."

"You never follow the instructions," Mai Lu objected.

"Instructions!" Concha scoffed. "A recipe is not a list of instructions. It's more like a series of recommendations."

Several of her more memorable meals had already been awarded a place in family oral history. But none was more renowned than her barbacoa. A recipe that she had from her cousin, Margarita. Who had it from her mother, María. Who had it from her mother-in-law, Sacramento. Who had it from some even more venerable ancestor, whose name, however, had already been consigned to the dustbin of time.

For the Innocents' Day dinner, Concha had prepared the sauce on Sunday night. With Mai Lu as her faithful apprentice. "There's a little trick here," she told her daughter-in-law. "Everybody knows that marinating gets the flavors deeper into the meat. But many people don't understand that the sauce is cooking the meat. So it needs less time in the oven. And that means it doesn't dry out as much."

Mai Lu had heard about this trick on a dozen previous occasions and knew her part well. "That's why the meat is always so tender."

"But you also need the right cut of beef," Concha cautioned. "This is a very strong sauce. So you need a strong cut of meat. Don't buy sirloin just because it's expensive and looks nice. It will go to pieces in the sauce. Buy chuck roasts and trim off some of the fat. Shank is good too. The round bone helps with the flavor. And cut it thick." She held up a three-inch cube of chuck roast. "About like this. You want the meat tender, but you don't want it to go to pieces."

"Is this enough?" Mai Lu gestured toward the small pile of chile ancho from which she had been removing the seeds and stems.

Concha picked up a handful of the dried pods and let them fall back onto the pile. "Two more," she pronounced. "Then about seven or eight of the chile guajillo."

When the meat was cut and the chiles cleaned, she started the marinade. She put the chiles into a deep pot. Over them she poured a cup of water. Then the pot went onto the stove over a low flame. When the chiles had softened, a half cup of vinegar would be added.

On a rectangular tray, she measured out her spices. Along one side of the tray, she built up five small mounds. First oregano, next thyme, then cumin seed, then coriander seed, and finally peppercorns. Along the other side, she spread a handful of salt, a half dozen bay leaves, two slivers of cinnamon, and three whole cloves. In the center of the tray she placed three quartered onions and the cloves of two bulbs of garlic. Then she stood back to appraise the array. After some study, she added two peppercorns and a smidgen of thyme and removed three cloves of garlic. "In Jachalco they go a little crazy with the garlic," she commented to her assistant.

Mai Lu knew her line. "Is that because the meat is mutton?"

"That's right. Mutton has a strong taste that some people don't like. So the cooks use lots of garlic in order to hide it." She paused for a final review of the ingredients. Then, "Time to find out what we've got." She put half the spices, half the onion and garlic, and half the chile and vinegar into the blender. Soon the other half followed. The sauce that resulted was thick, intense, and required just a little more salt." Another taste test. "Mmm," said Concha, "this is special. One for the storybooks." She poured the sauce over the thirty pounds of beef and moved the meat around until satisfied that she had bathed every veyne in swich licour. Then Mai Lu carried it to the basement where it would spend the night.

The rest of Monday evening's menu was discussed over brunch the following morning.

"So what would you like with the barbecue?" asked the head cook.

"I say go with the old reliable," Mai Lu suggested. "Beans and rice."

"You really don't want to try something different?"

"The beans are non-negotiable," said Loco, who ate very little meat.

"Something instead of rice then. Maybe a potato dish."

"Way too radical for this group," Mai Lu objected. "Two people will claim to have allergic reactions, and another pair will accuse you of trying to undermine their religion."

Concha chuckled. "What did you put in your coffee?"

Mai Lu was also smiling, but she stayed with her theme. "I came to this family as an outsider, and I've survived for fifteen years with one rule. When in doubt, go with the traditional. Beans and rice."

Loco agreed. "Beans and rice is the safe way to go."

Concha had another alternative. "How about a spaghetti casserole?"

Immediate concurrence from her son. "Ouh! Yeah!"

"Are you sure everybody eats that?" Mai Lu continued to doubt.

"I do," Loco assured. "And little Tony will think he's in heaven. He had four servings the last time."

"Even if they don't eat spaghetti, there's still lots of food," Concha reasoned. "But we do have one small problem. Somebody will have to go for cheese."

"No problem," said Loco. "I'm on my way."

"I still say beans and rice," Mai Lu insisted.

Monday afternoon, the barbecue went into the oven and the cooks went to work on the rest of the meal. Mai Lu started with the salad, which the family called pico de gallo.

She chopped five pounds of tomatoes, a pound of onions, three jalapeño peppers, three bell peppers, and half a bunch of fresh cilantro. Then she mixed the vegetables in a large bowl and seasoned them with salt, olive oil, and the juice of a lime. She tasted. "Pico de gallo," she acknowledged, "but something's missing."

Concha looked up. "Cheese," she said, then reached across the table for a sample. "And a little more jalapeño."

"You're right. I forgot the cheese. But that's enough chile. If I add more, the children won't eat it."

"Tienes razón," Concha conceded.

Mai Lu grated a half pound of the white Mexican cheese and mixed it with the salad. Again she tasted. "Much better." Then to Concha, "What's next?"

"Maybe you could mash the beans," Concha said. "The children

BOOK THREE, CHAPTER SEVENTEEN

prefer their frijoles planchados." And after a pause, "Then you can divide the beans into two serving dishes. And sprinkle some cheese on top. Let's try to make everything special tonight. All those extra little touches."

Concha returned her attention to the spaghetti casserole. She had already boiled three pounds of noodles and grated the cheese. Now she prepared the sauce. In a quarter cup of olive oil, she sauteed tomato, onion, garlic, and parsley. Then she cracked five eggs, separated the contents, beat the whites into a chiffon, and blended in the yolks. All was set for assembly.

Into two large butter-coated cakepans, she ladled a bit of the tomato sauce. She covered this with a blanket of noodles and a thin layer of grated cheese. Then more sauce and a coating of egg. And more spaghetti noodles. And more cheese. And again with the sauce. When the layering was completed, she topped the dish with a few dollops of butter and stood back to admire her work. She could not resist a smile. The recipe was another delight from Jachalco. Garnered from cousin Rogelio's wife, Leticia, following a single observation. It was simple. Only Mai Lu and possibly Victoria understood how easy it was to prepare. It was elegant. On one occasion provoking a reference to haute cuisine. It was appreciated. Even the children, who rarely paused to laud what they were eating, sang its praises. In fact, they had given the dish a special name. Because of its appearance and because it was served in squares, they called it spaghetti cake.

Concha covered the trays with foil and rearranged the pots of barbecue so as to accommodate the spaghetti in the oven. As the family straggled in by twos and threes, she made some hot sauce and some guacamole. While the tenson was being presented and discussed, she warmed the tortillas. When the discussion degenerated into bickering, QED, she announced dinner.

Food restored a friendlier mood to the dining room. Soon Concha was being rewarded for her labors by nearly unanimous praise.

"Sacaste un diez con la barbacoa," Victoria praised.

"De veras. It's super delicious," Toño concurred.

"It's the best ever," said Isabel.

"I'm telling you, Prima," said Noise, "you should seriously consider getting a job as a cook."

"It is pretty good," said Miguel. "I was expecting chicken nuggets."

For a second, no one understood. Then it quickly became clear that Miguel was using the line as a springboard for one of his shaggy dog stories. Which this time was about a fox, who was staggering home from the bar one night when he noticed a henhouse along the road. And there was no watchdog. He peeked in the window and started to count the nice fat hens that he would return for the following night. But counting made him drowsy, and soon he fell asleep. The next morning the farmer found him and went to get his shotgun. The fox barely escaped with his life.

"Now, you get your choice of morals for the story," concluded Miguel. "Either stay away from henhouses when you're out drinking, or don't count your chickens before they're snatched."

There were some polite titters. Mamá Margarita favored the group with one of her "This is what I have to put up with" looks.

"Are you sure that was a henhouse and not some other animal?" asked Noise.

"That's enough!" scolded Margarita.

The only discouraging word regarding the food came, predictably, from Marta. "What's the deal with all the cheese, Concha? There's cheese in the salad, cheese in the spaghetti, cheese on the beans. I know this is Wisconsin, but I think you got carried away just a little bit."

Mai Lu was sitting across the table from Loco. As Marta finished her criticism, their eyes met. Then in unison they pronounced, "Beans and rice."

Concha laughed. "I guess you're right."

Other than that, the meal was a wild success. Eventually the brandy and coffee began making the rounds. Later there would be a dessert prepared by Victoria.

But first it was time for Frances.

Frances, or more precisely, a story she had written, was the second half of the evening's entertainment. Her introduction was a model of brevity. "This is my story. It's about a princess named Helene," she announced and began reading.

At first they all lived happily ever after. The princess married a handsome prince. Her father grew old and began to mention resigning or abdicating or whatever it is that old kings do. Which meant that her husband would be the next king, and she would be the queen, and they would share the throne. And that whole bothersome question, about whether or not a woman might reign alone, could be avoided.

But, as things fell out, it couldn't. One day the prince, who was much too brave for his own good, went hunting wild pigs in the royal forest. Far out in front of the chase, he fell from his horse at the very moment which the male pig chose to whirl about and confront his pursuers. The prince was impaled on one of the giant hog's huge tusks.

"This is a bit of a bore," said Princess Helene. She also had been taught to conduct herself bravely in the face of adversity.

"Quite," said her principal adviser, Sofia.

"Now I suppose we will have that whole bothersome debate once again."

"Quite," responded a very laconic Sofia.

"Every antediluvian troglodyte will come out of the woodwork and begin moralizing on the perils of distaff rule."

"Precisamente," said Sofia, whose vices included bilingualism.

"They'll haul out every banal platitude that has ever been hurled at the topic."

"Presumably," said Sofia.

"So?"

"So?"

"So, you're the adviser. Start advising. What should we do?"

"The question is overly generic," Sofia advised.

"Sometimes you can really be a bitch," the princess complained.

"It is my job," Sofia replied calmly.

"So what should we do?"

"About?"

"About everything. About my dead husband."

"I recommend acquiring another consort as soon as decency will allow."

"Chosen again by my father?"

"You already have an heir. A girl, it's true. But still an heir. And your father is quite old. Presumably you will be allowed to choose this time."

"But how do I decide?"

"Make a list of the qualities you require in a male. Then select the five you consider essential for compatibility. Bring me the list at your earliest convenience."

Princess Helene prepared her list that same night. But for the next three days, there was no opportunity to discuss it with Sofia. First, the fallen prince must be buried with all due pomp and ceremony. With mournful wails and copious tears. And a sixty-four-gun farewell salute. Following which he was laid to rest in a crypt below the main altar of the principal cathedral of the realm.

The widow dutifully mourned her prince. But she was a practical sort. Before long she was discussing his replacement.

"Good news," she said one day to Sofia. "Father has decided. I am to inherit the kingdom. When he dies. Or when I have chosen a consort. Isn't that good news?"

"Quite," said Sofia.

"And one day my daughter will be my heir."

"Provided you have no sons," Sofia amended.

"How did you know about that?" demanded the princess.

"I have my sources. Did you bring the list?"

"I did. And I want you to know that this wasn't at all easy."

"Easy we left in Eden," Sofia quoted. "What's the first virtue that your consort must possess?"

"Sensitivity."

"Elucidate."

"In touch with more than his digestive system. When I've just finished reading a favorite poem, I want a response that shows some comprehension. At least I want to hear something other than, 'What's for dinner?' You can't imagine how infuriating that is."

"Actually it requires very little imagination," replied Sofia. "What's your second requirement?"

"A sense of humor."

"Rather vague," Sofia commented.

"Especially about himself. I mean, when you slip and take a tumble, as we all do from time to time, why is it so bloody important to look dignified about getting back on your pins? It's funny. Laugh."

"A sensitive type with a sense of humor," Sofia summarized. "What else?"

"He must show some spirit and style when it comes to dalliance," euphemized the princess. "Do you take my meaning?"

Sofia arched an eyebrow and replied, "I am not unacquainted with bedroom acrobatics. I take it that the former consort, en paz descanse, was a bit deficient in the spirit department."

"He was . . . how shall I put this . . . ? He was significantly more noble than mobile."

"Quite," said Sofia. "You would prefer a stud. What else?"

"Adventurous."

"Adventurous?"

"Yes. When I decide on a midnight ride to the pond in the royal forest for some skinny dipping, I don't want to hear twenty-seven reasons why it's not safe. I want him to lead the way."

"A sensitive adventurous stud with a sense of humor," Sofia updated the list. "And the last item?"

"I was saving the best. He must be a man of broad interests. Or at least not a single-subject soliloquist."

"You are referring to your late husband's all-consuming addiction to heraldry."

"Precisely. The man could put birds to sleep with his talk of armor and escutcheons."

"Similar to your first requirement. Which is helpful, since now we must reduce the list to three."

"Three!"

"Three," Sofia repeated firmly. "Even threes are rare. But fives, quite simply, do not exist. Choose."

"The last item is indispensable."

"Varied conversation."

"And the bedroom thing."

"A stud with varied conversation."

"And the sense of humor."

"A self-deprecating stud with varied conversation. Not an easy profile."

BOOK THREE, CHAPTER SEVENTEEN

"Can it be done?"

"We can try."

"How?"

"Resumes. Then interviews. Then maybe some performance tests."

"The first two of those are acceptable. But I will not engage in performance testing."

"Nor would anyone expect you to. I myself will see to the testing."

"You would do that for me?"

"Estoy para servirle," Sofia replied.

"Even the . . . you know what?"

"Even that," Sofia assured.

"You are truly without peer," said the princess.

"Quite," replied Sofia.

The following week the word went out to every province and territory. "Youthful widow seeks youthful male for possible lifetime partnership. Inquiries and resumes to the Castle."

Resumes arrived by the wagonload. Sofia began screening. She would select a hundred candidates at random, interview a dozen of those, and subject one or two to her performance tests. Occasionally a candidate would do so well that she would take him to spend a night at the pond in the royal forest. Only a handful passed that test. Even those who did were sent packing. But their files were kept in a special drawer mislabeled: Personal Hygiene Problems.

After receiving no referrals during the first six months, Princess Helene came to Sofia to complain about the delay.

"I'm sure you're being much too thorough, Sofia. Allow me to do some of the interviews."

"As you wish."

"When can I expect someone?"

"Tomorrow if you wish."

"I do wish."

Afterwards they exchanged notes. Sofia arched an eyebrow and said, "I trust that the young man was found satisfactory."

"The young man was found hideous. He was an expert in progressive geriatrics. Talked of nothing else. Are they all that bad?"

"He was one of the better sort. The other day I had a philosophy professor who misread the word coition. His response to the question was that cognition can be achieved in any position, prone or erect."

The process continued. Time passed. A year. Then another. Then a decade. The old king died. The princess became Queen Helene. Strife followed. A civil disturbance here. A small rebellion there. But the queen persevered. After a few years, the challenges ceased. Peace returned. Time once more to seek out a consort.

One day the queen was snooping about in Sofia's office. She found the file drawer marked: Personal Hygiene Problems. "These look interesting," she commented and carefully observed Sofia's reaction.

"Most intriguing," Sofia answered with feigned indifference. Then, crossing her fingers behind her back, she asked, "Shall I summon them for interviews with your highness?"

The queen was immediately wary. "Perhaps just one."

So he came. And strolled the royal garden with her majesty one summer afternoon. Pleasing the queen mightily with talk of history, travel, astronomy, and art. And as the sun went west, they nestled on a park bench cheek to cheek. She took his hand in hers and misquoted Huxley, "And here we sit in the evening calm, quietly sweating palm to palm." He looked into her eyes and his stomach rumbled as he asked, "So, what's for dinner?"

After that the queen ordered Sofia to discontinue the search. And the queen's daughter, the little princess, was officially crowned heir presumptive to the throne. The little princess was a most intelligent

BOOK THREE, CHAPTER SEVENTEEN

and very observant young woman, and on the day of her coronation, she told Sofia, "I have you to thank for this."

Sofia, of course, answered, "Estoy para servirle."

And only then did Sofia begin to introduce the queen to the men in the "Personal Hygiene" file. Eventually the queen selected one of them as her royal consort. Sofia herself consoled the others from time to time with a night at the pond in the royal forest. And that is the story of Princess Helene and how she came to be queen. Once upon a time.

Frances concluded her reading, and Loco led the applause.

"That's the second time I heard your story, and I liked it even more. It has a lightness. The people seem to waft along on cirrus clouds."

Tony submitted a somewhat more critical review. "It was a nice story, Frances. Except for the parts I didn't understand. And the once-upon-a-time is supposed to come at the beginning."

"¿Tú, que sabes?" said his sister, Alicia.

"Another vote for beans and rice," said Mai Lu.

"I took it as a spoof," said Noise. "Kind of a fractured fairy tale."

"The Sofia character is really impressive," said Marta. "I really like her."

"But she's such a manipulator," said Hannah.

"She does what she has to do," said Concha.

"Actually she's the fairy godmother of the story," explained Frances. "But with a tough streak."

Loco slapped himself up the side of the head. "I missed that! I completely missed that. And it's obvious now that you pointed it out. That's exactly who Sofia is." He paused. "I just knew she was a lot like my mother."

"You wrote this story for somebody in the family," said Mai Lu.

CONTINENTAL NEXUS

"Was it for my mother-in-law?"

"Actually," said Frances, "I wrote the story for Aunt Victoria."

Victoria had inspired the tale, albeit unwittingly. Two months earlier, Frances, now in her first year at the university, had been deploring the lack of maturity in her male classmates. Victoria had tried to comfort by describing her own futile early attempts to catch a prince. She, too, convinced that knighthood had already gone to seed. And every frog she kissed remained a frog. Until the day when Toño had appeared and carried her off to be his snow queen.

"Pero mi tío Toño no es nada de romántico."

"Ni en sus sueños," concurred Victoria. "Pero el principe que yo buscaba tenía que ser del tipo trabajador, también. Además tenía que mostrar cierta madurez para balancear lo chiflada que yo era."

"Maduro, romántico y trabajador."

"Y de los tres, tu tío mostraba dos."

"Y te conformaste con dos."

"Con dos. Y te digo la verdad. Después de discutir esta cuestión con otras mujeres, me considero bastante dichosa."

That, as it turned out, had been enough to stir the creative brew for Frances. And now Victoria found herself defending the resulting tale against, of all people, the writer's own brother, Nico.

"Nobody believes that nonsense about Mr. Right anymore. There are hundreds of acceptable matches for every woman."

"You mean that there are a hundred guys I could marry, and in each case my life would turn out exactly the same?" Frances questioned.

"I didn't say that." Nico looked to his girlfriend Sonia for help, but she was studying her coffee cup. "I just mean that you could be happy with a number of different husbands."

BOOK THREE, CHAPTER SEVENTEEN

"If I had a number of husbands, I would probably be deliriously happy," Frances teased.

Nico's ears turned red, and he attacked, "Anyway, what do you know about skinny-dipping at ponds in the forest?"

"As personal experience, nothing." Frances answered mildly.

"Then I suggest you stick to things you know something about."

"Wait a minute," Victoria intervened. "The pond is not a specific place. It's a place where you go with the person you love. Any place. A bedroom. A car. A pond in the woods. And everybody knows about places like that. You don't need to have personal experience."

"Okay, I'll give you that. But I still can't believe that women spend all that time agonizing about a perfect match."

"Maybe not all women," Marta interjected. "But not all women are the same. Why do you think some of us never marry? Because we have higher standards."

"I'm sure that's true," Nico carefully avoided contradicting his favorite aunt. "But that's not typical. I bet most of the time, it's very straightforward. You meet a guy. You check him out. You make a decision. Either you could live with this guy, or you couldn't."

"Of course that's how it happens," answered Victoria. "But you still prepare. When you're eighteen, that's all you do. You think about Mr. Right. You talk about Mr. Right. You dream about Mr. Right." She patted her husband on the shoulder. "Y luego te casas con Don Adecuado."

For once Toño had been paying attention. He patted himself on the other shoulder. "You could do worse than adecuado."

Everyone cheered. Noise cast a baleful look at La Rubia and asked, "¿Yo también soy Don Licuado?"

Everyone roared. Except, of course, Hannah, now adrift in a sea of bilingual ambiguity. Loco tried to explain to her what was happening and only succeeded in causing further mirth. Nico, however, seemed determined to end the discussion with at least one of his extremities entrenched firmly in his jaw. "Well, the story certainly leaves a wrong impression about the decision-making process. I mean, there has to be mutual consent. It's not just the woman who chooses."

The galaxy gasped. The herenow halted. The universe missed a beat. Every female eye in the room was redirected toward Nico. A massively maternal gaze. The sort ordinarily reserved for an inexperienced child who has just proposed some cosmically silly hypothesis.

Victoria to the rescue. "Time for dessert," she announced.

The galaxy exhaled. Miguel asked, "Did I ever tell you the one about . . . ?"

"Yes," answered at least ten voices in unison.

Victoria returned from the kitchen with a huge bowl of fruit salad and another of chocolate mousse. "Choose your calories," she invited. "The salad is a combination of grape, apple, banana, raisin, and walnut with a little lime juice on top."

Ouhs and Aahs were appropriately rendered.

"If you're beyond caring about scales and mirrors, I recommend the salad and mousse together," said Loco. "Based on a random sampling that occurred in the kitchen earlier this evening."

"How many people were in the random sampling?" Victoria asked.

"One," said Concha, indicating her son.

"But it was still a random sampling," Loco defended his method. "I closed my eyes and scooped some salad into a bowl. Then I arbitrarily blended in some mousse. Then I spooned a sample into my mouth. How random can you get?"

"You forgot the margin of error," said Marta.

"And the margin of error is zero," Loco added.

"I'll try the combination," said Miguel. "I'm actually watching my

BOOK THREE, CHAPTER SEVENTEEN

calories, but I need something to settle the brandy."

"I'm going to skip the first serving and start with seconds," Noise said. "What about you?" He winked at little Tony who also enjoyed a bit of nonsense.

"Me, too," said Tony. "I'm going to start with seconds. You can always go back for firsts." The kids gobbled their dessert, then coaxed Frances, Noise, and Loco into joining them in the kitchen for a game of rummy royale. Marta, Eddie, Nico, and Sonia went off to the movies. Miguel, Toño, and the Palafox brothers found a basketball game on the tube. The women took on a much weightier task: a discussion of the politics of food.

"Don't take this the wrong way," Hannah was saying. "The food was absolutely magnificent. But the feminists would say that you're out of touch with reality."

"Why is that?" Victoria asked.

"Most women are cooking less," Hannah explained. "And when they do cook, everything is simple. No fuss. No frills. No lime juice on the salad. No cheese on the beans."

"That's for the cooks to decide," Concha proclaimed.

"Of course. But the question remains. Why are you still spending so much time in the kitchen?"

Victoria did her best imitation of God on Mount Sinai. "A woman's place is not in the kitchen." Then in her normal voice, "Is that what you're saying?"

"I'm not associating myself with the notion," Hannah answered, "but, in a nutshell, that's the feminist position."

"I consider myself a feminist," Victoria answered. "I want my daughter, Alicia, to have more opportunities then I had. I want her to have more time to decide than I had. But I don't want her to forget her culture. I don't want her to forget her language. And I don't want her to forget her food."

"That's exactly my point," said Hannah. "You're saying that even if your daughter spends more time in the kitchen than other women, you still don't want her to forget."

"When you prepare a special meal for your family, you aren't watching the clock," Concha lectured. "You are hoping that they will enjoy the food. But at the same time, you are enjoying the work. Especially if you can share the work with other people who like to cook."

"Maybe this is too complicated for my English," said Victoria, "but I want to try." She paused for a deep breath. Then, "For thousands of years, women have cooked for their families. For thousands of years, we have called our families to come and share what there is. And that's the important word: share. Not eat. Share. People can eat alone. I'm not talking about just eating. I'm talking about sharing food. And while we share food, we also share other things. We share information, and that helps us stay in touch with the present. We share stories about yesterday and the old days, and that helps us stay in touch with our past. We share plans about tomorrow and next year, and that helps us stay in touch with our future. And there's more. When we share food we also share our feelings. We share our sadness when somebody is sick or when somebody dies. We share our happiness when two people decide to start a new family and when a baby is born. And we share the good feeling that we have when we are together." She paused. Everyone around the table was nodding affirmatively so she continued. "But the food is very important too. It's the stuff that keeps us alive. It's the stuff that gives us energy to work and play. Where would we be without it? It's what makes us grow and it's what makes us go. It's life sustaining life. So, of course, we want it to be tempting. We want it to attract. We want the herbs and spices to get into everybody's nose and bring them to the table. We want everybody to taste and say that it's good to be alive. We want everybody to remember our food and ask us when we're going to do it again." She paused, but only for an instant. "For me this is something really special. For me this is something that makes me feel proud. I like to be in my kitchen. That doesn't mean I'm somebody's slave. I like to cook for my family. That doesn't mean I'm somebody's robot. I don't believe a woman is more of a feminist because she stays away from the kitchen. I don't believe a woman is more liberated just because she doesn't know how to cook. I will not pretend that thousands of years of history were wasted. I am proud of what I do in my kitchen. I am proud of what women have done for thousands of years. I will never accept that cooking and calling my people to come and share food makes me less than a man."

Victoria stopped. For several moments, no one could pull herself free from the estrogen-soaked cloud in which the mesmerizing harangue had enclosed the group. Finally, Concha managed an "Amen," and the spell was broken.

"That was wonderful," said Mai Lu.

"It's too bad Sonia isn't here," said Isabel. "She's the one that needs this sermon."

"She doesn't like to cook?" asked Victoria.

"She can't tell a pot from a pan. The other day Nico asked her to make some three-minute eggs. When I told her there was no microwave, she didn't know what to do."

"But that's something Nico could do for himself," Concha protested.

The others agreed, and soon Isabel was defending her son against the entire sorority. Which gradually, logically, led to a review of the culinary prowess of each male in the group.

Loco's credentials were, of course, impeccable. The Palafox duo were championed by Lupe Silvas, who attested that both brothers had some cooking skills, albeit within a rather narrow range. Toño passed muster largely on the basis of goodwill. Nico and Eddie were pardoned because of their youth, as was Miguel because of his age.

So. It was not long before the full collective opprobrium of the sisterhood fell upon Noise.

Noise was always welcome at the children's card games. Not for his enthusiasm; that was Tony's forte. Nor for his knowledge of the rules; that was Juana's domain. Nor for his skill as an arbitrator; that was Alicia's jurisdiction. No. Noise's presence was welcome for a much less complicated reason. He could be counted on to lose.

The game didn't matter a whit. Pinochle. Poker. Euchre. Whist. Deal him a hand of cards, and his eyes blurred over. At once he began to envision rainbows with crocks of glowing metal at their source. At times, when playing with the children, he would lose by design. But that altered the outcome not a tittle. It only accelerated the process. As Miguel had once explained to Margarita, "In a poker game with five cards wild, your brother would bet on a pair."

Ordinarily, Noise could remain at the table by going deeper into his pocket. But on the night in question, he was undone by the house rules. Each player began a game of rummy royale with two dollars in chips. Once the game had started, no new money could enter. To equalize their chances with the more affluent adults, the children strictly enforced the limit. The ante for each hand was nine cents. Short of the ante, you were broke and therefore eliminated from the game. Not surprisingly, Noise was back in the living room in less than two hours.

As he served himself seconds from the salad bowl, he eavesdropped on the women. For some reason, they were discussing maternity clothes. He joined the men who were still sitting bug-eyed around the TV. The basketball game had just ended, and two guys in business suits were assuring each other that the winning team had

BOOK THREE, CHAPTER SEVENTEEN

outperformed the losers. Noise ate his fruit, then pretended to go to sleep.

The ploy worked. Within fifteen minutes, La Rubia was tapping him on the shoulder and asking if he wanted to leave.

At the door, Hannah paused to gush her gratitude. "Thanks everybody for a perfect evening. This was really great. The food. The entertainment. The conversation. Tonight I felt like I really belonged to this family. You're all wonderful. Thanks again."

It was Noise's turn. Assuming a voice in the female register, he began to parody Hannah. "I can't tell you how much I enjoyed this." Gesture of get-away. "You are all just too too wonderful." He knew better than to dawdle after that.

A cushion hurled by Miguel hit the door as sounds of, "¡Payaso!" and "Get lost already," and "¡Vete al carajo!" accompanied his exit. He turned to Hannah. Fortunately she was amused. They interlocked hands and started for home.

Halfway there, Hannah stepped off the sidewalk and flopped backward onto the snow. Then she spread her arms, joined them above her head, and moved them through the snow down to her sides. She sat up and threw one end of her scarf to Noise who pulled her to her feet. Back on the sidewalk she turned to admire her artistry.

"There! A perfect angel."

"How long since your last one?"

"At least a decade. Maybe longer."

"You should really be silly more often. Otherwise you're in danger of being declared an adult."

In their kitchen, Noise popped the lid on a Dos Equis and asked, "So, who's pregnant?"

"That was really funny," Hannah laughed. "Isabel thought that I was."

"You! Why?"

"Remember the night we went out for seafood? About two weeks ago. I got beastly sick just as we got home. Remember? I barely made it to the bathroom. You started referring to the restaurant as Salmonella Heaven. Don't you remember?"

"I remember. I remember. But what does that have to do with . . . ?"

"You were talking to Concha on the phone while I was being sick. I guess Isabel was there and overheard that I was vomiting and jumped to the conclusion that I was pregnant."

"Just because we're married now?"

"Actually, that's an interesting point. According to your sister and Marta and Concha, nothing is official until the church says it is."

Noise grinned and said, "I wonder if they're all holding their breath."

"Since they know you, probably not."

Noise sipped his beer and returned to his original question. "So, who's pregnant?"

"Lupe thought she was."

"Daniel's Lupe?"

"She is not Daniel's Lupe," Hannah lectured sternly. "But yes, the Lupe who cohabits with Daniel."

"And?"

"Her period was late. But it turned out to be just a tardanza. Is that the right word?"

"Get down, Hannah!" Noise congratulated. "It's exactly the right word."

Hannah beamed. "I guess it gave them quite a scare. Now they want to get married too. And they want you to be one of the witnesses. I told her you would probably say yes."

"Of course."

"I had a nice long chat with Lupe while we were eating."

BOOK THREE, CHAPTER SEVENTEEN

"I noticed. What was all that talk about immigration?"

"She and Daniel are participating in the amnesty process. Dante is undecided, but he'll probably also apply."

"That's right. The new immigration law. So Lupe qualifies?"

"Easily. She's been here since she was sixteen. And once she and Daniel get married, he'll also qualify. Dante is a tougher case, but somebody from the parish will probably vouch for him."

Noise was thoughtful for a moment. Then, "That thing Loco and the kids did. A tenson or whatever he called it."

Hannah doffed her professorial hat and interrupted, "Actually in English it's usually called a flyting."

"That thing. The new immigration law had something to do with that too."

"How so?"

"Loco and I were talking about the new law a while back, and he called it a breeze from the South."

"Really! He actually said breeze from the South?"

"His exact words. A breeze from the South." He paused to remember. "He was saying that the new law isn't like most laws that we have here in the North."

"In what way?"

"He kept using this idea of the brain and the body. He says in the North the brain gives the orders and the body obeys."

"That would make sense. Reason and restraint. They dominate in the North. But I don't see how he's going to make this work for the South."

"He says in the South the brain watches what the body is doing and then makes a law to say that's the way it should be."

"Instinct. The breeze from the South," Hannah recalled. "But I still don't see what that has to do with the new immigration law."

"I'm not sure I can get this right either. Loco's brain doesn't work

405

like mine."

"He's an original," Hannah concurred.

"Anyway. It's something like this. There are millions of people in this country without documents. The north wind wants to send them all home. But there are problems. That would be disruptive and expensive and probably impossible. So the south wind makes a suggestion. Let them stay and change the law so that they can become legal."

"Listen to the body and then have the law conform to what the body is already doing. This is really fascinating."

"And you see what Loco is saying? This is a new way of thinking about the law."

"Still a rational construct, but now with lots of input from the spontaneous and the instinctive."

"A breeze from the South."

"A breeze from the South. Instead of expending all the time and effort to send people back where they came from, change the law so that they can stay." She paused. "I'm even more impressed with the flyting now."

"The kids made it work."

"The kids and those costumes. You have a great family. I'm glad I decided to marry you."

There was a moment of silence. Then Hannah said, "Promise me something."

"Sure. What?"

"Some evening I would like to see the flyting again. I know Loco will let me read it and study the Spanish. But then I'd like to see another performance. Can you make that happen?"

"Why not? The girls always like to perform and Loco will be flattered that you asked."

Hannah assumed a pleading little-lost-girl voice. "But make it on an evening when Marta is too busy to attend."

Noise nearly rolled on the floor. "She can be a real saddlesore, can't she?"

Hannah had been moving around the room. Now she stopped behind the chair where Noise was seated. She embraced him, then pulled his head back and kissed his forehead. She borrowed his can of beer, sipped, and quickly handed it back. "I'll never understand how you can drink that stuff."

But the discussion about maternity clothes was still whispering inside Noise's head. "So nobody's pregnant?" he asked.

"Actually someone is. Guess."

When it came to naming life's major aggravations, Noise had a very short list. But guessing was right near the top. His usual response was a disagreeable obtuseness, and that was the tactic which he now employed. "Isabel? No. Concha? No. The Virgin of Guadalupe? Probably not. I give up."

"Mai Lu," Hannah announced in a whisper.

"Mai Lu!" Noise thundered as he rose from his chair. "Mai Lu and Loco are going to have another baby!" He stopped. "Are you sure? Isn't she too old?"

"Don't be ridiculous," Hannah countered. "She's no older than I am."

Uncharacteristically, Noise censored several possible responses. Then, "Did they really want another baby? Are they excited?"

"Are you kidding? Didn't you notice the way they were acting? Like a couple of giddy schoolkids. And why not? Mai Lu said that they've been trying to get pregnant for years. They never talked about it, because they were almost certain that it wouldn't happen. Even now Mai Lu waited for two months just to be sure."

Noise calculated, "Sometime next summer then."

"Probably the middle of July."

"A new addition to the family next year."

Hannah moved to him, circled his neck with her hands, pushed herself against him, and wiggled suggestively. "Maybe two, if we can get lucky." She tried to kiss him, but he held her off for a moment.

"We'll have to pretend we're the kid's grandparents."

"First let's do it. Then we can talk about pretending. Show some spirit, Grandpa."

And he did.

CHAPTER EIGHTEEN

It was a day like any day. A strong anticyclonic air mass had settled just to the north of Lake Superior, blocking the northern flow of sultry air from the Gulf in which Milwaukee had sweltered earlier in the week. Now on this end-of-summer Friday morning, the city was wrapped in a comforting breeze from the east. The classic cooler near the lake.

Loco, supine at his writing desk, stared at an aging aphorism on an otherwise empty page: *Order is the crumb that we snitch from Time when Chaos blinks.* The words were old, cold, comfortless. They were his. He could tell by the shape of the letters. They were all the words he had written for months. Since then. Since March. Since the day of the death in utero of the fetus. Which would have been his and his wife's second child. Which now would never be. Which almost had been the death also of the expectant mother.

Mai Lu herself had nearly brought on the second calamity. Understandably. She had so desperately wanted the baby. For two delusional days, she had silently clung to the wan hope that somehow the ominously still fetus would revive. Then the fever had overpowered her. She had collapsed. They had rushed her to the hospital and from there to surgery. Barely in time to save her life. And no one had been able to convincingly account for the death of the fetus. Nor could anyone explain precisely why the fetus had not spontaneously aborted. From that day to this, the sense of loss had pervaded all. Not overwhelming. But always there. Ingested with the food. Imbibed with the drink. Inhaled with the air. Inescapable. Except for that plaint against Chaos, his writing had ceased. Predictably. Awash in the pain of loss, the self diffused. Before creation could begin, energy evanesced. There was no concentration. There was no perspective. There was no focus.

Not that he could have written this day in any event. Even to begin required an ample expanse of leisure. And this day was thoroughly scheduled. In the afternoon, he would help with the tomato canning. In the evening, he would attend the housewarming for Daniel and Lupe.

Dear, gentle Lupe. The previous month, she had shyly approached to ask his blessing on the proposed party. Would it offend him and Mai Lu during their period of mourning? Would they attend? Would they consider music and drinks inappropriate? He had quietly reassured. At the time it had seemed such a trifling request. But then he began to reflect. What exquisite gentility! Here was a young woman of meager formal education who had the sensitivity to consider the feelings even of people not her blood relatives. And who, in a further gesture of civility, had approached Loco rather than Mai Lu so as to spare the bereaved woman any additional pain. "By such actions, the bodhisattvas vindicate the creation," he pronounced to the wall. Then, recalling that he was surrounded by Christians, he added, "Or, if you prefer, by such acts the world is redeemed."

A Jesuit voice from his past responded, "Civility may be a Buddhist virtue per se, but it is a Christian virtue only when enlightened by faith."

"Fine. Have the last word," said Loco.

"I shall," said the Jesuit.

BOOK THREE, CHAPTER EIGHTEEN

Dear, gentle Lupe. He knew so little about her. Only the biographic basics that Daniel had chosen to share. She was from a rancho near Durango. The third of five children. Sent north at fifteen with two older brothers. Worked for years in a sewing shop in Los Angeles. Then in the fields. Then in a restaurant. The brothers had married. The sisters-in-law had resented her presence. Away then. With a friend who had relatives in Milwaukee. And another sewing shop. Then an assembly job. Circuit boards. Slightly better pay. Some of which continued to go back home. To help support her parents and the siblings she hardly remembered. For recreation, dances on the weekends. At one of these she had met and begun to talk to Daniel Palafox. And as so frequently happens, one thing led to another. Now they were wed. And expecting a child. And tonight the clan would gather for their housewarming.

Lucky Lupe in a way. In stolid Daniel, she had encountered a nearly ideal partner. The two moved at the same persistent, unhurried pace. Which, now and again, here and there, was enough for a standoff with time. With their minimalist dreams and their condensed illusions, they were the salt of the earth. The unflashy hosts of everyday folks who carried on despite the horrors of history. It was they who had poured their blood and sweat and tears into the pyramids of Tula and Teotihuacán. It was they who had raised the temples of Tenochtitlán and then, when all was lost, it was they who had mixed their procreative juices with the runts and grunts of Iberia. Producing a people overly inclined to endurance. Facing the daily grind unblinking. Building and toiling through the long days. Stopping only for their nocturnal rest or the blessed sabbath or to bury their dead. As long as the daily gruel, however thin, was sufficient.

For a few seconds longer, Loco allowed the feel-good flood of fantasy to wash across his brain. Then, abruptly, he brought the interior monologue to a halt. "The masses," he scoffed aloud. "Brave perhaps, but hardly benign." The hordes of Genghis and Adolph provided cautionary overkill.

Fortunately, he had come to know Lupe and Daniel not as units of mass but as individuals. And part of the charm of individuals was their capacity for inconsistency. Sometimes they could even surprise, as on one occasion, Daniel had done.

It had happened during an English lesson. He and Dante were seated across from their teacher at Concha's kitchen table. Loco had initiated a drill for associating "am" and "is" and "are" with the corresponding form of the personal pronouns. Model question: where are you from? Model answer: I am from Puebla. The second person and first person plural would spin off from that context quite logically. The problem was the third person forms. Each of the brothers could refer to the other using the masculine singular form. And Concha was moving about the house and consequently available as the reference for the feminine singular. But what of the plural form? Daniel had solved the problem. On Concha's table there were two condiment shakers, one a male and the other a female figure. Daniel picked up the saltshaker and announced, "She is Maria." Loco's jaw dropped a half foot. Then he nearly lost that appendage when Dante had asked, "Where she from?" Without missing a beat, Daniel had responded, "Monterrey." Then he picked up the pepper shaker and declared, "He is Juan." Right on cue, Dante questioned, "Where he from?"

Daniel's response was, "Monterrey también."

Loco had intervened, "Where are Maria and Juan from, Dante?"

"Monterrey."

"Complete answer, Dante. They are from Monterrey."

Dante had tried, "They from Monterrey."

"Where are Maria and Juan from, Daniel?"

BOOK THREE, CHAPTER EIGHTEEN

"They from Monterrey."

"They are," Loco insisted. "They are from Monterrey. Repeat: They are from Monterrey."

"They are Monterrey," said Daniel.

And the magic moment had vanished. Never to return. Loco had replayed the scene in memory again and again, in an effort to convince himself that a breakthrough had occurred. And in a search for the trigger of that epiphany. But all for naught. In the months that followed, nothing remotely similar had come to pass. He let the memory waft away and then almost unconsciously picked up a pen and wrote: *Reflective individuals can make good community members because they understand the limitations of individuality while at the same time recognizing that community can be based on a mutuality of shared strengths.*

He dropped the pen, recoiling from what he had just done. Then he read what he had written. It was okay. He could live with that. It could serve as a new beginning. Individuals were the strength of a community. In fact, you could gauge the strength of a community by noting the extent to which individuality was allowed self-expression. A group that respected eccentricity was almost sure to be a healthy community.

And so in a flow of free association, the morning passed. In the early afternoon, the kitchen screendoor banged and the voice of Noise announced, "Prima, vengo por mis enchiladas."

Loco descended to meet him. "You got volunteered, too?"

"Your mom laid this guilt trip on me about how I'm always mooching a free lunch. And how she never says no. And what do I ever do for her? You know the routine."

Loco laughed. "She's shameless when she needs help." He paused. "Change of subject, Daniel and Lupe. Mai Lu and I want to get them something for the housewarming, but we don't have any idea what they need."

"You're asking the wrong guy. Hannah got them something. I think she said it was a comforter. What the hell is a comforter anyway?"

"Like a bedspread."

"Maybe they need two."

Concha ascended from the basement. "I suppose you won't work if I don't feed you."

"It's not that I won't," countered Noise. "It's that I won't be able."

"¿Chilaquiles?"

"Perfect. Chilaquiles will get you at least two hours of forced labor."

"Necesito seis horas. Chilaquiles, frijoles planchados, y una Dos Equis."

"Echale."

Isabel arrived all in a fluster. "What a morning. Se me olvidó la party de Lupe. Fui a comprarle un presente and then I had my hair done y luego fui a pagar unos biles. Todo de carrera y ya estoy bien tired y apenas vamos con los tomates."

"¿Qué le compraste a Lupe?" Concha asked.

"Unos frying pans de Teflon."

"Buena idea," Concha praised. "Le van a gustar."

The four settled down to lunch. Then they descended to the basement to confront three bushels of ripe tomatoes, and two pressure cookers already atop the venerable stove.

Concha assigned tasks. The men would peel the tomatoes. Isabel would wash and scald the jars. Concha herself would fill the jars and tend the pressure cookers. Any questions?

"Isn't anyone else coming?" asked Loco.

"Marta said she would try to get away early and give us a hand," Concha answered. "But you know Marta."

BOOK THREE, CHAPTER EIGHTEEN

Marta had promised to leave work early on Friday in order to help with the canning. She was admirably faithful to the first half of the pledge. But she conveniently forgot the second. Instead she went shopping at her favorite suburban mall. Where for an hour or two she could feel like she belonged. With people who were more her type. People who dressed and moved with a sense of style. And munched the latest faddish snack. And sipped the latest faddish fizz. And gossiped and joked about the latest scandals in Hollywood or Washington or some other entertainment capital. Where people gathered to see and be seen, thereby reassuring themselves and the others that this was what it was all about. For those who could afford the rewards of a consumer society.

Unlike her dotty, dowdy relatives, who dressed and behaved like riffraff refugees from another century. Exhibit A: Lupe Silvas, for whom she was now shopping. Pobrecita. The girl had gone from tattered adolescent to frowzy housewife with no apparent transition. One week she had been an impoverished working girl with little but the weekend dances to brighten her life. The next week, still a member of the working poor, she had also become the cook and laundry maid for a spouse and a live-in brother-in-law whose notion of a really satisfying Saturday night was a bango action flick and a pair of six-packs. And now, Dios nos libre, the girl was pregnant. And everyone was acting like she was the latest apparition to Juan Diego. Impregnated by divine intervention. Instead of having her slut button punched by Daniel's twinky.

But Mamá Margarita had been firm. If not exactly precise. "I want you to find something nice for Daniel and Lupe."

"Like what?"

"Something practical for the house."

"Pots and pans?"

"Not necessarily. Something they can use, but they probably

wouldn't buy for themselves."

"A food processor?"

"She has a blender. That's really all you need for sopa and mole and salsa."

"What then?"

"You'll think of something. It doesn't have to be for the kitchen."

That was vague enough. So here she was. In housewares. As per instructions, finding something nice. A set of Teflon pans. Price range right. But associated with last-second desperation. The kind of thing Isabel would buy. Popcorn poppers, no. Coffee makers, no. Crock pots, no. Hey. Wait. There it was. A waffle maker. What could possibly be nicer for Daniel and Lupe? They would be ecstatic. They would adore it. They would probably even have her over for brunch. The following Sunday. Yeah. Right. Give me a break. Microwave ovens, pricey. Jello molds, mixing bowls, casseroles, cheap, cheap, cheap. On to home furnishings.

On her way, she paused at a snack bar for a glass of iced tea. And to rest her high-heeled feet. This whole thing was beginning to irk. She was wasting a lovely Friday afternoon, probably one of the summer's best, trying to find the perfect gift for a shirttail relative and his incredibly dismal bride. No. Dismal was not too harsh. If anything, dismal was excessively kind. The woman had once confessed that she had never in her life read an entire book. Confessed it. Openly. Blandly. Certainly not with pride. But with no shame either. Confessed it the way people state that they once had chicken pox. Like it was beyond her control. Which, thinking it over, it probably was to some extent. She had finally finished primary school at the age of fourteen. Her parents were of the ilk that view their children as resources. To be harvested. The way you harvest apples year after year. So Lupe was sent to Los Angeles to earn money and send it home.

BOOK THREE, CHAPTER EIGHTEEN

But still. There were always things you could do to improve yourself. Nobody was entirely blameless for not getting ahead. Especially when there were so many opportunities for adult education. Of course, you had to learn about managing your time a lot better. And maybe forget about dancing the weekend away.

In the furniture department, she ignored the bulkier items. Small was all. Whatever else the gift might be, it had to be easily portable. No lazyboys. No futons. No rocking chairs. No back up to the loading dock and we'll tie it to the roof of your car. Yeah. Right. So you can drive away looking like some idiotic urbanized hillbilly.

Hey. There. The lamp. Keep that in mind. That was a definite possibility. Much too elegant. But if push came to puchar. The price was right. And that was the key. Display your ability to spend, but don't overplay it. Or look. Over there. A center table for a livingroom group. Pure functionality. A board with a hole in the middle for a piece of very plain glass. It would match the most nondescript sofa in creation. Which was exactly what the Palafox couple had. But not the right finish. Too blonde. She would ask about maple or walnut. But not right now.

Hunger pains announced their approach with a sounding off of tripas. Time to reconsider the decision to go without lunch. So. Away to the nearest salad bar. But by stages. Maybe they had that blouse in her size. And how could she resist sampling a few perfumes? Or noticing a purse? And then a belt. And then a hat.

Finally the salad bar. Some romaine for a base. Shaved carrot. Julienned onion and green pepper. Some of those cute little cherry tomatoes. Should be fresh since it was tomato . . . Oh my god! She had told Concha that she would help with the canning. Quick check of the watch. Well, she had to eat lunch anyway. Besides, Concha probably had a mob of helpers. And she still had to find a gift. So where was the problem? She would stop by when her shopping was completed. If the canners had finished when she got there, it meant that they hadn't really needed her anyway.

What were those chopped nuts? Pecans probably. Oily. But delicious. Maybe just two little scoops. Okay, two and a half. Skip the sprouts; that was for impressing friends. Garnish with some sprigs of cilantro. Then the vinegar and oil. As she replaced the second cruet, she noticed a garlic shaker. Yes, she would have some. But hey! This might also be a brainstorm. Spices. There wasn't a Mexican cook on the planet who didn't adore spices. And she had seen a spice rack somewhere earlier in the afternoon. She would go back and find it. Then she would swing by the spice store and load it up. Garlic. Ground pepper. Oregano. Tomillo. Cominos. Parsley. Paprika. Maybe get a little crazy with some fennel, marjoram, tarragon, and sage. It was perfect. Everybody would love it.

She slithered into a booth and attacked the salad. Relieved to be done deciding on a gift. Now if she could somehow survive the party. Yes, she would be there. Regarding her attendance, Mamá Margarita had been most explicit.

"I don't want to hear that you dropped off a present and left. This is the first time that we will be celebrating something for Daniel and Lupe. I'm counting on you to be there."

"Counting on you," as pronounced by her mother, conjured up the sound of anathemas and the smell of burning faggots. You tended to do as directed. But coercion was not the only salt in her C-cups. There was the whole outrageous fuss. It was not just incredible. It was unintelligible. A party. A housewarming. For a pair of bodoques who had been screwing for months before they finally decided to get married. And who had married only after they found out that Lupe was pregnant.

And who still had no plans for a church wedding. Even though they would soon have a kid who would need baptizing. Gente! Come

BOOK THREE, CHAPTER EIGHTEEN

on people! Does this make any sense? Can somebody please explain? This is not considered acceptable Christian practice. I know we're supposed to love the sinner. But throwing them a party! Madre santa! Give me a break already.

But that was vintage Mamá Margarita. And her famous double standard. Marta and Toño were expected to behave in a certain way and were royally roasted for any deviation. People like Daniel and Lupe were judged by a different standard. They could screw up, no pun intended, and you had to smile and forgive.

But that didn't entirely explain why the welcome mat had been stretched so far for Lupe Silvas. Sure, the girl was without the protection which a family ordinarily provided. And it was also true that she worked hard and learned quickly and didn't whine when things went sour. And yes, she was friendly and reserved. But if you shopped around long enough, you could find puppy dogs with all those characteristics. No. There was something else going on here. Something elemental. Something primal. Down at the level where the progesterone bubbled and the estrogen flowed. Something so obvious that it could be overlooked. Something so simple that it could be missed. Lupe Silvas was a breeder. Distasteful. Primitive. Even a little gross. But there it was. To survive, the family had to grow. And who else was there? Victoria had made it abundantly clear that her nuclear unit was complete. Mai Lu had recently failed. Hannah was apparently infertile. All the other females were menopausal. Go, Lupe.

Not that it mattered. Her mother could pretend to adopt Daniel, but she couldn't magically alter his genes. The infant would be welcome. But calling it an addition to the family was an exercise in semantic contortion. Still, having a child to cuddle again would be very nice. It seemed like years since little Tony had allowed her even a small hug, much less a good old-fashioned poke and tickle. "They grow up so fast." She had unwittingly spoken aloud.

A passing busboy paused to ask, "Are you talking to me?"

"No. No." She responded too loudly and then added absurdly, "I was talking about time." He favored her with that compassionate gaze reserved for the cerebrally deficient and turned away.

¿Quién sabe? There was no way to say how she would react to this new infant. She might even babysit. Provided they asked. And provided it was only an occasional request. She would have to be firm about that. She wouldn't want them to start counting on her for every whim and pretext. She didn't appreciate being taken for granted like some old piece of furniture.

But enough of this woolgathering. The hourglass trickled down, and there were a dozen things to do. The spice rack. Then the spices. Then home to wrap the gift and prepare a card. Then a quick shower. And then? No more excuses. She would cross the street and face the wrath of Concha.

Concha had noted Marta's nonappearance much as one might mark the absence of mosquitos on a warm summer night. In fact, she was flush with helpers. Two being all that she really required, and these had been quickly identified. Her son had volunteered, and Isabel's presence was a given, since she annually requested her summer vacation during canning season. Noise's participation would be welcome, albeit superfluous. He could fetch and carry, help with the peeling, and provide some comic relief.

The canning process itself was a series of simple, repetitive steps. Blanch the tomatoes. Remove the skins, cores, and any defects. Wash and scald the jars. Fill the jars and close each with a lid and screwcap. Place jars in pressure cooker in batches of seven. Cook at five pounds of pressure for ten minutes. Shut off heat. Allow cooker to cool. Remove jars. Proceed with next batch. All very low-tech. Soon the chatter began. "Tonight's the housewarming," Isabel said.

"Who's cooking?" Noise asked.

"Your sister. She and Victoria are showing Lupe how to make mole poblano."

"Somebody from Durango making mole poblano. That's illegal, isn't it?"

Years of dealing with this sort of relajo aided Isabel in formulating a response. "I think she got special permission from the archbishop."

"No kidding." He was relentless. "That must have cost a bundle."

As the banter continued, Concha listened to the silence of her son. Often she had heard him refer to himself as a citizen of the planet. That might be true. What did she know about such things? But in at least one way, he was puro mexicano. His soul.

Concha believed in soul. Not as some inner sanctum, which the sinner sullied and confession cleansed. Such tonterias were the inventions of silly priests to scare little girls and old maids. Nor did she believe in the soul as some ethereal self-sustaining entity that entered the body at conception and exited the body at death and then went on to some glorious future in a place called heaven. Such tonterias were the invention of not-so-silly priests who used the can't-take-it-with-you rationale to improve their alms collections. No. Concha believed (and this would have delighted her son had he known of it) that the soul is that part of all living things by which they access the lifeforce. In the case of humans, she thought of it as a sort of opening in the person. More or less permeable. More or less elastic. And the relative permeability and the relative elasticity determined the degree of liveliness of the person. People with great elasticity but little permeability were very lively but in a superficial way. Concha thought of Caribbean people as representative of this group. Other people with little elasticity but great permeability were less lively but more profoundly affected when something did touch them. Concha thought that this was more typical of mainlanders. And her son, Dios lo bendiga, was the consummate mainlander.

There had to be a way to release him from the morose self-captivation he had been in since they lost the baby. Maybe she could get him talking about the family. "Daniel y Dante han cambiado mucho desde que llegaron de Puebla, ¿verdad?"

"Dante, un poco," Noise responded. "Daniel, casi nada." Then, "I still can't get either one to say three words in English." A brief pause. "I guess we have to take into account who their teacher was."

Loco cast him a wry smile and answered, "Saben defenderse."

"Eso sí es cierto," Noise agreed. "The other day this guy came into the shop. Un tal Rodriguez. Asking about a tune-up. The guy's got nopales growing out of his ears, but he knows a few more words in English than Dante does. So he's trying to impress everybody with his English. Dante keeps explaining in Spanish and the guy keeps pretending not to understand. Finally, Dante gets fed up and tells the guy he can have a tune-up in Spanish for sixty dollars or a tune-up in English for eighty."

"He liked the sixty dollars better," Isabel predicted.

"Spanish all the way," Noise confirmed. Then, "Daniel is a different type. He likes the traditional stuff. He had a big fight with Lupe about quitting her job when they got married."

"But she didn't quit," said Isabel. "Good for her."

"That's only half the story. She agreed to quit in her last month of the pregnancy. And she promised not to go back until Daniel says it's okay."

"Men!" Concha editorialized succinctly.

"Southern men," Noise corrected. "Mi vieja can work two jobs if she wants."

BOOK THREE, CHAPTER EIGHTEEN

Concha laughed.

"It's in everything down there," Noise expanded his theme. "Remember when we went for Tía Pilar's funeral? Dante and Daniel asked me to get copies of their birth certificates while I was there. So I went to this government office and told them what I needed, and after about two hours they brought me these copies. Extra long legal size papers full of words. I thought I was reading a short story. So I asked the guy in the office why they put so much extra information into the documents. And you know what he told me?"

Without missing a beat, Concha answered, "We've always done it that way."

"Like you were standing next to me," Noise confirmed.

"That's what I mean. In the South, tradition rules."

"But to them it makes sense," Loco challenged. "To them it's the most prudent way to deal with novelty."

Holding her breath, Concha asked, "What do you mean by novelty?"

"Novelty. The new. The unexpected. Whatever you haven't experienced before."

"I don't get the connection," Concha released her breath. He was showing signs of interest. "How do you connect tradition with novelty?" She took another deep breath and observed with delight his way of collecting himself before delivering a lecture.

"Every society works to preserve itself," Loco began. "That means fending off dangers. And one of the most serious dangers is novelty. What do you do with the new?" He paused to separate the inquiry from the response. "One way to deal with novelty is to incorporate it. But in such a way and at such a pace that you render it harmless. That's the job of tradition in the South."

"Me dejaste en la terminal," Concha answered with what she hoped was not excessive glee. "I need an example to understand this."

"And I have one for you. It's a classic. I got most of this from a conversation with Victoria. Remember when women in the South couldn't wear pants?"

"Of course. Thirty or forty years ago, a woman who wore pants was considered a marimacho."

"But why was that?"

"Because men were the ones who wore pants."

"So what happened?"

"I guess some women just kept doing it until, little by little, people started accepting it."

"Actually it was tradition that intervened. First, tradition resisted the change firmly. That slowed the pace of change so that gradually people could rethink the issue. And when people started to rethink the issue, it began to occur to them that the issue could be reframed. Tradition provided another way to view the whole question." He paused.

Concha interjected, "I don't know what you mean by reframed."

"I'm getting to that. At first the traditional view was that pants on a female was a challenge to the males. But tradition also says that the female is frail and needs to be protected in every way possible from the predatory male. So now we stop thinking of pants on a female as a challenge to the male. And we start thinking of pants on our females as additional protection against other bad-intentioned males. Now what happens?" He paused to catch his breath. "Suddenly fathers, husbands, and brothers are finding reasons not only for condoning but actually for favoring the use of pants by their womenfolk." He paused and then concluded, "Another triumph for tradition."

"Would you believe it?" Concha was genuinely confounded. "I lived through that whole thing and I never once thought about what you just said. But now that you said it, it's obvious."

BOOK THREE, CHAPTER EIGHTEEN

"Victoria gave me another example," Loco continued. "But this one is different. It shows that sometimes tradition can deliver a knockout blow to novelty." He paused and stifled a giggle. Then, "Picture, if you can, a group of women from Puebla out shopping and wearing shorts."

Concha noted that even Isabel, who had never been within a thousand miles of Puebla, recognized that as a howler.

Laughter all around. At the next pause Concha asked, "So why didn't the gringos have a problem with shorts?"

"Because a citizen's way of dressing here in the North is connected to freedom of expression. And freedom of expression is a constitutional guarantee." He paused to regain his line of thought. "And from that, you can see how here in the North people confront novelty in a very different way."

"They sure don't believe in tradition," Concha agreed.

"That's right. Instead of tradition, we have law. The women's movement has a dozen examples. Take the issue of wages. Women complain that they receive less pay for doing the same jobs as men. How does society react? With a change in law to guarantee equal pay for equal work." He paused and found another example. "Women complain that they are disproportionately represented in public sector employment. How does society react? With a court ruling that women must be hired in greater than equal numbers until some semblance of parity is reached." Another pause. "But there is some similarity. Both tradition and law resist change. So resistance in both cases has to be gradually broken down by sustaining the pressure for change."

"I prefer to take my chances with the law," said Concha.

"That makes sense. The law is definitely more rational. Although probably not as rational as it pretends. And tradition probably protects a larger majority of people than the law." He paused and caught his breath. "But it all depends on the society. In a healthy democracy, where the citizens really participate, the law will certainly be preferable." He paused and rephrased the issue. "Where's the power? That's the bottom-line question."

After that there was no going back. The keg had been tapped and a veritable multitude of vermiforms tumbled forth. What was power? Where was it supposed to reside? Where did it actually reside? Everyone was heard from. At times by turns. At times in chorus. Laudations of the law gave way to tributes to tradition. Acclamations were heard for every form of political organization known to humans, plus a couple that were invented willy-nilly in the heat of the verbal embroil. At one point, Noise played devil's advocate and insisted that, since real power ultimately resided in the planet, all discussion of a just human society was so much bibulous babble. Loco conceded the argument in theory, but went on to counter that in practice the discussion of a just society was essential, since it constituted a search for meaning. Then he indulged in the ultimate self-flattery by quoting himself, "Man can no more live without meaning than a lion can live without meat."

Concha smiled ever wider as the talk continued. This was more like it. This was her son. A little verbose. Even pompous, when stirred to a defense of his principles. But who, in spite of the peculiar way in which he had been raised, had learned to care for others.

Now. If only there was a way to help him carry the mood into the evening festivities. And maybe there was. She would talk to Victoria and Frances.

Frances was at the university library. Collecting data for a research paper. For a course in Latin American studies. She had posed this question: Why had the creative outburst that followed the Mexican Revolution expressed itself in muralism rather than in some literary form? Her hypothesis was that the passions that had provoked and energized the revolution were so elemental as to render them impervious to verbalization and consequently inaccessible except to artists working in nonverbal media.

The underpinnings of her argument were sound. The foot soldiers of the revolutionary armies had been peasants. Their revolutionary fervor had been accumulating for centuries, during which its expression had been effectively blocked. Social mobility, a safety valve in most societies, had been discouraged or even outlawed. The fiesta, another potential release point, had been manipulated by the church and monitored by the hacienda. The only religious innovation of the society, the Guadalupe myth, had been promoted by the church and landowners to reinforce resignation in the worshipers. So far so good.

But there were problems. Where were her sources? The histories could abundantly attest that the peasants were mum, but that did not prove that they were mute. So. She had found herself at the mercy of the muralists themselves. More precisely, she had spent most of the afternoon wading through a dreary biography of Diego Rivera. For a pair of lame quotations that reflected rather poorly on the artist while doing precious little for her theme.

She dropped the book, closed her eyes, and let her lower lip slip into a peevish pout. Everything annoyed. Her hideous hypothesis. The endlessly enduring peasants. Rivera's sycophantic itch for fame. Any pretext for quitting would be welcome. Any trifle at all. She opened her eyes. And there he was. Harold the Handsome. Duke of Dork. The young man who sat next to her in Latin American studies. And showered her with unwelcome attentions. Whose modest cerebral talents had been displayed the day she had explained that education was doubly difficult for bilinguals since they had to learn everything twice. He had responded, "That makes sense."

Fortunately, he had not seen her. She jammed her things into her backpack and maneuvered through the stacks. And so to the entrance and down the front steps. A quick left turn. A sudden fraternal collision.

"Eddie! What are you doing here?"

He checked for dislocated parts and answered, "I was supposed to meet somebody. There must have been a mix-up about the time. I'll call him later. Want to get a drink or something?"

"Coffee maybe." She looked him over more carefully. Did he want to talk? Maybe not. Play it by ear.

Seated across from him in a coffee shop she asked, "So, what did you get for Lupe and Daniel?"

"The bath towels. Like you told me." He paused to display what she called his funereal face. "I was thinking maybe you could drop off my present. I don't really want to go."

She did a bilingual count to ten. Then, "Eddie, this is not about you. This is about Lupe and Daniel's first-ever invitation to the family. Not going is not one of your options."

Eddie did his best imitation of defiance. "Okay. If I have to go, then I'm going to bring someone." He paused and added lamely, "A friend."

She giggled. "Meaning that you gave some consideration to bringing an enemy?"

Eddie the irritated: "I'm being serious, Frances. You don't know what it's like."

That merited the wag of a warning finger. "I told you about that, Eddie. Don't do that if you want me to keep listening. It just makes me mad. We're all human. We all hurt. We're all human. We all empathize. So. Don't pretend that you're a special case. You're not."

Eddie the chastened: "I just mean that it's hard, Frances. Every time we have one of these family things, Nico shows up with Sonia.

And everybody knows they're doing it. But that's okay. He's a stud. Right?"

"Is that what this is about? Nico can bring a friend and you can't? That's crazy. Of course you can. Bring him."

"It's not the same. Everybody approves of Nico."

"Because Nico and Sonia have a statistically more standard relationship than you and your friend. That's just numbers, Eddie."

"No, it's not. Nico knows that people approve of him. So he has a lot of confidence. I know that people disapprove of me. So I don't have the same kind of confidence."

That was not easily disputed. Time for a frontal attack. "Are you going to change yourself so that people will approve of you?"

"You know I can't do that."

"So you need the family to accept you the way you are." She paused. Then firmly, "Eddie, they've already started to do that."

Eddie the intransigent: "That's right. They started to accept me. But alone. Not with somebody. If I take my friend to the party, I'll probably spoil everything."

Frances studied him for a few moments. Then, "You know something? You're right. Bringing your friend to a family thing is the next logical step. So do it. Tonight. Bring your friend."

Eddie the incredulous: "You approve?"

She shook her head. "Eddie, what have we been talking about? You have to take the leap and let people do whatever they do."

"I understand that. I don't need your approval. But I still want it. Frances, you are my favorite person in the whole world. I want you to say you approve."

That left her silent for a moment. Then she put a hand atop one of his. "Okay. I approve. But don't make too much of that. In this family I'm still a lightweight. Just like you." Then, in a bouncier tone, "Tell me about your friend. What's he like?"

Eddie the ingenuous: "He's got big ears."

She giggled. "Big ears!"

"Well, he does. That's the first thing everybody notices."

"Does he have a name?"

"Paul Quiles. He's from New York. He's in his third year at the university. His people came from South America, but he can't speak Spanish. He's taking courses, and I'm trying to help him. But it's tough. He keeps asking me why we say things a certain way, and all I can tell him is that it sounds right." He paused and asked, "What's a subjunctive anyway?"

"It's the verb form when you talk about something being doubtful or possible instead of factual."

"See, that's the kind of stuff I don't get. And Paul knows all that stuff. But he still can't talk."

"So what do you two have in common?"

Again he displayed the funereal face. She stifled a grin and amended her question, "Aside from that."

His face went to a scrunched concentration. "Let's see. We both like to swim and we both like country music. And we both want to live out in the woods some day."

"What's he studying?"

"Political science."

"Don't tell me. He wants to be an ambassador."

"No. He never mentioned that. But he does have some weird ideas."

"Like what?"

"Lately all he talks about is something he calls a worthy national purpose. He says we don't have a worthy national purpose, so the country is just drifting."

"Continental drift. It's unavoidable."

"He wants to start a campaign to make everybody computer

literate within ten years. What do you think?"

"About mass movements? Mostly I think yuck. I like individual people to have their own individual projects. Then there's a chance for real community when the projects converge."

Eddie the enthusiastic: "Maybe you two could discuss this some time."

"Maybe. What's your favorite thing about him?"

"That's an easy one. He's organized. He has goals. He knows what he wants."

"Another classic instance of opposites attracting. What's his favorite thing about you?"

Eddie the earnest: "The fact that I don't have to hide from my family about being gay."

"Ouch! That sounds like his family doesn't know about him."

"They don't. And his situation is worse. He's the only male child in the family."

The imp in her could not resist. "Are they rich?"

Eddie the offended: "Frances! That's none of our business."

"I know. But are they?"

"Actually I think they are. He drives a Jaguar. It was a present for his eighteenth birthday."

"Hecho! Bring him to the party. When his parents throw him out, we'll adopt him." She paused. "And now, speaking of cars, can you give me a ride home? I promised to help with the food for tonight."

Back at the house, she surprised Nico as he was about to raid the refrigerator. "Frances!" he crooned. "Perfect timing. I didn't have any lunch. How about making me a couple tacos? Beans and egg. Please. I'll tell everybody you're my favorite sister. Please."

He was not half as charming as he fancied himself. But she might need him on her side for Eddie's sake later that night. So she swallowed hard and answered, "Sure. Why not?" while he raced up the stairs.

She heated some oil in a frying pan and sautéed some chopped onion and chile. Into this mixture she dumped some cooked beans and mashed them as they warmed. Leaving them to simmer, she whisked two eggs and added them to the pan. She heated the comal, warmed a half dozen tortillas, and covered them with a cloth napkin. Then she put the beans, tortillas, some hot sauce, and a glass of juice on the table and yelled up the stairs that the food was ready. And from on high he descended. King Nico. Followed closely by a sexually satisfied Sonia, clad only, Frances was certain, in her cynical brother's bathrobe. "Hi," the queen of bedroom high jinks beamed.

"Excuse me," said Frances and ran to the bathroom. She immediately raised her skirt, lowered her panty and settled onto the toilet seat. But she was so outraged that it was a full five minutes before she could relax enough to pee. Meanwhile, she counted the ways by which she could remove the supercilious smile from Sonia's face. Acid was too violent. Irony could be ignored. And then, as she released a small fart, it came to her. The beans. She had seasoned them with chile and onion. Now she would add a dash of doubt.

She exited the bathroom and smiled broadly at Sonia and Nico as she measured her steps toward the kitchen door. "Good luck with those beans. I don't know how long they were in the refrigerator. They smelled okay when I took them out, but you never know about beans." And after the slightest pause. "Okay then. Got to run. I promised to help with the cooking for tonight." The screen door closed behind her with a bang.

A few moments later, still giggling, she entered the kitchen across the street and greeted Lupe, Mamá Margarita, and Tía Victoria.

Victoria was pleased. With Lupe, who had arrived early for her mole poblano lesson and had stayed to wash the breakfast dishes.

BOOK THREE, CHAPTER EIGHTEEN

With Mamá Margarita, who, noting that Lupe was available for stirring the mole, had volunteered to cook the rice. With herself, for expediting the mole-making process by a daring act of heresy.

Preparing mole poblano from scratch involves the frying of multiple ingredients. No self-respecting poblana would ever employ anything but an earthenware cazuela for this purpose. Some degenerate northernized impostor might compromise with a metal skillet. But Victoria was committing an even more impious act of cultural iniquity. She was using a wok. Which Mai Lu had presented to her the previous Christmas. Which Victoria had put off using until just such a day as this. And now, East was meeting South in an oleaginous kiss.

Each of the ingredients was fried individually. First into the wok went a handful of almonds. When done, they were removed with a perforated scoop, drained against the side of the wok and dropped into a bowl of hot broth from the already boiled chicken. The almonds were followed by a handful of peanuts. Next came a heap of raisins, a stack of semisweet crackers and two plátanos machos cut into tostones. Then, in no particular order, small measures of cinnamon, anise seed, sesame seed, and a chunk of genuine Mexican chocolate. Finally, the dried chile was given a quick dip in the oil: first a sizable mound of chile mulato, then a smaller amount of chile pasilla.

The wok proved to be both more efficient and more effective than a skillet. Since the heat was more concentrated, the ingredients fried more quickly and more evenly. Since the ingredients could be removed more easily, they drained better and less oil went into the sauce. Victoria was pleased. She smiled. "Va muy bien esto."

Lupe nodded agreeably. "Yo he comido este mole muchas veces. Pero es la primera vez que veo como se hace. Está muy curiosa la receta."

"Más que curiosa," Victoria answered. "¿A quién se le ocurrió la idea de combinar chile con chocolate?"

Lupe shook her head but attempted no response.

"Lo que yo digo es que fue pura chiripa," Victoria continued. "A alguna cocinera de aquella época se le cayó el chocolate en el mole. Ella no chistaba nada a la gente que vino a comer. Y como a todos les gustaba su mole, ella se decidió por cambiar la receta."

Lupe laughed. "A lo mejor así fue."

The two returned their attention to the sauce. Victoria half-filled the blender with some of the fried ingredients and some of the broth. As the machine worked, she thinned the mixture with water. Satisfied with the consistency, she stopped the machine, poured the blender's contents into a large mixing bowl, and repeated the process.

When the ingredients of the mole had been blended, Victoria began the process of blending the flavors. Into a cazuelota, she poured some oil, heated it, then ladled in the sauce. She thinned it with more of the chicken broth, lowered the heat to a simmer, and provided Lupe with a large wooden stirring spoon and a short course in mole amalgamation. "El cucharón se mueve lentamente de un lado a otro. Siempre tocando el fondo. De manera a que no se pegue el mole abajo. Eso es lo que tenemos que evitar. Porque pegándose en el fondo, se va a quemar. Y si se quema, olvídate. Tú solita te vas a comer el mole."

Lupe tried. Victoria approved. "Así exactamente. Que no se pegue. Es todo el chiste. Y despacito. Al estilo de la tortuga. Tocando todo el fondo. Así es." She moved a high stool next to the stove and said, "Siéntate."

"No, gracias," Lupe responded. "Yo estoy acostumbrada a trabajar de pié. No me canso."

"Como quieras. Pero te digo de una vez. Este proceso toma casi dos horas. Al rato te vas a arrepentir."

"No creo," her helper countered. "Soy de buena pierna."

BOOK THREE, CHAPTER EIGHTEEN

"Es lo que dice Daniel."

Lupe blushed furiously and laughed. "Apenas estoy acostumbrándome a las bromas de ustedes. Es algo nuevo para mí. En mi casa teníamos que medir las palabras con mucho cuidado. Y ustedes no. Ustedes bromean de todo. Hasta del sexo." She blushed again.

"Es verdad. En el sur, la mujer que cuenta chistes lo hace con sus comadres. Donde hay hombres, se queda callada. Y acá en el norte, como dicen mis cuñadas, la mujer es mas atrevida." Victoria reflected on that for a moment or two. Then, following a feat of cerebral acrobatics, she started off in a new direction. "¿Y qué tiene de malo? Los chistes dan sabor a la vida."

The transition was stressful for Lupe. But she puzzled along as Victoria, now firmly astride a favorite rhetorical pony, raced ahead. "Ponte a pensar, Lupe. ¿Cómo sería un mundo sin sabores?"

Lupe hobbled from puzzled to bewildered and Victoria was forced to adjust her pace.

"Con un ejemplo, mejor. Vamos a la comida. A ti te gusta el chile, ¿verdad?"

"¿Cómo no?"

"Y te gusta el limón."

"También."

"¿Y la tortilla y los frijoles y el queso?"

"Todo eso me gusta."

"Pero cada una de esas comidas tiene un sabor distinto."

"Es cierto."

"Y nos gusta la variedad de sabores."

"Claro que sí."

"Bien. Ahora imagina un mundo en que toda la comida tenga el mismo sabor."

"Sería un mundo desabrido."

"Sería un mundo muerto. Ahora. Ponte a pensar otra vez. ¿Cómo sería un mundo sin cuentos y bromas y chistes y juegos de palabras?"

Lupe chose to treat the question as rhetorical.

Victoria stormed ahead. "Sería un mundo igual de desabrido. Los discursos sin gusto. Las pláticas sin pique. Como dices tú, '¿Qué chiste?'"

Lupe summarized. "Entonces las bromas y los chistes son como los sabores de la comida."

"Efectivamente. La persona que tiene maña para los chistes saca las pláticas más sabrosas."

All unconsciously, Lupe produced an instance of Victoria's theme. "Entonces el chiste colorado ha de ser como la salsa verde."

Victoria amended. "Salsa verde, no. Para chiste colorado, tiene que ser salsa roja." The two laughed. "Ya ves lo que te digo," Victoria crowed. "Ahí está el ejemplo."

The afternoon advanced lazily. More and more the kitchen took on an aura of warmth. The veggie tray grew by mounds of radishes, carrot sticks, quartered bell peppers, scallions, and cherry tomatoes. The mole bubbled gently along. Victoria pretended not to notice as Lupe eased a cheek and then both onto the stool. But the seated posture emphasized the distension of her belly. That brought on the next wave of conversation.

"¿Estás haciendo tus citas regularmente con el doctor?" Victoria quizzed.

"Sí. Voy cada mes," Lupe answered. "Pero es doctora."

"Mejor. Así hay mas confianza. ¿Y qué dice la doctora?"

"Ella dice que todo está progresando muy bien. Pero yo tengo mucho miedo."

"¿Por qué?"

"No sé. Como que algo me va a suceder. Me acuerdo mucho de cosas que contaron en la casa hace años."

"Son historias de antes," Victoria tried to reassure, "cuando la

BOOK THREE, CHAPTER EIGHTEEN

mujer que contaba con la ayuda de la partera se consideraba muy dichosa. Pero ya no es así. La doctora va a estar contigo."

"¿Y no dicen que la naturaleza manda?"

"Es cierto. La naturaleza manda. Por eso. Ten fe en ella."

"¿Y qué pasó con la esposa de tu primo entonces?"

So that was the burr in her saddle. "Estás hablando de Mai Lu. Pero no. Fue solo un caso en un millón."

Lupe was not so easily put off. "Como que ella no se compone."

"Tienes razón. No se ha compuesto bien. Pero no se trata del embarazo."

"¿Entonces?"

Victoria measured her response. Regardless of how she phrased it, what she was about to say could be construed as gossip. And she detested all such prattle. But Lupe needed reassuring. So. "Físicamente, Mai Lu está bien. Moralmente, sigue sufriendo. Y es porque le falta la comprensión de su esposo. Ahora es cuando ella más necesita compartir su tristeza con él. Pero él prefiere sufrir solito." She fought to maintain control but anger took hold. "Como todos los hombres cuando confrontan lo último. La muerte los deja hipnotizados. Y la mujer llorando solita." She brushed a corner of her apron across her eyes, forced a smile, and altered her tone. "Pero estábamos hablando de tu caso. Mira Lupe, yo tengo mi trabajo y mi familia, pero eso no quiere decir que no puedes contar conmigo. En caso de una emergencia, desde luego. Pero para cualquier problema o pregunta también. ¿Me entiendes?"

"Sí, Victoria. Gracias. Todas ustedes son muy buenas conmigo. Aquí me siento mas protegida que cuando vivía con mis hermanos en California. Pero el miedo no se me quita."

"¿Miedo de qué?"

"Tengo pesadillas. De que voy a morir y mi hijo va a quedar sin madre."

"¿Y has hablado de esto con Daniel?"

"No. Olvídate. El ya está harto de mis quejas."

"No. No puede estar harto. El embarazo es de los dos. Te tiene que aguantar todas tus quejas. El es el papá. Parte de su responsabilidad es de aguantar tus quejas. Es su trabajo. Tienes que insistir, Lupe. Estos hombres tienen que aprender que el embarazo es de los dos. Y nosotras tenemos que ser las maestras."

"¿Pero, qué le digo?"

"Dile todo lo que sientes. Y si empieza a protestar, pregúntale si él no es el papá del bebito. Rápido vas a tener su atención muy concentrada en ti."

"Es fácil para ti," Lupe objected. "Tú tienes mucha educación."

"Lo que acabas de decir es totalmente falso," Victoria countered. "Yo no tengo más educación que tú. Tengo más años de estudio en la escuela. Eso sí. Pero más educación, no. Mira Lupe. La verdadera educación viene de la vida, no del estudio. Y en la vida tú has visto cosas que yo no conozco ni en pesadillas."

The usually docile, diffident Lupe met her gaze unflinchingly for a full fifteen seconds. Then she asked, "¿Eso piensas de verdad?"

"De verdad. Por eso voy a esperar la misma firmeza de ti que espero de mí misma." As Lupe continued to stare Victoria added, "Ya atiende ese mole. Si se echa a perder, todos los hambrientos van a estar hartos de ti."

It took forever, and to Lupe it probably seemed longer, but eventually the mole was done. By that time, Margarita had returned to announce that the rice was ready. Frances had entered and entertained the group with her story of Nico, Sonia, and the beans. The four women had migrated to the front room, where they had made an early start on a pitcher of piña colada.

"Lo que hace falta ahora es un hombre para llevar todo esto a la casa de Lupe," Victoria said.

BOOK THREE, CHAPTER EIGHTEEN

"Somebody with a weak mind and a strong back," joked Margarita. As she spoke, she looked across the street at Concha's house. She blinked. There he was. As if on cue. Standing in the doorway. Her brother Noise.

Noise performed his transport of the cooking vessels with all the impassivity of the average donkey. First, he and Frances lugged the cazuela of mole poblano to Lupe's house. Then he hoisted the veggie tray atop his shoulder and repeated the trek. He did a third trip with a kettle of cooked chicken dangling from each arm, and a fourth with the rice from his sister's kitchen.

Meanwhile, the womenfolk tippled and giggled. Soon Isabel and Concha joined them, and the gathering took on an aura of conspiracy. Which aroused no trepidation in the donkey. The women were oblivious to his comings and goings. So clearly he was not the object of their plotting. But some hapless male was having his past exhumed or his future planned.

Noise completed his beast-of-burden morph, reassumed his human guise, and went home to shower. Then he grabbed a beer and settled into a chair on the back porch, awaiting Hannah.

She would be on time. She was always on time. In that way, she was a standard Northerner. Not so in a number of other ways. Not so when it came to religion. Not by a light-year. Based on her sermon of the previous evening, she was some kind of unregenerate bolshevik. He still had no idea what had brought that on.

He had been in the bathroom tinkering with a leaky faucet. Suddenly she had appeared in the doorway. "You know what I just decided? It's a lie about religion being a basic human need. The basic need is not for religion. The basic need is for purpose. And we let religion fill our need for purpose because we're lazy. We don't want to do the hard work of creating purpose for ourselves from scratch. So we settle for the canned stuff off the shelf. The prediluted predigested formulas. And they come with womb-to-tomb service and a guarantee. So who could resist when all you have to do is buy the package."

"What's wrong with being lazy?" Noise had objected.

"Nothing really. I'm not big on effort either. But that's not my point. My point is that we let ourselves be controlled by the witch doctors and the priests and the shamans and the other pranksters. And what they're doing is something we could be doing for ourselves."

"Why make it so complicated?" he had protested. "Why all the heavy lifting to get yourself a purpose? Just live. That's enough purpose for everybody."

By which, of course, he meant that it was enough for him. But he also knew that she would never share his simple creed. She was like one of those mechanics that go right on monkeying with a car even after it's running perfectly.

He must have dozed off for a minute. His next recollection was of Hannah tapping him on the shoulder and saying, "We're late. Everyone is already next door."

As it turned out, their tardiness proved advantageous. Some of the clan had already finished eating. There was immediate seating at the kitchen table, where they joined Isabel and Frances, and were in turn joined by Eddie and his friend, Paul Quiles. Soon all were sampling the mole.

"This is exquisite," said Paul. "Edward was attempting to explain about this sauce, but obviously he could not do it justice."

"Edward?" Noise arched an eyebrow at his wife. Hannah scowled ferociously, and he quickly amended. "Oh. Of course. Eddie."

"He calls me Edward," Eddie explained, and then with further redundancy, "It's Paul's first time eating mole."

"First time!" Noise feigned umbrage. "I thought you said his last name is Quiles. What planet is he from?"

"He's from New York," Eddie responded innocently.

"Well, everybody has to be from somewhere. We won't hold that against him."

"Edward told me about an uncle who's sort of a genius with cars. Is that you?"

"I'm a mechanic. If that's what he meant. Why?"

"I have a Jaguar that needs some service work. Would that interest you?"

Noise nearly choked. Was the young man bereft of his senses? How could he even construe such a question? Would working on a Jaguar interest a mechanic? Did fish swim? Did birds fly? Did coyotes ever have a craving for lamb? Would he be interested in working on a Jaguar? Mole, beans, and rice wafted away into realms ethereal. Eddie, Hannah, Frances, and all the others faded into a cloud of unknowing. Bells summoned the faithful to worship. Pilgrims slouched toward the sacred grove. Noise entered the holy ground on penitent knees. And beheld. A power plant divine. Precision in every line. A vision of felicity. A high performance deity. The monster god of the century. Da car.

A half hour after the meal, Hannah returned and forcefully led him away to the dance floor, where cousin Dante was in charge of the music. Wonderful stuff issuing from the boombox. Big band. Latin sounds. Cumbias. Salsa. Danzones. Cha Cha. Merengue. And the occasional unavoidable polka. And people really dancing. Miguel and Margarita. Lupe and Daniel. Frances and Loco. And then Hannah and Noise.

The meager furnishings of the Palafox living room had been pushed against the walls. So there was ample room for four couples. Even mainlanders. Even from the Alvarez clan. Noise had overindulged himself in the mole, however, and he was a taco too heavy for sustained gyration. He managed a polka with his wife and a cumbia with Frances. Then he slipped outside into the cooler evening air.

In the shadows on the north side of the house, he nearly bumped into Marta. "Sorry. I didn't expect anyone to be here."

"It's so hot inside," she justified her presence.

For a minute or two, there was some labored small talk. Then Noise asked, "As long as you're here, can we talk about something?"

"Sure, I suppose so. What's up?"

"Lupe is pregnant," Noise began ceremoniously.

"If you're trying to be newsy, you'll have to do better than that."

"It's their first baby," Noise continued to belabor the obvious, "so they're all excited. And one night we got talking about some things. Stuff that won't happen for months. But you know how people are when they're looking ahead to some big deal."

"When you say people, you're talking about Lupe and Daniel."

"Right. So the subject of names for the baby came up. And that led to some talk about baptism. And that got them started about godparents and all that mess."

"And they want you to be the godfather," Marta guessed.

"That's right. But I reminded them that I never go to church. So there's no way that the padre is going to let me be the godfather. Isn't that right?"

"That's probably true. But why are you telling me this?"

"Because they want you to be the godmother."

"Me? Why would they think of me? I'm not even a relative."

"A bunch of reasons. You and the padre are friends, so there wouldn't be any problem with the arrangements. And maybe, since you're a good Christian, the padre might think that one good godparent would be enough. So he'd let me be the godfather."

BOOK THREE, CHAPTER EIGHTEEN

"So that's what this is about. You want to ride along on my coattails."

"Not at all. Regardless of what the padre says about me, they still want you to be the godmother."

"Then why don't they talk directly to me about this? Instead of sending a messenger."

"I'm not the messenger. They didn't send me. They don't know that I'm doing this." He paused to carefully construe his next sentence. But nothing came to him. Finally he blurted out, "Lupe is afraid of you."

"Afraid? Of what? That I'll say no?"

"Lupe thinks you live in a different world." He raised a hand to detain Marta's response. "I'm not kidding. That's what she said. Except in Spanish. Ella piensa que tú vives en el mundo elegante. Hablaba del estilo que tiene tu ropa, y que tu cabello siempre está perfecto, y que conoces las películas y libros que están de moda. All that stuff. The word she kept coming back to was elegante."

Marta's reaction was a mix of doubt and delight, with the latter clearly in the ascendancy. "She thinks of me as elegant? She really said that?"

"Only a few dozen times."

"And you're sure that they really want me? I was their first choice?"

"You were the only person they talked about. But it's like I'm telling you. Lupe is afraid to ask. She thinks you'll be offended."

Marta stared at him intensely for several moments. "You're not just making this up?"

Noise snorted, "Marta, for christsake! Why would I possibly make this up?"

She was unrelenting. "Lupe really used the word elegante?"

"Elegante. I'm telling you. She gave us about three dozen examples of how elegante you walk and talk and dress."

Marta preened and pranced as she pretended to weigh the various and sundry considerations. Then she issued her pronouncement, "Tell them I said yes." With an elaborate gesture she reassured herself that coiffure and diadem were still in place. Then she brushed regally past him on her way to rejoin the group. Five paces off, she stopped, turned, and, after a majestic pause, amended, "No. Tell them I would be honored."

"Serendipity," Noise whispered at her departing back. He raised his gaze to the night sky, winked, and repeated, "Serendipity." Then he too rejoined the dancers.

Inside, the atmosphere had turned purposeful. Isabel, Lupe, and Frances seemed determined to keep Loco on the dance floor. Toño and Daniel dedicated themselves to doing the same with Mai Lu. Then, in the course of a polka or cumbia, a switch would occur, and Loco would be partnered with his wife. Finally he took the hint and invited her to dance.

Almost immediately the rhythm issuing from the boombox went from salsa to slow dance. At a signal from Concha, the women pulled their men to the dance floor. Then all the adults formed a circle around Loco and Mai Lu. They locked arms and began swaying to the easy cadence. Mai Lu buried her face in her husband's shoulder, but that provided but a momentary refuge. Soon someone started a chant of, "Beso. Beso. Beso." Which crescendoed until the hapless harassed couple obliged. Compliance, however, brought no respite. The kiss was critiqued and appraised from every angle. Then there were shouts of, "Put some feeling into it" and "Echale ganas." And no sooner had the lips of the harried couple parted, when someone started a chant of "Otro. Otro." Following some further osculation, Victoria pushed her way into the circle with two champagne glasses filled with piña colada. The pseudo-newlyweds interlocked arms and drank until the glasses were drained. At that point, Miguel got caught up in the fun and insisted on dancing with the novia. So Margarita followed his example with Loco. Then the others joined in and played out the ritual, males dancing a few steps with the bride and females with the groom. Even little Tony took a turn with Mai Lu.

When the piece finally ended, Loco announced, "I think we'll be going home now."

Concha did her part. "Juana is spending the night with Alicia. I intend to stay here and dance some of these youngsters into the floor. You two lock up the house. Noise can let me sleep on his sofa."

"No problem," Noise quickly agreed.

As Loco and Mai Lu departed, Hannah eased Noise away from the group. "What a lovely spontaneous happening," she gushed.

"Are you kidding!" Noise scoffed. "That was about as spontaneous as a parade."

"But what was it all about?"

"It looks like my primas decided that Mai Lu and Loco were starting to lose the old flame. That's my best guess. To tell you the truth, I never noticed any problem."

Hannah nodded. "Impressive. I'm glad I was here. It was really nice to be a part of this. And who knows? Maybe someday the family will have to do the same thing for us."

Noise laughed. "You could get some long odds on that."

CHAPTER NINETEEN

It was a day like no other day. A day to be remembered. Even if you were not the birthday child. Nor the long-laboring mother. Nor the agitated father. Nor the self-possessed midwife. But just some dumb-stricken witness to the fury of snow and wind.

For most of the previous week, the jet stream had exhibited a zonal flow from Pacific to Atlantic along the forty-fifth parallel with hardly a hitch or wrinkle in its progress. Then, inexplicably, it had taken a mighty dip down the eastern slope of the Rockies. As if the continent had reached up to remind of its basic north-south predisposition. Immediately, a wave of hyper-frigid Arctic air had darted south as far as the Rio Bravo. There, above the plains, it had met and mingled with the hyper-humid air of the Gulf.

Back in Milwaukee, Lupe Silvas moved with the aura and pace of a sleepwalker. She was no longer her self. An ungovernable force had overtaken her body. She had become the repository of the most basic drive and striving of her species, the plaything of purpose.

On Tuesday, the obstetrician had repeated her status report of the preceding Friday. "Any day now. Everything looks ready. It should be a normal birth. I don't expect any surprises. Something should happen this week. If not, then we might have to consider inducing labor."

On Wednesday, Lupe had busied herself with the laundry.

BOOK THREE, CHAPTER NINETEEN

Huffing and puffing up the basement steps like some overweight octogenarian. "El ejercicio te hace bien," everyone encouraged. That same day the meteorologists began talking about a storm system that was slowly getting organized over the southern plains.

On Thursday, Lupe watered her houseplants and nearly fell off a chair while ministering to a peperomia in the kitchen. "Ya no puedes hacer esas cosas," everyone scolded. "¿Cómo crees?" That same day, the meteorologists began talking about a major storm that was slowly moving out of the southern plains.

On Friday, Lupe revisited the obstetrician, who again assured, "Any day now. Everything looks ready. Something should happen this week." That same day the meteorologists reported that the Texas panhandle had been clobbered by every form of winter precipitation known to humans.

Throughout that day, the blizzard maintained a northeasterly bearing. By midnight, it had reached southern Illinois. Where it seemed to hesitate. As an unsure traveler might pause to study a road map. Weather experts, who had confidently plotted the storm's course along the Ohio River, also paused. And began to hedge their bets. "Almost certainly" was replaced by "probably," which was soon downgraded to "maybe." Head-scratching gave way to hair-pulling. One savvy veteran summarized, "Don't take your eye off this one. This monster is as predictable as a horse with a hornet in his ear." And while not long on precision, his forecast proved to be as accurate as any. The blizzard took a left turn and headed for Chicago.

On Saturday, Lupe was overcome by the culinary imperative. As soon as brunch was finished and the dishes washed, she began with a large pot of beans. Then in another pot, she boiled a four-pound potroast. By adding corn, squash, green beans, and potatoes, plus a sauce that was a blend of tomato, peppers, onions, and garlic, all ingredients from the previous summer's garden, she produced a huge kettle of mole rojo. From there she went on to a cazuela of rice. That would suffice for the evening meal. With plenty left over for the men to reheat while she was hospitalized. Or so she projected.

But then Noise, whose wife was away visiting her mother, came by and found the Palafox brothers in the basement, sipping beer and tinkering with the clothes dryer, and who could resist such felicity. In the late afternoon, Loco and Mai Lu dropped by to see how she was doing, and not inviting them for dinner would have been unthinkable. Then Isabel and Frances showed up to check on her progress, and certainly there would be enough for them as well. And what with more eaters than expected, and most of them with larger appetites than anticipated, the mole disappeared, the beans nearly vanished, and the leftover rice would not have nourished an anorexic sparrow.

The day's weather would have received mixed reviews. Had you solicited a comment from a veteran of Wisconsin winters regarding the forecast of a heavy snowfall, he might have scoffed, "It's January. Big deal." A less hardened critic might have been more perceptive. To such a one, the patches of lake-effect precipitation that fell in the afternoon might have appeared as prologue for the next day's drama. And justified the air of eery expectancy that seemed to settle over the city.

Following dinner at the Palafox home, the invitees ordered Lupe to rest while they did the dishes and attempted to reassure her regarding the imminent arrival of her firstborn.

"Nada mas ponte a pensar, Lupe. El sábado que viene, vas a estar sentada en la misma silla dándole el pecho a tu hijo," Frances enthused.

"Tú estás joven," Mai Lu tried her Spanish. "Todo va a estar bien. No te preocupes."

"En otra semana, no vas a recordar estos días," Loco added.

"Yo sí me acuerdo de la first time," Isabel recalled. "Fui al doctor

BOOK THREE, CHAPTER NINETEEN

y le dije que tengo symptoms de la flu y me sale con la surprise de que estoy pregnant."

The chatter continued. The effort to keep it light persisted. But by nine o'clock, Lupe was yawning profusely. Twenty minutes later, she was dozing. In the perennial pronouncement of Frances, even a bilingual could figure out that it was time for "Hasta mañana."

Meanwhile, the storm advanced. By eleven o'clock, the wind at its leading edge was cavorting and disporting in the streets of Milwaukee. Within a half hour, it was penetrating every nick and crack in the Palafox home. Music ensued. But of a savagely postmodern mode. The apertures around the windows and doors differed as to narrowness and length. So there was some variety of pitch. But with no diversity of instrumentation and no direction or arrangement, the result was pure cacophony. A Saturday night carouser stumbling into Lupe's kitchen might have concluded that he had joined a brotherhood of woozy whistlers.

And then it was Sunday. A day like no other day. A day to be remembered. And Lupe slept on. As one long deprived of rest might abandon oneself to sleep. Unaware of the lashing gale without. Unaware of the more subtle stirrings within. Until about three o'clock. She awakened with a shudder. Or so it seemed. Something had tugged at her lower abdomen. Briefly. Then it passed. Again she closed her eyes. But no longer to find profound sleep. The wee hours would be a bout with vex and fret.

There was no dawn to the memorable day. A careful observer might have noted a lighter tinge to the gloom. But a mere glimmer at best. And little change as the day advanced. Everywhere white-out conditions prevailed.

At six o'clock, the weather forecasters bravely stated that ten inches of snow had accumulated overnight. But anyone who had bothered to go outside could have told them that the word accumulation in the present context was meaningless. In some places, the wind had whipped together drifts of five feet or more. In others, the ground was nearly bare.

A little after six, Lupe got up to pee for the third time in two hours. As she lay down again, her husband stirred.

"¿Qué te pasa? Estás muy inquieta."

Lupe's casual response was, "Parece que este va a ser el día."

Comprehension took a second or two. Then he tried to swallow. Twice. And gave up. "¿Qué hago?"

"Nada," she gave him a reassuring pat on the shoulder. "Falta mucho tiempo todavía."

That was a little like announcing to a child that it was Christmas but too early to open the presents. Rational responses were not to be expected. Nor were they forthcoming. Daniel got up and began to pull on his jeans. Backwards. That he could rectify easily enough. But then he looked out the window and his stomach dropped to his ankles. There was nothing out there. Nothing but blowing snow. They would never get to the hospital. He should have expected it. He was always screwing up. But this time it was happening with something really important. And he had to do something to make it right. Anything. There must be something he could do. Then it came to him. He could go for help. He could brave the storm and bring back someone who could help. A woman. Someone who would know about these things. Victoria. Yes. Perfect. She was practically a doctor. She had all the answers.

He took a deep breath. Straightened his shoulders. Stiffened his spine. He must hide his fear from his wife. Fear was contagious. If he showed the slightest sign, his wife would become terrified, and everything would be lost.

He turned to her. "Victoria," he announced. "La voy a traer."

She smiled. "Sí, Daniel. Pero más tarde. Es como te digo. Falta

BOOK THREE, CHAPTER NINETEEN

mucho tiempo todavía."

"Mejor de una vez," he answered. "Así podemos formar un plan de como vamos a llevarte al hospital."

She laughed. "Todavía no, Daniel." She tried to sense his mood. "Mira, si ya no puedes dormir, vamos a la cocina. Te hago unos blanquillos con rajas."

That seemed to anger him. "¿Cómo crees que te voy a tener cocinando en estos momentos?" He jerked himself into his winter coat and, without even covering his head, went out the front door.

A blast of bone-numbing air raked his face and knocked him down the front steps. He pulled himself to his feet. On an ordinary day it was a mere four paces out to the sidewalk, but today he could barely locate the front gate. He took the first step and fell again. After that he crawled to the gate. And made a decision. An incredibly illogical decision. Which probably saved his life. He would abandon the plan to go to Victoria's house. He would get Noise instead. Noise would know what to do.

Along the front of the Palafox yard and continuing along Noise's yard was a wire mesh fence. Daniel used the fence to claw his way to Noise's gate. Then he crawled inside and up the front steps. The house had a covered entryway, and, by dragging himself inside, he finally escaped from the wind. He caught his breath, pulled himself to his feet, and began banging on the front door.

His luck held. Noise had fallen asleep on the couch in the living room. Even with the wind howling in the background, the pounding of Daniel's fists and feet eventually awakened him. He opened the door. For a few seconds the two men just stared at each other. Then Daniel yelled, "El niño viene." It was such an odd and unexpected greeting that Noise actually looked over Daniel's shoulder to see if someone else was there. Then it dawned on him. The niño was the baby. He grabbed his nephew by the coat, pulled him inside, and slammed the door.

"¿Los dolores? ¿Cada cuánto tiempo?"

"No sé," Daniel answered. "Me dice Lupe que falta mucho todavía."

He stood on the doormat, eyes and nose dripping, looking quite forlorn. But he had said the right words. "Falta mucho," was exactly what Noise wanted to hear. He led Daniel back to the kitchen, poured a generous three fingers of brandy into a glass, and said, "Toma."

"No pero . . . " his nephew objected.

"Drink, damn it," Noise roared. "Si no te compones de los nervios, no me vas a servir para nada."

Daniel complied. Noise went to his bedroom, peeled off his jeans, and pulled on some thermal underwear. Then he carefully layered himself in shirt, sweatshirt, hooded sweatshirt, and jacket. He found a ski mask and his insulated boots. He clomped back to the kitchen, opened a drawer, and took out some safety goggles and a flashlight. "Okay. Vamos."

They fought their way back to the Palafox front door and struggled inside. Noise pulled off the ski mask and stared at Lupe for a long second. Clearly she was handling the situation better than Daniel.

"¿Qué pasó?" She looked at her husband. "¿No fuiste a la casa de Victoria?"

"No es tan fácil," Noise answered. "Ni puedes ver la casa de Victoria. Pero ahorita vamos a hacer algo."

He knocked some snow off his boots and walked back to the kitchen. He lifted the phone and got a dial tone. Serendipity. He dialed Victoria's number. An ecstatic Alicia answered, "Uncle Noise! Did you see the storm? Isn't it awesome?" It was a full minute before her mother could gain control of the line. But it took her only three or four questions to grasp the parameter of their predicament.

BOOK THREE, CHAPTER NINETEEN

"Yo puedo alistarme en veinte minutos. ¿Pero cómo voy a llegar allí?"

"No problem. I'm working on that even as we speak," he assured her. He hung up and turned to Daniel. "¿No tienen una cuerda bastante larga?"

"La que usamos para colgar ropa afuera."

"Algo más larga. Quiero estirar una cuerda de la entrada de ustedes hasta la entrada de Victoria. Así ella puede venir guiándose por la cuerda hasta con los ojos cerrados."

Lupe raised a hand as if about to speak. Then instead she bent over the kitchen table and began to pant. One. Two. Three. Blow. One. Two. Three. Blow. Again and again. Dante's face took on a "¡Dios mío! ¿Qué hago?" cast but Noise caught his eye and delivered a "Don't you dare" message. The moment passed. Lupe pulled herself erect.

"Ese sí, estuvo mas sabroso." She blinked away the last of the pain and said, "Cuando trabajan con los coches en el verano, usan un cable muy largo."

Noise slapped himself on the side of his head. "¡Pendejo! An extension cord. I've got a two-hundred-foot beauty in my basement." He gave Lupe a hug and headed for the front door. Ten minutes later, he returned to find Dante in the kitchen innocently inquiring about all the fuss. "Hey sobrino, apúrate. Vamos a visitar a Victoria." Then he ordered him back to his bedroom to suit up for blizzard conditions.

The plan was fairly simple. Daniel was sent to secure one end of the extension cord to a post at the front gate. From there Noise and Dante would work their way south to the corner and attach the line to a parking signpost. Then they would turn east and make their way along the sidewalk toward a utility pole, about halfway down the block, where they would again secure the line. From there it was but a few jumps to Victoria's gateway. Wherever the snow depth would allow, they would not shovel but, instead, trample it underfoot. Hand signals would be the means of communication. Questions? Ready. Go.

The first leg of the trek was almost exhilarating. Along the west side of the block, the snow had drifted into the yards, leaving the sidewalk slippery but nearly bare. With minimal exertion, Noise and Dante reached the corner signpost. They did their loop and hitch as planned. But then they turned east, and everything changed. Now the gale hit them squarely in the face, forcing them to turn away in order to breathe. And even that tactic was unreliable. At times, the attack would come in a whirl or swirl, leaving the men stumbling and disheartened. And the wind was not the only impediment. The snow was nearly knee-deep, and the effort to raise their legs to that height in order to beat it down soon had them panting and near exhaustion. "At least the line is there. We can always go back," Noise consoled himself internally. But then he remembered Lupe's words, "Esc sí estuvo sabroso." There was no more thought about a quick return.

Gradually he found a rhythm for the task. He turned his body sideways and took five short sidesteps, packing the snow beneath his boots. Then he hunkered down to escape the full force of the wind and regain his breath. After three such cycles, he would push Dante to the fore, and the younger man would do his own three cycles. By such effort, after a full twenty minutes, they came within sight of the light pole. There they faced another barrier. A snowbank almost as high as their noses stretched between them and the post. Noise could feel his nephew hesitate. He jerked the shovel from Dante's hands and threw himself at the drift. And soon discovered that the height of the bank was actually advantageous. It shielded them somewhat from the wind. Even so, he was soon panting again, and he handed the tool to his helper. After ten hard minutes, they broke through the bank and . . . Glory Hallelujah . . . the sidewalk on the

BOOK THREE, CHAPTER NINETEEN

other side had been swept clean by the wind all the way to Victoria's gate.

They did a loop-and-hitch around the utility pole, staggered to the gatepost, and repeated the process. Then it was just a ten-pace scramble to Victoria's entryway and an assault on her front door. She greeted them with a cup of hot broth and a tongue-lashing. "¿Cómo voy a creer que esperan hasta esta hora para acordarse de mí? ¿Por qué no me hablaron desde anoche?" Noise and Dante were not about to waste some perfectly delicious oxygen on a pre-doomed response. Victoria allowed them about five minutes with the broth, then handed Noise her medical kit, pushed them back out into the storm, and followed.

The return trek was a virtual cakewalk. The lifeline functioned exactly as Noise had envisioned. By maintaining a hold on the line while walking parallel to it, they were assured of staying on course even when blinded by the blizzard. The wind, at least at first, also became an unintentional ally as it pushed them toward the west end of the block. In ten minutes, they were dripping on the floor of the Palafox kitchen.

"En doce años acá, jamás he visto una tormenta como esta," Victoria declared. No one contradicted her. She removed her coat and gloves, and rubbed her hands together to warm them. Then she led Lupe to the bedroom for a preliminary exam. Five minutes later, she returned to the kitchen to announce, "Cuatro centímetros ya. No cabe la menor duda. Vamos a tener un bebito hoy."

She called the hospital and learned that her obstetrical associate, Doctor Howe, had been stranded there overnight, and was seeing the world through gloom-tinted glasses. "Even if you could get Lupe here, which I doubt, I wouldn't advise it. Everybody here is far into a forced double shift, and they're as testy as a bunch of caged cats. Take my word for it. Lupe will get better care if she delivers at home."

Victoria relayed the message to Noise and added, "I'm going to count on you to keep Daniel occupied. He's just too hyper to be near his wife. If he can maintain control, I'll let him in at the end. But right now, no way."

Noise studied her for a second. "You've done this before."

"Of course, dozens of times."

"I mean alone. By yourself."

"Actually, no. This is the first time alone," she beamed at him.

"Maybe we should keep that to ourselves," he cautioned.

Victoria went back to the bedroom. Noise conferred with the Palafox brothers. He explained that Victoria would attend to the delivery. But she might need some assistance. And who better to help than the godmother whom they had chosen for the baby. So. The brothers should fix themselves some brunch while Noise talked to Marta. Then if she agreed to come, Daniel and Dante would brave the blizzard again and bring her back.

Marta was very apprehensive. "What could I do? I don't know anything about childbirth."

"You agreed to be the godmother."

"I know but . . ."

"Lupe needs a lot of moral support. She's a little nervous. She wasn't expecting to have this baby at home. She was expecting a hospital with all the trimmings. She needs people around to tell her that everything is going to work out."

"I suppose I could do that." There was a long pause. "What should I wear?"

It was the kind of straight line that Noise lived for. "Anything casual is fine. The baby won't know the difference."

"¡Payaso! Estoy hablando del frío."

"Oh that. Right. Dress warm. Daniel and Dante will be there in a half hour." He hung up.

The men made some tacos from eggs scrambled with onion and chile. Then the Palafox brothers headed out into the storm, and Noise went to assist the midwife.

"¿No has comido nada?" Victoria was asking.

From her answer it was clear that Lupe understood the intent of the question. "Nada. Ayer comí poquito. Pero en la noche me dio diarrea. No tengo nada."

"¿Y te explicaron de los dolores?"

"Entiendo que van a atacar con más fuerza y más seguido como va pasando el tiempo. Mai Lu y su esposo me enseñaron a respirar para ayudar a mi bebito."

Victoria observed the next contraction closely. Lupe did a gasp-gasp-gasp-blow-routine for the rise to crest, then shifted to a rapid pant for the downside and ease away. There was every indication of preparation. There was not a hint of panic. When the breathing had normalized, Victoria asked, "¿En qué estás pensando?"

"Mai Lu me dijo que soy un río. En eso tengo que concentrarme." She paused and her eyes went a little glassy. "El río va a traer a mi hijo. Y yo estoy aquí mirando como llega."

"Yo sabía," Victoria nodded admiringly. "This is pure Mai Lu. That woman is a witch."

"Maybe she should be here," said Noise.

"Can you arrange that?"

"No problem. We got you here, didn't we?"

"Good. Bring Concha too. Pero primero, ayúdame con esta cama. Trae dos sillas de la cocina."

Noise fetched the chairs. Then he and Victoria lifted the mattress at the head of the bed, and on each side slipped in a chair with the back against the mattress and the feet aimed at the wall. They thus pitched the mattress at an inclination more or less suitable for a birthing bed.

Back in the kitchen, Noise called Victoria's house. Alicia answered. Yes, the Palafox brothers had arrived. They were making a path to Miguel's house across the backyard. "Good. Tell them to borrow an extension cord from Miguel." She agreed to everything. Then the pleading started.

"Can I come back with them? Please. I'll stay out of the way. I promise. Dad and Tony are watching football. There's nothing to do here. Please."

"Hold on. I'll ask your mom."

"No. Don't ask. She might say no. You can say yes. Once I'm there, she won't send me home. Please."

He surrendered. But not before threatening her with several forms of extinction if she did not dress warmly. Then he cleared the permission with her father, hung up, and served himself a cup of coffee. Before he had taken the first sip, the phone rang. It was Alicia's cousin, Juana.

"Uncle Noise, Alicia says Lupe's baby is coming, and she gets to be there. That's not fair, Uncle Noise. I'm as old as she is. Let me come too. Please? I can help. I can wash dishes. Okay? Please. I can change diapers." Even she stopped to giggle at that whopper.

"Let me talk to your grandma."

Juana passed the phone to Concha. Noise recounted the morning's events and explained how things stood at the moment. Then Concha talked to Victoria. When she resumed her conversation with him, she sounded positively perky.

"You're doing great. Send the men here as soon as you can. In the meantime, we'll try to clear the walk to the front gate."

By noon Marta and Alicia had arrived. Then an hour later, the house really began to fill as they were joined by Concha, Mai Lu, Loco, Juana, and Frances. When Victoria announced to the group that Lupe's dilation was approaching six centimeters, there was collective applause. But then the process seemed to reach a plateau. For more than an hour, there was no apparent progress. Dilation became dilatory. Contraction intervals varied little. Neither did their intensity increase. About two-thirty, the amniotic fluid began to appear.

"Agua bendita," whispered Victoria.

"The juices of life," mumbled Concha.

The two women smiled at each other, both supposing that the amniotomy signaled a rapid transition to second-stage labor. It didn't happen. Meanwhile the other family members began to assign themselves tasks. Mai Lu took up her position as Lupe's coach and masseuse. Frances ministered to Lupe's face and neck with a cool sponge and asked lots of questions. Marta moved her chair into a corner of the birthing room and recited the rosary. Dante and Daniel, having burned their adrenaline reserves in their battle with the storm, pulled off their coats and boots, and crashed, one at each end of the sofa. Concha ushered the others into the kitchen.

"What are we supposed to do now? Boil water?" Loco asked his mother.

"Of course not," she answered. "You do the Mexican equivalent of boiling water."

"Which is?"

"You make soup."

And they did. Soon Alicia and Juana were peeling potatoes. Which they then passed on to Noise, who diced them and passed them on to Loco. As the chef du jour, Loco browned some ground beef in a skillet and seasoned it with salt, pepper, and parsley. While that sizzled, he sauteed some onion, garlic, and tomato. When the meat was nearly done, he drained off most of the fat. Then he combined all the ingredients in a large soup pot and added several liters of water. He waited for it to come to a boil, then added the diced potatoes and reduced the flame so that the cooking continued at a simmer. In less than an hour, there was a huge pot of potato soup. But no one ate. Instead everyone seemed to be holding their breath, waiting for Lupe.

By four o'clock, the blizzard began to relent. The wind lost a little of its ferocity. The barometric pressure rose slightly. Occasional gale-force gusts still whipped the snow from one drift to another, but there was little additional accumulation. The brunt of the storm had moved up the lake to wreak its wrath on Manitowoc and Manistique and Sault Sainte Marie and eventually on to Ontario.

About the same time, Lupe's labor abruptly began to move forward. The interval between contractions shortened while the intensity of the pain increased. Catching Lupe by surprise. The previous respite had lulled and gulled her into a belief that the difficulties of labor had been exaggerated. Now she quickly became acquainted with the travail of advanced parturition.

"Ya no puedo," she whined as the second major contraction subsided.

"Ocho pulgadas," Victoria cheered. "Vamos a buen paso."

As the next contraction began, Lupe gave way to panic. "No puedo más," she screamed.

"You're losing control," Mai Lu warned and tried to regain the laboring woman's attention.

Lupe fought clear of the pain. Then, "¡Háblame en cristiano, Tonta!" she yelled at her coach.

"Que te controles," Victoria translated. "Es todo lo que te dijo."

But by then, control was a sometime thing. The pleasant meander of the early afternoon had given way to a raging torrent.

"Voy a morir," Lupe screamed at the next contraction.

The usually unflappable Frances began to cry silently. Marta started to pray en voz alta.

"Nadie va a morir," Victoria reassured. Then to Mai Lu, "Look for a position where she can see you doing the breathing exercise. That way she can follow you better."

BOOK THREE, CHAPTER NINETEEN

An excellent suggestion. But on the next contraction, Mai Lu discovered that the adjusted position brought her face within range of Lupe's claws. Concha stepped in, eased Frances aside, and grabbed Lupe's arms. Lupe shifted her attention toward the older woman, and tried to wrestle free. But it seemed that her wrists were locked in a grip of steel. "Quiero morir," she wailed.

"Sí. Sí. Vas a morir," Concha concurred. "Y lo puedes hacer cualquier día de estos. Menos hoy. Ahora vas a dar a luz a la pobre criatura que tienes adentro. ¡Orale mujer, a trabajar!"

The pain crested and ebbed. Lupe stared at Concha. The older woman was not simply composed. She had the look of someone who had witnessed all this far too often, and, quite frankly, failed to see what all the fuss was about. If she had yawned, Lupe would not have been shocked. She was not human. She was some kind of monster.

The next wave approached. Lupe returned her attention to her coach. But this time, fully attuned to Mai Lu's lead, she pushed the panic away and withstood the pain. Then, as the wave subsided, she fixed Concha with a ferocious glare, and flicked her a nod that expressed emphatically, "¿Qué tal? ¡Bruja Vieja!" After that there was no further talk of dying. In fact, the whole process took on an aura of magic.

Following another dozen contractions, Lupe grunted, "Quiero empujar ya."

Victoria checked, "Diez centimetros. Ahora sí, puedes. Pero ya sabes. Cuando la cabeza esté a medias, tienes que detenerte. Yo te digo."

Another few pushy contractions and the baby's head crowned. Soon the head was half-birthed. Lupe paused as instructed, while Victoria eased the tissues around the head. Then, in almost no time, the baby slithered out. Victoria cleaned the small face and lay the boy on his mother's belly while the blood receded from the umbilical. Then she clamped and cut the cord and passed the boy to his mother. Arturo Alvarez Palafox y Silvas, for so he would be named officially, still a bit wrinkled and crinkled of face from his recent voyage, immediately declared to the world that he had mixed feelings about his birthday. But Lupe put his mouth to one of her nipples and there were no further complaints.

Noise, who as godfather was already in the room, proclaimed, "No cabe duda. Es hijo de su Papá."

That helped to dispel a little of the reverential awe which had settled over the room. Concha challenged Noise's hypothesis, "Daniel no es el único chupador en el vecindario." Which produced some further laughter.

Soon the placenta was birthed. Victoria examined it scrupulously and pronounced it intact. Meanwhile, Concha and Mai Lu performed some preliminary hygiene on the new mother. Then they removed the chairs from under the mattress so that Lupe could find a more comfortable nursing position.

"Do you think we can get the new papá in here to meet his son?" Victoria wondered.

"I'll twist his arm if I have to," answered Noise.

Daniel had been awakened by Lupe's first scream. Noise found him scrunched into a corner of the living room, covering his face with his hands.

"Ya levántate hombre. Tienes un hijo."

A reluctant Daniel answered, "Siento una vergüenza muy grande."

"Lupe va a pensar que tienes vergüenza de ella si no te acercas."

Noise hauled the younger man to his feet and pushed him into the bedroom. Daniel was speechless. Which was fine. No speeches were required. He smiled tentatively at Lupe and she smiled broadly back at him. Then she took his hand and touched it to the baby. Daniel

BOOK THREE, CHAPTER NINETEEN

gingerly moved his hand along the baby's arm, then withdrew it.

"¿No quieres cargarlo?" Lupe asked.

"Mejor mañana. Cuando me puedas enseñar," he answered.

That seemed like a good plan. Arturito soon finished nursing, whereupon he was more thoroughly examined by the medical team as they bathed and clothed him. Then Godmother Marta stepped in and took possession. She called the children together and explained what would come to be known as Marta's rules. "Juana and Alicia, you can hold the baby. For short periods. As long as you show responsibility. You can change the baby's diaper. But only after Victoria gives you a demonstration. No one bathes the baby except adults, but you two can watch and fetch if Lupe allows it."

After that the atmosphere lightened. Toño showed up with little Tony and a camera and several bottles of champagne left over from New Year's. The spontaneous celebration continued for a good half hour. Handshakes. Abrazos. Expressions of gratitude. Congratulations. Exchanges of smiles and backpats. Comments about the child's resemblance to one parent or the other. Mild disagreements on that subject. More smiles. More congratulations. More backpats. Gradually the emotional energy of the house began to return to a more everyday level. People, beginning predictably with the children and the men, turned to thoughts of food. Soon Loco was ladling out his pot of soup.

The children ate first. In her usual role as peacekeeper, Frances joined them, and her mediation skills were almost immediately put to work.

"Alicia says that you're a cousin to Arturito and we're not," Tony complained.

Frances thought that over.

"Well, are we?" Tony demanded.

"I don't see how," Alicia interjected.

"My dad said that you need a common . . . what was that, Dad?" Juana asked.

Loco was listening. "Ancestor."

"That's the word," Juana enthused. "A common ancestor. Frances and Arturito have a common ancestor. But we don't."

"I think we should all just act like cousins," said Frances.

"That's a nice way to look at it," Alicia concurred, "but strictly speaking, we're not really cousins."

"Why do you get to be a cousin and we don't, Frances?" Tony asked in a voice that implied that here was another of life's outrageous and unfathomable injustices.

Frances attempted a new tack. "Some scientists say that all humans have a common ancestor. A woman who lived in Africa a few million years ago. If that turns out to be a fact, then we are all cousins."

"A few million years ago," Tony scoffed. "That's not like having the same grandmother. That's really lame, Frances."

Eventually the children finished and were eased away from the table. Loco, Toño, and the Palafox brothers ate next. Finally, about nine o'clock, the last of the family moved toward the kitchen. Except for Marta, who refused to surrender the swaddled infant to anyone. She stayed behind with Lupe. Toño poured a glass of champagne for everyone. Noise offered a toast.

"To Arturito and a new beginning."

Victoria clinked her glass to his but countered with, "Why not a happy ending instead?"

Concha provided the resolution, "Let's do both."

This was greeted by a mighty chorus of "¡Salud!"